John Stuart

DARK AS THE GRAVE

BOOKS BY MALCOLM LOWRY

DARK AS THE GRAVE WHEREIN MY FRIEND IS LAID

LUNAR CAUSTIC

HEAR US O LORD FROM HEAVEN THY DWELLING PLACE

UNDER THE VOLCANO

ULTRAMARINE

WHEREIN MY FRIEND IS LAID

DARK

BY

MALCOLM LOWRY

EDITED BY

Douglas Day & Margerie Lowry

AS THE GRAVE

WHEREIN

MY FRIEND

IS LAID

MERIDIAN BOOKS
The World Publishing Company
NEW YORK AND CLEVELAND

A MERIDIAN BOOK

Published by The World Publishing Company
2231 West 110th Street, Cleveland, Ohio 44102
Published simultaneously in Canada by
Nelson, Foster & Scott Ltd.

First Meridian Printing—1969

Reprinted by arrangement with
The New American Library, Inc.

Manufactured at World Publishing Press, a division of
The World Publishing Company, Cleveland, Ohio

Library of Congress Catalog Card Number: 68-26029

PRINTED IN THE UNITED STATES OF AMERICA

WORLD PUBLISHING
TIMES MIRROR

PREFACE

ONE MUST BEGIN BY realizing that Malcolm Lowry was not really a novelist, except by accident. It is difficult to know what to call him: diarist, compulsive notetaker, poet *manqué,* alcoholic philosophizing rambler—any of these would do for a start, but only for a start. When one talks to those who knew him, the word one hears most often used to describe Lowry is *genius;* and the word, for once, is apt. Even his least successful works are clearly the products of a mind and a sensibility quite different from yours and mine. The second most frequently used epithet is *unique,* and it applies as well as *genius* does: there has never been, one is sure, anyone even remotely like Lowry. A man sly and deceptive, yet shy and ingenuous; a drunk of gargantuan proportions, yet a man who seems never to have let go an almost preternatural degree of self-awareness, even when face down on the floor of a pub or a cantina; a great liar (or, more charitably, inventor of autobiographical fictions), but—in his writing especially—one of the most painfully honest men who ever lived. A great trial to all his friends; but a man of such charm that someone once said of him: "Just one look at the old bastard makes me happy for a week." A happy, even silly, man; a suicide.

There are other paradoxes in the Lowry character, to be sure. For practical purposes, the most important of these is the fact

ix

that he was a man obsessed by the need to write, while at the same time being almost totally unable to write. The published Lowry canon is small: *Ultramarine* (1933), his undergraduate novel about a young man's dubious life-initiation at sea; *Lunar Caustic* (written first in 1934–35, but thus far published in English only in *Paris Review*, Winter 1963), a surrealist novella set in the psychiatric ward of Bellevue Hospital; *Hear Us O Lord from Heaven Thy Dwelling Place* (1961), an anthology of seven short stories and novellas collected (and in some instances completed) by Mrs. Lowry in the years after her husband's death; a small volume of poems, published in 1962; a few random stories and scraps of novels that have appeared in various magazines from time to time—and, of course, the magnificent *Under the Volcano* (1947), the keystone of Lowry's work, the center of his life, a great novel.

Except for a collection of his letters, published in 1965, that is the corpus of Lowry's published work—a pitifully small amount, when one considers the fact that hardly a day in his life from his early adolescence to his death in 1957 passed without his writing something: notes, journals, tentative paragraphs and chapters for work in progress, revisions of earlier work, revisions of revisions, and so on. For every published Lowry page, there must be two hundred unpublished, either in his impossibly tiny and illegible handwriting, or typed by Margerie Bonner Lowry. There remain three unfinished novels, six or seven stories, and literally hundreds of poems.

Why was so much begun, and so little completed? There are a number of reasons. First, Lowry's method of composition was eccentric, to say the least. He saw all his works, those published as well as those yet unwritten, as part of a vast continuum to be called *The Voyage That Never Ends,* the central novel of which was to have been *Under the Volcano;* and he refused to see any part of this continuum as complete until all of its parts were complete. As the consequence of this ambitious Proustian scheme, it was necessarily impossible for him ever to put a work aside; ideally, he should have been able to compose them all simultaneously; but practically, he had to skip from one to another, always revising, always polishing, always discarding—and never ending.

Another reason lies deeper within Lowry's character. He was never able to define himself *to* himself, partly because he was afraid of what he would see if he looked deeply enough into his psyche. But like most visionary artists, he was acutely egocentric: his gaze was almost always inward, so much so that he was very nearly blind to the world outside—except in so far as it reflected his own thoughts and feelings. From time to time he would try mightily to focus on something outside himself—the world situation, friends, wives, the sound of a voice, the color of a sky—and hope that alcohol would help him get through such adventures. But, of course, it only helped him back inside himself, where an elusive inner Malcolm Lowry alternately laughed at and sorrowed with his brilliant, incompetent outer self. Such a man could write only about himself, which is precisely what Lowry did. It would be a cliché to say that he wrote "thinly veiled autobiographies"; but it would be the truth. Very rarely he tried to invent characters, but he did not know enough about any other human being to do this—which, incidentally, is why his secondary characters, especially his women, seem shadowy and ill-defined—and so he would return to his only true interest: Malcolm Lowry. But he could never bring himself to face Malcolm Lowry completely, and so was unable to finish any of his self-portraits. (He regarded even *Under the Volcano* as incomplete.)

It was his fancy to give extravagant and resounding names to his personae: he could be Kennish Drumgold Cosnahan, Roderick McGregor Fairhaven, William Plantagenet—or Sigbjørn Wilderness, the protagonist of *Dark As the Grave Wherein My Friend Is Laid.* Less flamboyantly, but ultimately no less memorably, he could be Dana Hilliot or Geoffrey Firmin; but whatever the name, it was always Malcolm Lowry who was the subject. It is important to note, though, that Lowry had no very high opinion of his fictional selves: egocentricity is not synonymous with conceit. When he tried once in a letter to explain Sigbjørn Wilderness to a friend, he revealed his reservations:

Wilderness is not, in the ordinary sense in which one encounters novelists or the author in novels, a novelist. He simply doesn't know what he is. He is a sort of underground man. Also he is Ortega's fellow, making up his life as he goes along, and trying to find his vocation . . . he is disinterested in literature, uncultured, incredibly unobservant, in many respects ignorant, without faith in himself, and lacking nearly all the qualities you normally associate with a novelist or writer. . . . His very methods of writing are absurd and he sees practically nothing at all, even through his wife's eyes, though he gradually comes to *see.* I believe this can make him a very original character, both human and pathetically inhuman at once.

One reason, perhaps, that Lowry's reputation has until recently been quantitatively small is that readers have sought to find in his works what is not there, except peripherally: external action—"plot," as we used to call it—and realized conflict between characters. Nobody moves anywhere; nothing *happens.* But if there is no external action, there is almost a surfeit of movement internally; and there is enough tension within the mind of the protagonist to render any other conflict superfluous. Lowry was really, for all his romanticism, for all the exoticism of his prose, the most cerebral of writers, a real intellectual's delight. What sustains all his works is not plot, nor dialogue, nor movement, but the spinning up and down of a mind which is genuinely amazing, in all the senses of the word. The pace of this mind is such that it generates great tension and excitement, so that the "plot" of a Lowry novel is the movement of the mind of the author—or, shall we say, the mind of the protagonist. Whenever he lets his protagonist think, Lowry becomes a great writer. Whenever he tries to invent action, or dialogue, or to create believable characters other than himself, he is on very thin ice indeed. Sometimes, as with Juan Fernando Martinez in *Dark As the Grave,* he succeeds in interesting us in another person—but Juan Fernando never appears in the novel, except as remembered by Sigbjørn Wilderness. And when, in this novel, we are moved by the awesome Mexican landscape, we must realize that it is not Mexican at all (except by accident of geography): it is an inner landscape, Sigbjørn-Lowry's, the same abyssal landscape that Gerard Manley Hopkins had described:

> O the mind, mind has mountains; cliffs of fall
> Frightful, sheer, no-man-fathomed. Hold them cheap
> May who ne'er hung there.

In early December, 1945, Malcolm and Margerie Bonner Lowry flew from Vancouver, British Columbia, to Mexico City. They traveled by bus down to Cuernavaca, where Lowry had lived with his first wife, Jan, in 1936, and where he had begun *Under the Volcano*. On New Year's Eve Lowry heard from Jonathan Cape, to whom the completed manuscript of *Under the Volcano* had been sent, that they could not accept the novel as it stood: many revisions were needed. For the next two weeks Lowry spent most of his time writing one of the most remarkable literary documents of our time: a letter to Cape, in which he dissected and analyzed every chapter of *Under the Volcano*, explaining why every detail had to be left as it was. This task was hardly impeded by the events of the night of January 10, when Lowry made a halfhearted and spontaneously conceived attempt to slash his wrists. On January 16 the two set out for Oaxaca, where Lowry hoped to find a Mexican friend from his first stay in that country. They discovered that the man had been dead for some years; and, their reason for being in Oaxaca being nonexistent, they left for Acapulco via Mexico City the following day.

This much is the matter of *Dark As the Grave Wherein My Friend Is Laid*. During the entire trip both Lowry and his wife made notes as they went along—dialogues, descriptions, copies of signs along the way, all sorts of random observations. After a dreadful series of comic catastrophes in Acapulco and Mexico City, which culminated in their deportation from the country (and about which Lowry wrote yet another unfinished novel, *La Mordida*), they returned to Canada. Some short time afterwards, Lowry looked through all the notes of the Mexican journey, exclaimed, "By God, we have a novel here!" and fell to work on *Dark As the Grave*.

In August of 1947 Lowry wrote to Albert Erskine, the American editor of the now-accepted *Under the Volcano: "I've written the first of the first draft of Dark is* [sic] *the Grave* and have started on the second. I can't make the first chapter come out right, but when I do I'll send it along." By October he was ready to send installments to Erskine:

> I am writing what can fairly be described as a good book—
> I'm not sure, of course, precisely, being a kind of side-street to

my own consciousness; however, the report of what is going on from my own point of view would seem to be pretty good, as an objective observer I would like to wander miles to queue up, as a subjective one I would say without any qualification at all that it is *tremendo siniestro:* at all events, *pazienza*—you will receive it in driblets, I will have a time to go through before I finish and some of what I send you may seem a little wild. We progress toward equilibrium this time instead of in the opposite direction, and the result is considerably more exciting, if not even more horrible, more inspiring is probably the word.

This burst of energy was interrupted by the Lowrys' trip to Europe (the first stages of which are described in "Through the Panama," one of the novellas in *Hear Us O Lord from Heaven Thy Dwelling Place,* in which Sigbjørn Wilderness is once again the Lowry-persona), but it was resumed by 1951, when Lowry, back in Canada, could write his agent that *Dark As the Grave* was "still cooking." In early 1952 Lowry wrote to Erskine that he was now thinking of the novel as part of a trilogy, with *Eridanus* (which today exists only as a fragment) and *La Mordida* as the other components. In May of the same year he wrote again to Erskine: *"Dark As the Grave* is still going along being typed by Margie from my execrable pencil notes," and in August came his final words on the book: *"Dark As the Grave*—700 pages of notes and drafts—is deposited in the bank; *La Mordida* has been started on the long haul of typing. I didn't send you any of the former because in toto it is not in a fit state to read and it would take a lot of time to make suitable selections."

And so things stood until two years ago, when I read through all the Lowry manuscripts on deposit at the University of British Columbia Library, came across *Dark As the Grave,* and agreed with Lowry that "By God, we have a novel here!" So did Mrs. Lowry, and so did the publishers; and so the present edition was undertaken.

What we had to work from was a formidable mess. The whole "bolus," as Lowry liked to call it, was, in fact, 705 pages of typescript, already yellowing and crumbling. At first, the task seemed rather straightforward, textually speaking: there were within the "bolus" three distinct texts, of 383, 174, and 148 pages respectively. The three seemed to run consecutively, so that it would require only a minimal amount of housekeeping duties to provide ourselves with a respectable text. But such optimism was naïve. We found out very quickly that Lowry had *not* really worked through the three texts consecutively—that, instead, he had done an uncommon amount of backing and filling, of retracing his steps, of setting off on false starts, and even of throwing in a good deal of material that belonged elsewhere, in other novels and stories ("just for safekeeping," as he would say). In several cases, one incident existed in as many as five different versions, none immediately obvious as superior in quality to the others. Neither was it possible always—or even often —to assume blindly that the most recent version of an incident was the most finished, or even the one preferred by the author: quite frequently Lowry would write a passage, then modify it, then delete the modifications, then try others, then delete the entire passage—then reinsert it fifty pages later. There were many repetitions, and more than once we had to decide which of three identical passages, occurring in as many chapters, we were to retain. Characters were predicted who never appeared, characters appeared who had nothing much to do, and so drifted out after a few pages of embarrassed standing about.

Worse yet, in many places the notebooks had barely begun to be translated into fiction, so that from time to time we had to cross out "Malcolm said" and replace this with "Sigbjørn said"; and there were many other names that had to be changed as well. Primrose is, of course, Margerie Bonner Lowry. Daniel is Conrad Aiken, Lowry's friend, mentor, and father-surrogate for many years. Erikson is Nordahl Grieg, the Norse novelist. Ruth is Jan, Lowry's first wife. Eddie Kent, Dr. Hippolyte, John Stanford, and Juan Fernando Martinez are our names for genuine Lowry friends and enemies. *The Valley of the Shadow of Death* was Lowry's original title for *Under the Volcano* (this was Lowry's change, not ours); and *Swinging the Maelstrom* was one of his original titles for *Lunar Caustic*. *Drunkard's Rigadoon* was Lowry's substitute for Charles Jackson's *The Lost Weekend*, about which Lowry was more than a little paranoiac for many years, and needlessly so: there is almost no similarity between *The Lost Weekend* and *Under the Volcano*. In general, characters, books, hotels, cantinas, and so on were given new names—a legal, not aesthetic, necessity. *In Ballast to the White Sea*, incidentally, was the real title for a Lowry work which burned with the shack in Dollarton.

The chief textual problem thus became one of splicing and cutting—tricky work, calling for patience and restraint. One had to find a mean somewhere between two extremes: we could either leave the "bolus" just as it was, and present it to the reader as a brilliant but bewildering—and often boring—work in progress; or we could step in and finish it for Lowry. That is, rewrite, expand, revise, expunge, polish—anything that would make *Dark As the Grave* a smoother product. The first alternative was intriguing, especially to the scholar. It would have given readers a rare opportunity to see a writer actually, as it were, in the process of creation—a book to study, full of anguish, torment, and clumsiness often left uncorrected. There would have been bad passages crossed out and rudely condemned by the author's marginal comment, then revised, then re-revised, and finally allowed to stand—tentatively. There would have been Lowry's occasional pauses to lecture himself on the art of fiction, these lectures occurring in the middle of, say, a piece of dialogue or exposition.

The second alternative was, of course, totally unacceptable for the obvious reason that it would have been both unethical and unaesthetic. There could be no word in the text that was not written by Malcolm Lowry. Even when we were quite convinced of what Lowry would have done in one place or another, we could not allow ourselves to act on this conviction without some evidence for it in Lowry's own hand. All we could do was cut out what was repetitious, demonstrably not integral to the book, or still not begun to be incorporated from the notebooks into it.

Such "smoothing" as we refrained from doing was aesthetically proscribed because Lowry was never a "smooth" writer. He was more than Scott Fitzgerald's putter-inner: he was a crammer-inner. His work was at its best when he filled it full of ideas, images, allusions, word-play, all superimposed on one another; when he allowed the imagination of his protagonist to wander, to seek all manner of obscure and bizarre correspondences, and most especially to bore further down into his psyche than any reader could follow. To have made *Dark As the Grave* neater, smoother, would have been to rob it of its only claim to importance: its status as an accurate reflection of the splendidly chaotic mind of a genius. So we had to leave it rough, not only because we had no right to tamper with a dead man's work, but also because to have done so would have been to diminish it cruelly.

The facts of the Lowrys' journey to Mexico in 1945–46 are only the bare bones of *Dark As the Grave*. Lowry was nothing if not a symbolizer: whatever happened, whatever he heard or saw, had to *mean* something, however obliquely. Sometimes he could be embarrassingly amateurish in his symbolizing, as when in Chapter VI he evokes "the bilingual moonlight, that spoke at once the language of love and madness." But at his best—which is occasionally in *Ultramarine, Lunar Caustic,* and *Dark As the Grave,* and almost always in *Under the Volcano*—his mind reaches deeply and broadly, drawing from the world, from his own considerable intellect, from his subconscious, new visions of the great old symbols. Not the authentic simple forms of vine, plate, wine, stone, woman, tree—Lowry was after bigger game: the archetypal daemonic forms of abyss, labyrinth, burnt forest, monster, blighted garden, ruined castle, dark and ominous forces at work in an ancient and dangerous world. Thus Sigbjørn Wilderness is not simply Malcolm Lowry taking his wife on a vacation to Mexico: he is a Dante or a Virgil on his way down into the Inferno. And more than they, because he is going back a second time. And the hell is no one else's but his own.

The first swooping, breathless paragraph of *Dark As the Grave* throws us and Sigbjørn in this downward direction. There he is, pretending he is on a vacation, this writer who cannot write, this would-be hero who has missed World War II (just as his alter ego, Geoffrey Firmin of *Under the Volcano,* had missed the Spanish Civil War), this reformed drunk who has begun to drink again. He has left the security of his Canadian home be-

cause a malignant fate has burned it down, and he and his wife
have not had the will to finish rebuilding it. He is a middle-aged
Lord Jim who no longer has illusions about his honor; he admits
his fear of everything but death—which is actually what he is
seeking in Mexico. His fear of other people is enough to make
him sit in the rear of the plane's passenger compartment. As his
"ghostly ballet of fears" testifies, he is afraid of exposure as a
plagiarist (which Lowry always imagined himself to be, but
which he was not); afraid of disease (Lowry was convinced
through most of his adult life that he either had syphilis, or was
about to contract it); afraid of losing his wife, since his recent
behavior has caused their marriage to slip; afraid of himself;
afraid of fire (another Lowry obsession); afraid of authority; and
afraid of Mexico—as well he might be. In Mexico he hopes to
find Juan Fernando Martinez, whom he thinks of as his good
angel—a fellow drunk, but one of nature's noblemen: horseman, swordsman, idealist, true friend. (This same man had also
been a presence in *Under the Volcano,* both as the offstage hero
Juan Cerillo, and the bibulously *simpático* Dr. Vigil.) Juan
Fernando is really the key to Sigbjørn Wilderness, and to this
book, in spite of the fact that he never appears: for Sigbjørn
comes ultimately to realize (in Chapter IX) that, though he has
all these years thought of Juan Fernando as a symbol for life and
vitality, he actually is equally symbolic of *death,* in its most attractive forms. When Sigbjørn learns this, he knows then the real
reason for the pilgrimage that he is making into his past, which
he had hitherto thought of as sordid: he had somehow been
happy in the bad old days; he had possessed something then that
had slipped away from him in the intervening years. This
"something" emerges as more than youth, or inspiration, or
happy irresponsibility, though these were parts of it: really,
what he had known then was the exhilaration that comes from
proximity to danger—and the danger for him had not simply
been physical, but spiritual as well. In the old days he had been,
like Faust, flirting with damnation, and enjoying the flirtation.
For Primrose, his pleasant yet not overly perceptive wife, the
pilgrimage has the function of vacation-*cum*-exorcism: Sigbjørn
is to visit the scenes of his earlier downfall, and lay the ghosts

that have plagued him ever since. But Sigbjørn learns that he really does not *want* to lay the ghosts, but to rejoin them—and this is what makes his descent into the Mexican hell truly perilous. As Sigbjørn says of himself in Chapter IV: "It was as if the ghost of a man who had hanged himself had returned to the scene of his suicide, not out of morbid curiosity, but out of sheer nostalgia to drink the drinks again that had nerved him to do it, and wonder perhaps that he had ever had the courage."

But this early insight is a fleeting one for Sigbjørn; for some time he feels more terror than anything else about what he is doing. Again, from Chapter IV, as he and Primrose enter a cantina, one of his old haunts: "it was much as if by so entering the past, he had stumbled into a labyrinth, with no thread to guide him, where the minotaur threatened at every step, and which was moreover a labyrinth that now at each turn led infallibly to a precipice, over which one might fall at any moment, at the bottom of which was the abyss." Later, the minotaur will turn out to be Sigbjørn himself, or a piece of him; but now it is monstrous, and Sigbjørn is afraid.

Or, to put it another way, use an image, not of descent and death, but of ascent and rebirth. This image, that of the phoenix rising out of its funeral pyre, was a Lowry favorite, a gift from Conrad Aiken; and Lowry uses it when he lets Sigbjørn speculate that

> It was as if the funeral pile had proved inadequate to the phoenix, and he had to look around him for another kind of immolation in the depths of the past. And he would find his old self here in Mexico if anywhere, if not quite the old self he had meant: he would come here, if anywhere, face to face as well as with, he hoped Fernando, with everything that that self had imperfectly transcended.

Sigbjørn's burning home in Canada had not been sufficient to transform him into a new, better self; perhaps the old destructive forces of Mexico could complete the job. And, in fact, so they do, yet not in the way Sigbjørn expects.

But this journey is nevertheless a descent, at least at first, and Sigbjørn's life accordingly deteriorates. No sooner have they reached their hotel in Mexico City when the *accidia* that is his worst enemy attacks Sigbjørn, and he must send the cheerful, touring Primrose down for a bottle of habanero, instead of going himself. Little, practical tasks have never been easy for Sigbjørn, but now he can hardly bring himself to buy Primrose a *torta,* or to find the right bus to the right town, or keep from being cheated by very nearly everyone he meets. This deadly sloth grows in him until, by Chapter VIII, he finds it difficult to move at all. Primrose is renewed, to be sure, but not Sigbjørn: he can only lie inert, blind, incurious, unloving, "cast into some anguish of the past, into some agony of self, chained by fear, whipped in the tentacles of the past, like some gloomy Laocoön."

Finally, tossed all the way into despair by the apparent rejection of his novel, Sigbjørn quarrels bitterly with Primrose, gets drunk, and slashes his wrist. This is the nadir, and from here on in *Dark As the Grave* the movement, though almost imperceptible at first, is upward. He finds himself able to talk (and talk, and talk) with friends about his dubious literary career, and he musters enough courage and energy to take Primrose with him to Oaxaca, most dreadful of cities, home of his worst moments in the past.

It is in Oaxaca that they hope to find Juan Fernando Martinez, and (for the sake of the ingenuous Primrose) to revisit the Farolito, the cantina where the worst danger resides. But first they meet John Stanford, another and very different sort of ghost from the past. For reasons which Lowry never develops, Stanford represents for Sigbjørn his evil angel—a perfect antithesis to Juan Fernando. But when he appears, Stanford is only a banal old lecher, himself rather afraid of Sigbjørn, and thus no threat at all.

And Juan Fernando is dead, murdered years before while drunk in a cantina. Sigbjørn's friend is laid in his dark grave—but so is the threat to Sigbjørn now buried. Sigbjørn is on his own, now able to live with some degree of hope for the future for himself and Primrose. This becomes clear to him, and to us, when Sigbjørn is able to pray for Juan Fernando, and—more important—to bless John Stanford as well. As he realizes during the visit to Mitla in the last chapter, he can now see himself as no longer simply a fictive character, a whim of some semicompetent daemon who is writing out Sigbjørn's life for him, but instead as the director of his own life, capable of controlling his own destiny. He is a Roderick Usher who has escaped destruction in the collapse of his home. Significantly, Sigbjørn discovers early the next day that the old Farolito no longer exists. And he and Primrose ride out of Oaxaca, sitting in the front of the bus, while all around them they see evidence of Juan Fernando's benevolence: the barren countryside is blooming, thanks to the work of Juan Fernando's Banco Ejidal. The fields of Etla have become a garden of paradise. Rebirth is upon them: Sigbjørn has willed a happy ending, and he has got it.

Now, this book is no *Under the Volcano*. It might have been but it isn't. There are too many loose ends, too many undeveloped ideas, too many images of intended great significance which never seem more than vaguely portentous. Sometimes Lowry's prose is hasty, even slovenly. The dialogue is often surprisingly wooden. The flight to Mexico with which the novel begins is probably the longest literary journey since that of the *Pequod;* and the evening that Sigbjørn spends talking about his fiction with Eddie and Hippolyte is nearly as lengthy. And improbable to boot: who could talk as long as Sigbjørn does? Who could listen as long as Eddie and Hippolyte do? And who, really, *are* Eddie and Hippolyte, other than receptacles for Sigbjørn's prolixity? Why is Primrose such a lightweight, alternately gushing and carping? How can one understand what is going on in *Dark As the Grave* unless he has a copy of *Under the Volcano* beside him as he reads, in order to keep track of the allusions, to recall characters and incidents?

In fairness to Lowry, we can say only that this work is a fragment, a notebook on its way to becoming a novel—and that Lowry would have needed at least four more years to bring it all together. It is frustrating (yet reassuring, when one wishes to defend Lowry's ability) to recall that his notes to himself in the "bolus" suggest what he would have done had there been time. The *longeurs* of the plane trip, for instance, were to have been alleviated by making Hippolyte a fellow passenger—which would also have had the effect of making the long night of exegesis in Cuernavaca a little more interesting. The *Drunkard's Rigadoon* business would, mercifully, have been pared down. There was to have been much more about John Stanford. Wilderness, the wife-slayer, was to have been a running theme, and not just a semi-waking dream, in the finished manuscript, with Sigbjørn following the slayer's movements and trial via newspaper reports throughout the trip. There were to have been many more allusions to *Parsifal* and *Tristan*. *Dark As the Grave* would, in fact, have been given the same treatment that *Under the Volcano* got: Lowry would have applied to it layer upon symbolic layer, tied together all his images in a tremendously complicated network of correspondences, and brought Sigbjørn Wilderness' quest into much sharper focus. But he never got very far along in his project, and our loss is not a small one.

Yet in spite of all its flaws, *Dark As the Grave Wherein My Friend Is Laid* needs only so many apologies; for the book has genuine merit as it stands. There is real Lowryesque comedy in it: the impossible bathroom in the Hotel Cornada; Sigbjørn's envious reflections about the robust virility of other novelists; the picture of Sigbjørn in the old Palacio de Bellas Artes, sitting all alone with his tequila for two hours while the surrealist film he has come to see is being shown upstairs in an anteroom; Sigbjørn's morning swim; Sigbjørn with a hangover—and so on. There is the occasional piece of description that stuns us with its grandeur, like the view from the hill in Yautepec:

> They laughed and then stopped. For beyond the volcanoes far, far, beyond the horizon, impossibly far away, almost like the White Sea and Arabia, almost like a dream, beyond the farthest mountains, as might have appeared the Promised Land to the Children of Israel, or Ceylon at three bells to the seaman chipping rust, it had seemed to Sigbjørn, pointing, that there, dimly and for the first time, was a shadowy hint of Oaxaca.

And above all, there is Sigbjørn Wilderness himself, frightened, shaky, inept—pulling himself together, then collapsing, then laughing at his collapse; then somehow, so quietly at first that we almost do not notice it, climbing out of his personal abyss and discovering that the dead world outside has come alive again. *Dark As the Grave Wherein My Friend Is Laid* is a work of embryonic greatness. We can lament its imperfect state, but we can also be glad to have it even as it is. Sigbjørn Wilderness, like his creator, was a man worth knowing.

Douglas Day

University of Virginia
August, 1967

DARK AS THE GRAVE

WHEREIN MY FRIEND IS LAID

I

THE SENSE OF SPEED, OF gigantic transition, of going southward, downward, over three countries, the tremendous mountain ranges, the sense at once of descent, tremendous regression, and of moving, not moving, but in another way dropping straight down the world, straight down the map, as of the imminence of something great, phenomenal, and yet the moving shadow of the plane below them, the eternal moving cross, less fleeting and more substantial than the dim shadow of the significance of what they were actually doing that Sigbjørn held in his mind: and yet it was possible only to focus on that shadow, and at that only for short periods: they were enclosed by the thing itself as by the huge bouncing machine with its vast monotonous purring, pouring din, in which they sat none too comfortably, Sigbjørn with his foot up embarrassedly, for he had taken his shoe off, a moving, deafening, continually renewed time-defeating destiny by which they were enclosed but of which they were able only to see the inside, for so to speak of the streamlined platinum-colored object itself they could only glimpse a wing, a propeller, through the small, foolish, narrow oblong windows. Nonetheless, the sense of adventure, if Sigbjørn participated in it mostly for Primrose's sake, was tremendous, too, and now, as they sat hand-in-hand, Primrose ecstatic at the window (the thunderous, dumbfounding voice of the plane), the sense of relief, of joy, they were through, yes, they were beyond the barrier—or one barrier, this much was certain—they were through the customs, they were away, they were in America; to the left was Oregon, to the right the Pacific coast ranges, but the sense of joy did not wholly mitigate those other gnawing feelings, which Sigbjørn took care to keep out of his face, of sorrow, of crashing failure, and, even now, when there seemed little to worry him at the moment, of blind and all-possessing, of permanent panic.

Leaving Oregon at sunset, clouds carved out of black basalt, and a rim of turquoise-jade-green—did they have jade mines in Oaxaca?—and light flowing pure gold-orange: "You never saw such a sunset on earth," Primrose said, and indeed you did not, Sigbjørn thought, so dark and terrible, this great black basalt sunset over the burned forests of Oregon, the burning gold and great shafts of burning light against ten-mile-high piles of black clouds shot through with these shafts of unearthly light and unearthly foreboding. "We're through!" Primrose said. "Now do you see how wrong you were!"

"We're late too," Sigbjørn said, glancing at his new French antimagnetic wristwatch, a pre-wedding-anniversary present from Primrose.

"But we're in America, and you said you'd never be able to go to America again."

"In America, but not in Mexico yet," said Sigbjørn, and Primrose Wilderness laughed. "Still I imagine Fernando can wait another week or so, having waited more than seven years," he added. "But it's true. Here we are, and I never thought we would get through, even to America."

"And we're on our honeymoon."

"We're always on our honeymoon."

"Five years—"

They sat at the back of the plane (at the back so that no one would see *him*) and Sigbjørn kissed her.

To their right a star shone out in the western agony on the horizon. "Altair," Primrose said.

"And soon we'll see the Southern Cross."

"Tomorrow perhaps . . . *and* all of Eridanus."

And it was true, they were through, beyond the barrier, or the first barrier, and there away to the right stretched the Pacific coast ranges and the sea, the same ranges in whose shadow, back in Canada, they lived, which ran right down to Tierra del Fuego itself, to Cape Horn, the same sea on which they lived too, and which lapped on the shores of Acapulco Bay, of dubious memory, and of what promise for the future?

It was as if, since that day of ruination on June 6, 1944 (tomorrow would be December 7—December 7!—1945), that Sigbjørn had, little by little, let slip his hold on his life: in a subtle sense both of them had: they had not let go, altogether, but they had fallen, and they were now on a lower ledge than before: their marriage, and their life even, was in danger, and he knew it, and was doing nothing about it (his marriage in fact was an almost exact counterpoint of his house: it had fallen asunder and had not yet properly been put together again); he was using his wife's necessity and the fact that she had never visited a foreign country as an excuse for indulging his own necessity—for what, was it—what was it but death? Or was this trip, ostensibly for Primrose, something that nature, destiny, was giving him, in return for the loss of his book . . . ?

Just as he had taken his first drink for three years on June 6, 1944, now today—after another period of abstinence—he had begun drinking, a little, not much, to celebrate. Why had he been so disappointed that they had some kind of prohibition in Portland? What did San Francisco mean to him but another drink? this time of Scotch, which he couldn't get in Canada. Why had he used Fernando Martinez of all people, as a kind of excuse for going to Mexico? What did his friend, his character Dr. Vigil, mean to him, but a nostalgia for delirium? Or oblivion. And his meeting with him another excuse, even such as the Consul liked to find, for "celebration."

Nonetheless, Sigbjørn had a sense of hope: or at any rate, after his illness, and his wife's, a sense of it, not great, rather poignant, as if one had risen one winter morning and looked out into the garden to see a wild apple tree in bloom.

It had been a day of darkness and murk and rain. By the time they started for Vancouver airport it was drizzling rain, and when their plane finally took off, it was a blizzard: swirls and lashes of rain across the Seattle airport, Customs inspectors in pools—Sigbjørn shuddered. Customs inspectors! How afraid of such creatures he was—would he ever get over it? And the memory of that morning more than six years ago when he had been turned back to Canada at the American border came heavily and clammily about him once more. That was September, 1939, and he had been trying to enter America by bus through Blaine, Washington, in order to see Primrose herself at San Francisco— "for the last time," as he had tactlessly put it to the Immigration inspectors. And now here they were anyway, over that border, beyond it, and a great sense of freedom possessed him at this idea, of flying right down America, right down the western side of the map, over this once forbidden territory (ravaged here by fire too as far as the eye could reach), forbidden not only because he had been designated as a person liable to be a public charge upon it, but because the territory itself was at that time neutral, and he proposed crossing it in order also to fight in a foreign war in which, incidentally, he had not finally participated in any capacity whatsoever; so it was true that that misfortune could be seen as having saved his life, something for which he forgot too often to be grateful—was he ever really grateful save when he read this as "our lives together"?—down, down over the western ranges, beating the sunset; but down into complete darkness now, flying into Frisco spitting fire, lights like a bowknot, cities like rock candy, lights like a question mark, a bus station of pearls—they got out to have a drink. It was fine weather at the San Francisco airport, with the stars clear. "Alıs volat propriis," Sigbjørn remarked, turning, for a moment toward the faithful plane in its more unfamiliar mood of being stationary and silent, a meek appurtenance of a field.

"What does that mean?"

"Does an Englishman have to tell you your own state motto? She flies with her own wings, unlike the nonexistent bird with one. Well, it's either Oregon or California's."

"It isn't California's. So you've made San Francisco at last." Primrose could laugh now.

"Is this your first trip by air?" a fellow passenger was asking them.

"No, but it's our first decent drink of Scotch in half a decade,"

Sigbjørn said, though now he had it, it tasted rather medicinal, and far from ordering another, he gave Primrose half his.

"You folks from Seattle?"

"Canada. . . . That is, my wife's American. I'm—well—anyway."

"Fifty cents for a snort," Primrose was saying. "It certainly costs."

"And how. On holiday?"

"We're on our honeymoon."

"Ah . . ."

"We're off to see a pal of mine in Mexico if he's still there. . . . We've been married for five years, but we're still on our honeymoon," Sigbjørn explained hastily. "Only," he added a little later, "our house burned down but we saved the forest."

Though this latter event had taken place eighteen months ago, the Wildernesses still evidently had to talk about it. But had that anything to do with why he, Sigbjørn, felt such a ridiculous need to give an *account* of himself? And why had he brought in that honeymoon, an intimate little joke between Primrose and himself? Why did he do such things? And what the devil was everybody still so suspicious for? What bloody right had they to question one? Sigbjørn wondered as they boarded the plane again, wishing now he hadn't mentioned Mexico either, which might seem suspicious in itself. And at that, three months after the war was over. Perhaps it was Primrose's Arctic skunk coat, his own preanniversary present to her, that was the trouble: people might think she was a Russian spy. There was a spy scare in Canada just now, and to judge from all accounts, an even worse one in America. In fact merely to have come from Canada, with its relative proximity to Russia, might seem even more suspicious than to be going to Mexico. Sigbjørn was so absurdly shaken, though in all seriousness, by this, that he now wished he had not given half of his drink to Primrose; he was finding difficulty with his safety belt, and after the new stewardess had admiringly hung up the beautiful coat, Primrose had to adjust the strap for him. They were soaring above San Francisco; he leaned over to see the lights again behind and below in the distance, and Sigbjørn thought of the diatonic booming of the

foghorn in the great bridge. That time he had been turned back
at the border he had been visualizing walking over the bridge
with Primrose. He couldn't bear even now to think of her waiting vainly for him in this city, for waited she had. His first mes-
sages had somehow miscarried. Still, it all worked to a joyous
ending; Primrose instead came to Canada; and now, happily
married for years, they were flying over the bridge, had literally
risen above it, as she would say. When they had unfastened their
belts, Primrose prepared to sleep on Sigbjørn's shoulder, while
Sigbjørn wondered if he had sufficient courage to take his shoes
off. He decided, despite their seat at the back, that he had not.
Refraining from smoking for fear of disturbing her, Sigbjørn
contrived somehow to keep his right foot up: both feet were still
swollen slightly, the right was the worst one. Five hundred miles
to go for the next stop, Los Angeles. And, overpraised method of
travel though flying might be, this was at least better than sitting
with both those feet in a bucket of hot water, five minutes after a
bucket of cold water, in their poor beloved rainy house in Eridanus, British Columbia, that they had been building on what remained of their old burned site, between the forest and the inlet
—better, certainly for poor Primrose, who had had, now their
well was dry, to drag down the water herself from the store, and
this after having not long recovered from a dangerous infection
herself.

"Come over here, son, you can get a better view." The passenger who had spoken to them in the bar was leaning over the aisle,
and Sigbjørn, seeing there was now a vacant seat beside him,
smiled at Primrose, and went over and sat down in the other
place, wondering at the same time why he had allowed his will
to be presumed on. Perhaps it was the "son" that did it; somehow it moved him, not unnaturally, for Sigbjørn was thirty-six, a
fact that he immediately remembered when the man added: "A
lot of water has flowed under that thing since I was last here."

The remote lights of the bridge were now almost immediately
beneath them, their plane was circling for height. "We've got a
very beautiful one in Vancouver too, not so big as this of course.
Unfortunately people are always jumping off it," Sigbjørn said.

"Ever been to San Francisco before?" asked the man, who had
a rather deep voice.

"Yes," answered Sigbjørn. "As a matter of fact I have. Twice, to be exact. I went to Mexico from here once before. That was in 1936, September, 1936, when I was about twenty-seven. Panama Pacific. On the *Pennsylvania*. We sailed right down under that bridge to San Pedro, and then down the Lower California coast past Mazatlán to Acapulco, where we landed."

"Oh, you've been to Mexico before too? What did you do there?"

"Drank mostly," Sigbjørn answered, after taking some thought.

"Oh yes, we can all do a bit of that, ha ha."

"Well, I was a journalist at times," Sigbjørn thought of saying, though it would have been almost a lie, and kept silent, though not for that reason.

"Will you have a snifter?" The man produced a flask, as the plane roared on southward through the night.

"No thanks. . . . Though I will have a smoke. Thanks. Thanks a lot."

"Fire is a very terrible thing," said the other, blowing out the proffered match.

Sigbjørn went on after a pause: "My mother often spoke of my grandfather sailing from San Francisco. That was in England, of course. My grandfather was a skipper in sail, he was wrecked, and drowned in the Bay of Bengal. Actually, his ship was blown up. He had a rather heroic death. . . . It became quite a legend. They were in the doldrums. The crew had cholera." Sigbjørn stopped. "But that would be before the bridge was built," he added.

"Were you insured?"

"You're talking about our house? No, it was just a cabin on government land we'd bought for a hundred dollars from a blacksmith," Sigbjørn said shortly. "But it was our first home and we loved it. We've been building another one now on almost the same site, not quite the same, unfortunately. We've built it mostly out of the lumber from a dismantled sawmill." Sigbjørn thought of the big windows they'd wangled from the machine shop and how proud Primrose was when, with Mauger's help, they had finally fitted them into their frames. *Nine-light windows that never saw the sun. Now face the east in a house that's scarce begun. Who once lent grudging day to a machine, what joys and agonies would they someday light within?* Too many days, too much light. Or it was, could be, almost, a poem. "We've been working on the place since last March, and we hoped to get it finished for this winter," he continued. "But we had accident after accident, and the going got too tough for us all round. We really had to put yet another roof on the place to make it habitable, and the weather's just been too bad to do it. I would say altogether it was too hard on my wife." Sigbjørn looked round to see if this well-intentioned half-lie had reached Primrose's ears for if truth were told it had more than equally proved too hard on him.

"You don't mean to tell me that you were doing this work yourselves?"

"Who else would do it? But it's a fishing village, and the fishermen gave us help, when they were there." But if he thought of the unfinished house with sadness, it was also with pride. Yes, frightened though he had become at almost everything now, they together had been courageous, though he said it himself, with their everlasting terror of fire, and considering everything that had happened, to rebuild there, in that place. And considering everything that had gone on happening, to go on rebuilding. To have done this with their own hands was the least thing about it. And especially had it been courageous of Primrose, who in her own way had become more frightened than he. The difference between them was that it was possible that Primrose had left her fright behind in Eridanus and he fervently hoped he could help, by this trip, for this to remain so, never to be assumed when they returned: for her, much depended on him, but his own road was more complicated.

"What's the name of your village?" his companion was inquiring. "Perhaps I know it. I've hunted up in British Columbia once or twice."

"Eridanus. It's down an inlet of the same name fairly near Vancouver. But that doesn't mean anything, for there's every kind of wilderness fairly near Vancouver, come to that."

"I've done a little navigation in my day. Am I wrong, or isn't Eridanus the name of a star?"

"It's the name of a constellation, the one south of Orion. It looks like a river and to the ancients was identified with the River Styx. That's about all I know about it, except that it's also been called the river of youth, possibly because it was associated with Phaeton, a man who insisted on driving the chariot of the sun against his father's orders, and as a consequence burned the earth up. Thus it's been called both the river of death and the river of youth. You can't see the whole constellation up north where we are and we were hoping to see the rest of it in Mexico. The inlet got its name from another windjammer belonging to a company that liked to christen its ships after the constellations and she was apparently driven ashore in a violent chinook. Some of the very old-timers claimed to remember when parts of the wreck were still on the beach and she was said to have carried a very pleasant cargo of marble and cherries-in-brine and wine from Portugal."

"How did your first house catch fire?" the persistent fellow was asking him, when Sigbjørn excused himself and returned to his seat by Primrose, who was now fast asleep, breathing gently like a child, with her head cushioned on her arm. God, how innocent and beautiful, even angelic she looked, with her lips slightly parted and the lamplight falling on her face like that. You would not have thought she had ever suffered. And you would have thought she was at least fifteen years younger than he was, whereas in fact she was slightly older—thirty-nine. Nor had the light anything to do with it. She looked younger still by daylight. In fact Sigbjørn had been at pains to bring his marriage license with him, not merely lest he be impeached in America under the Mann Act, the white slave traffic ruling, that must be so baffling to Frenchmen, which forbids your taking a woman not your wife across any border, under pain of hanging or electrocution, but—talk about freedom from fear—under the California law that would have baffled his own father and mother, which forbids a man's cohabitation with any woman below the age of consent, under pain of ninety-nine years' incarceration for rape. Or so, quite seriously, these laws had taken form in his mind. Sigbjørn switched his lamp off, as he did so noticing that his fellow passenger had done the same. Suddenly what remained of the feeling of pride and pleasure that he had had while talking about the house, as well as his feeling of tolerance for the man, was succeeded by one of violent shame. Idiot! Buffoon! Oaf! Here he had been maundering to himself about people's inquisitiveness, and what precisely had this damn fellow drawn out of him! Everything, or almost everything. And what had he, Sigbjørn, whose business it might be considered so to glean, learned about the man? Nothing, or almost nothing. Why, he could not now—the man was slightly ahead of them, he was dozing and had turned the light off, and Sigbjørn saw only the vague shape of his back—he could not now have told what sort of clothes the man wore, how tall he was, though he had seen he was taller than himself in the bar, whether he was fat or thin, whether he was an American or a German or even an Armenian. He was not even a face. He was nothing but a voice, a rather deep voice, and what was so awful, Sigbjørn was content that he should be so, he had no curiosity about him in the slightest. The only thing he remembered clearly, or perhaps had looked at, was the flask and now he wished he'd accepted a drink from it, just as he had wished earlier that he had not only not given Primrose half his whiskey at the bar, but ordered another one. Perhaps he'd only refused the drink because of the flask itself, which was one of those yellow leather-clad contraptions he particularly disliked, whose declining contents were marked by pictorial gradations: Half full, Quarter full, a little man becoming more and more borracho, with at the bottom a picture of a pig, labeled Damn Fool, which hinted (though what Sigbjørn possibly despised most about them was that they always held less than a pint) that those contents might be as cheaply unamusing as its exterior; and that was all, absolutely all—unless you counted that the man had once hunted, or said he had once hunted, in Canada, and once done a little navigation, or said he'd done a little navigation—that Sigbjørn knew about him. Now could you build the man up from the synecdoche of the porcine flask, which most likely had been given him as a parting present, as some gag at the airport, and had little bearing on his character at all. One had been presented to Sigbjørn himself years ago with conceivably better reason. But if he had not learned anything

whatsoever about him, by this very defection was not so much
more revealed about Sigbjørn himself to himself? For Sigbjørn
had not quite given away the most salient point, that <u>he was, if a
monumentally unsuccessful one, and of late silent, a writer.</u> It
was thus that their positions were, so to say, reversed; the voice
having behaved as a writer was supposed to behave, and himself
as his potential subject. And how easily he had fallen into the
trap! He had been enticed into it like a son, and then had found
himself talking like a father, or as a father might, were his intention less to instruct than to make himself important, or to justify
himself. The immature father and the inquisitive son. The subject and object. Yes, to justify himself. Why? For it seemed to
him now that it was not only that he hadn't grasped the opportunity to learn anything about this individual, it was almost as if
he'd felt obliged—and this went far beyond his former thought
of the necessity of giving an account of himself—to make some
excuse or explanation for being on earth at all. Or was this in his
imagination? First he was as much secretly flattered, whatever
his later reactions, as outraged, at being spoken to in the first
place. Yet while he was glad that the man was interested in his
life, since this was indeed interest in his work at one remove,
nonetheless he was very much afraid that he would be asked embarrassing questions, which was why he had to talk, to supply
even symbolical answers to those questions in advance to forestall their being asked, such questions as: "Were you in any of
the services?" He still felt that at this point of history in this
hemisphere, to the greater part of humanity, even if its immediate representative had never been within a thousand miles of a
war, a man simply possessed no cognizable value whatsoever who
had not been precisely in one of those services. Sigbjørn lit a
cigarette and kicked off his shoes angrily. *Al stereless and in a
boot am I, amid the sea, between windes two, that in contrarie
standen evermo.* And those contrarie windes, what were they?
Were not those improbable winds, the subjective wind, and the
objective wind, that blew out of who knew how much more improbable immensities? Objective wind indeed! Sigbjørn now
went back over his shameful recital, as it now seemed to him,
and if for no better reason than it had been made at all, and

tried to imagine what he himself would have learned from it, had he been in the other's place.

He could not help laughing at himself. And all that because he had not said he was a writer. Take that away, and his life, objectively considered, seemed to have no meaning at all. Did all creative writers, in one way or another, suffer from this ghastly alienation? If they did, they certainly tried their best these days to keep it dark. On the face of it, you would think they—and by "they" he meant all the better writers in his own language he could think of at the moment—were the kind of people who rose early and shot pheasants boisterously out of the sky, were capable of gigantic feats of farming or engineering or even stone masonry, had muscles like barbellmen, hurtled through Belgium on motorcycles, fought in wars like young Charlemagnes, were traitors, or became heroes of the people, like Erikson, with equal zest, and even when they were geniuses, like Daniel, turned out their work as easily as if it came out of some celestial sausage machine. And they had one thing in common: with very few exceptions they all seemed, at bottom, to be incorrigible optimists, even when their works were most despairing. Or this was what they took care to have known. Such people might go into exile, forcibly or as a protest, but you could never think of them being turned back from a border as a person likely to be a public charge. No, you felt that the very exuberance of their bloody optimism would carry them through any border, if necessary, without a passport. Sigbjørn had scarcely ever read a genuine book about a writer. Usually if the writer wanted to talk about his own struggles, he disguised them as those of a sculptor, or a musician, or of any other character, as though he were ashamed of his profession. It was a pity. For to learn something of the mechanics of his kind of creation, was not that to learn something of the mechanism of destiny? There was even a sort of unwritten law about it. Indeed it was the first thing you learned: the reader does not want to hear about your rejected play. That was true: still, why not? Half the world was like a writer who has had his play rejected. In fact the world at times seemed very like a rejected play itself. Or a rejected novel; like for instance, *The Valley of the Shadow of Death,* by Sigbjørn

Wilderness. A world in suspense, a world in delirium, a drunken world in fear. But fear, that was another thing. With him there were too many fears, so that the word too, like himself, was liable to lose all meaning—it was high time he categorized them.

At this moment there was a brilliant flash throughout the plane, the machine gave a lurch upward, bounced, lurched upward again, and simultaneously with the appearance of the sign ahead bidding them fasten their safety belts, there was a single tremendous thunderpeal. But the lightning, a good writer, did not repeat itself. The plane roared on.

A ballet, yes. Such form, through his half closed eyes, Sigbjørn could now almost imagine he perceived hovering above the passengers all sitting bound to their seats under the ceiling lights, as though the plane had suddenly been invaded by skyway robbers, like a ballet, or something in some old morality play, or a ghostly animated cartoon. There was a dancer, (a) alpha for acrophobia, the fear of heights, whose white mask was set in a fixed muted yell, as if perpetually contemplating a vast drop below him; there was a dancer (b), the fear of discovery, a jester— for even Sigbjørn could not bear that he be wholly serious, yet with an implacable mask who carried newspapers under his arm with such headlines as Wilderness's Works Written by Erikson, or Writer Confesses Old Murder, or Wilderness Admitted Liar; there was (y), a grinning witless mask, but more familiar than any of the others, for he had perhaps been with him the longest, the fear of disease; and dancer (z), with a mask that wept, the fear of losing Primrose; there was the fear of Primrose's fear, with a mask that screamed; and with Wilderness's own face streaming with blood, the fear of himself, and with his head turned always Dantesquely facing backward, with a sombrero, and a bottle of mescal in his hand, who was fear of Mexico; there was the motor face of fear of accidents and traffic, and the frenzied roaring face of fear of fire whom he could not contemplate for a second; and all of them were chased about, herded, ordered, and finally set to dance together by a master choreographer, a giant in the brutal boot-faced mask of an Immigration officer, or a border official, or a Consul, or a policeman, though his mien was military and he wore a uniform covered with medals, with two guns at the hip, who was fear of authority. One dancer who did not seem to be present was the fear of death, which was an odd thing, but perhaps he was not so much a fear as a medium in which one lived. Or possibly he was disguised as the fear of losing Primrose or the fear of sorrow. Though in another sense the fear of death in so far as it existed was his one unselfish fear, for it was the fear of Primrose's sorrow. A ghastly alienation indeed! Did any hint appear in his face that such appalling tableaux were invariably shaping themselves before his inner eye, even at his happiest moments? And was this the real reason why he had been selected all those years ago as the person to turn back from the border? The sign went off, and Sigbjørn unfastened their safety belts, and though they seemed to have come out of the storm the plane still rocked and bounced. They could not be more than an hour now from Los Angeles. Would there be any formalities to go through there? For the stewardess had said that it was not certain in this weather that the Los Angeles-El Paso-Monterrey flight would be "on," in which case they might have to go straight down through Mazatlán, and Los Angeles would be their port of exit. This would mean delay too, for he had tried for that flight, as being the more exciting of the two, but had failed to get tickets. Oh well, throw away your mind, as dear old Fernando would say. It was not easy. According to some Scandinavian writer, you always remember the moods when you were thinking hardest.

A scene that had taken place just this morning at the Vancouver airport came back to him vividly. When their airliner limousine had drawn in at the airport entrance, a police car had been standing in the rain outside, and possibly it was this that had put him off. Sigbjørn had fumbled and dropped his tickets, forgotten to give one bag in to be weighed, and become covered with confusion, and it was not until Primrose and he were seated finally on a bench waiting for the southern flight to be called that it occurred to him that the presence of the police car was probably a matter of course. Then he seemed to remember that police cars nearly always were to be found standing outside airports, a war measure that no doubt someone had forgotten to cancel, or was still in operation, for the very good reason that peace had technically not yet been signed. With this realization Sigbjørn sighed with relief and was able to give himself for a while wholly to Primrose and their excitement. Meantime they had watched, through the French windows of the waiting room, a big plane arriving from Seattle. It maneuvered for position, the ramp was wheeled up, and the passengers began to hurry down it through the downpour, over the tarmac, and toward the wicket, where their tickets were taken by cloaked officials. Sigbjørn now suddenly became aware that he was watching these passengers narrowly, that the whole process of their arrival had become something of extraordinary importance to him. Many of these passengers were obviously American and thus were landing in what was, for them, a foreign country. How would they, his cousins, his brothers from across the border, meet the ordeal of examination on this side? Well-dressed for the most part, cheerful, exhibiting an unusual patience despite the weather, they gave in their tickets and passed through the gate as thoughtlessly as though they were going into a cinema. And now here stepped one young fellow out onto the ramp, who evidently regarded his ordeal with such indifference he hadn't even bothered to shave or comb his hair. Here now, he approached hatless, chewing gum, the wind blowing his fair hair about, whereas Sigbjørn for fifteen minutes prior to landing would not have had a moment's peace about his hair; he would have been dodging in and out of the lavatory and plaguing Primrose as to whether he looked "all right" (as only too soon now, as they came ever nearer to Los Angeles, he would begin plaguing Primrose) and as this man drew closer, sauntering nonchalantly across the tarmac with his friend, and then past the gate, a minute or two later, was to be seen just as nonchalantly going through the Customs, even daring to smoke, Sigbjørn discovered that his whole mind had become focused upon him, that for a moment he filled his world, blotting out all else. For that moment the man seemed to him the epitome of everything that he would like to be, and in being that, he *was* him. It was precisely the reverse of what had just taken place on the plane between himself and his fellow passenger. So absolutely did his being seem to enter into that of this other totally different and carefree person that it was like one of those identities of subject with object that are the end of certain mystical disciplines and Sigbjørn almost had the feeling that if he did not hold on to himself he would disappear altogether. This man also, it now struck Sigbjørn, resembled in that respect one of those optimistic writers he had been thinking about, a person who would get through any Customs, any border, do what he would, by virtue perhaps of his very volition, of the impossibility of any idea of any hitch entering his head.

Was this a good sign? Sigbjørn now wondered. Certainly it was rather a second-rate ambition to be an optimist, but was there a suggestion, in all this, that some part of him at least felt capable of writing again? Had he not once, he now recalled, transcended his own experience of having been turned back at the border by writing about it? Or if not transcended it, turned it to account, made it *work*. He had. He had, once, written a poem about it, and though he had not thought of this poem, which he had never sold and had lost completely in the fire, for years, it now, queerly, began to come back to him:

> *A singing smell of tar, of the highway,*
> *Fills the gray Vancouver Bus Terminal*
> *Crowned by dreaming names, Portland, New Orleans,*
> *Spokane, Chicago—and Los Angeles!*
> *City of the angels and my luck—*

How did it go on? If he had the energy, he would write it down, if he could remember any more. How pleased Primrose would be with him! But now he felt sleepy, and besides there was another obstruction against writing anything down. *A singing smell of tar, of the highway.* Then that would seem to mean also that he too had once been as carefree, so far as any trouble at the border was concerned, as that tousled fellow landing from the Seattle plane. His longing to see Primrose, and his joy at the expectation of meeting her again, had been so great that it had even wiped out the fear that, for all he knew to the contrary, even when he did see her, he would have to part from her again soon.

Yes indeed. His joy had been great. What kind of poem,

though, had he been trying to write? A kind of sestina, though more elaborate than a sestina, of eight verses, of ten lines each with, to begin with instead of the end words being repeated, the last line of the second verse rhyming, or rhyming falsely, or striking an assonance with the first line of the first. But what had been his general purpose in choosing such a form? Sigbjørn remembered that he had wanted to give the impression of the bus going one way, toward the border and the future, and, at the same time, of the shopwindows and streets flashing by into the past: he had wished to do that, but something more: since the poem was to be about his being turned *back* at the border, these shopwindows and streets that he was so glibly imagining in the past were in the future too, for tonight and at the end of the poem he would have to return *from* the border by a similar bus along exactly the same route, that is, in both an opposite direction, and an opposite mood. But he hadn't got to the border yet so he set out afresh to do the same thing as before with another unit of two verses. How did it go on?

Primrose was shaking him, to put on his safety belt. My God! Here they were at Los Angeles itself. Lights were all round them and he was not going to have time to comb his hair. But there was no need, Primrose was saying. The El Paso flight was on.

II

THE LOBBY OF A GREAT
American airport such as Los Angeles at this period of history
was rather like the major part of a stage divided into compart-
ments where one of those symbolic plays is being performed
whose playwright delights in manipulating great masses of people, his interest being in groups, rather than individuals. At
one moment this part of the stage seems full of soldiers. At the
next, sailors. At the next the member of a nomadic dance band is
inquiring at the desk if there is room for him to take his bass
fiddle. But by that time your interest is focused upon the coffee
shop, which is monopolized by marines. Back to the lobby again,
and you see it is full of priests, all bound for a religious conven-
tion. Yet there is this difference. The groups of people change
with bewildering rapidity, but late at night, like this, having
made vast journeys out of one immensity into another, they are
mostly silent. Most of the dialogue is taken care of by a loudspeaker that barks at regular intervals: "Will the passengers on
the Eastern flight to Denver and Salt Lake City please have their
tickets ready." Or Chicago–Detroit–Cleveland–Boston. Or El
Paso–Monterrey–Mexico City, as it happened to be.

This last was the call that the Wildernesses were waiting for
but their flight went out at midnight so they had plenty of time.
Since there were no formalities to be gone through Sigbjørn had

a pleasant feeling of freedom in which to exercise a revived curiosity. It was also, in spite of his having been round the world as a sailor and their having lived in Los Angeles before, a new experience for them both. The airport was new too, but it was not that which was of such interest, though neither happened to have seen it. Nor was it that in appearance Los Angeles differed so greatly from any other large airports on their route. Nor were they complete strangers to flying, if they had flown before only for short distances. It was that the mode of travel on this great scale was new itself, and no airport could have more absolutely expressed this newness than Los Angeles, than this huge gray-sounding place with its tremendous sense of *junction*, to north, south, east, and west. So Sigbjørn reflected must Herman Melville, masquerading as Redburn, have felt at Euston Station, in London, over a hundred years ago, if Euston could be called a junction. Meantime the only people apparently not tired, they wandered round the airport taking in everything, as happily as a couple of Australians in their first snowstorm.

"I'm dying for a cup of coffee," Primrose said finally.

"Do you remember what a tremendous dissipation that used to be in this town?" Sigbjørn said, pushing the swing door open for her. The coffee shop, crowded five minutes before, was now empty, so that they could go on stretching their legs and talking freely without embarrassment. But after a while Sigbjørn sat down to rest his feet, putting his right one up on a neighboring seat.

"Something a bit too much like the motion of too many other writers," he was saying, "with the syllables counted rather than the iambics flowing. Here, let me finish writing it down for you. But not bad. I feel encouraged. Of course I suppose I was a better cartoonist, not to say game warden, if not fire warden, than I'll ever be a poet. But even after all these years it seems to have something original about it. I don't know how it was I came to remember it all, just like that. Nothing like it's ever happened to me before."

"Oh Sigbjørn, I'm so excited, it *is* a good omen. I've always loved that poem."

"Do you mind telling me—this isn't a dirty crack—if you remembered I'd lost it in the fire?"

"Of course I did," Primrose said. "I worked on it with you. You called it 'The Canadian Turned Back at the Border.' How could I have forgotten?"

"Very easily indeed. *I* did. Primrose, you look marvelous. . . . Something very special."

"Do I, darling?" Primrose said, patting her hair and grimacing in the mirror. "Really I look terrible. I couldn't get into the washroom on the plane to put on a face. And I couldn't get in the airport one either. It was full of Waves or Wacs or whatever you call them."

"You don't need to put on a face. You look all the sweeter with it a bit dirty. Look out, here comes your second cup of coffee."

A flushed and hatless young man on a swivel stool asked the waitress: "Have you see that film *Drunkard's Rigadoon?*"

"Ugh."

"All about a drunk. Damndest thing you ever saw in your life. It's the biggest hit in town. They're getting all the drunks and all the anti's. Turning them away by the thousands." The young man did not order anything. Sigbjørn finished his coffee. Then without looking at Primrose, he rose and went out to the washroom where a tall man adjusting a bow tie in a mirror was saying to a soldier in khaki vigorously drying his hands on a paper towel: "I haven't had a drink since I saw that God damn thing. . . . Pretty good, eh . . . you know, that scene where he swipes the blind man's money box. Quite a kick." *Kilroy was here. El Grafe was looking*.

"That Jake Sawson, eh?"

"In line for the Oscar."

Sigbjørn looked out of the transom: *Supreme Pictures Grand Premiere Drunkard's Rigadoon*—"*Tops them all*," *Gabbler Hooples*, glared an advertisement; on the other side—it was a pyramidal hoarding—appeared, cunningly placed, an advertisement for Old Grand-Dad whiskey, a cocker spaniel with a benign air holding his master's slippers while his master, with a fatuous expression, drank a big snort of Old Grand-Dad. Sigbjørn laughed.

The Wildernesses drifted into the airport cocktail bar upstairs, which seemed, however, on the point of closing. It was

raining slowly outside. Both advertisements, which were off by
the highway, were illuminated by neon lights against which the
raindrops seemed to hang, large, luminous, and menacing.
Tilted planes of glistening aluminum lay staggered about the
concrete area. Wet lights shone in the runways. The road led
between an inexpressible desolation of hoardings into darkness,
the barren deathscape of Los Angeles. And yet it was in this hell
that they had met.

"What is it, darling?"

"All right. You heard."

"It's purely a clinical study; it's only a small part of yours."

drinking "Like hell it's a small part. At all events it's meant to be the
best part. And it's the most important part."

"It could be anything else, not drinking."

Sigbjørn was silent.

"Let him have his little triumph. When there's so much *more*
in your book."

"A work of art should have but one subject, Yeats at any rate
said."

"Now I really know why Fernando called you the maker of
tragedies."

"And to my mind, it's by no means a little triumph."

"Oh, *Sig*bjørn!"

"No, no, not tonight," Sigbjørn said, jumping to his feet.
"Anything but that tonight. Let's have another drink." He held
up two fingers, noticing that the mark of his craft, the small blis-
ter on the inside of his second finger, was not altogether faded.
"Dos, por favor. I mean two."

"Can't you unalloyedly be happy just this once, on the eve of
our wedding anniversary, must there always be *something*—!"
Primrose began, as was sometimes her habit, using the very con-
text of his own implied apology to prolong the quarrel, just
when he thought all was made up. But Sigbjørn smiled with love
toward her at that word "unalloyedly." This was what came of
being married to him. At this rate it would be only a matter of
time before "unalloyedly" crept into one of her papers on the
glaucionetta clangula. Or would it be the trogon ambiguus ambiguus?

"Yes, I certainly can be unalloyedly happy, as you put it," Sigbjørn chuckled.

The drinks were brought by the barman who, though he had already pulled down the blinds, seemed now disposed to linger.

"And here's to you, Primrose darling. It's been a marvelous day and I'm not going to let anything spoil it."

"Here's to you, sweetheart," But Primrose was on the verge of tears and went out to powder her nose.

"What's the matter with the little lady?"

"Have *you* seen this *Drunkard's Rigadoon?*" Sigbjørn asked after a pause.

"Get all kinds of people here," answered the other, wiping the bar. "Crazy in the feet, crazy in the head, crazy in the stomach. Screwballs. Well, I once read a book, ha ha."

"I wasn't talking about a book, I mean the movie."

Well, at least *some*one had not seen it.

But my God, what a cruel trick this was, coming just at this moment, and all done so casually too! He had known all about the book being written, of course, had found out, indeed, just before the fire, just when he had to be putting the finishing touches on *The Valley of the Shadow of Death*. Should he tell the barman this? The eternal confessional of the bar. According to statistics, the highest suicide rate was among barmen. He had told Primrose, years and years ago, half fearing it might happen, that should another book be published on that theme—not on that mere theme, but which entered as tremendously far as he flattered himself he was going into the calamitous suffering drink could cause to the drinker—he would kill himself. Had then the greater disaster of the fire, with the destruction of *In Ballast to the White Sea*, the third part of the trilogy he was writing with his portrait of Erikson in it, saved him? He had been fortunate, prior to the fire, in having read only a mediocre review of *Drunkard's Rigadoon*. Had he known at that time, as he was to know later, in Niagara, that the book was becoming a household word, he might indeed have killed himself, even though his threat to Primrose had not been altogether serious. Might he? Perhaps not. And if he had *read* the book then? He had been saved by the isolation of his position in Eridanus—by that, and by two things he had always deplored, Canada's ineffably vulgar taste and her barbarous and loutish ruling that prevented, while permitting pulp magazines of all kinds, any intellectual periodicals to cross the border from America during the war. So, by the miracle of that one review, while the news had appalled him, he had not been particularly encouraged to buy the book, and so was not to learn its true and, for him, heartbreaking, merit and fame till later. Gilbert Reid in Niagara had been privileged by his profession to cross and recross the border, so that his status was not much different from that of an American. He had his finger on the pulse of everything. On the pulse of *Drunkard's Rigadoon*. And, most especially, on the pulse of something else. For was it not Gilbert who had told him—told him without even knowing that Sigbjørn knew him—that Erikson was dead too? Yes, for when they had gone to Niagara in refuge from their fire, it was only to discover that he had died, like the book that contained his portrait, in flames, and when had he died? He had died in what would be, in one hour, two years ago tonight, and what had been, then, six months before, also on their wedding anniversary, in a bomber, in the great raids over Berlin, on December 7, 1943. And so, what was their day of rejoicing, to him, would also be forever a day of mourning. Could he tell the barman that? Tell God that? Remind Primrose of it? Intimate it, to the cheerful ghost of Erikson, who would hate it and tell him to drop the idea instantly? So he would, so he was trying to, and so now he had the film of *Drunkard's Rigadoon* to bother him. Oh, throw away your mind, old maker of tragedies. It had meant everything to him, the writing of *The Valley of the Shadow of Death,* the feeling of turning his greatest weakness—he loathed the phrase—into his greatest strength, and together with Primrose, her helping him to do it, the feeling that he, who up to that time had been haunted by the suspicion that he would never write anything original, that he was destined to copy all his life, had sunk his teeth into that appalling theme, that he was breaking not merely new ground, but building a terra nova, achieving something that was unique, in a sort of ultima thule of the spirit. And now, even should that book be published, and it was highly unlikely that after *Drunk-*

ard's Rigadoon it would, he would merely be told, as he had already been as much as told by his agent and the two American publishers who had so far rejected it, that—and had they stopped to think they must have known it could not have been so—it was merely a copy of *Drunkard's Rigadoon!* Throw away your mind, indeed! It was too much. It would be the same in England too. They had said they were looking forward to reading the book, promised him a telegram when they had read it; that was months ago, and up to their departure no telegram had arrived. It was hopeless. It was hopelessly hopeless. Or would be now, after the film. Substance and shadow! The book and the film. He had known too they were making a film, for by this time the book was so famous that it would have been strange indeed if the advance publicity had not reached their ears in Canada, yes, even in Eridanus, even the fishermen's ears, the fishermen to whom he could never tell again the theme of *The Valley of the Shadow of Death,* or give the book itself, as he had longed to, as a proof that he was not, which he was, shiftless, and was a worker even as one of them, which he was not. He had known, but he had been certain that Hollywood would make a mess of it. Unsportingly he had found himself hoping that far from reviving interest in the book, it would convince everybody that the book must also be of no account. Now he could not be sure. Tops them all, Gabbler Hooples. Even he was not proof against Gabbler Hooples. But that this had to happen tonight and at the very moment when it was so necessary for him to say something sympathetic and decently jolly to Primrose! This was where they had first met. There were tendernesses and memories and thoughts that were good. There were thoughts about how far they had gone since those old days. And there should have been some sympathy, above all, with *her* thoughts. A word would have helped, but he had not yet uttered that word. Immediately upon getting off the plane he had felt too happy because there were no formalities, and now he was too miserable. And he hated Los Angeles so violently at the moment that all he could think of was that it was a hell. Yes, outside there, beyond those curtains, was the sort of hell his spirit would have wandered to *had* he killed himself, yes, into that deathscape of bleary hoardings, there, no doubt to be confronted by yet another advertisement for a movie: Sigbjørn Wilderness in *Wilderness's Rigadoon*. Featuring Primrose Wilderness. With Don Fernando Martinez and Bjørnson Erikson. And an unprecedented cast of omens, joys, terrors, delights, demons, dentists, doctors, and coincidences. Bottoms up, Gabbler Hooples. Hullo, old maker of tragedies. Are you making more tragedies? He was. "Yes," Sigbjørn said, reflecting that all these thoughts that had he written them down would have taken him at least an hour had passed through his mind, like one of those dreams in which you live a lifetime, in less than two minutes. He took out his little notebook and began to write. "We're going to Mexico," he said, without looking up.

(a) Try to make Primrose as happy as essentially she had tried to make me, by casting, for Christ's sake, a little more joy (strength through joy, ha ha).

"Once went to Tijuana," the barman was saying.

(b) Definitely to see reasons for some kind of self-control.

"They tried to roll me. Never again, boy. Made out I'd forged a check. And do you know what it was, it was the police that did it. Yes, *sir!*"

"I was there once before and never had much trouble," Sigbjørn said so absently he almost did not know he was lying: (b) Definitely to see reasons for some kind of self-control: this such a blind quality and property of self-preservation it has come to seem almost unworthy.

"They don't like you to drink down there."

(c) But happiness may come from it, in that it protects us from external compulsion.

"How do you mean, they don't like to see you drink down there?"

"Not every day they don't. They like to drink themselves. But they don't like to see you drink. Makes them mad," the barman said. "Say, I've got a drop of tequila here. Like a drop? Get it from over the border sometimes."

Sigbjørn was aware of the waiter standing poised with a siphon-snouted tequila bottle of familiar build held over his glass, then of himself shaking his head, and then nodding: he took it and drank it at a gulp without benefit of salt or lemon and handed the glass back.

"Your wife's a long time."

"She's had a long journey," Sigbjørn said. "We're not keeping you?"

"No."

(d) Cast out fear, which is utterly impossible without (1) faith in God (2) complete hopelessness.

(e) The latter is living death, so discard it.

(f) The problem of selfishness.

(g) Is it true, as Helge Krig says, that two people who love one another need eventually a cause outside them etc., etc.?

(h) N.B. Remember that one is, essentially, a humorist.

"Yes, they'd steal Christ off the cross, those characters would," the barman said. "Mexico's a good place to stay out of."

"My God, you'd better not say that in front of my wife," Sigbjørn answered, folding the notes he'd been making and putting them in his pocket.

"Better not say what in front of your wife," said Primrose, coming in at that moment.

"We were talking about offensive language." She looked young and slim and fresh in her new blue traveling suit, and her large and beautiful flowerlike eyes, with their long lashes, showed no sign that she had been crying. She could have forgotten, for ever since they began making preparations for this trip, her moods had taken to changing as swiftly as her eyes did color. They were now green and wore an expression of innocent and childlike but almost exhilarating excitement. When they were first married, and before, it was a sign of willfulness in her when a dark mood was protracted. But after the fire, that had altered in her and those moods had grown, beyond control, darker and longer. Now it was nearly again as it had been in the old days. She was all eagerness, like a child; the sadness had passed as quickly as shadows running away on a sunny morning. It gave him a curious sense of responsibility, as well as a curious sense of being old, not at all like that of a husband or a lover, but rather like that of a grandfather, someone who is entrusted for a while with a child's dreams, and is trying to make something out of the

New York Battery on a Sunday. At the same time, if he figured in these dreams at all, which he sometimes doubted, it was, or should be, he felt, as a sort of knight-errant. He had unlocked her from the prison of Los Angeles, where she had been working her heart out in the soulless labor of animating cartoons, led her through a secret door from that dungeon in the castle, opened another, and there was Eridanus, opened yet another, and behold, there below her, stretched the world, mountains, beautiful, with its rills and rivers and little church spires, rolling over the hills and far away to Oaxaca, to, God knows, God. What was odd, too, he didn't think she was grateful to him for those rolling vistas, any more than a child is for being born. One could scarcely let oneself be hurt for this. It was justice, and it was her birthright. Nonetheless, it secretly grieved him a little. But it was that eagerness in her that was so touching and yet so vulnerable and that he did not wish to spoil or hurt. What unfathomable gay adventures of the spirit she looked into when those equally unfathomable eyes saw Mexico he did not know: but above all he did not want to disturb or enshroud by any gloom of his its brightness and enchantment. He reflected that she was his wife and one aspect of that gloom could come from love itself, should he allow himself to brood upon its awful seriousness. For it was with love, as with the phases of Venus. When Venus stands between the sun and ourselves upon the earth, she is dark. It is only beyond the sun that she is brightest and at the full. Thus it follows that we should attempt anyhow, when well we may, to keep the sun between ourselves and love. All of which should be just as possible under these circumstances at eleven o'clock at night in Los Angeles in a desolate barroom when it is raining outside, as anywhere else. But it can be difficult. "And you haven't got a drink," she said.

"No, thanks," Sigbjørn answered. "I don't want one." It was true: he didn't want one drink: he wanted seventy. Yet on the other hand it was precisely the wrong thing to have said, just what he had been guarding against doing. Now he had met her warmth with a chill and a shadow. But Primrose was shaking him by the arm.

"Come on, old boy, it's our wedding anniversary."

"Rye and a Scotch," said the barman.

"There was something," Sigbjørn began in a sudden inspired effort at joviality, while the barman's back was turned, "I wanted to ask you about women's washrooms—"

"Oh *Sigbjørn!*"

"What is it?"

"You tell me that I'm looking perfectly beautiful when I'm looking perfectly foul and now when I've gone to all this trouble to make myself look ravishing for you, you talk about women's washrooms!"

"I'm sorry, I am a bloody fool. I was under the impression I'd just made a long speech telling you how charming you looked. Is it too late now?"

"It certainly is not."

"I dare say it was the tequila. I cheated when you were out—the barman offered me a tequila. Would *you* like one? Though I think I had the last drop in the bottle."

"No," Primrose said, "I want to keep that for Mexico. I want to have the thrill of having my first tequila in one of your special bars."

"You shall," Sigbjørn said, their drinks having arrived. "I think I know the very one. You'll laugh when I take you there." They toasted each other silently. "Though I wouldn't guarantee the thrill." Wouldn't he? Sigbjørn wondered. And yet that had been one important reason why he had once drunk. It was not for the "thrill," no, and by thrill Primrose had meant something different; she would see a place familiar so far only on paper take actual form; but it was certainly something that was related to sensation, or at least to consciousness, or had become so, after oblivion became too difficult. But oblivion was not what he had been after at all most of the while: fundamentally the truth, or part of the truth, about his own drinking was to be found in William James. "It heightened the metaphysical consciousness in man," he said. Whatever that was, he vaguely suspected such an effect now, and wanted it prolonged and intensified. And had not James said somewhere too that it was the poor man's symphony? Sigbjørn was that poor man. A skillful performer, in his limited way, he knew little about music. He could count the symphony concerts he had been to on the fingers of one hand. With three of them amputated. At one concert he had heard Beethoven's Ninth Symphony whose mighty harmonies merely gave him the impression while listening that he wanted to do the same thing in prose. While apart from the fact that his use of voices seemed to him a negation of the kind of art Beethoven was driving at, the wooden semblance of the singers standing up there stiffly and angrily in their uncomfortable Sunday suits and looking as little like brothers as possible had merely served to call his attention to the awe-inspiring translation of Schiller's words on the program. He didn't take pride in this state; on the contrary he was always meaning to learn a true appreciation of music and taking books out of the library about it. But at this rate too, there was little enough to relate him to the fellow in *Drunkard's Rigadoon*. Except damn it, the suffering. Yes, he had forgotten the suffering. But then that went equally for Beethoven and perhaps for all men.

"Do you think the house will be all right?" he asked. "The tide will be coming in now, at this very minute."

"Of course, Quaggan'll look after it. They're only half tides now. They're cutting after the new moon."

"When we get back, we'll have to paint the boat," he said.

"Are you longing for it so much already, Sigbjørn?"

"I didn't mean that." He offered Primrose a cigarette, one to the barman, took one himself, lit the two other cigarettes with one match, then struck a match for his own. "And tomorrow we'll be in Mexico. Oblation!" Sigbjørn observed, holding up his glass. "An oblation to the gods of old Mexico. Perhaps that fellow who said drinking was a vicious circle meant 'oblate.' A state flattened and depressed at the poles."

"What fellow?"

"The fellow in the *Rigadoon* thing. But to get back to the ladies' washrooms, I saw something very peculiar in the men's place here. As you know, men's toilets are always covered with obscene drawings—"

"How would I know?" Primrose laughed.

"I first saw it in Seattle, just a sign in chalk on the wall: *Kilroy was here*. I didn't think much of that, Kilroy had been there, so what? In fact I didn't remember it till I went out in the bar at Frisco and found Kilroy was here too. This seemed mildly funny, but here it was again, in Los Angeles: this time it said: *Kilroy passed a stone here. El Grafe was looking.*"

"Well?"

"This time it struck me as positively sinister. And even a little bit frightening, with the Latin American influence beginning to creep in as you approach Mexico. What I wanted to ask you was whether anything similar went on in the ladies' side?"

"Sigbjørn, you do expect me to be an expert on the weirdest subjects." Primrose was laughing.

Sigbjørn grinned to himself at the barman's face, which appeared shocked and rather wounded, indeed he was engaged in withdrawing himself slowly to the far end of the bar with the evening newspaper. "This wasn't too obscence, as I said. It just struck and strikes me as strange. It gives almost a feeling of being pursued down the coast by this Kilroy moron. And how like man that is, with all the world to choose from, to seek to establish his immortality in a public urinal. Do you suppose these things are all over the country? And if so, where do they stop? Just think of the power an infectious catch phrase like that could wield. Suppose that, instead of Kilroy, you had, Forgive Your Enemies. Or say, Read *The Valley of the Shadow of Death.*"

"Oh darling, don't grieve," Primrose said. "You'll hear soon. Don't worry my honey lamb."

"It certainly wouldn't be much use," Sigbjørn said, "putting an advertisement in a public lavatory suggesting that a publisher simply read it. For one thing, if their bowels are anything like as petrified as their hearts seem to be, Kilroy's deed as witnessed by El Grafe notwithstanding, they never go to one."

"Christ, what a maze of complicated suffering and interrelated nonsense everything is," Primrose said.

Ding deeng dang deng. . . . Suddenly a radio, from behind the counter, chimed in: chimed, literally, the quarter hour, while beneath it deep organ tones swelled out prior to an announcement, to be followed by a musical program or the news, an announcement, from the awful tragic progression of the chords, one would have imagined to be of the crack of doom, though actually it was from a sponsor bidding the world drink Coca-Cola: nothing is sadder than these unearthly chimes, than the music of these brief interludes heard in an empty place, nothing more homeless than these sounds that strike into so many thousands of homes including that loneliest of all, an empty barroom, or a full one for that matter, for it still remains lonely and homeless, and so do you; perhaps it is that the chimes themselves bring back to the listener memories of other chimes, the friendly personal clock striking at home, where it has itself for most purposes been replaced by the more impersonal radio: or perhaps, since these chimes spell the passage of time itself, they evoke, together with that tragic musical accompaniment, the whole addled *morbidezza,* out of their lostness, belonging everywhere and yet to no one place, lost time, lost other times, lost love. Later you will look back upon these moments with such a baffled longing you will think you were happy. As, by gosh, perhaps you were. As indeed perhaps Primrose and he were, loneliness, bad temper, and all, standing there with their oblationary glasses half full, the kind words unsaid, the wedding anniversary turned momentarily for him again into a wake for Erikson, dead, two years ago in three quarters of an hour, in a blazing plane. Eleven fifteen.

How in its echoing on in the mind too, in a barroom such as this, called back also the voices and snatches of music blown in the wind in delirium to the lonely drinker, voices and music both real and imaginary, the chopping mumbling of steam music, faint marimbas of misery in Oaxaca, the wooden twangling and metallic thudding, all mingled with the muted chatter that is at once some real hubbub far away, and the mutterings of conscience or remorse, as if, out of the memories of lost deliriums, those voices, that music now, were calling to you, my dear Sigbjørn, my old maker of tragedies, and as though, yes, they themselves felt a bit lost without you, even almost loved you, as you, almost, them.

How would the Consul, his aficionado of *The Valley of the Shadow of Death,* have liked this airport bar? Sigbjørn could now quite imagine himself becoming attached to a place like this, seeing it as exotic, much as a friend of his had once confessed to him that he always felt compelled to return to the habits of his puberty in railway trains. Once Sigbjørn himself had liked to drink in railway stations. This was a place to put in his collection beside the saloon adjoining the bus terminal in Washington, D.C., where he had once sat with Ruth and where, over the door, to welcome one, appeared the words: *Through these portals pass the most damned people in the world.* ~Dante~

These thoughts were, no doubt, the consequence of his rash tequila; they were also, though, as if developed in reverse from that, the negative of everything sweet he had clearly visualized himself saying to Primrose. But now, as they still stood there in silence, their drinks still undrunk, those kind words still unsaid, the urgency of the hour gripped him: at any moment they would be called, and, anyhow, they should go: they smiled, touched glasses, and finished their whiskies. And it was better they said nothing; a silence broken the wrong way may cause a longer one, later on. All he hoped was, as he paid for the drinks and helped Primrose on with her Arctic skunk coat, that these gloomy thoughts were not the result of some kind of actual prescience of disaster; what, for instance, if they should crash themselves? How did it feel? he wondered. How had Erikson felt when he knew they were going down? Sigbjørn, with a friend of his, a game warden, had once gone on an expedition up a mountain near Eridanus in search for a lost aircraft. There had been a honeymoon couple on board. Most of the passengers had been eaten by bears. A wedding dress, impaled on a rock, floated in the wind on top of the mountain.

And now already reconciled without a word, their spirits lifted with the sinking sensation that was becoming familiar as the loudspeaker spoke.

"Will the passengers for the United Air Lines Los Angeles–El Paso–Monterrey–Mexico City flight please go to the lobby and weigh in or check their baggage. Please have your tickets ready. Thank you."

They weighed in. They had too much luggage and had to pay extra. Sigbjørn was not feeling efficient, and was efficient. It was those two distant dramatic and impossible words *Mexico City* perhaps that canalized almost everything that jarred within them both into sheer anticipation. He could even briefly reflect without too much pain upon the reason for their having so much luggage, which included his guitar and two typewriters.

"They won't let us take the guitar inside with us this time. What shall we do, Primrose? All right," he went on, without waiting for an answer, "We'll risk it. Have to anyway," he remarked to her. He had made a fuss about this at Vancouver, now it didn't seem to matter, despite the fact that the little instrument was dear to him.

Everything was being arranged. Or what was not, he was arranging. For since they were changing planes, each item of luggage had to be rechecked. The airport people seemed to him slow, and Sigbjørn worked like a stevedore, shifting bags onto the weighing machine himself. One reason for so much excess baggage was that, though they would not admit it or discuss it, they were probably bewildered as to the actual permanence of their move. It was not merely a matter of not having a complete home to return to. "Auto camps of the better class," their besetting nightmare, they might find when they returned, the forest felled, their own house knocked down and ugliness and an urban subsection beginning to move in. Their bags were full of all kinds of paraphernalia, even junk, you would never expect to make use of on a short vacation. But here, unexpectedly, Sigbjørn himself was the greater villain. For in addition to what few clothes Primrose had brought, there were fragments of manuscript, piles of it, even burned and unintelligent manuscript that Sigbjørn could never hope to put together again but which, equally, seemed too precious to be left behind, or to be trusted with anyone else. There were even the burned remnants of the manuscript of *In Ballast to the White Sea* in there, that had once contained his portrait of Erikson, four almost perfect circles of page fragments, upon each of which, in the faded typescript of the text appeared, terrifyingly enough, the word "fire."

"Well, that's done," he said. "Yes, right through to Mexico City."

Sigbjørn looked at Primrose as if to say: "You see, I have no difficulty with this kind of thing," and turning tenderly yet expertly to help her with her fur coat—a rite at which as a rule he was phenomenally clumsy—which she now wanted to put on like a cape, caught sight of himself doing this in a mirror, and without recognizing either himself or Primrose for the moment actually thought: who is that incredibly lovely girl talking to the nice-looking young fellow with rather German manners?

They began to take their place in a queue consisting largely of soldiers in uniform. Elsewhere the lobby was taken up by chalky-faced sailors, with wide trousers, nursing large seabags, each containing a Monte Cristo. They seemed mostly machinists, with the insignia of propellers sewn to their sleeves. Sailors often never learned the virtue of traveling light, shipshape though they might be in other respects. Still, these sailors, or many of them, were clearly going home, that was different. Innocent, with bare necessities, and narrow shoulders, they had once set out. And heavyset, with curios originally made in Japan and re-exported from Baltimore to the Far East, with a kinkajou on a leash, and a dose of clap, they returned whencesoever they came. And all this, too, was new to him: airborne sailors. Well, well. Gradually Primrose and he moved up in the queue. Both the sailors and soldiers had this in common: they looked deathly tired. So many people moving about, going back to their homes, to broken homes, leaving their homes, sailors half homesick for another sea, soldiers half seasick for another war. Not all his aloofness and standing askance from anyone in uniform could keep Sigbjørn from some pity. Before he was twenty he had been a seaman and a fireman himself in the British merchant service. A good school for writers, Erikson had said. Perhaps: but to the sailor it was only a good, or bad school for being a sailor. Or a good school, a most enlightened and progressive school, for death. But meanwhile it was as if the war had sent the quicksilver of human lives scattering in every direction. God absently peered down through the glass, tilted the closed box again, and the scattered bits of mercury began to run back into their proper burrows. But no, here were a couple of bright little globules that refused to go in. . . . Primrose and Sigbjørn shuffled up, step by step. In one sense a cycle of their life together was over. Having met here in Los Angeles, they started from Los

Angeles again. At midnight, beyond that barrier, their fortunes
together began once more. Though they would return, leaving
Eridanus had been a sort of ecdysis. And Sigbjørn could almost
feel, as if created by the airplane propellers outside, their being
caught in that suction of the future.

"Oh, the shearwaters," Primrose said, suddenly and delightedly taking his arm.

Sigbjørn smiled. "The good shearwaters," he replied, bending
to put his head against hers.

From where he stood Sigbjørn could hear some people con-
versing in a language that sounded vaguely transliterated, but
that language, however ancient, was clumsy and inexpressive
compared with this of the Wildernesses. Yet it was susceptible,
he reflected, of explanation.

The most supernatural and mysterious of birds, like the alba-
tross almost in their mode and beauty of flight, shearwaters
glided, rather than flew, making use of the currents of air in
their vast and lonely voyages. There was a moving story about
the shearwater. An English scientist, having ringed a bird and
conveyed it thither, released one in Rome, and it had found its
way home, presumably over the Alps, to its remote Danish rock,
in less than a week, there to be found deep in earnest conversation with his mate and chicks.

But if by mentioning the shearwaters Primrose conveyed all
these things, she also implied such a wealth of others as to make
their speech, considered on these terms, as incomprehensible to
anyone overhearing it as that of the shearwaters themselves in
their nest: it was the word, if word were now needed, of their
reconciliation, of their having "made up," in one breath it con-
gratulated Sigbjørn upon his supernatural efficiency with the
baggage, and the two of them for having managed to arrive here
at all: it forgave Sigbjørn, if forgiveness were needed, for his tact-
lessness in bringing up her difficulties with her ornithological
work, begotten, he could not help feeling, from his own difficulties, for had Sigbjørn not been a writer, Primrose might have
been content to remain an observing ornithologist, and never
bothered to write a book about birds and thus saved herself un-
told anguish: the "shearwaters," on the more serious plane, took

account of the drama of their wild journey that lay ahead, as well as of that part already behind. Since the word was plural, and since, according to the special reality of this kind of private esperanto totemistically speaking, they were, almost, by God, shearwaters, it reminded them how far out "at sea," how far from home they actually were, and in so doing, by wistfully seeming to share it, excused Sigbjørn for betraying his homesickness. And since shearwaters were supposed loyal to their mates it reestablished *consciously* between them the unity of their marriage. And on top of all that, Sigbjørn thought, it could suggest to one the absurdity of taking five pages, to say in prose, what one could say in one word in poetry.

"The admirable, the clever shearwaters," he repeated. "Just look where they've flown to."

Probably most married couples, united for so long, and on the whole, as merrily, as the Wildernesses, have acquired a private language such as this, if not so ambiguous, a language that at lowest, when overheard, affects us as being just too cute and loathsome for words, but that, should you reflect on the matter more kindly, is merely a mutual acknowledgement of their uniqueness one to the other. Here perhaps in many cases the uniqueness stops. The Wildernesses were, no doubt, not unique either. But if this connected the Wildernesses with other married couples, it was also a measure of their isolation, if it was their fashion too, of laughing at it.

For certainly they didn't fit in, at least not into this queue of human lives. Though they themselves might belong to the "American plan," to the best movement that had made America, they were almost more American than these Americans themselves. The majority of these people when they went home, if they went home, went, figuratively and for the large part, to the very urban subsection that threatened the Wildernesses. They possessed telephones, electric lights, inside toilets, most of them automobiles. It would have been much the same had they been miners, not soldiers and sailors. But how much less did any of these people, here on this quintessential cross section of America, ever think of home in such a guise as the Wildernesses? How many of these people in this queue here, when they thought of *home,* thought of the ocean breaking under the house, or the green forest bending in a chinook? It was in their dreams, perhaps. It was in their songs, surely. But how many of them *knew* the actual benison of oil lamps, hauled and chopped their own wood, or had the privilege of diving off the front porch into the sea every day? Or, not to become lyrical about the scenery and spoil it in another way, how many of them had the privilege of *not* turning on an electric light, of *not* hearing a telephone ring, but from one year's end to another? Or, as Primrose might say in a moment of exasperation, of *not* having a fire engine to come to the rescue when your house caught fire, or, when your wife was sick, of *not* being able to get a doctor in time?

It was easy to romanticize their own kind of life. But it often seemed so much better to Sigbjørn than any other, for them, despite its disadvantages, that even to contemplate any other made him feel physically sick. Unfortunately it was the same the other way round. Few people could understand why they liked what they did. And sometimes Sigbjørn couldn't himself, how what had begun out of sheer economic necessity had ended as a spiritual necessity. And sometimes they didn't. The truth was, they had it both ways. Without an occasional plunge into civilization, they wouldn't have enjoyed what they had so much. As other people went to the seaside, so did they to the city. This was true even of shearwaters, who for very sport, it seemed, rather than greed, were not above going to the city themselves in the guise of following a steamer, sometimes for many days. But even shearwaters on their rock had more sense of society than did the Wildernesses.

Sigbjørn remembered that the forest he had been thinking about as so primeval had once, at the beginning of this century, been planned as a park. Once upon a time where their old house stood, there had been a Japanese shingle mill. Where there was jungle now there had been a bandstand. And the *Eridanus* herself, when she had been wrecked, had been due to berth, all those years ago, at that very sawmill, flourishing then, but from whose dismantled timbers Sigbjørn and Primrose had themselves built their home. And Primrose and he were starting again, were they? Setting out into the future, were they? In a way they were, or she was. But yet it seemed an unusually strange way to go about it, by setting out smack into the past. Still, perhaps it was merely a foreshadowing, of what he'd been thinking, of precisely what everyone else, in their different ways, had to do too, but this time more *consciously*. Just, as Nietzsche says, one stepped back to take a spring. Or the ship went astern from the wharf, before swinging round to the open sea. All at once Sigbjørn's attention was taken by two people talking immediately ahead of them. One, a tall, carelessly but expensively dressed man, gaunt and spectacled, and wearing, queerly, worn-out shoes, did not seem in the queue. The other, who was standing in line, wore a tight-fitting immaculate suit, with the trousers very narrow at the bottom, and a stiff collar with a rather loud bow tie, a combination that Sigbjørn seemed to remember having been fashionable here years before and which, like the out-of-date trousers, as they also seemed to Sigbjørn, were now presumably fashionable again.

It reminded Sigbjørn that with the exception of some Primrose had recently insisted upon for the trip, and a pair of dungarees, he had bought no clothes for himself since before the war and had lost most of those in the fire. The clothes he was wearing now, a well-tailored brown corduroy jacket and trousers—and God knows how old *they* were—had been given him by his uncle's lawyer who had sought refuge with his family in Canada during the German blitzkrieg of London. They had belonged to the lawyer's brother, a Christian Science practitioner who had died of general paralysis of the insane. In fact of what he had on, only his handsome Irish tweed topcoat and brown shoes which he had bought seven years ago in Los Angeles itself, and his tie, a Christmas gift from Primrose, really belonged to Sigbjørn. His white shirt was even a relic of Mexico, and a very good shirt it was, for it was more than seven years old to his certain knowledge and still as good as new. It was Stanford's. The hotel manager of the Tarleton in Mexico City had given it to him with sundry other belongings of Stanford's when, before Sigbjørn left Mexico, more than seven years ago, he had paid finally at that hotel both Stanford's bill and his own. And when he had met

Stanford first in Acapulco, Sigbjørn had been wearing, he now remembered, the white linen suit Juan Fernando Martinez had as good as given him, for a token five pesos, in Cuicitlán. And that was the nearest Stanford had even been to meeting Fernando. Curious—for they were, so to speak, his good and evil angels of that whole memory: Stanford, most remarkably so he reflected, being the evil one. Now it gave him an odd feeling to be wearing the evil one's shirt. But it began to give him a much odder feeling still to be wearing the other poor devil's corduroy suit, the suit of someone he was sure was dead, and died in what a way! And where would Stanford be? Dead, probably, also, in the South Pacific or somewhere, his quid pro quo for Acapulco. He had left Mexico, sticking Sigbjørn with his hotel bill, before Sigbjørn himself, and was the sort of beefy person that would be dead in the war, or if not, ought to be. Nonetheless, Sigbjørn could not escape a pang. It was eerie too, that all these garments fitted so perfectly. And now, confronted with that new stiff collar and bow tie of the person ahead of him, and new tight-fitting suit with the narrow trousers, Sigbjørn felt overwhelmingly, in his clothes of the dead and the probably dead, his sense of isolation coming back.

Yes, even his thoughts were backtracking on his own solutions, but knowledge of that didn't help. Suddenly it seemed to him that it was exactly as if he had come out of a cave: yes, that was it, Primrose and he had been in a cave for five years. Fashions had changed, come back, changed again, and returned, the worst war in history had been fought, whole populations had been thrown into confusion and dispossessed, a new age in which sailors flew had been born, they had emerged from their cave into a certain awareness of all this, and yet, for them, it was as though nothing had happened. In this growth—and what fantastic changes in Los Angeles alone!—in those sufferings, they had had no part whatever. It made him feel a bit like Rip Van Winkle, that fortunate man who had waked after twenty years to discover that at least some part of his house was still there. So, for that matter, was Shakespeare's tomb. But their house had burned to the ground. . . . Ah! So it was the fire that came to the rescue again, this then was what connected them. And it was true. War was often more merciful.

Turning your greatest weakness into your greatest strength! Once more the phrase, also Yeats's, came to him. But it was somehow more than that, if there could be any more, for the phrase which had started out at him like an uncoiled spring from *A Vision,* a book he had only glanced at, could also call to mind a man with a weak stomach who in a few years manages to win the world's barbell record for the abdominal raise. Here, it required nothing less than an organic turning of oneself inside out, the setting to work of all the headlong down-driving machinery of a colossal lethiferous debauch in the reverse direction. The writing of such a book was in fact itself a form of prolonged concentrated debauch, with the great difference that throughout it one was obliged to tell the truth. In brief it was the highest thing that, allowing for all the shortcomings of the type of consciousness that could entertain such a notion, and the shocks, bald necessities, and brute facts that had brought one to the pitch of doing it, an artist of that type could attempt.

A maze of complicated suffering and interrelated nonsense indeed! What was especially funny about it all was that, as he realized, it might well be only alcohol that had put the charming idea in his head that he ever *could* transcend it. And if so, how?

Here he was, standing in a queue with a group of people most of whom seemed more than ever to have come from the moon, a writer who not only couldn't write any longer, but had nothing, he thought, to write about, unless he were to write about his cave, or Primrose's troubles, or the very act of writing itself. His recollection of that poem about the border, he seemed to feel now, though this thought was not painful either, was infuriatingly pathetic rather than anything else. If he had to recall in toto something he'd written as long ago as that and which was not very good anyway, it merely revealed his dreadful poverty of creative spirit and the pass he had come to. Would you like to see my etchings? It's true that I have no etchings, I lost them in a bad accident, of which I will not speak, but if you will have a little patience, I will try to recall what their subject was, and perhaps we may even recreate them a little. And it was much the same with those disgusting fragments of *In Ballast to the White Sea* that he had preserved. So here he was, out of his cave, in his Sunday go-to-meeting garments belonging to a man who had died of general paralysis of the insane, the most dramatic events of history having swept by him like a liner in the fog.

But what of the author of *Drunkard's Rigadoon?* Must he not have been in a bit of a cave too, if not a combustible one? How even much more interesting than the book he had written would have been a book about his actual struggle with whatever it was he was struggling with, if only his own material, for one thing that was strange about *Drunkard's Rigadoon* was that it did not seem autobiographical. It was a new thought. Had not Proust wondered the same about Dostoevski? And Gide about someone else? What was the relation between Sigbjørn and the Consul? Was it sufficient to say that he had, in *The Valley of the Shadow of Death,* transferred his sense of guilt to a figure of authority, who happened to be a Consul, but who might as well have been an Immigration inspector, and, during a period of sobriety roughly coinciding what that of the world's drunkenness, let fate and his unconscious do the rest?

It was not so simple. For that matter, was his own relationship to the protagonist, or to the author of *Drunkard's Rigadoon,* so simple? It was not. There were other complex relationships that like a man who possesses the evidence of his own eyes for the knowledge that he has developed the symptoms of some fearful and fatal disease, but with a part of his mind persists in telling himself that this is merely the clue to the morbid workings of another part of that mind, or to error—as it well may be, for this is something to treat with reverence, as is the case with anyone else's religion, but there is again, alas, that damning evidence—like that very poor man perhaps Sigbjørn thought, with a sudden oblique, not sharp, and almost comic fear, whose trousers he was wearing, he scarcely dared even to mention to himself: not that these relationships were serious on the surface; they were not, it was only when they were pursued to their logical end that they became frightening, for at one blow it knocked everything we know as reason on the head and at a standstill.

Sigbjørn smiled to himself and lit a cigarette, an operation in which he fancied he rather resembled the publicity photographs of Arthur Koestler: a winning Hungarian quality of the intelligentsia plus the British Tommy with the ball at his feet.

Coincidences, yes, the sort of coincidences in his life of which there seemed no end. But were they, strictly speaking, coincidences? Were they something less, or more? A maze of complicated suffering and interrelated nonsense! Yes, but still, what a more-than-Pirandellian theme was here for someone, if not for him. Every man his own Laocoön! As Daniel might say. And here would be the trick, he thought, in one's life to be amused by them, in one's work, rather to study them, to be the detached haruspex of them. For were he to take them all seriously, and he was still thinking of only a fraction, he might well go the way of that protagonist, or of the late owner of his elegant corduroy trousers.

All this time, as they stood in the queue, Sigbjørn had kept anxiously consulting his watch, fearing that in the confusion of going through the barrier he would miss the exact minute of midnight when he could say "Happy anniversary" to Primrose: he made it still less than five to: but now it was as if, as the second fingers moved on, the two excitements, that of being about to go, and the other became one: and combined with the other tensions of the day and his attempt to keep his suffering below the surface, *because somewhere at the back of his mind too among other things was always the feeling of: "when it was before the fire," and "when I had the field to myself,"* were transformed into something else, a feeling almost of having been brought to the brink of a discovery: it was more even than that, he had suddenly a glimpse of a flowing like an eternal river; he seemed to see how life flowed into art: how art gives life a form and meaning and flows on into life, yet life has not stood still; that was what was always forgotten: how life transformed by art sought further meaning through art transformed by life; and now it was as if this flowing, this river, changed, without appearing to change, became a flowing of consciousness, of mind, so that it seemed that for them too, Primrose and he, just beyond that barrier, lay some meaning, or the key to a mystery that would give some meaning to their ways on earth: it was as if he stood on the brink of an illumination, on the near side of something tremendous, which was to be explained beyond, in that midnight darkness, but which his consciousness streamed into,

and was continuous with, as in an inexplicable way, everybody
else's seemed to be continuous with it and flowing into it, and
this flowing current appeared to him now in the guise of something irreversible, like that current in the Fraser River at New
Westminster back home in British Columbia that is so strong
that not even the incoming tide, like God's will vainly struggling with man's, could turn it, and it was like too the black star-
laden current of Eridanus itself: suddenly the loudspeaker
broke into his thoughts, and his spirits dropped as Primrose said
behind: "I knew it.They've put off the flight." Now the whole
queue began to move forward in a body toward the barrier:
"No, it's for El Paso." They laughed, were unable to stop laughing, Sigbjørn had his tickets ready, and they kissed uncaring of
the others, so delighted were they by that announcement.

*Fasten your safety belts. . . . No smoking. . . . Stewardess
Miss Gleason.*

And now, once more a stewardess—and she had her name up
in lights anyhow—with a fixed faint smile, was wafted, balanced,
downhill between the seats that seemed to tilt you back into
some kind of tyrannous human fixative: once more there was
the grip and tug of wild blowing excitement and once more the
thunderous voice of the lifting, salient plane. . . .

"Happy anniversary."

"Happy anniversary."

It was midnight, past midnight by Primrose's own present,
the French antimagnetic wristwarch, secondhand, with gold
soldered onto lead; perhaps it was even more precious to him
because in the secret dreams of the noncombatant he imagined
it as having been through the Battle of the Bulge; the safety-belt
sign had faded without their knowledge and it was time for him
to bring out his own token gift, a phial of Chanel perfume he
had kept hidden since his last painful trip to town. With what
love he gave it to her! Primrose with an air of secrecy now took
her token from the pocket of the seat in front, which at that
moment slanted back violently in his face, and both laughed as
Sigbjørn unwrapped the parcel. "I know this will make you think
of a Charles Addams cartoon," she said as he kissed her. Sigbjørn
was delighted. "Wonderful. But thanks, darling, an awful lot."

Sigbjørn collected first editions in a mild way, or had before the fire, and this, the first edition of the English translation of Julian Green's *The Dark Journey*, that Primrose had picked up at a secondhand bookstore in Vancouver, was one he had been looking for a long time. That it happened to be a work of the most monumental gloom and could have been perceived as anything but a jovial presage, seemed not merely beside the point but even for some reason seemed to render the occasion merrier. I've often wondered what a struggle morticians' wives must have giving something suitable to their husbands, he thought of saying. The book was a link too, strangely with Erikson and hence with *In Ballast to the White Sea*—though had she known that? Could he ever have told her? It was a link with everything, in the great chain of the infernal machine of his life. And he thought again of the occasion he had first bought, fourteen years ago, not the first edition, but a Tauchnitz, on the first dramatic occasion of his having met Erikson and just after they had parted in the street, in the dark stormy tree-tossed Bygdø Alle in Oslo, in the little bookshop near the huge Biblioteket. Stamped in since by how many Teuton boots? What hint of that time, what message for the future was there in that now? They embraced, loving one another; perhaps they embraced themselves, they were so close (he thought that), these two little people.

"I love you."

"I love you."

They sat for a long time too happy and excited to talk. Sigbjørn wondered how could you explain all this to another person, should one have wanted to. That a gloomy anatomy of man's misery like *The Dark Journey* had here, this quite without one's tongue in one's cheek, become a symbol of thoughtfulness and love. Only great innocence of heart could have prompted her, even though she was not unaware of the morbidly funny side of it. No, the ways and usages of lovers were largely incommunicable, as was the significance of the book to him, and he thought too that this incidence could only have pleased its author, whose life had quite another significance to Sigbjørn, could he, Green, but be aware of it. The plane thundered on into darkness: out of the window far below, the Supreme Pictures cinema passed, where they were showing *Drunkard's Rigadoon,* and Nuestra Señora de la etc. whose population had increased by such and such, slowly faded into the darkness.

The Dark Journey. . . . Well, the same thing could be done, with malicious intent. Just prior to his first journey to Mexico, Ruth had presented him, caustically, and at a bad moment, with Arthur Schnitzler's *Flight into Darkness.* Now another spiral had wound its way upward, as Erikson would say. For that matter, one of his most prized possessions at home in Eridanus was another token present from Primrose—an ancient pewter demi-liter tankard that Primrose must have chased up and down all God's heaven looking for. What if Ahab's young wife, knowing he liked gingerbread, had presented him, on the eve of his setting out on board the *Pequod,* with a gingerbread whale? With these and other gayer and more triumphant fancies, Sigbjørn occupied his mind drifting off into sleep. And yet, as the drinks wore off, becoming ever more and more wakeful.

Leviathan, that had been the French name for *The Dark Journey,* the Leviathan that lies in wait, the crocodile-whale-dragon, and was not today also—he remembered again—the anniversary of the real Erikson's death, of Sigbjørn's death, and would he ever be able to forget that, oh maker of tragedies? and why should books like *The Dark Journey* start up at you just when you are trying to make a journey into life, he asked himself, as Primrose fell asleep on his shoulder and the plane roared and crackled· sarcastically on into the night, always night, and always down, down, or so it seemed—for in fact they were headed slantwise toward Arizona (sitting at the back to be out of sight); they offer you coffee—what do you want? mescal perhaps?—you half refuse and half drink it.

Now Sigbjørn knew he was not going to be able to sleep for some time. Every night, for as long as he could remember, Sigbjørn had closed his eyes with the notion that just before he slept, the perfect poem would suggest itself to him: it was true that a poem of sorts invariably did suggest itself, and this poem, somewhat under the influence of Lewis Carroll, and which always ran as now, much in the same way, came now: but even before it began he knew it was not going to work, at least as a remedy for sleep:

The boomboom gumgums abumbum
and toodley toodley too
and twaddley the twem je twimtwam
in the boomboom's boodley doo

Bingtwoom by the twim twot twicktwad
Twing twoom twing twaddley twock
Twing twick twack twock, twick twick twach
Twing plockerly twockerly plock

Ah there's twockerly perplock a plumplum
Or plon ple plom plam ple ploo
the boom boom gumgums abumbum
And so, by Christ, are you.

Why did people travel? God knows Sigbjørn hated it all over
again. Travel to him was the extension of every anxiety, which
man tried to get rid of by having a quiet home. A continual
fever, an endless telephone alarm, perpetual heart attack. A continual anxiety. An unending fire-alarm. A prodigious prolonged jumping conniption. Is my passport in order? How shall
I prevent being robbed? How can I get my papers out of my
pocket in this position? without dropping half my money? But
it's too dark to see. How can I get hold of my overcoat? How
much do I have to tip some hateful pimply bastard for confusing
and embarrassing and distressing me? It isn't that he's hateful
either, I believe, so to speak, in the brotherhood of man. Or
pimply, so used I to be: or a bastard, so am I, in many ways. In
most ways, probably it would be better were I really a bastard,
but how can I tip myself? Fortunately such questions don't arise
on a plane, though when you get out it's a different matter. But
have I dropped all my passports out onto the floor? I can't
move, I can't see. How can I prevent myself making a fool of
myself? Horripilation. Fingerprintings—and, ah, that had done
it, those fingerprintings at the American Consulate, that had
taken away the last of one's freedom. Consulates. Customs. Conniption all over again. Double conniption. Bribery and conniption. Treble conniption. It is going into hell, inviting it, going
from the society of people you are not quite sure like you,
among people whom you know for certain despise you; who—

consciously—would do it? Out of an environment to which one bore little relation into one to which one bore none. (When you were a sailor you did not, of course, have to think of these things. Or you were too young to think of them.) Primrose did not, of course, know quite how he felt either, which was not so violently as this anyway all the time, and Sigbjørn was going to be unselfish and not show it, as he had made up his mind not to before. But travel is a neurosis, so how should one expect that it would not make you neurotic? And when you have no home, or only half a new home—the other being burned—that was different, his thoughts mumbled to himself. (And besides this was the first real trip she had ever taken in her life.)

At Phoenix, Arizona—Phoenix—and had the phoenix clapped his wings? Daniel had written him—Phoenix, a lonely clean new airport station, a freezing clear night, and the stars bright, with Jupiter overhead, a cowboy suddenly seen through the door of the tilted stationary plane, etched in brilliant electric light, his face under the gray Stetson, young and weather-beaten, walking away forever, just like Hugh, in *The Valley of the Shadow of Death,* lost, under a big dusty palm.

III

SIGBJØRN PUT OUT HIS
light wearily and tried once more to sleep. But the next minute
he switched it on again and even accepted the offer of another
coffee from Miss Gleason who happened to be passing. They had
been delayed at Phoenix and so were not stopping at Tucson,
she said, but were going straight through to El Paso. Sigbjørn
began to feel restless and excited and at the same time again
extremely nervous and worried. Though it was true they were
still in America—flying over Arizona as far as he knew—and
would be still, in a sense, in the same position at El Paso, this
new border town now seemed far too near. As his coffee arrived
and he sipped at it, he tried to think again of the extreme courtesy with which they had been treated by the American officials
in Seattle and how different that was to the way he had been
treated in Blaine in 1939. Sigbjørn had the impression, though he
had never been there, that El Paso was not a border town in the
same sense that Blaine could be considered so or even perhaps
Nuevo Laredo, and a moment's reflection reminded him that
airport formalities were not to be confused with an actual border crossing by bus. Now he tried to take comfort from the fact
that he seemed to remember having seen that the actual crossing
over the Rio Grande was at Ciudad Juárez, famous for tamale
pie, and that the formalities must be much worse there than at

49

El Paso. Nonetheless, that didn't alter the fact that their papers would have to be examined twice, so he thought, at El Paso, once on the American side, and once (though they would still be in America) on the Mexican. In a year or two, when air travel of this kind had become more general and less of a luxury, doubtless there would not be much to choose between the toughness of the two types of border officials.

But El Paso was in Texas anyhow and Sigbjørn was predisposed in favor of Texans. His father had owned some oil wells in Texas and he had only pleasant memories of the genial Texans he had met in England. They might be tough too, but in his experience there seemed to be ground for belief, held also, it is said, by the Texans, that they were a race apart. At worst, they would still be gentlemen. Still it was not the American side anyhow he was now afraid of—was it—but the Mexican. . . . How would the Mexicans react to his Form H, on which appeared the forbidding words: *Refused entry at Blaine, Washington, as a person liable to be a public charge: September 15, 1939.* The thought of any trouble, but far more of Primrose's disappointment should he actually be turned back from Mexico itself, unnerved him to such an extent that he was not able even to put his hand in his inside pocket to verify whether this form were indeed still there. He half hoped, perhaps, he had lost it. He found that his hands were trembling as he gave back the coffee cup to Miss Gleason, and, though he had not drunk enough to warrant it, he wondered what he would do if his hand trembled like that if he had anything very much to sign, and, to take his mind off such an eventuality, he reached into the seat pocket for *The Dark Journey,* which he opened at random.

Gloomy passage, he thought. This was indeed genius, perhaps, but genius in its most baffling and tragic form, genius on its way to some sort of sainthood-mysticism perhaps, judging from Green's later works. Just as Erikson's had been genius on its way to political canonization and Daniel's genius on its way to more genius and the Nobel Prize. "It seemed to him," he read, "as though time had rolled back, and that all the anguish and terror of those last months were suddenly reduced to nothing. Perhaps nothing had happened since he had been there; the house and the cobbles seemed the same. If he had really committed a crime, would he risk himself thus in a place where everyone was eager to denounce him?"

Sigbjørn shut the book with a shudder and replaced it in the pocket; he was still shaking, the more so because this reminded him of the passage in *The Valley of the Shadow of Death* where he compared Yvonne's return to the tower to a murderer's return. The plane began to bump and the safety-belt sign went on and he recovered himself and managed to fasten Primrose in without waking her. Well, he was not known at El Paso and he had not (although he felt uneasy on the subject) ever precisely committed a crime—had he not?—and certainly not—had he?—in Mexico. Why should he be afraid of El Paso anyhow? Especially with his safety belt on? He had left Mexico before, and God all these goings and returnings, in July, 1938—more than seven years ago—through Douglas, Arizona, from Sonora in Mexico, passing into this very state they were flying through transversely now, after having made that never-to-be-thought-of awful delirious trip by rail in the Pullman coach *Aristotle,* from Mexico City. And even then, with the shakes, because that impossible Mexican Pullman porter, doubtless out of misdirected kindness, at seven in the morning and just when the Immigration inspectors were coming on board, had refused him another tequila; still he had not been turned back even then. He may not have been a Texan but the American had had a good heart who had said, and when he had some right on this occasion to refuse him entrance, for Sigbjørn's condition on that occasion had certainly raised a doubt: "All right, I'd been going to refuse you. But under the circumstances I've decided to let you in, if you promise it'll be only for six months." Sigbjørn hadn't been able quite to keep his promise, for it had been almost a year before he left for Canada. But that had scarcely been his fault. There had been his divorce, there had been the approaching war, and his meeting of Primrose. And under the circumstances! God, what circumstances they were! Even the man who during these very hours, so he-read in the American papers and he remembered because at the time it was his own twenty-ninth birthday, was making up his mind whether to jump out of a New York hotel window or not standing on the parapet there with the faces and the roofs of taxicabs below him, had seemed to him luckier and more lucid than he; and certainly less lonely. It was not until he was approaching Los Angeles—where on arrival he found he had forgotten Ruth's address—that he remembered that his tobacco pouch was full, together with his Balboa Screme, of marihuana and he emptied it into the toilet. What folly! What a danger he had escaped! It was not that he was in the habit of smoking marihuana—perhaps he would have acquired it had his sole experience had the slightest discoverable effect—some imbecile had in fact given it to him as a gag, as a parting present, and he had said, "Very well, I'll put it in my pipe, in my tobacco pouch," but that his contact with reality was so slight that it had not occurred to him what peril he ran in crossing the border with it, in fact had he been discovered he might even now be still in the hoosegow, and it bore thinking of too that so great had his need for a drink been that blazing morning in the train at the border at Douglas, Arizona, that it had never occurred to him he possessed the marihuana. Well, he had been in his twenties then and all that was left behind. Sigbjørn, seeing that the sign was now off again and they were flying steadily, sought more reading material. He had not bothered to take his topcoat off and in the pocket, folded, was this morning's Vancouver paper, or should one say, yesterday's. How strange it was to think that only this morning they had been five thousand miles away. How swiftly, and on more levels than one, could a man's circumstances change. And if it was five thousand miles away just so had he once left his twenties five thousand miles behind; his late twenties, the essences and landscape of which he was now so mysteriously approaching once more.

Sigbjørn switched the light out and held Primrose tighter, listening to the roar of the plane that at that moment suddenly began to get an attack of arrhythmia again, bumping in a sudden swooping air pocket, and he hoped that the safety-belt warning would not go on and Primrose be waked up. The poor child had not slept for nights with the excitement. The sign went on and he secured her. The plane was drumming into real weather. Sigbjørn thought of their wedding night in Eridanus on December 7, 1940, the uncertainty then, and now, as then, hugging her, he felt as if he were protecting her again against the awfulness of the world outside. Yet what a joyful, tremendous night that had been, and what an awakening at dawn in the cabin in the forest with the gray sea and whitecaps almost level with the windows, and the rain dashing against them, and the sea crashing and hissing inshore under the house, causing dumbfounding commotions of logs, the smoke of the factories that worked all night during the war far over in Barnet a rainy blue, leaves falling into the sea, their boat hurling itself about down below in awful jeopardy, and the sound of breaking branches in the forest, the green maple tree would seethe and roar, the windows rattle with the wind, while the rain beat deafeningly against them. It was unbearable to think of their new little house, alone, in the sea, and unprotected, in the dreadful weather they had left it to.

Awake, and with a vengeance. For the experience that now followed Sigbjørn had no precedence. Because involved with dream, even hallucination, nothing could persuade him, from the moment it began, that it was a dream. It was as if, and this was to happen with the experience itself, he had opened his eyes upon another reality.

There was nothing but the desert outside to look at, or even to pretend to look at, so while Primrose dozed happily on his shoulder, Sigbjørn busied himself with the New Orleans Times-Picayune, *which he had bought in El Paso although before he read the headlines again—$15 Billion for Red Arms, Exceeds U.S.—he asked himself why precisely, since New Orleans was thousands of miles away from El Paso, he should have bought this particular paper and not the El Paso Herald. Sigbjørn felt, for a moment, a complicated emotion, that was like love, that was like several kinds of love indeed, all at once, for Primrose, for Mexico, and also for New Orleans where, had they gone to Haiti their original plan, they would have now been regarding the iron tracery on the French Quarter and waiting for a ship to Port-au-Prince. It was, Sigbjørn knew, scarcely*

looking at the phrase Coldest December Day in 31 Years—
*for what British Columbians would care how cold it was in
New Orleans?—because of Fernando, who always answered
his gratitude by saying, "Well, one day we'll have a plate of
beans, when I am not so perfectament borracho, hombre,
in New Orleans." It was a catch phrase, a bit like a song
too, "But I owe you sixty pesos, Fernando, as well as my
life." "Never mind, one day I will ask you to a plate of
beans, in New Orleans." Sigbjørn turned, crackled the
pages back again in the manner of his father. Canada was
in the American news. And more especially British Columbia was.* Medos To Hang, *Canada, it seemed, was all the
way up America save for her spurs so that she was even
committing her murders for her. Never, as in this period
immediately succeeding the war, had there been so much
crime there before, and especially in Vancouver, only fifteen miles from Eridanus.* Medos To Hang. *He had shot
a couple of policemen in Seattle apparently because he'd
had some terrible trouble convincing a bartender that a
Canadian dollar was as good as an American one. Well,
without approving, he felt a sort of defiant approval. Then
Sigbjørn's hair walked on cold feet down the back of his
head. At the same time he chuckled in a manner he could
not help feeling was rather obscene. That bloody man
Wilderness—and, of course, he should have known it, since
everyone knew he was in New Orleans by this time—the
wife slayer who, having confessed, last night it seemed to
Sigbjørn, could now sleep, was in the news again too.*
Wilderness Returned Here for Trial, *he read.* Canadian
Police Ignore U.S. Ban. Bring Murder Suspect Back via
Airlines. *Sigbjørn, who had seen a little farther down the
page, lit another cigarette in such a deliberate way that he
almost saw himself doing it in the act of being photo-
graphed, his two rather stumpy fingers pressing themselves
against the cigarette and almost squeezing the self-conscious
cinematic smoke out into a plume that was blasted away by
the air current they had turned full on since it was hot in
the plane.* Sigbjørn Wilderness, *he read,* accused of the

murder of his thirty-nine-year-old wife, in Eridanus last June 6, was returned to Vancouver today to stand trial for his life. . . . Wilderness, clean-shaven and wearing an un-pressed (*impassioned, he read it first*) blue double-breasted jacket, shirt open at the neck, and odd trousers flew from New Orleans incognito with Provincial Police Dt. Cpl. Geoff Elmsley. Despite American aeronautics board regula-tions, which forbid the carrying of prisoners in passenger planes, Wilderness was brought here by three separate air-lines. Airlines hostesses and passengers did not know until they landed that Wilderness allegedly hit his wife over the head with a hammer and stabbed her sixty-seven times. *Sigbjørn read it again. It said he stabbed her sixty-seven times.*

But the next moment it seemed he was awake again. Suddenly he came still more to his senses and stretched out his hand to touch Primrose sitting beside him. Most of the lights were on and people were talking in low voices. *He would not remember.* Others were going toward the lavatory; but it could scarcely be El Paso yet, only a moment since he had seemed to have the whole night before him. Primrose was still asleep, and when the stewardess asked in a low voice if he would like to have his breakfast now he shook his head.

"How long to El Paso?" he whispered.

"About an hour and a half yet, sir." Miss Gleason looked at her wristwatch. "Would you like some chewing gum, sir?"

Sigbjørn shook his head. "In about half an hour then, is that all right?" The stewardess nodded and departed.

Dawn at El Paso, with Venus burning on the red horizon in a sky still blue-black overhead, the incredible purity and coldness of that dawn, the hope, but was that hope a lie? Probably it was a lie, with the mountains rising straight from the flat plain, deep rose with cobalt sky and in the field silver planes glittering in the sunrise and an olive green military plane with a tiny orange one beside it like an outrider, against the cool clear delicious blue; but now once more there was the agony of the papers, the passports; then imperceptibly, unbelievably, fatally, innocently, they were in old Mexico itself: for there had been no trouble, no trouble only delay and that due to some engine trouble, no one had even bothered to look at his Form H—"And what do you know, he wanted to look at my Form H," one woman had said, "the idea!"—delay while they wandered about; but now they were in old Mexico itself, the land of the pulques and chinches (Daniel's phrase all those years ago: "We are chuffing down to see you in the land of the pulques and chinches," he had written), with the tiny shadow of the great aircraft following them in the desert, flying over the abysses and canyons, the barrancas, the arroyos, and then, nothing, a sense of limitless, unparalleled dun- and biscuit-colored nothing.

In the distance there were velvet foothills fading into a pure turquoise sky: formations below in shapes of lizards or giraffes: alkali like breaking waves, roads rambling across the desert like canals on Mars. Flying, flying, over Chihuahua—and ever the roaring propeller, the wing—they were above a lunar landscape.

Slate-blue smoke from a train, or smoke like a crow's wing—he saw the smoke from the train and the shadow crawling underneath it, but no train was visible; along the eastern horizon to the left was more smoke like that from some celestial tramp-steamer.

And below now were swirling patterns, water courses, dry round dunes, wooly, like a certain sort of soft tweed, or in herringbone patterns, water courses, dry streams like planned trails, arroyos secos, and nubbly salmon-colored sand.

A landscape like innumerable striped sphinxes lying on their backs, a landscape of frozen waves, a land of inconceivable desolation and in the midst of this was a single farm by a waterhole with fields smoother than golf greens in Hoylake, England.

Sunken waterholes in the desert, far rock formations like Inca cities, pools of alkali like frozen rivers, wrinkled rhinoceros hide of the foothills, like pyramids too, tender blue sky with one long motionless still white cloud a benign unwinking swordfish, blur of horizon mist and purple desert producing almost rainbowlike effects, and far to the west were clouds like polar bears tinged with blue, or balls of smoke hanging over the horizon, as from perhaps that same steamer, as they overhauled it, or it was overhauling them as they were overhauling time, or vice versa, or both, and still the tiny shadow of the plane on the desert, the tiny cross, the abysses and canyons, and then again, nothing—nothing—nothing.

"The old place hasn't changed much in eight years," Sigbjørn said.

A lake in the distance. Blue? Green? Or a mirage? Suddenly in the middle of the desert below them appeared a geometrical group of farms squared off by black roads, the fields green, the houses neatly placed in the corners, the road ran straight across the desert and vanished, it seemed, over the rim of the world. And this was the land of his friend Fernando, the land—could it be?—where he wanted to die.

In the plane Sigbjørn looked at Primrose, so pretty, and so vivaciously absorbed, so hypnotized by what was after all only desert, so full of life: already she was beginning to show signs of benefitting from the trip. Was it possible anybody so gay, so adaptable, so courageous, and the same time so lovely and intelligent — though perceptive was more the right word — could exist, let alone be his wife? Good heavens, what a God-awful description. And yet, that was the way he thought. Descriptions were his weak point and probably he should not be a writer at all. He was fooling himself. Besides was that, or something like it really what he thought, even was thinking at the moment, even while she was relishing her ice cream, still impossible to purchase in Canada. Well, it was true, so far as it went. And by God, it was certainly true that he was lucky. Who else would have put up with what she had had to put up with in the last few years? And he thought of her again—their well dry still this autumn, in spite of the bloody weather, the haunted well that apart from their beloved pier, their first attempt at building, had been about all that had survived of their old house, carting down those heavy buckets of water through the forest from the store, and heating them for him to soak his feet on the God-awful secondhand stove in the house they had not been able to make even inhabitable for the winter. And Sigbjørn really saw the new house all right. Yes, that was something he really did see, not something he just pretended he ought to see, or was seeing for an ulterior motive. Sigbjørn saw the unfinished house standing there helpless, all but unprotected, at the mercy of the shipwrecks, and battering weather, something indeed like their own loves.

Now Sigbjørn, following the suit of a man on the other side of the aisle, wearing a service badge, who had abstracted some papers from an important looking briefcase, did likewise: that is, he also took a rather small black notebook from his briefcase, another present to him from Primrose, and began to glance through it with an air of conscious puzzlement, as though, which was indeed the case, he wished everyone on the plane to know that he had as much right there as they, a sentiment he was so far from feeling that he thought he should do some hard writing immediately to establish it: ah, the ghastly alienation of writers, in no time at all he knew that he was not absorbing what was written there, but merely hoping he was being observed in the act of looking intelligent, or of being like other people—thank God there were no GI's, flamethrowers in uniform anymore— the perfect gentleman, or at least justifying himself as the perfect converse of this, so intense was the feeling that he became hot and, finding that he had read nothing whatsoever, had to look up to ease the strain: no one was looking at him at all, and taking courage from this, he directed his gaze at the man with the briefcase whom he now saw was shamelessly making out a horoscope: and since this could not in one way be called precisely behaving like other people or even being the perfect gentleman, Sigbjørn returned to his notes with less embarrassment: the black notebook, together with its notes, had a peculiar history but was remarkable in this that, while he had lost so much else, it contained some observations he had made years before, on his previous visits to Oaxaca, and which, in one form or another, mostly in the first chapter, he had already incorporated into *The Valley of the Shadow of Death:* one or other of them had saved it (it was Primrose, of course) from their holocaust, but he certainly would have forgotten all about it had not Primrose produced it the other day, since when, during his moments of anguish with his feet, he had amused himself by making certain additions, as though indeed they were but a kind of prelude to the work that was being created now, or created by another through him by virtue of his return: since at all events it was not a horoscope—or was it?—Sigbjørn took some interest in what he had written. He read:

Juan Fernando's ancestry. Fernando traces his ancestry back —sometimes under the influence of mescal—to a king of the Zapotecans, on his mother's side, which anyone would believe to see his kingly bearing, whose name was Cosijoeza. This king, according to legend, became displeased with certain merchants, who came from other kingdoms to trade, and had them killed at Mitla. The Aztec emperor, being advised by the Chalca merchants, sent to Mitla to take revenge, and set fire to the town, and killed the inhabitants, having no mercy on anyone.

His great-grandfather was a pure-blooded Spaniard, an engineer who had been in California at the time it was lost to America, and who had married an American. Driven south by necessity he had settled first of all in Tabasco and then in Mexico City, where his wife gave birth to a son, Fernando's grandfather, who married an English woman, the daughter of one of the directors of the Oaxaca railway, the very narrow-gauge line that had been built by the English, over as long a route as possible, since they were paid by the kilometer. Fernando's father had come to Oaxaca to live where he married a pure-blooded Zapotecan from whom came Fernando's royal descent.

But what is important is that his father had been a man of intellectual persuasion, his mother had been a pure-blooded Zapotecan, and that somewhere among his collateral relations was an English renegade, who had drunk himself to death in Oaxaca, where he was allowed to remain because he was under the protection of the British Consul, likewise a relative. Fernando had been trained as a chemist: but the horrible incident of his operation on his sister, for whom his father would not call a doctor, his father who had even stopped the operation before Fernando was finished, had resulted in his leaving home forever.

Mescal. Mexican drinks have been maligned, tequila is a pure drink, the evils that dwell in rye dwell not in it, though others,

*worse, may: mescal is a pure drink too. Its consumption: from
small glasses, and ritual demands a steady hand and a sober social
interest, mescal drunk thus is therefore a civilized drink. But
mescal, it is said, will go to the brain—any barman will demon-
strate to you, while giving you another one, just how it does this
(though it must not be supposed that the Indians, for whom
once drunkenness held the death penalty, approve of drinking
on the part of others than themselves). When that happens the
brain as often as not dictates, as with any other drink, that
mescal should not be a ritual, but drunk by the bottle. Ochas
is boiled orange leaves and should be drunk hot with raw alcohol put into it. But mescal put into it is still more exciting.
Just as Mexican drinks have been maligned so the friendships
of two people of similar alcoholic capacity with every intention
of drinking to the bottom of the bowl and remaining intelligent
is sealed by alcohol as by nothing else. It becomes a sort of blood
brotherhood. This is true of friendships formed over beer, but
less true over rye. But in mescal lies the principle of that godlike or daemonic force in Mexico that, anyone who had lived
there knows, remains to this day unappeased. Under the influence of mescal, the best of friends in sober life will do their
best to murder each other. But a friendship that, begotten of
mescal, survives it, will survive anything.*

And their friendship had more than survived. He read:

*6 Enero 1938. Sigbjørn: I went there at 8 o'clock and I did
not find you. Now, at this time, I am not able to go and have a
talk with you, so if you are so kind write me a note and send it
to me. Tell me your tragedies of this day and also tell me if you
are drunk. I will see you tomorrow at 8 o'clock P.M. at that
place, but try to be there exactly at that time. Did you went to
the Post office as I proposed you? Did you had that talk with
Lomilla? Did you keep out of drinking today? Is there no more
remedy than cut out our friendship if you are continuing on
drinking? Sincerely yours, Juan Fernando.*

So far these were the notes of eight years ago. Sigbjørn now smoked his rather foul pipe and read the notes that he'd made at Eridanus within the last month:

For a long short story or short novel begin with 1936-37-38 the material in Mexican notebook, which is all the protagonist knows about Mexico etc., but now after writing book (unpublished) about Mexico, he is going back there at the end of 1945. Letter from English publishers: "I have never looked forward to reading a book with more expectation than I do The Valley of the Shadow of Death. *I will send you a telegram as soon as I have finished it." Waiting for the telegram, which never arrives. Tension piling unbearably. Subplot should again be the drink conflict, with its analogue of the abuse of mystical powers—only this time really* conflict.

Sigbjørn smiled, though in fact he felt more like weeping.

Beneath these notes he had made some jottings for a short story to be called "Via Dolorosa," and which dealt with the last time in his life he ever saw Ruth, when she had left him in December, 1937, at the Hotel Cornada in Mexico City. This story would have dealt with that period and been set at the time immediately prior to his having gone to Oaxaca for the second time. Sigbjørn had actually—he reflected for the second time, having forgotten that he'd thought of it before—used much of this material in *The Valley of the Shadow of Death* and for a moment, as the plane suddenly sprang upward like a distorted spring, he was surprised at the poverty of an imagination that had driven him back upon old and used material: but doubtless he had had no intention of writing the story, in fact he very much wondered if he would ever write anything again, so perhaps it didn't—but what about Primrose?—much matter.

"Primrose," Sigbjørn said suddenly, replacing the notebook in the briefcase, and the briefcase in the seat pocket, "did we return the Chaliapin book to the library?"

"Oh yes," Primrose said. "Don't you remember I returned all the books the last time I went into town. Why?"

"No reason. I just found a few notes I'd taken from it. I'm

fond of that old Vancouver library. I used to love getting the books out and then coming home in the bus and finding you waiting for me at Eridanus. And then having a swim off the pier before tea."

"What is it, my precious darling? Are you homesick already?"

"No, just a motiveless, incomprehensible nostalgia. I was worried about Pushkin. I mean the little cat."

"Ah. . . . But Quaggan'll look after him all right. He loves Quaggan."

"Quaggan'll feed Pushkin too much fish. And then he'll become too attached to Quaggan and he won't meet us in the woods anymore. And I'm afraid before that, he'll miss us and fret and become neurotic or something. What's that you're reading?"

"Darling, how long would it take us to get to Taxco from Mexico City?"

Sigbjørn shared the folder she was studying with its picture of Taxco, reading: *You step into a different world the moment you board a clipper for Magic Mexico. . . . The magic of the high plateaux and hill towns of Mexico and Guatemala is calling. . . . Calling you to a* different *kind of vacation in 1946. . . . And that magic starts the moment you board your clipper at Miami, New Orleans, Houston, Brownsville, Nuevo Laredo.* "I wonder how many people who read that advertisement remember what a peacetime vacation was like," Sigbjørn was saying, or not saying to himself. "No, it's fairly easy to get to Taxco. It's about three or four hours from Mexico City by bus. No more than an hour or two from Cuernavaca. When I first went to Mexico I went by boat and landed in Acapulco. So Taxco was the first interesting town I saw. There was a bloody awful road from Acapulco to Taxco but I dare say they've finished the highway they were beginning by now."

"Oh, Sigbjørn, can we *really* go to Taxco? It looks dreamy."

"There used to be pleasant tin objects." Sigbjørn, as if seeking perhaps the tin objects in question, regarded, below the colored photo of Taxco they were looking at, with its twin churrigueresque towers of Borda's cathedral, and the dome with seven pointed—seven!—white starfish on a blue background on it, and in front of a low Spanish-tiled building—La Asturiana something de Abarrotes—the obvious honeymoon couple, the man with his Hawaiian white sport shirt with green-and-orange spirochetes on it and brown trousers, and the girl in her Cuernavaca outfit and Spanish skirt. The man was taking a photograph (presumably with steady hand). *The unforgettable beauty of Taxco is typical of the Mexican highlands in summer. . . . The altitude here is 5600 feet.* Meantime in Sigbjørn's mind Hart Crane rang the bells their dreadful peal away up in the church tower, *and all my countrymen rush to one stall*—one could almost see the stall in question, which was Doña Berta's cantina— while Sigbjørn himself slept on the church steps in 1936, slept also on the balcony of the great-doored bare hotel, while pigeons walked over his feet and hands in the sun, while the altitude meant: *Exile is thus purgatory, not such as Dante built, but rather like a patchwork than a quilt.* And the bells: *And what hours they forget to chime I'll know, as one whose altitude, at one time, was not so.* The same honeymoon couple were also to be seen partaking, in another picture, of some kind of vintage near the parapet, say, of Los Arcos, or the Rancho Selva—or was it the restaurant with all the delirium tremens all over the wall?— served by a sharp-chinned Mexican who looked like a captain in full wardroom kit on board a French battleship in a film about Indo-China, and obviously so glad to be doing it, and not inwardly despising them, not hating them with everything in his being; Borda's cathedral with its twin crosses on its twin spires was also in evidence here, but in a farther background. *Modern luxury in an old setting,* it said. *In the temperate climate of these high regions, enjoy modern hotels with ancient cathedrals in the background. Burros climb narrow cobbled streets between white houses roofed with red tiles. . . .* Ah yes, Sigbjørn could feel Primrose identifying herself already with that pretty girl in the photograph and himself, Sigbjørn, with the man taking the photograph. Perhaps she also thought of herself as dressed in the elaborate Tijuana skirt—and indeed why not?—in the picture of the Tehuacán girl below, who lent authority and at the same time a thoroughly hypocritical welcome. *You step into a different world the moment you board a clipper for—*

"Sigbjørn, are we really in Mexico darling? Tell me that we're really *in* Mexico."

Sigbjørn pressed her hand, noticing at the same time that the man had put away his horoscope. "Perhaps we'll be in Taxco this time next week," he said. "And you'll be wearing a Tijuana costume—"

And then out of nowhere it seemed, the cold and fog and the sense of the whistling air draft, and mountains: he had the feeling of going slowly, far too slowly—*Fasten Your Safety Belts*—the sense of danger and steering by instruments. Fog, fog, fog. Occasionally he had a glimpse of what seemed to be sides of mountains. The plane shuddered and bounced. It was like feeling your way along in dead reckoning; the plane seemed to be going dead slow and wallowing like a ship. But perhaps the fog would make them late, they would not have to go through Customs at Monterrey—but Sigbjørn combed his hair in preparation for the Customs—or perhaps, better still, they would crash and not reach Monterrey. It was suddenly much colder too, at any moment one expected to see an iceberg sailing through the shifting mists. *In Ballast to the White Sea?* What about the ships, the real ships that had gone down or been wrecked while he had been writing that now burned work? The *Ariadne N. Pandelis,* the *Herzogin Cecelia.* That awful business of the coincidence of Erikson! Ah, the maker of tragedies. The uncertainty had now, he reflected, gone on for so long that everyone at least must be possessed of the idea of some kind of fright, if only, so to speak, as something required of them. And was it not? For one thing it had been the worst month in the history of commercial aviation.

It was one long continuous moan—a wild chorus shrieking to heaven. Tears for the dead who shall not come homeward to any shore on any shore on any tide. A tablet will be unveiled to the *Titanic* survivors. The Oratorio society will follow by a rendering of the Damrosch Brahms *German Requiem,* thus bringing the first part of the program to an end. The second will open by an appropriate orchestral selection, "The Liebestod," followed by Mr. Rinaldo Strappo and Mary Garden singing, say, "It Happened in Monterrey One Afternoon in December." Signor Ernest Consolo will render "Get With Child a Fallen Constellation" . . . followed by a Bach concerto in D minor (first movement); Enrico Caruso will sing "The Lost Chord," by Sullivan, in English. Prince Pierre Troubetzkoy has finished a painting called "Spirit Triumphant," which is to be reproduced on postcards to be sold at the performance this evening for the survivors. The painting represents a beautiful woman with a triumphant expression rising from dark waters while in the background towers the burning outline of a ship. Why burning? . . . Sigbjørn tried to fix his mind on the last time he had seen Eridanus, the little new still unfinished house below, the cedar tree, the foreshortened pier, their boat hoisted up and overturned on the platform for safety during their absence, but it had been raining then, stormy, and he wanted a composed picture of it in his mind, but for some reason he found himself thinking of Kristbjorg, who also brought disturbing thoughts. What was worse, the sign forward in the plane now said *No Smoking* and Sigbjørn obediently stubbed out his cigarette. But it was soon apparent that this was not prior to any intention of landing. Had they lost their way? They were groping their way with an even greater uncertainty, and even greater slowness.

They sideslipped and perhaps they were going to make a forced landing. No, though quivering through their entire length like their own house when a high wind and sea drove an unruly log against the hemlock piles, now they were quite obviously gaining height. . . . He imagined Kristbjorg as pretending not to be too surprised when news eventually reached him that their plane had crashed and that Primrose and he had been killed. He would like it to be understood that he had foreseen it in a way, had even said as much, or if it hadn't been one thing it would have been another; he had had a suspicion, he would never see them again. That was what he would say; however, he would miss them. But Kristbjorg was in his way a maker of tragedies too. Indeed Sigbjørn had quarreled with him on that score in Eridanus. Yes, he would have liked to have made it up more and he was sorry for it, for it was the only quarrel he had ever had with him, the only quarrel, save with Primrose, he had ever had in Eridanus. Yes, he would have liked to have made it up more positively with Kristbjorg before they left, even though they had stopped by his shack and all had a beer together on the last day.

What if it were now too late completely to rectify it, after all
Kristbjorg's kindness? He could console himself at least that he
had done it in part. The quarrel had come about this way.
Kristbjorg, like Glaucous, was a fisherman. When he went! Yes,
but that time, at that moment of complete forgiveness, at that
moment when Sigbjørn realized, Endymion-like—though it
would perhaps be more subtle to leave Endymion to the end—
that it was within his power, such is the life of those who dwell
on the window of existence, the life of those with endless
thoughts, as it were on a nickel at the edge of eternity, to make
Kristbjorg perhaps fatally miserable but that he was not going
to use that power, it was then, as he sat watching the scend and
dive of the boat that he made up his mind to take Primrose to
Mexico. . . . Yes, it had been then, that the decision was made,
the one decision in fact springing directly out of the other, the
action from the abnegation of action, and as against the terrific
sunlit mountains above the blue glittering choppy water continually swayed the cross. . . . Had he done right? Quién sabe?.

The plane made another drop and Sigbjørn visualized the
crash, in fact almost experienced it. First the motor conking out
and making a terrible rumbling noise, then falling, at least two
hundred feet, without breathing. First this dropping—then the
leveling off—the emergency power pulled from somewhere,
then the falling toward the ground and the certainty one was
going to crash, the agony about Primrose, the screams and yells
of the passengers still with straps round their waists—then striking the apartment building, the turning upside down, striking
something else, the ground, the ship skimming along, then suddenly the fiery nightmare, the helplessness, the not knowing
whether one was alive or dead, or if one would get out of the
ship, one's body still twisted upside down, but still struggling to
free Primrose, then the heroic rescue of Primrose and the other
passengers struggling and crawling out of holes, and others
struggling, the flames leaping round them, the bodies and the
wreckage strewn all over the field, wanting to help but unable to
do anything, but Primrose was safe, heroically rescued. Then
the bottle of tequila, and the Royal Humane Society's Medal,
presented by Aleman, or the Minister of the Interior.

There were exclamations and sighs of relief in the plane that had now emerged from the fog. The clipper was flying down the same gulch between mountains as before, though it was losing height rapidly. Through the window Sigbjørn could see that the gulch took a slow surprising turn to the left, which they were following, sideslipping, and after each sideslip the plane strained upward a little like a kite, and then began to drop down again, banking, steeply, and turning steadily to the left, as they approached a long somewhat swampy looking valley at the far end of which appeared to be a smallish town of gasworks and railway lines, the railway metals running through the swamps, and a few tall rain-shrouded factory chimneys, the whole surrounded by huge gray humped mountains in murk and rain, so that it seemed for a moment with this chaos of fog and storm for a background almost as though they were in Canada once more.

So great was everyone's relief, doubtless, at emerging from the fog that it did not seem to occur to anyone as they descended bumpily that they might be making a forced landing even now after all. Such was not the case: Sigbjørn combed his hair hurriedly; now a few isolated planes stood about below among what looked like reeds, and it was the Monterrey airport, and he did not give the Customs another thought till they emerged from the belly of the plane onto the field, where they were immediately assured that due to the delay they would not go through the Customs till Mexico City, which in fact was the more usual procedure. They were to have only a short stop. The plane stood on the runway before what looked like a small clubhouse for a nine-hole golf course, on whose windows was written *Carta Blanca, Cerveza Monterrey.*

It was raining in abrupt windy gusts and the wind itself howled and whined desolately round the clubhouse. It was freezing cold so they made for the clubhouse where with the other passengers they stretched their legs; but it was late afternoon and the bar was shut so they came out onto the porch. What a lugubrious impression! The mountains stood around desolately in the rain and those few distant factory chimneys, a few shacks and huts, and the swampy desolate Gogolian landscape was, as is the way with airports for that matter in relation to most large towns, all one could see of the metropolis. When he had been in Mexico previously someone had suggested that he come here, which was possibly why he had one of those sudden impressions of having been here before, which he had not, even that they had been in some sort of deadly peril, and that Primrose had strayed away and got lost: he took her arm protectively, wishing too somehow to counteract the disappointment, for here, at last, they had set foot in the dark mysterious country itself. But Primrose was pointing loyally up into the murk, loyally for she must certainly have noticed them before in California, at some birds like dirty flying dishcloths that were circling, flapping slowly, in a melancholy procession.

"Oh Sigbjørn, your xopilotes!"

"Another Charles Addams." Sigbjørn chuckled, warmed, however, by the reference, which was to *The Valley of the Shadow of Death* where the Promethean creatures were supposed to play a part perhaps a shade less obvious than in every other book about war or Mexico or death. "You should say, 'Oh *dar*ling, our first vultures!' "

But they were called on board and had to run for the plane. "She's headed for the barn!" Primrose called delightedly over her shoulder to Sigbjørn limping behind her up the ramp.

"I just overheard that according to Mexican law they have to land in Mexico City before sunset."

"Who the vultures?"

"No, the plane, idiot."

Up, up, they climbed, ever higher into the Sierra Madre, mountains beyond mountains beyond mountains, where on those mountains the farmers sowed their seed crops and left them, upon seemingly inaccessible peaks—far below, there were even signs of cultivation—and where, the stewardess told them, the farmers sowed once and just left their crops to fructify, without even bothering to keep an eye on them, not looking at them for a year at a time, when they would pay a difficult pilgrimage up there, making the occasion doubtless one of celebration, at which period they would be found to have flourished spendidly, as did Parsifal's flowers in his absence. And what a lesson there was for a writer in this; it was an ascension into heaven itself.

Sigbjørn had been sitting on the left, and now he moved over to the right to see which was the better view. They continually changed from one side to the other and from one seat to another; they were rebuked by Miss Gleason, blasé about the scenery, but Sigbjørn paid no attention, the departure of so many passengers had freed him, had liberated his soul, and made him bold and unselfconscious. It was going to be worth it, Sigbjørn thought, and he felt a joyous pride eating his rump steak above these gigantic abysses, for was it not he himself whom Primrose must thank for making all these wonders possible? And what a difference, what a triumphant difference from the way he had left it.

Mountains beyond mountains, abysses beyond abysses, ranging away below while the whole sky—shafts of sunlight, roiled wild clouds, tender blue rifts, and wisps of fog—came rolling toward them as if caught in one gigantic whirlwind, huge ethereal tumbleweeds, a northward odyssey of eternity itself. While later at eighteen thousand feet, bouncing crazily along, hastening into the sunset above an ocean of clouds like boiling cotton wool, sprinting drunkenly, tripping over skyey boulders but never reducing their speed, with to the westward the summits of enormous volcanoes seeming like quite low mountains with their bases washed by the kind of white seething sea sailors call white water, and in which you expected at any moment to see that same celestial tramp steamer beating itself to death against the black rocks, it was not like life at all—even if Bergsonianly it reflected a process of life—it was like sailing into the pages of Shelley—or was it perhaps ultimately sailing into the pages of one's own book?—into *Prometheus Unbound,* so that it was almost with relief that you turned to go on eating your corn and sweet potatoes, even if you had missed seeing whistling by to windward, the winter palace of the Demogorgon. Here, from this point of view of sublimity, it was possible to look back upon one's life without too much pain, or triumph, being beyond both: but he would have been inhuman indeed, as sitting together once more, if he had not reflected upon the contrast between this triumphal entry and his ghastly drunken ignominious exit more than seven years before in the Pullman car named *Aristotle;* what was extraordinary though, as Primrose who was, to his delight, excitedly looking for Popocatepetl and Ixtaccihuatl. "Is that it? Is *that* it?" "Yes . . . yes . . . yes . . . No . . . no . . ." "There . . . there . . ." "No, we have to wait a bit. Or perhaps we can't see them," what was extraordinary was to reflect that beneath this mass of boiling cotton wool, beneath these reefs and wild white seas of clouds, far far beneath these peaks of volcanoes and fabulous summits, far far below Mexico was still there, without doubt, largely unchanged, had been there all this time, carrying on without him, Sigbjørn: yes, as if he were a god, and could lift this lid of cloud, there, he saw in his mind's eye, it all was below him, as if he were a god who had just lifted the lid to a box of toys, the burros, the flowers, the tortillas, the little pigs, the Indian women, the dancers in fringes of scarlet (they had timed their arrival to coincide with the festivities for the Virgin of Guadalupe at the basilica of Guadalupe itself), the straggling villages and vast shrouded slopes, the cargadores carrying their terrific loads, the buses to Tlalpán or the trams to Xochimilco, and Cuernavaca, the town of his novel; yes there it all was, and how different from Vancouver. He was so much filled with joy on his own account, at the miracle of his return, that he scarcely noticed that Primrose had at last found Popocatepetl: "There it is—" "Yes . . . Yes . . . there," and Sigbjørn kissed her with delight: privately he was a little disappointed, for the sacred and majestic peak was considerably diminished by the enormous height at which they were flying, it was not much bigger than a slag heap, in fact, but then of course, come to that, they would be landing on a high level too at Mexico City, and here they were not far from doing just that, coming out of the clouds, yes, here was his lake bed, his volcano bed, ugly, beyond belief, they would be landing soon—landing indeed now, the sunset had stood still for them since they were an American plane, and now he didn't want to be doing so at all, did not want to go through the Customs—as if they were coming to earth on a half-flooded planet in which some great catastrophe had taken place, though what seemed to have been there previously was not the landscape of floating islands and verdure of fantasy, nor the sort of quasi-Venetian barbaric civilization of fact, but some ravaged glass factory town in Lancashire; now the throttles were retarded, they were sinking, they had landed.

IV

I<small>T WAS VERY COLD, WHICH</small>
reminded Sigbjørn that Mexico City was after all eight thousand
feet up in the clouds, so that Primrose did not even have much
reason to be disappointed about the comparatively small size (as
yet, he thought, a trifle grimly) of Popocatepetl. There had
been the usual tension at the Customs of course, nothing very
much, the chief Customs officer very pleasant, chalking their
luggage without a word, while others, for example an American
rash enough to bring a bottle of rye with him, were not so lucky.
True there had been the slight annoyance caused by the assist-
ant Customs officer, a mere boy, who kept shouting, almost heck-
ling: "Half eh moment, chief! Half eh moment, chief! O.K.
chief, let's go!" And then it had been an annoyance to have to
make up their minds on the spot what hotel they were going to,
but quite as much a triumph to have resisted the attempts at the
airport to make them take an expensive hotel: "Nosotros no
somos americanos ricos," they had said, and how many times
would they be saying that again, Sigbjørn wondered (as the taxi
at the moment began to pass a half-familiar pulquería called
The Line of Fire, went down a bystreet, then came out on the
main road), before they returned to Canada, "Nosotros somos
canadianos *pobres*"; and it had seemed quite natural, as if they
were following a preordained path indeed, to find themselves
taking the last taxi from the airfield in the gathering chilly dusk

through the ghastly gingerbread suburban-broken Aleman-scarred landscape toward the Hotel Cornada itself. Nor had the exchange been too bad either; they cashed some traveler's checks at the airport without trouble, Sigbjørn had even signed them without trouble, and, shifting his decimal point just as Miss Gleason suggested, felt proud that he was dealing with matters intelligently and practically (not to say operatically, for, as in Italy, there was always a latent operatic air about the smallest transactions in Mexico, which could be forced should they threaten to become serious) without putting too much of the burden upon Primrose. To be sure, it was extremely difficult, having lived as they had, having saved as they had in Canada, and after the relatively precious unit of the dollar to think again in terms of pesos: it slightly embittered Sigbjørn, for instance, journeying through the sunset then, to realize that at the airport ten pesos had already been extorted in advance for the taxi fare: still, by the cunning mental manipulation once more of Miss Gleason's decimal point, the knowledge could be held in the mind for a while that this was only two dollars: moreover Sigbjørn had done it all before—seven years ago the peso had been crashing, every week it had fallen—and he should have known better than to attach too much importance to the unit "peso": nonetheless, then he had thought in pounds, he had had more money than he knew what to do with and usually threw it away as soon as possible: now things had changed, it was up to him to make, for Primrose's sake, as much use as he could of the money, and even though he knew that in the end, despite all his resolutions, he might find himself leaving everything to Primrose (when she could spend almost as much as she liked and it wouldn't matter, so long as he didn't have to hear about it), for the moment he was the responsible fellow. In fact it was part of the plan, part of being her guide, her Virgil, through these intricate regions of ancient fire and purge and transcendent beauty, that he should be, and were their roles to be reversed, it would amount to a very considerable failure on his part. Their taxi was caterwauling its way slowly yet savagely through the narrow streets like a fogbound steamer. Ah well, Mexico City, whose rush hour it was, seemed much the same, smells, noise,

open cutouts, with which went the same invitation to get out of
it as soon as possible: pulquerías, exactly as he had visualized
them; the same peons; women with rebozos; cantinas; humped
churches; so far at least there seemed little difference, save that
there were more beer shops than formerly, and this inordinate
number of ill-advised signs ordering one to drink ice-cold Coca-
Cola; and though every crowded street crawled with the milli-
pedes of memory, this represented finally a concatenation of emo-
tion one had no need to disguise, even when wholly unpleasant,
especially in the face of Primrose's almost speechless excitement,
for since it was with a genuine catch of the breath that one
grated oneself against the familiar street names, Isabel la Católica, Cinco de Mayo, and the rest, and drew up at last at the
Hotel Cornada, the luminous name of which above the main
entrance had been, rather holophrastically, significantly as it
turned out, reduced by three red letters, so that, as one might
have seen this arrival in a dream, what seemed only to welcome
them were the words *Hotel Nada.*   ̽ ̽ ̽ [*liVe SHELL siqn*]

"Veinte pesos son todos, señor. Todos son pagados," Sigbjørn
had said, still chuckling at this drollery of fate.

"No, señor. Diez pesos mas."

"Pero—Primrose, I seem to be having difficulty with my ears."

"That's it darling, it's the plane. We're not down to earth
properly yet."

"I'll say we're not. Hotel Nada—ha ha ha! Ugh! Es todos,
señor. Por favor, mon bagliagli—"

"You must ah pay extra for the luggage," said the taxi driver.

"But we've already paid."

"Americanos?"

"No, hombre. Nosotros no somos americanos ricos. Nosotros—"

"Nosotros somos canadianos *pobres.*" Primrose, with a significant gesture accompanying the *pobres,* helped Sigbjørn out loyally.

"Ten pesos more."

"All right then." Sigbjørn cheerfully paid the driver. "Down
with the North American tyrants! Damn it, Primrose, it's our
first night anyhow, don't let's spoil it."

"Bagliagli indeed, what a love you are," Primrose commented.

"Sorry, I forgot my medieval Latin. I meant impedimenta. Now for our winter quarters."

But after this flight even the Hotel Cornada in Mexico City was not a letdown. Always a nasty little hotel, yet a few years ago seeming so modern (if cheap—and certainly central), it appeared like a cross between a ruined cotton exchange and a tenement. The street, the Cinco de Mayo overflowed into a carpetless dark lobby where shoeshine boys mingled freely with hawkers selling their wares and even beggars. This praiseworthy democratic impression, if not altogether deceptive, meant nothing however. Sigbjørn's restaurant of his last morning when Ruth had left, and he had gone to Oaxaca—neither of them ever to see the other again—the restaurant abutting the hotel lobby, through which a man with a look of an executioner had dragged the shrieking fawns to slit their throats behind the barroom door, was still a restaurant, though much more respectable looking, with white tablecloths, such as one sees at some country stations in America, but the bar had been altogether removed. Upstairs the decaying modern outfitting produced a weird effect. Tiers of washing hung outside the windows like a scene in an old Soviet movie. Whole families, obviously in poverty, inhabited some of the rooms and in places seemed actually to be camping out in the corridors. On the other hand the occasional flashily dressed Mexican would emerge, lock his door, and stand awaiting the elevator, opposite one of the cheap electric-blue-velvet, stuffed and decaying divans that confronted the entrance on every floor, smoking a cigar, with every appearance of prosperity and of living there too. The hot water system in the rooms they were shown of course did not work; it never had. What was surprising was the degree of desuetude in an establishment built not ten years before so that as has been said the fittings—it was or had been a place of harsh rectangles, large steel-rimmed windows, of blocks and violent angular contrasts of color, so that at one time it had suggested to Sigbjørn some super modern yet even so jerry-built apartment house in Vienna or Berlin left unfinished from lack of money and then completed on a still cheaper plan while still preserving this illusion of the "modern" —were already falling into ruin and decrepitude. The Hotel Nada indeed. The Hotel Cornada was originally a copy of an American copy of a cheap German copy of its own typical Berlin architecture. Evidently it was not even adapted to decay, as might have been the case with a more ancient or solid building. Sigbjørn had seen families who had fashioned a comfortable home of sorts out of the complete wreckage of what was once a small room in a summer palace of Maximilian's or a section of burned building in an old hacienda. Though apparently people were doing it for whatever reason, you could not here somehow imagine anything similar being done when the place completely fell to pieces.

Nevertheless, they secured one of the better rooms on the very top floor; the light in the bedroom was too dim, that in the bathroom a glare, but this didn't seem to matter. Primrose was in high spirits and Sigbjørn in such a daze that left to himself he probably would have drifted straight out into the city, but for that lobby, without even bothering to unpack.

"It would be nice to have a drink," Primrose said.

"Weren't we going out to get one?"

"I mean in here."

Sigbjørn, who had already mentioned, possibly to elicit just such a response, that he'd noticed a liquor store next door to the hotel, lit his pipe. "Do you know, Primrose, it's a strange feeling, because somehow or other I just don't feel I can face going through that lobby again right at the moment."

"Oh, I'll go." Primrose had already put on her Arctic skunk fur coat like a cape. "It'll be an adventure. What shall I get?"

"Say, 'por favor, dame Berreteaga,' it's only four pesos, I saw it on the bottle, and it's good."

By the door Primrose burst out laughing. "It's just occurred to me you'll have to go through the lobby *some*time, darling," she said, "unless you want to stay in this room all the while we're in Mexico."

"I was just thinking the same thing, sweetheart. I don't know what's got into me. Be sure the bottle's got a little gadget attached, or get them to open it, or I'll have to go down anyhow to borrow a corkscrew and I've forgotten the word for it. Thank you."

Now why have I done that? he asked himself, once she had gone. What he had really meant was: I just don't feel I can face going downstairs to the lobby, going through the lobby, or, worst of all, coming back through the lobby, carrying a bottle in case they see me, without a drink first. A significant beginning, though Primrose would see no significance in it probably. When she had gone, he looked at himself in a mirror. Why, he asked himself aloud, of all places did I have to bring her *here,* anyway, to the Hotel Cornada? By what indraft? The first was a question that did not want to get itself answered, even while, as a certain school of philosophy maintains, the answer was no doubt contained within it. But what did it all mean? Why *had* he brought her here? To this ugly, damn, bloody, uncomfortable—Is it fun for her? Somehow he felt it was, so far, but any thoughtful person would have taken her to the Reforma or the Regis or at least the Tarleton, somewhere where she could above all have a shower or a hot bath to begin with. He remembered that the expensive hotels held bitter memories for him too, especially the last, where, after Oaxaca and Acapulco, he had stayed with Stanford. And he could justify himself on the ground that the Cornada was not "recognized"—and Sigbjørn hated "recognized" places, all the more so when they were recognized by officials under the guise of hospitality at the airport; the only reason probably apart from the rake-off on the taxi and the hotel itself that they asked you to declare your hotel, or advised one, was that they wanted to keep an eye on you—that he supposed it was still relatively cheap, and its location was convenient. He could not have known—Hell!—however that might be, the ramifications of the questions were too many—he had only to reread the notes he had glanced at on the plane for his projected story "Via Dolorosa" to find all too many good reasons why he should never have set foot in the Hotel Cornada again, he had only to read. He felt them stifling him, literally, and he pushed at the hotel window, which had got stuck, was supposed to open outward like a visor—and what was the name of that glass, triplex? duplex? homo triplex?—though their room in the Hotel Cornada was unheated. But to get some air; a big wind had sprung up suddenly outside, now the sun had gone down. So that was the first thing he had done, to send her out into the storm to get a bottle—he could barely push the window on its injured hinges against the wind, so he shut it again. Homo duplex, he thought, at least . . .

The Hotel Coranada had been, of course, a place of decision, the scene perhaps of the most purely destructive and negative decision he had ever made in his life unless since, had he not made it he might never have met Primrose, and certainly would never have written *The Valley of the Shadow of Death*, it was the most ruthlessly constructive and positive one. But constructive or destructive, it had been sad, the results seemed unending, it was the lowest ebb—and was there a clue in this platitude, were the tides of our life inexorably drawn back in some fashion to that lowest ebb?—of his life perhaps. It was as if the ghost of a man who had hanged himself had returned to the scene of his suicide, not out of morbid curiosity, but out of sheer nostalgia to drink the drinks again that had nerved him to do it, and wonder perhaps that he had ever had the courage. Here once, in the Hotel Cornada, he had separated from Ruth, chopped his life in half as surely as if he had done it with a meat cleaver; and here Primrose gaily came with the bottle of habanero.

The Hotel Cornada! It was odd to think, as he did think, after they had savored their first drink of Berreteaga, that it was to this hotel, when he had left Cuernavaca as he had thought forever, with Ruth, that he had come with her, if for no better reason than that it was the first hotel at which he and Ruth had ever stayed in Mexico City: that it was from here, after Ruth had gone, he had departed for Oaxaca: that it was to the Hotel Cornada, after Oaxaca, after Fernando, he had returned: that it was from here that he had gone to Acapulco that second and fateful time, and after Stanford and the Tarleton, it was to this Hotel Cornada that he had returned once more, and from here also, that he had left Mexico altogether, so humiliatingly, more than seven years before, never, as he thought, to return, again. There's another thing too. There was his youth. No wonder he did not want to go down in the lift! It was like a station of the cross, in the unfinished Oberammergau of his life, shadowy understudy even in that, it was much as if he'd left his cross here, while he went off and got drunk on Pilsener one night and then had done something else, and forgotten the part he was playing: and now he'd had to come back here to pick it up again and finish whatever it was he had begun. Or was it he had left his cross in Oaxaca, c/o Fernando Martinez, to be left till called for?

"You didn't have any trouble?"

"No, the man was sweet. Oh, Sigbjørn, I know I'm going to love Mexico. . . . And the bottle's got the little gadget on it, as you said, and he opened it for me."

And the shy, childish, sweet faith of that, Sigbjørn thought, pouring drinks into the two tumblers, not a word about the lousy hotel, not a word about being sent out into the storm to buy a bottle of habanero even before you had a chance to wash in a strange and dangerous country but turning the whole thing into a little adventure, and I know I'm going to love Mexico.

"Habanero, it's wonderful." Primrose laughed. "Here's to our stay in Mexico!"

"Here's to it," Sigbjørn said.

One of the features of the Hotel Cornada in all the better rooms was still, Sigbjørn noted, a shower nozzle placed directly over the toilet seat, so it was necessary to take a shower either sitting down or standing on the seat, an action that in either case resulted in the complete flooding of the bathroom, as if this were a sardonic commentary upon such conveniences in general. The toilet, with its soaking, for its part would not flush, the nozzle could never in those days properly be turned off, here at least time had wrought a subtle mercy, if not an improvement, for not only was the shower itself broken, but the cold taps did not work either.

Neither, upon a different plane, in the dark lobby, at the too familiar desk downstairs, behind which still hung the enigmatic picture of the Canadian Rockies, but where the picture of President Cárdenas was replaced by one of President Camacho, and another one depicting the Mexican eagle gnawing at the Nazi flag, did their almost indigenous plea of "Nosotros no somos americanos ricos, nosotros somos canadianos *pobres*," to which Sigbjørn, who thought he recognized one of the two managers, added an earnest, "y *amigos*, hace mucho tiempo," for he was trying for a reduced rate, should they stay a week, and now after the habanero, to be recognized as a guest in an advantageous light; but it instead was not surprising he wasn't, he'd worn a beard from time to time in the old days, and even then had not infrequently been mistaken while stopping here for the all-in wrestler who'd lived on the floor above. "Pero un otro vaso, por favor, señor," he demanded sternly. "Sí, señor." The manager, who now looked as though he recognized him after all, smiled. "An othair glass."

"Well, you can't blame them in one way for not building anything durable," Sigbjørn told Primrose as they went through the swinging doors.

"Why?"

"Mexico City is sinking into the lake bed and Mexico itself will be desert in a few hundred years. Or so they say."

"How cheerful you are."

"That's exactly what I am."

Outside the wind blew with a dark melancholy wailing. They turned up their coat collars and walked arm-in-arm. Imperceptibly his feet were taking him into his old sinister haunts, although this was common sense too, in this fashion they were going toward the opera house and the Paseo de la Reforma. The streets were dark and much less crowded, and those who remained in the city seemed making for home in a great hurry. Streetcar bells clanged down the gale. It gave Sigbjørn an uncanny feeling of doing several things at once, or rather, both of approaching and of moving upon several thresholds. In one way he was just walking happily down the street with Primrose, delighted at the completion of the first part of their trip and with his sense of triumph no whit abated, and looking forward to the future, to an enchanting holiday with her, and above all the opportunity of showing her Mexico, though they wouldn't see much tonight. In another he was treading, walking, much more seriously over a sort of spiritual battlefield, in which Sigbjørn, Cortez-like, was the conqueror, the horrors of experience here that had been so far transcended by the completion of his book and his presence in Mexico at all being the defeated enemy. In yet another there was the sense that he had perhaps used treacherous forces to bring about his conquest—he could not have said quite how or why—and by walking straight into the past like this, it was asking for them to have their revenge. On this level the future scarcely existed, and the more he traveled upon it in his mind, the less like any kind of conquest was it, did it seem. Indeed it felt here more like a defeat, a monstrous defeat, a noche triste in fact—only now even the sense of battlefield disappeared.

It was much as if, he thought, when they came to the Bach, an underground café, the entrance to which led from behind a kiosk shutting up for the night, and began to go downstairs—it was much as if by so entering the past, he had stumbled into a labyrinth, with no thread to guide him, where the minotaur threatened at every step, and which was moreover a labyrinth that now at each turn led infallibly to a precipice, over which one might fall at any moment, at the bottom of which was the abyss. The Bach was in fact a gloomy spot with a long bar on one side and high black wooden booths, almost deserted save for a Mexican officer with a girl sitting on his lap, and it had about the same mixed effect on Sigbjørn as he imagined an empty stadium would upon a superannuated bullfighter, or, he reflected as they took their seats in one of the booths, and he tried to attract the attention of the waiter—an eternal funereal figure with a white cloth over his arm who in a million different places, in three score and ten countries, was probably yawning at the counter over some evening paper just like this—of a superannuated golfer confronted with an empty clubhouse after having quite unobserved done a hole in two. But it had another effect too, rather more subtle.

"Is this one of your favorite old places?" Primrose said.

Sigbjørn laughed guardedly, waiting. "Well, perhaps hardly. But I used to sit here all day sometimes. Wrestling with the odd sonnet. What shall we have?"

"Oh, Sigbørn, I want to drink what you drank and do everything that you did."

"God forbid. . . . What about a tequila then. . . . The Mexicans don't let women into half their cantinas," he added, as the tequilas were finally brought. "And now I suppose I should teach you the ritual of the salt and lemon."

"Good heavens"—Primrose choked—"it *has* got authority. Give me that lemon, quick! I don't think I like it as much as the habanero. So this is what the Consul would call a cantina?"

"No, but I'll be able to show you some of those places later." Sigbjørn lit his pipe and then fell silent.

The tequila, a virulent and tasty variety, was as good or bad as ever. It is a drink that if it does not swiftly make you drunk promotes meditation, not always of a cheerful nature, especially on top of habanero.

"I love to see you smoking a pipe, Sigbjørn. You scarcely have since the fire."

"Daniel used to say that it was always a good sign in an ex-pipe smoker who'd taken to cigarettes. With him it used to mean, when he was in a doldrums, that he'd start writing again soon."

"I hope it means that with you, darling."

Why had he thought of Daniel, Sigbjørn wondered. He knew the reason. Had he not identified himself with a character of Daniel's—if not with Daniel himself? And a similar thing had happened with Erikson, who two years ago today had died. My first day of death, he might have said to himself. God, how deep existence was. Deep, deep, deep. Depths beyond depths beyond depths. And again Sigbjørn felt himself looking into an abyss.

"You're awfully loyal."

"Did you love her so much?" Primrose said suddenly.

"I—"

"But we've never talked about it before. I won't be hurt."

"That's not the point." Sigbjørn let out a groan.

"What are you thinking, Sigbjørn?"

"If you really want to know I was thinking that I'm more actually afraid of Oaxaca than anywhere else in the world."

"Then let's go to Oaxaca," Primrose said immediately and gaily and as if this had not been thought of before.

"Unless it's Cuernavaca."

"Then let's go to Cuernavaca as soon as we can," Primrose said just as gaily.

At this moment with an abrupt crash and whine the jukebox began to bawl: "I'm dreaming of a white Christmas." "American," cheerfully announced the Mexican soldier, weaving about beside it again. "Song! You like American music."

"Muchas gracias, señor," Primrose and Sigbjørn said, and then, whispering across the table to each other: "Pero nosotros no somos—"

But the leprous chagrin of the half-beautiful maudlin melody drove them out into the storm again, laughing, and they left the Mexican soldier to his girl. Yet had that been when, with the half-jesting admission of fear, that fear itself—as if all the other anxieties and lesser fears connected with their trip and other essences and velleities of fears piling up behind it, had poked, pushed it through into his full consciousness—entered in? They wandered down Gante (which for the first time he realized rhymed with Dante) to look for an old German restaurant called the Münchener Kindl, where there had once been good food. It was no more—changed this time into a cantina of the Consul's kind where women were not allowed. Only it was garishly floodlit and a jukebox snarled just within the door. An unruly drunk, they saw, who had been battering for entrance as they approached, having meanwhile managed to get in, was on the point of being put out again. No, he would not go out, and he too was like fear, or like Sigbjørn's fear: nothing but a drink would induce him to leave for a while, and even then he always came back by another door. Fear the thumper! They stood watching the scene for a minute. Idiotic nostalgias! How often he had behaved just like that drunk, or sat in the Münchener Kindl talking to his own neurosis, his own pain, his own solitude. Or to his nemesis, the wretched and doomed, beefy, San Franciscan, Stanford, one of whose white shirts he was even now wearing. And working too—think of that—working, while drinking the cup of astonishment and desolation, even while listening for his own strike of the hour, in the whirlwind of his self-destruction. Yes, Sigbjørn could grow almost biblical about it. Once when he had been temporarily broke he had left Stanford's hat there as security, and Stanford, in spite of the fact that he owed Sigbjørn a considerable sum of money, had raised an unholy shindy. "That's something I don't *like*," he had said. How explain this senseless supernatural attraction, that, despite the wind, he had almost to wrench himself away from what had been the Münchener Kindl. They passed into the Paseo de la Reforma and it was the same there. It had been a Gethsemane, or a parody of one, and yet it produced in him almost the sensation of setting foot upon some long-dreamed-of soil. He could have understood it better had there been one single happy memory to fall back upon. But there was none. His memories were all of suffering, hideous anxiety, or the escape from, or more powerfully into, these through tequila or mescal—of the certainty that his life was falling to pieces, was over, but above all, of solitude, or a companionship that was worse than solitude. Fernando was the only saving grace of Mexico, or Fernando and two quixotic actions were, but Fernando belonged to Oaxaca, not here. It had an element of the ludicrous too. Over there was the Palacio de Bellas Artes, the old opera house, that he was pointing out for Primrose with such a knowing air, as if it contained some treasured recollection, as, by God, it did. It was the occasion that absolutely alone with a bottle of tequila, in that enormous opera house, he had sat before the glass curtain with its elaborate absurd painting of the two volcanoes on it, for two solid hours, waiting for the surrealist movie to begin that all the while was being played upstairs in an anteroom. And yet he was indicating the Bellas Artes with as much pride as if he had once held a successful exhibition of his paintings there. Still, so much had been turned to account, thanks to Primrose, and he gripped her arm more firmly. But God, these avenues, these melancholy bells! The streets were dark and quite empty now, reminding one rather of Cambridge on a Sunday night, and above them the sky, without stars, was dark too, save where a lacteous portion screened the moon driving her dim path in the second quarter. Meantime another favorite German restaurant proved now a jeweler's shop, a place of Viennese architecture and excellent food, once ably managed by an affable Negro, was shut forever, as was, beyond the tree-lined square, the incompar-

able Broadway. Almost next door to this, a little Mexican restaurant that Sigbjørn had in mind was open, although it no
longer had the same name, in fact it had no name at all. And it
was larger and more loudly lighted. They went in and Sigbjørn
ordered scrambled eggs with chorizos, frijoles, and beer. It was
under new management, indeed the management seemed largely
Chinese, so that they might have been back in Vancouver
again. Despite having dined on the plane, they were both
hungry and Primrose was delighted with the chorizos. But the
door kept blowing open, and it was so cold they had to eat with
their coats on.

"Here," Sigbjørn said, "there always was a jukebox. Stanford
used to play a tune called 'Tipitipitin' on it until it nearly drove
me mad."

"The Café Nada too?" Primrose was smiling.

"No, this was once the El Petate," Sigbjørn said with his
mouth full. "Don't you remember the poem of the Consul's that
Yvonne and Hugh found on the menu in the old Popo—just
before Yvonne's death, when they set out for the Farolito?
*Strange hellish tales are told of this poor foundered soul, who
once fled north.* Well, I wrote that on the menu here, the one
with the lottery woman on it, that turned up after the fire, and
we found we had it with us in Niagara."

"Oh, my God, yes!"

"That's all. Here we are. We kept the name El Petate in chapter eleven for another cantina where Hugh and Yvonne failed to
find the Consul, the cantina that was all that was left of the
'burned Anochitlán'—by which I really meant Nochitlán in
Oaxaca, where I went with Fernando to deliver money for the
Ejidal to the two villages Andoa and Chindoa that were fighting
each other across the ravine. Anochitlán isn't very far from
Parián, where Fernando and I had to say good-bye. Or Doctor
Vigil and I, Juan Cerillo and I, just as you like to call him. Fernando had to go back to Cuicitlán where he'd been transferred
from Oaxaca, and I to the Hotel La Luna, in Oaxaca itself. All
that will be about eight years ago, in a couple of months. I left
Oaxaca altogether a few days after that, and returned here to
Mexico City, to the Cornada. Then, Primrose, years later, we

used the menu of the old El Pelate with the Consul's poem on it, as being the menu of the El Popo, where Yvonne got tight, and Hugh bought the guitar. I remember writing the poem here. what there was of it, at about five A.M., with 'Tipitipitin' playing and Stanford and a lot of drunks milling around.''

"That wouldn't be so long before you fled north yourself."

"So to speak." But the Consul had not fled north, thought Sigbjørn, he had fled to the Farolito, in Parián, there to meet his death. And they, Primrose and he, had not fled north either, at least not yet. They had flown south, a hell of a way south, and pretty soon, "as soon as we can," they would be flying even further south, to the Farolito too—who knew?—for the Farolito was not in Parián, but in Oaxaca city itself, that part of it, of course, that was not El Bosque in Oaxaca or La Universal in Cuernavaca, to which, should they also go there "as soon as they could," they would also be flying south. And in Oaxaca they might even put up at the Hotel La Luna if it still existed, from which Sigbjørn used to stumble at four A.M. to the Farolito. And meantime, after their supper of sausages and eggs, they would fly back to the Hotel Cornada, with no sign of this drama upon their brows for the hotel clerk to read in the dark lobby. It was very singular.

"Tell me more about Stanford, you must have been very fond of him," Primrose said.

"No, I loathed him. . . . On the other hand I'll always be grateful to him for saving *In Ballast to the White Sea*."

"If only for me not to save it."

"Don't let's go into that again, Primrose. . . . That wasn't your fault. Besides, don't I owe the existence of *The Valley* to you, in more ways than one?" Sigbjørn pushed away his plate and began to fill his pipe. "Besides, it was fate, or whatever. And besides, *this* is the book."

"This is what book?"

"The real book. Now, it's as if everything we do is part of it. I can't write it, of course."

"But at least you're smoking your pipe again, Sigbjørn darling."

"And if I did, it would probably be unreadable. I

Even the mistakes we make seem part of what that blight intends—and perhaps these are the parts he crosses out the next morning when he sets up his precious desk again strung between two stars. If he ever sleeps. Or eats. Myself, I think he just drinks."

"What *are* you talking about, Sigbjørn?"

"He's not a blight either, far from it. It's just that his notions of art, while sometimes perhaps not unlike ours, are simply wider. That he isn't altogether a blight I know because I can feel him wanting me, wanting us to do good, to be good. The trouble is—it is his trouble too—we are liable to get out of hand by taking the bit of his sentences in our own teeth. Then we become filled up with self-reliance of the wrong kind and that in turn fills him with despair, because in fact we're utterly dependent upon him and have to ask his help at every turn instead of our own. That indeed is his principal headache, because having given us life of a sort, he also has given us a will. Whether or not that operates constructively, as we call it, is utterly beside the point. Or without what we call desire, in our own terms. But it's important on his; because if ours is strong enough on the distaff side, he can't conquer it. We might insist on a tragic ending and get it, when what he intends is a happy one. It is at such moments that he burns our house down or destroys three quarters of our life work, just to remind us that he is on the job. Does that satisfy your tragic instincts, he seems to be saying, now then let us see what you do. Perhaps you'll think that that's the end. But with me, it is only a beginning. It isn't that he demands humility in the narrowest sense but that he can do nothing unless we're humble, a word that needs some redefining because Uriah Heep seems to have corrupted it."

"It sounds as if you were talking about God."

"Perhaps I am. Perhaps I've got religion. Or perhaps the point of our being here is that we shall discover that we can't live without God. But I hadn't intended to talk about God. I thought I was talking about that tutelary gent known to writers as the daemon, and it was my idea that my daemon was trying his hand at writing a book himself, rather than making me do it, since I've kept rather silent since the fire, and moreover have signally failed to see the joke in *that,* whether it was his work or God's."

"I wouldn't have thought that your daemon specialized in happy endings."

"I think I began with the daemon and then in the course of my rather smug conversation found myself talking about God."

"And if your good blight decides that you should try and write this unreadable book?"

"Then I suppose I'd try to write it."

On their way back from the old El Petate, they got lost and found themselves in the Via Dolorosa, a transverse street, that looked precisely the same whether you looked up or down it. Sigbjørn could not tell, be finally sure in which direction they were going. But for some reason he felt no pain. Several of the infrequent passersby had courteously tried to show them the direction, Sigbjørn pretended he understood them better than he did in order not to betray his lack of Spanish, and it was more good luck that really guided them back to the Hotel Cornada. Primrose, dead tired, soon fell asleep. Sigbjørn could not sleep at all. It was as if he were still continuing the conversation with himself that he had had earlier and which had been interrupted by Primrose's return with the bottle of Berreteaga, now in the bathroom. Yes, why indeed had he brought her to the Hotel Cornada? And yet he felt he could scarcely have brought her anywhere else.

The Cornada is where he had made a great objective decision that changed the whole course of his life: it was the tower where he made the Consul—Consul indeed, that was as funny as Hotel Nada—try to make a similar decision: but it was more. Here he had separated from Ruth. It was a decision that had been held in abeyance right until the last minute, had been in abeyance after they had left Cuernavaca, while he made his obscure difficult arrangements with Hölscher to try and get to Spain from Salina Cruz, or imagined he was making those arrangements, while those arrangements having been made he slept with prostitute after prostitute with passion such as he had never known until then in an effort to lose or project through or connect his suffering with something, in abeyance all that dreadful last night in the Via Dolorosa, right up to the last minute she had kept the decision open, not to leave and go back to America.

But there was a price, a price he had been unwilling to pay, the Consul's price, a price, now one came to think of it, that should never have been asked, just as he had foreborne to create a character so unsympathetic that she would ask it. "Darling, if I stay with you, will you stop drinking? . . ." "Right off, today?" A suffering that was as long drawn out as the tension about the syphilis with the doctor, he had thought he was suffering from her. "Yes, now." "Well, my answer to that is No. What do you expect? I'll carry your bag down." (At least Primrose would never make a fuss about his drinking should that ever become a problem again; in fact he had been drinking when he met her, and even had he not happened to fall in love with her, it would almost have been worth while marrying her because she was the sort of person who didn't make a fuss; or to put it another way, had she not seemed that sort of person, he would never have thought it worth while to stop drinking at all. And he had taken the bag—his first and last service to Ruth, he thought—to where the car with the two Americans was waiting to take her to California, stopping at the bar downstairs for a mescal. It was this scene that kept repeating itself, over and over again, like a disrupted film repeating itself (and that disrupted film was uncomfortably an image of himself too), the going down in the lift with the bag, the sense of unreality, the Americans waiting in the two-seater with the open rumble seat outside the Cornada on the opposite side of the road for Ruth to come down and then, when she appeared: "Are you sure you won't change your mind, darling—even now, it's not too late. We could go to Yucatán." "Perfectly sure. I'll arrange about the money." "Sigbjørn—" "It's not a question of changing my mind, Ruth. Or if it is, it's necessary first of all to acquire the kind of a mind you approve of to change." But for a moment Ruth had still lingered there on the threshold of the Cornada, almost dumbly, a finger on her lips, perplexed, like a child, and it was only the thought, perhaps, of the tyranny of children, or his own dead one, of which she herself was the murderess, that prevented him from relenting. "But won't this be ruining your life?" she asked.

"Sort of." "You'll be sorry, you know." "If I am, you won't know anything about it. Anyhow, even if you stay, I'm going to Spain." "To Spain, huh!" she broke out contemptuously, and turned away. "And you seem to have forgotten, but I'm *working.*" "Working—*hee!*" "But don't go like that," Sigbjørn added, almost in tears, however. "Oh darling, you don't love me and never have. But good-bye and God bless you. Good luck." "Good-bye." "Sigbjørn, I'm sorry for you." "Cut out the sorrow. I've got enough for myself, and," he called after her, "I'm glad if you've got enough of other things up your sleeve that I don't have to feel sorry for you."

And then the mescals and the slaughtered fawns: Hölscher and Oaxaca and Fernando Martinez: and later, Stanford and Acapulco. The parting had taken place almost eight years ago to the day, to the very hour, since it had been in the morning too. "You don't love me and never have." It was true; more than that neither of them had genuinely—according to the categories through which such things are perceived—to quote Lucretius, to quote the Consul, to quote himself, loved each other. He had never discussed the whole business with Primrose for fear of hurting her, any more than she had discussed an equal anguish with him: both could read between the lines so far as their pasts were concerned, Primrose especially since, as he sympathetically pointed out, she had to type so much of his. But had she known the truth she would scarcely have been hurt: quite the contrary, unless it was on his account.

All of which did not explain the suffering, that the days in Oaxaca, and then later in Acapulco, and then later still here in Mexico City again, before he had left Mexico so humiliatingly by train and as he thought forever—had been the saddest of his life. When Sigbjørn thought of love such as existed between Primrose and himself—or had existed between his own parents, or his brothers and their wives for that matter—he always thought of something like durmast oak, dark, heavy, tough, but also elastic, blessed by the sun, bright or somber according to season, but surviving lightning and great rains and trouble, and always, mysteriously, somehow growing. Or, he often thought too, it was like their brave pier, most particularly and damnably like that very brave pier, which was not as might first appear a barren symbol, for it was capable, if not of infinite, of continual extension, moreover it was always having to be repaired, and while it had the strongest of foundations, it possessed also the lightest of structures, and yet had borne the most violent tempests. Nor had it been built altogether by love: love never is. They had often cursed like stokers building it and quarreled infamously. Just as they had with the house, which was a better symbol still, since it was more obviously uncompleted, or would have been a better one had they not in a sense recklessly abandoned it, if only for the time being. But again, this suffering, or its recrudescence—and perhaps this was the only explanation—represented, and had always represented a *displacement,* it was out of order in his life; it came to him with a sort of terror that perhaps it was like a warning, anterior to an event that he must prevent at all costs, it would be like that, if through his own fault, now more fully, he were to lose Primrose.

But if that was true about love, that is, that in that case it had not existed, what was true about the suffering? Had what was not love turned into suffering, or was it possible, through loss of what might have been, to fall not, as the obvious saying is, in love with suffering but in suffering, as one was supposed to fall in love. Time, with his blunt rod of steel, his useful nailset, had driven these agonies below the surface of his mind. Now they came up flush with it. Flattened and indurated they were still into his very being: but there, nonetheless, now they were, as they had not been, plainly for his visible eye to see, for years, and they hurt. But suffering at least, that of the mind, the soul, will not stand any concrete description. Nails, even the cross, from which we take our hope, are of the earth. But the suffering itself seemed to come from somewhere else, was from elsewhere and doesn't want to be described, and it seems in perpetual metamorphosis, and frenzied mixed metaphor, impossible simile. Like blood, like smoke, like flame, seeping up through the floor, blooming through the window, drowning, stifling him, in spasms of anguish, sadness, and suffocation. And then like a roaring of water that never ceases, though it rises and falls like the sea smashing into a cave. Like this, but not this. And not like this either, but something like what such words might evoke out of their confusion, out, yes, of their very incompetence of arrangement, as if suffering belongs to an order in which incompetence were a valid quality, like, indeed, the cliché again, come true—nothing on earth at all.

When a man allows himself to be completely overwhelmed by catastrophe, he will tend to forget in fact, even though he still automatically mourns them, the heights he has formerly reached, and the obstacles he had overcome to reach those heights: and the old self regards the new with such absolute contempt for giving in that, fearful, the latter shuns his terrible look over the years altogether, forgets him, for all purposes too, in the end; and for all that it is the merciful brain that is responsible for this excretion of memory there is, in this process, in the deepest sense, absolutely no mercy. And whatever excuses there might be, had he not allowed himself nearly to be overwhelmed? And Primrose too, in the process. Looked at like this, it was tempting fate indeed, this trip, it was not ignoble, even if one ruled out what he could persuade himself was unselfishness toward Primrose. And if there was a certain admission of failure about it, it was on, he could altogether persuade himself, the grand scale. It was as if the funeral pile had proved inadequate to the phoenix, and he had to look around him for another kind of immolation in the depths of the past. And he would find his old self here in Mexico if anywhere, if not quite the old self he had meant: he would come here, if anywhere, face to face as well as with, he hoped Fernando, with everything that that self had imperfectly transcended.

"Throw away your mind," the voice of his blood brother said to him, his voice on its familiar dying fall: "Think what you have to do. What are you doing now, making more tragedies? Poor my friend!" That was all very well, Sigbjørn thought; then, yes, I want to go to Oaxaca, Fernando, I do indeed long to see you, my blood brother, more than anything else in the world.

Had, as Daniel jovially asked him, the phoenix clapped his wings? No, alas, Sigbjørn now could unfortunately answer the question, the phoenix had not. Not yet. True, he could see Mexico itself as utter ruination, in itself a charred ruin, the damnation from which he had risen, phoenixlike, to write his trilogy. But merely to have written *The Valley* or to now have *The Valley* as a fait accompli was apparently not enough. What else was required of him remained in doubt but he could scarcely be said to have risen until his house had been completed. Yet it was as if he was back in another disaster from which he had not risen either. Perhaps being in Mexico was, as it were, the spiritual analogue of the second disaster, when their house burned down, from which conflagration he had far from risen, and in the midst of which, spiritually speaking, he still stood. Tonight he had thought of the streets, the dark dark streets, the melancholy bells, that sometimes made Mexico City remind him of Cambridge, and even now, he could remember those wonderful clear clear sunlit mornings only in terms of alcohol, which he had observed at that arc of bar with its cracked brown paint near the railway station, with the girls and students going to the races, with the wind blowing and no company but fear, the protracted fear that goes with waiting for the incubation of a dreaded disease. He thought of his first poems, all lost, but it was something to remember the extraordinary concentration of those times, the amazing narrowing down to a single point of thought, so that on one occasion a dead lemon in an ashtray had taken on the aspect of a cowled old woman shivering sitting in the cold rainy snow. Fernando was the only saving grace of all this, and yet the symbol of all Mexico. What then, in the name of goodness, was its attraction, its supernatural influence over him?

There had been a brief thunderstorm (out of season too, just as it happened in his book) which had wakened Primrose, and as he lay with his arms round her, and Primrose, as she liked one or the other of them to do, told him some story, he had thought it was as if some self within him, like the friend of Roderick Usher when Usher stood aghast at the casement thrown open to the storm, at the whirlwind, the velocity with which the clouds, glowing with unseen lightnings, flew careening from all points against each other around the doomed house of Usher, was saying to him: "You must not, you shall not behold this. Here is one of your favorite romances. I will read, you shall listen—and so we will pass away this terrible night together" and this while the night was not terrible at all, but even joyful. It was this friend, this "I," of Roderick Usher that he had to try, was now indeed trying, to keep uppermost, for Primrose's benefit as well as his own: but unfortunately as he could not expel fear without it, here again, it began to look as though he could not bring him to the surface without drinking. Still, nothing had really gone wrong as yet. And the evening had been a success. In one way? But on the other hand, it was during the night, their first night in Mexico, that there had begun slowly to be borne in upon him the real positive psychic, if obscure, danger in which he stood and to which he had deliberately, and even delightedly, brought himself, deliberately and delightedly brought them: Primrose was aware of this in a fashion. After all, she knew *The Valley of the Shadow of Death* backward: with her it was a matter, in her concern for him, of laying ghosts. But with him it was rather different. But for one thing by far the most potent ghost he had to encounter was himself, and he had very considerable doubts as to whether it wanted to be laid at all.

V

T HEIR BUS TO CUERNAVACA,
with open cutout and a noise of tearing canvas, made little
spurts of speed in its last attempts to shake off the city, like
Nietzsche's outworks of the ideal (though Mexico City was far
from being an ideal), its outer garb (of ugsome Parisian subur-
bia), its masquerade (of pulquerías), and its temporary hard-
ening (of the plaster of new apartment buildings), stiffening as
of skeletal structures never to be finished, and dogmatizing
Aleman-Moralización. And now the bus began its weary circling
up toward the Tres Marías through scenery that was not unlike
that of New Hampshire or the Cotswolds; jammed in the second-
class bus and scarcely daring to breathe, the thought struck him
that their journey might have a larger meaning, for them, if he
reflected upon it. Was it not as if they themselves were making a
pilgrimage? As if almost to the shrine, or to the oracle of miracle, to place their ignorance at the foot of the cross in humility
and ask if there was any meaning, after what had happened, in
their lives? Strange things had happened to them with such fre-
quency during the past years it was almost as though a force
were trying to din some matter of import into their minds. But
the fact remained that something almost imperceptible had altered in both of them. He thought back over the last week. They
had begun to haunt churches, and even today before setting off

with their bags and hangovers for the Plaza Netzalcuayatl, in the Church of Isabel la Católica they had made a devout prayer to the Saint of Dangerous and Desperate Causes. But what, Sigbjørn, too hypocritical to put anything in the collection box, asked himself, as once more they changed gears and began slowly to round another hairpin bend, past the familiar sign, Euzkadi, another Vulcanización—was dangerous or desperate about it all? What indeed was the cause or causes? A partial answer to his question seemed to arise from the road before and above him winding up ever higher and higher to the mists and chevals de frise of the Tres Marías. No wonder it was like coming home. For had he not lived in Cuernavaca before, and made this journey, backward and forward, many times before, both in happiness and sorrow, and then later, in absolute crushing despair, going to and from Acapulco, shunning his eyes from Cuernavaca every time he came to it as if his soul, as he had written, had been tied to the tail of a runaway horse? That last grim time he had come back from Acapulco with Stanford—no, he would not think of it: perhaps that had not been quite the last time: at any rate he did not want now to make sure which was the very last time. And yet he had the mysterious feeling that this road from Mexico City to Cuernavaca had something to teach him—alas, or thank God, them too; for better or worse, Primrose was caught up in it—some obscure lesson that he had not, when he was here before, succeeded in learning, and that he must traverse this route many, many times again, backward and forward, before it was learned to the satisfaction of whatever force moved his ways. But after all—dangerous and desperate cause.

Partly due to his stubbornness they were on a second-class bus and not in a turismo. This time the trouble had begun in the Plaza Netzalcuayatl by a misunderstanding on Sigbjørn's part. While he had not wanted to take the Flecha Roja, or simply the Flecha, the second-class bus, for they had too much luggage and were unlikely to get a seat, he *had* wanted to get a bus, namely the first-class one, the Estrella de Oro, for which, just as in the old days, you booked your seat and then, since passengers were not allowed to stand, were entitled to that seat and sat upon it. It was a good arrangement. Nonetheless having booked such a seat he was told—which was an evident lie; before he had finished his argument the Estrella de Oro came and departed without them—that the first-class bus was not going, and that he must take a touring car, a turismo: the price was legally not much more but what with their luggage, and the portentous presence of Primrose's fur coat—now upon their lap; they were almost glad of it for they were reaching the Tres Marías—it came to three times as much. Almost immediately another half dozen pesos or so were added, to be paid in advance. Though it was merely a question of sixty cents, American or Canadian, Sigbjørn refused, and this time Primrose herself was the more indignant.

"Pero, señor, nosotros no somos americanos ricos," she said excitedly, and Sigbjørn added, "No—nosotros somos canadianos *pobres*."

Although two expensively dressed Mexicans, an almost Italian-looking man and a woman with marmalade-colored hair, had risen courteously to their defense, their luggage—fortunately Sigbjørn held on to his guitar—was rudely thrown off the car and two other Mexicans took their places. Meantime the dispatcher for the Flecha, which started from the opposite side of the street, who'd been having a lemonade next door, apparently on hearing the word *canadianos,* strolled over to see what was going on.

"Winnipeg—you know Winnipeg?"

"Sí, sí, conozco Winnipeg un poco": they had visited that strange mirage of a city on the way to see the Reids after the fire. That was the extent of their conversation, but he had taken pleasure in seeing them on his own bus (the number of which Sigbjørn was too exhausted to notïce) even suggesting that two other passengers, these were Indians, give up their seats, which they did with graciousness, and in a manner brooking no denial, and to make even more certain that they would not be further embarrassed, the dispatcher who had been to Winnipeg wrote down the price, including that of the extra luggage, which came to about a third of the other, upon a piece of paper that he handed to them through the window, exhorting them to pay precisely that and no more. And at this moment their fares were taken, from outside, just as in *The Valley,* he paid that and no more, the man gave him a torn ticket with a print of a huge stone god on it.

Meantime, they were going to Cuernavaca.

The bus journey from Mexico City to Cuernavaca was deceptive, as Sigbjørn knew of old. Although it was only forty or fifty miles, this gives little idea of its nature. A long, dreary, dusty road leads out of Mexico City itself, and then, half an hour later, the long circuitous climb to Tres Marías begins. Having started at an altitude of eight thousand feet you ascend to an altitude of ten thousand. At the highest point of the route, a desolate clapboard of decaying huts named Tres Cumbres in the Tres Marías, where you may encounter a blizzard, you begin to descend, unwinding, by a similar circuitous road, until, in Cuernavaca, you find yourself at an altitude of some three thousand feet, that is at a point rather lower than the one in which you have started: in this regard the journey had always struck Sigbjørn as rather like life itself. Repeat the journey many times and you have the eerie sense of repeating an existence over and over again, which, although perhaps true of any journey, seems for some reason particularly true of this one. One is liable because of the altitude and abrupt change of temperature, to feel exhausted, and when one arrives finally in Cuernavaca, quite worn out. But Primrose and Sigbjørn, if not for travel, shared, other things being equal, a love of bus journeys, which was all to the good.

And Sigbjørn could feel Primrose was enjoying herself, taking in the beautiful scenery, the flowers, the straggling adobe villages, the little pigs, the delicate ankles of the Mexican women. A vast shrouded slope loomed before them, the Tres Marías. They reached Tres Cumbres, where they stopped briefly and Sigbjørn without any haggling at all, of which he was beginning to have a dread, to her delight secured her a torta, through the window from a scolding old woman. This, for him, was a feat as well as being unselfish: for there was something in his nature that loathed to break the rhythm; only more than stopping at all did he hate to move on, lulled into a certain mood. To the right there was a signpost pointing down a windy road: *A Zampoala.*

It was a lake, very high in the mountains, which Sigbjørn re-membered he had seen and he made up his mind to take her there. It was a possible happiness for Primrose over there, lakes, heights, choices, superterrestrial or sublacustrine.

As they rolled forward again, Sigbjørn remembered the visit they had made to the basilica at Guadalupe a few days earlier. They had taken the bus by Bellas Artes, and at the basilica Sig-bjørn had been delighted by the sideshow: *La Maldición de Dios . . . ¡No deje de ver este asombroso aparato de óptica! La cabeza que habla su cuerpo fue devorado por las ratas.* The mal-ediction of God! Step up ladies and gents and see the spectacle of the head who has his body devoured by rats. Primrose had been enchanted with the women, however poor, who wore exquisite silver earrings, and had lovely ankles and hands and often gor-geous rebozos, and carried themselves like queens, and the danc-ers: one man in fringes of scarlet with feathers two feet high on his head, the other wearing a horrible grinning mask on the back of his head.

They drank marvelous beer in a little booth at one side facing the basilica: the figurine of the Virgin looked like a model in an American department store window of 1917 or so, dressed in bright print and carrying in one hand a lamp—a boy of sixteen or so stood by her, leaning on her shoulder. They watched the little families sitting under trees with their sweet quick smiles, and then they wandered through the basilica of Guadalupe— they who had not been in a church in twenty years. Sigbjørn felt the sense of complete faith when Primrose knelt and prayed at the altar, and he watched the expression of passionate sincerity on people's faces, the father with the little girl, showing her how to cross herself, the old woman touching the glass case and rub-bing the baby's face with it, Mexican babies, aware of man's tragic end, do not cry: "I slept here once," Sigbjørn did not say, meaning on the floor of the basilica itself, tight, in a borrowed mackintosh, in December, 1936. They smelt the smell of Mexico City, the familar smell, to him, of gasoline, excrement, and oranges, and drank beautiful Saturno for forty-five centavos.

Then something happened, or nearly went wrong, wrong enough at all events, wrong enough, so that, had he been writing about it, he would have preserved it as the "first bass chord." They were wandering, mingling with the crowd at Guadalupe, scarcely knowing where they were going; such a crowd indeed that unable to make any progress they turned into a little tiendita in which as in many such, they sold beer and spirits. People were drinking and talking at the counter, but way was courteously made for them. They ordered Carta Blanca and were drinking happily but watching the scene outside, rather than inside. A blind woman tottered past carrying a dead dog. A borracho, in a state of drunkenness almost unique, carrying a stick, and so far as Sigbjørn could see without the slightest provocation suddenly began striking her brutally with the stick and then struck the dead dog, which fell to the pavement with a horrible smack. The blind woman, furious, with obscene grief, groped, felt for the dead dog, and finding it, clutched it to her bosom again. Meantime the crowd had turned as a body from the counter and pressed toward the open doorway to watch what was happening, in the course of which Primrose's bottle of Carta Blanca, which had been standing on the counter, was knocked over by a whiskerando Indian and smashed. This Indian generously apologized and began to pick up the pieces, Sigbjørn helping him, and then, because of the chaos, thought that for Primrose's sake it was time to pay the bill.

"Nosotros no somos americanos ricos," Sigbjørn began, since by the price list on the wall they were being charged a peso a bottle more for seventy-five-cent beer. This, however, was the signal for the borracho to turn on Primrose and him. The broken bottle etc., they must pay. Americanos! Abajo los tiránicos americanos! Sigbjørn refused but seeing that the whiskerando was offering to pay, offered to pay himself. But now, the borracho insisted that five extra pesos be paid, and there were cries of "Policía!" The police already had arrived for that matter and were talking angrily to the blind woman. And while everyone was arguing they made their escape as best they could.

"It's our fault," Primrose said. "The Americans come down here and throw their money around. What can you expect?"

"Pero nosotros no somos americanos," Sigbjørn said gently, at which moment also noticing he had been robbed of his tobacco, someone doubtless having mistaken it for his notecase. "Nosotros somos canadianos *pobres*." In spite of his calm however, now they were safe, even if in another tiendita, the cruel and bestial little scene had made a fearful impression on him. He knew only too well to what such things could lead in Mexico. And their crime would have been that they were not being muy correcto, and behaving like Americans, in drinking at a lowly cantina. In fact, in a subtle manner, they had not even any right to have a look at the image of the Virgin of Guadalupe at all. Sigbjørn didn't like the dead dog any better, which itself seemed exhumed out of *The Valley of the Shadow of Death.* It was an incident at least such as he might have used and perhaps it was not too late to use it.

The tumultuous scene about the basilica was very curious: the merry-go-rounds and obscene or gruesome sideshows, and yet tents of shade in the tremendous heat (he had only visited the basilica before at night) with the shouts of "Step up ladies and gentlemen and see the amazing spectacle of the head that has his body devoured by rats," the wild pagan dances, the sense of freedom and confinement at once, and the feeling of definite *pilgrimage* toward the basilica, and yet the virtual impossibility of moving a step, or one found that one was only going round and round the square, the sense of sacred miracle preserved in the midst of all this chaos, the contrast of the bishop speaking, or rather mutely opening and closing his mouth, so that he might have been Mynheer Peeperkorn prior to his suicide making his final speech before the clamor of the waterfall in *The Magic Mountain* for all one heard, and yet pronouncing in the midst of all this his benediction, almost as it were his encyclical to a closed order, on all present, even Sigbjørn and Primrose, as the yelling jukeboxes shrieked and whinnied in English louder and louder, "I'm dreaming of a white Christmas"—all this had an absurdity and horror, would have been justified as an experience simply by its overwhelming effect of absurdity and ugliness, but for the equally overwhelming sense of something sublime everywhere present, of faith.

You could not say it was a simple faith, omnipresent as the jukeboxes and a curious sign that he had observed, *Kilroy was*

here; you could not pin it down at all. For that matter even a
devout Catholic—Primrose was descended from a Catholic-
burning bishop and Sigbjørn from practicing Manx sorceresses
—of the usual Western type would have been equally disgusted,
and have been far more critical than he of the tasteless votive
symbols of that belief, while in Sigbjørn himself—probably far
more highly superstitious and less skeptical a person, and yet
reluctant to submit himself to the discipline of any church, dis-
believing indeed in public worship—he might have detected an
element of pride, in many respects humble indeed as Uriah
Heep, humble though he was, that would have immediately
placed him among the damned. And yet again, there was the
overpowering sense of something irrefutably sublime, of faith,
or a complex faith.

Now as they commenced the unwinding descent to Cuernavaca, Sigbjørn could not help reflecting on the strange vagueness
of their plans. They had, in fact, no plans at all, unless Sigbjørn's
to have a drink as soon as possible could be called such; perhaps
Primrose imagined that he had, but he had not thought of
where to put up in Cuernavaca and for all he knew all the hotels
would be full, or prohibitively expensive. They were drawn on
as by an invisible cord. But these thoughts were held in abeyance for the moment by the wild excitement at seeing the volcanoes again, for Primrose loyally wanted to see them exactly as
they appeared in his book. If this feeling were indeed to be
compared to anything whatever, Sigbjørn thought, it would
strangely be to reading a book. Yes, precisely a book that, while
the terrain is so vividly communicated that it seems familiar,
that indeed has become, even as we read, familiar, is exasperat-
ing in that we are being held up continually by the notion (conviction) that we can do it better ourselves. In this case, he supposed, it was, if inexactly, as though in part this book were his
own, and the passages in question equivalent to that village
here, or that mountain peak there, were conjured up by either a
sense of their omission or ineptitude, or even a phrase of the
flowers, a straggling village, the novelty of the tortas, a little pig.
I didn't get that! Damn it, how could I have missed that? If he
felt at this moment any clear belief that he would write again,

he would have spoilt his enjoyment by making notes in the margin, or in the notebook that, alas, he carried no longer.

On the other hand, and far more powerfully, this book that he was reading was like a book that, paradoxically, had not yet been wholly written, and probably never would be, but that was, in some transcendental manner, *being* written as they went along. Viewed in this light by Sigbjørn what he read was more enthralling still. The temptation here, however, was, due to the anxiety as to what was going to happen to the protagonists, to skip ahead and see. Since this was impossible, and at least in part up to fate, and since they themselves were the protagonists, although self-absorption could perhaps not go much further, what actually seemed to happen was that from time to time they seemed on the point of disappearing altogether, a sensation so pleasurable that one forgot that one had a hangover and wished to protract it forever.

Coming back to earth at this moment with the realization however of this hangover, with which simultaneously came, once more, terror (perhaps one deliberately courted hangovers because it was the closest analogy of the feeling inspired by helpless love), it was to realize that a drink at the earliest possible moment was the best manner to protract this sensation. More or less in this way, at all events, just as he could explain his reluctance at making any move at Tres Cumbres, even to buy a sandwich for Primrose, Sigbjørn could explain to himself the vagueness of his plans. On the most obvious level of thinking anyhow it certainly was extremely odd to be going back to this town, so odd that Sigbjørn would have been quite at a loss to interpret these thoughts logically, which perhaps were so weird indeed that Sigbjørn began to find that the drink was their only essential feature. But those thoughts were held in abeyance anyhow for the moment by Primrose's loyal yet genuine wild excitement at the prospect of seeing the volcanoes again in what Sigbjørn had assured her was their most admirable setting, exactly that was, as they had appeared in his book. "Look, no, there, no there," she was searching as excitedly as she had done in the plane. They were hidden, however. It perhaps, he thought, emphasized the shadow-line quality in both their lives: both were leaving their youth behind. Nothing, however, could be more deceptive than this gloomy and logical notion, because just as in the song in *The Maid of the Mountains,* it is at this moment that perhaps your youth opens up before you all its possibilities that you were not mature enough to see before. Far more often is it than in adolescence we experience the stultifications we associate with old age. And in old age itself recapture the wonder that is popularly supposed to be correlative of childhood, when in fact we often, still as blind as starved kittens and still as unwanted, are in danger of being sent down to the bottom of the ocean with a stone in the sack. It was hard to explain this to Primrose. How often do you read: "She was a woman of middle age" or approximately forty. Have we noticed this, the more often perhaps as approaching forty, ourselves, and never without a shudder. Take heart! It is not true, for this at least is one way in which the world has advanced. Ten years ago it was sufficient for a protagonist to be approaching thirty. With the Victorians "She would never see twenty-five again" was sufficient to suggest that the apple was about to fall off the tree. As for himself, in his mid-thirties, Sigbjørn thought: if ever he should write an autobiographical novel he would begin it: "I was now approaching the critical age of five."

Although Cuernavaca itself was now clearly to be seen far down below them at regular intervals as they rounded the corners, a sort of violet haze hanging over the whole valley obscured the volcanoes from sight, and although it was a fine hot day, becoming ever hotter as they descended, it did not seem to Sigbjørn from what he could remember of the climate that this haze would lift in time for them to see the mountains before sunset. Still it was not far from the full moon, and perhaps Primrose would see them tonight by moonlight, which would be still better. To Sigbjørn's eye a suggestion of bulk in the distance, an inkling of a sloping shape within the haze, gave a hint as of some great presence there, rendered them to him even more impressive in their defection.

Now the road straightened out and they began to pass through the outskirts of Cuernavaca itself and a little later, opposite a large barracks that had not been there before, appeared a sign *Quauhnahuac,* Cuernavaca's Aztec name, with its translation in Spanish, Near the Wood. This was an innovation. Nine years ago Sigbjørn, who had not then read Prescott, had been at pains to discover what this Aztec name was and had thought, by using it, that the fact that the scene of his book was largely in Cuernavaca would be thereby disguised. Now in the event of that book coming out, and in spite of the delay in his hearing from England, and the disappointing reports from America, his hopes were not yet altogether dashed, anyone who had visited Cuernavaca recently would know. They would suppose too that he had got the geography wrong due to his lack of observation, whereas in truth this was because that part of his terrain that was not wholly imaginative was equally based upon the city of Oaxaca and sus anexas. The bus passed, still going down, the Cuernavaca Inn, to which they were making certain obscure additions. Yet hideous buildings were going up everywhere, Bebe Coca-Cola, the huge stone statue; the new bus stop—his old Terminal Cantina was no more; and where would Señora Gregorio be?—was below Cortez Palace, so that almost immediately on getting out, they were confronted with a view of the Rivera murals that he had described in his Chapter VII of *The Valley*. The wall below Cortez Palace was being reinforced, however, and the path that the Consul and Yvonne had taken when she returned to him through the rubbish heap was no more; they would now have had to come down some stone steps.

After some difficulty they checked their bags at the bus stop, with the exception of Primrose's fur coat, and on Sigbjørn's suggestion strolled up to the square. They paused by Cortez Palace to look once more in vain for the volcanoes. He guided their steps to a cantina called La Universal, which he had immediately noticed was still there, and where he once knew the proprietor, a Spaniard with whom he played dice and who always "bumped the dice" on his head. Jukeboxes, at least twenty of them apparently, kept up an endless caterwauling. La Universal was where, inside, he had obtained some of the dialogue that he had put in his Chapter XII, which he made actually take place in an awful place called the Farolito in Oaxaca—it was partly the Farolito and partly another place in the city of Oaxaca called El Bosque, that also meant The Wood.

The Universal always had been a sidewalk café and it was still.

They sat down, tired, at a round table, and Sigbjørn having ordered two beers draped Primrose's coat upon a neighboring chair. With the forethought that had often been lacking during the many years he had not been drinking, he had insisted that she bring it, for it had struck him that it might be some time before they left the Universal, and the nights were cold, and the checking room at the bus station might be shut. The beer was black and delicious; they toasted each other, and ordered another one. Every now and then the cathedral let loose a jangling gaggle of bells. "I wish Juan Fernando would just happen by." He had meant to add, then we wouldn't have to go to Oaxaca, but refrained for that would hurt Primrose, who said something of the sort and Sigbjørn said, "Well, we'd go to Oaxaca anyhow. Perhaps with Fernando."

In the square, as Primrose pointed out, there was even a Ferris wheel and a few roundabouts not in use, to welcome him; although this Ferris wheel had the air of a permanent feature rather than an appurtenance, as it was in his book of a fiesta, it was swarming with Americans, in every kind of costume and all with the air of having a great deal of money. Many were in uniform. Many, however, paused at the Universal; they seemed to favor it and another little sidewalk café between theirs and the Hotel Bella Vista. Luxurious American cars made their way slowly past and occasionally an isolated tourist, or a couple, in shorts, with packs upon the backs and looks of wonder: if he could only be like that, Sigbjørn thought. Still, perhaps, why not, since doubtless he had more wondrous things to look upon than any tourist. The jukeboxes bellowed.

The second beer arrived and they waited for fate to step in. Meantime, however, the aspect of things seemed to change for Sigbjørn. He began to feel excited. How on earth could one communicate—or for that matter, excommunicate—the extraordinary drama of all this to him? There must be some way: but how do it. Then again, perhaps it was not interesting, save to him. All these thoughts that had been amorphously in his mind before now, with the proximity of their realization, took concrete shape. Every now and then the little Chapultepec bus drove up, stopped, drove away. That was the bus in his book that went to Tomalín. Before him, on that park bench, was where the Consul had sat. And down beyond Cortez Palace, in a direction that he scarcely had let himself think about, down that street at the end, lay, would it be there, that madhouse of M. Laruelle's, which even Yvonne actually *forgot* was there when Sigbjørn had caused her to return? Would it still be there? And would the writing on the wall still be there, *No se puede vivir sin amar?* And would the Calle Humboldt be the same as Yvonne had found it? And would the Consul's house at number 65, which had once been his, Sigbjørn's and Ruth's, still be there? Good God! Laruelle's house, where the Consul had made his act of will.

Sigbjørn went inside to find out what the price of beer was—Nosotros no somos americanos ricos—and when he returned, it was to find the marmalade-haired Spanish woman and her man seated with Primrose. They had seen the Wildernesses deceived in the Plaza Netzalcuayatl. "We are ashamed of my country."

They began to have a party and the day became triumphant. Señor Kent, the proprietor of the café, came by and was introduced. "Haven't I seen you before?"

Sigbjørn had stood up politely. "Why yes . . ."

"Don't you remember me?" Señor Kent gave him his card, but at the moment simultaneously his attention was called by someone in the road and Sigbjørn, catching the table in imbalance, spilled the tequila in the Mexican's lap, and the next moment, he dropped the card. They were helped by a rather slovenly waitress, who later charged them too much. Quite apart from anything else, what was continental in Sigbjørn required, even as Don Quixote, a café of some sort as a center of his circle, this was a necessity of travel to him, if he must travel, and La Universal—which so to speak was a divided character leading a double life, Dr. Jekyll outside and Mr. Hyde within, while sometimes at night the two would mix, clearly would not do. Things began now to happen very swiftly in Sigbjørn's mind.

"Do you know what, Sigbjørn," Primrose said excitedly, "he says he thinks he knows of an apartment to let in the Calle Nicaragua—I mean the Calle Humboldt."

"In the where!" Sigbjørn's heart began to thump loudly.

"Good heavens, Well, there usen't to be any apartments there in my day. They're all private houses." Sigbjørn was feeling very strange indeed.

Primrose went off and returned, enchanted with everything she had seen, the masses of flowers, the men on horses and burros, the terrific loads that they carried.

And then, Primrose was saying even more excitedly, "I've been to the Calle Humboldt and it's still just like you describe it. . . . And do you know what, Mr. Laruelle's tower's still there—it's just like you say only there're not so many gewgaws on it, and there's no writing outside on the wall. But it's wonderful inside."

"I've never been inside. I made it all up."

"And do you know, I was so excited I almost forgot to tell you. It's been turned into apartments and we can have one there. There's a swimming pool and an enormous garden and it's called the Quinta Dolores."

"Are you quite sure?"

"Sure about what?"

"Sure that there's no writing on the wall."

"Perfectly sure."

"It's all right. It's only my joke."

But Sigbjørn had never been inside it. Good heavens, what a thought! What if he were, after living in it, so to speak, so long, to go inside it, to live *in*side the tower, now, if this tower should become, for a while, their home, and this again, by simply what was known as coincidence, for he had not moved a muscle in that direction, had not, apart from vaguely having moved them —the most obvious, the most logical, the, indeed, almost inevitable move to anyone who is acquainted with Mexico at all and cannot bear the city and does not have the most specific plans— toward Cuernavaca itself made any move at all. What if this were to happen? What would that be like? Surely it bankrupted the imagination, or at least invested it with powers that were normally held to be beyond it, unless they were in truth so far below it and behind it, that it had the same effect: it was enough to drive you crazy, or make you think that you were on the track of some new truth that everyone had somehow overlooked and yet was somehow bound up with some fundamental law of human destiny.

The Quinta Dolores itself was largely a garden that stretched right down from the Calle Humboldt to the barranca. It was uncultivated on the slope and where the declivity began, on level ground, was a swimming pool. The nearest approximate to the establishment in America or Canada was indeed one of those "drive-ins" or "auto camps of the better class" that had threatened and were threatening Primrose and Sigbjørn's existence in Eridanus. This however was unfair to the Quinta Dolores. Grotesque in design, as it was deficient in plumbing, roomy yet uncomfortable at the same time, the whole place nonetheless had a beauty, not to say splendor, usually quite lacking in its more efficient American counterpart.

They settled for one hundred and five pesos a week, and afterward Sigbjørn took Primrose for a walk up the Calle Morelos, down which they had come early that afternoon on the bus: the glimpse through the archway of the old man and the boy on the bench, the cobbled court and stone building at right, then rolling hills and fields and sense of light and space with low afternoon sun and marvelous piles of clouds: later, the black horses running across the tilted fields, Popo in magnificent form, a cloud like a hat turning into a cloud streaming off the top as though erupting, then the barranca!—*the* barranca: just as he had described it.

Primrose said, "Is it? I must know."

"It's not *the* place, of course."

Though this was not *the* place, it was vast, threatening, gloomy, dark, frightening: the terrific drop, the darkness below. They lingered long on the scene, and Primrose beautifully remarked: roads that are laid straight east and west, those get the sun all day, but roads that go north and south get the sun later, and lose it by three o'clock in the afternoon. It was like a poem. It was difficult to see how any happiness could come—for the Consul, his hero, it would not—out of this but so it did, floating like an essence. It was the happiness engendered, strangely enough, by work itself, by the transformation of the nefarious poetic pit into sober or upright prose, even if jostled occasionally by Calderón, or it was the happiness engendered by the memory of work finished, of happy days, other evening walks, or rather, more accurately, of the memory of their escape—from some or other part of that transformation, after tea, when they discussed it to some sort of conclusion, and in this respect purposely of turning evil into good—to see Mauger, the fisherman with his tales of salmon drowning eagles, or of how the wind blowing wildly seemed to keep the tide high up a whole day, or of beaked fish with green bones.

And of other walks in Eridanus, the time they had called on old William Blake, for instance, an Englishman too, who was making a garden by the forest. His house was very clean, with fresh shingles and scarlet sills. "It is the best built house on the beach," he said proudly. "Aye, and the inside's good too. On the shore," he added, "'ave you seen them? They're *crabs wot jump!*" His speech was such, or so he persuaded himself, as Wordsworth dreamed to record, humble and good as plates on a farmhouse shelf. He fed the chipmunks, then showed them the spring where the deer came down to drink. "The deer come right down to the lighthouse, swimming right across the sound." In winter time they were tame, you could feed them. Then, because it was the beginning of their life in Eridanus, and Primrose and he did not know the way well, he showed them their trail, the trail now widened by loutish loggers, loutish not for being loggers, but because they practiced high rig logging, who had left nothing but a vicious slash behind. "Keep to the left," he said, "and you can tell when you are almost home, because the trail bends, and where you look out to sea the trees are thinner, where you can see the light in the sky." Then there was the time, long before their own fire, and there was even happiness in this memory, because it *was* at that time, when they stumbled on a burned house in the wood. The eaves lay to one side: a smashed barrel-tree the owners had planted, and smashed pint bottles in a pool, limp dungarees, the washing pole overgrown with vine. Thus was disaster's message without word.

Now they walked higher up into the town for a view of moonrise over the volcanoes, meaning to drop in afterward to the Cuernavaca Inn, which was kept by a Señor Pepe, who should have known Sigbjørn of old. As they approached the inn the full moon, seen over an orange junkyard filled with broken and rusted tin cans, was already rising above Ixtaccihuatl. At her summit a veil of cloud was billowing in the moonlight. Entering the inn, Sigbjørn said:

"This is the place where Hugh really used to offer the Consul strychnine. However that's a long story, I don't know if I've ever told you."

But all Don Pepe could say was "Mucho tiempo, mucho tiempo"; he didn't really remember after eight years and Sigbjørn was more than half relieved. The inn was much changed, the old swimming pool now hidden by a huge wall, no one lived in the ramshackle old building.

When Sigbjørn and Primrose came out, it was to see an extraordinary sight. Over Ixtaccihuatl the moon was in eclipse, which, as they walked to the Quinta Dolores, catching strange glimpses of the ever-increasing horrendous shadow of Tellus, the earth, on the moon between houses, became total. They had mysterious glimpses of it down narrow streets, and as they walked watching, little by little the shadow of the old earth drew across the moon; everybody else ignored it save one Chinese boy in the zócalo with opera glasses and a man carrying a baby down the Calle Humboldt, which was his old Calle Nicaragua. How sinister and yet exciting in this shadow blacker than night had Laruelle's house, had the Quinta Dolores seemed then. What sinister omen did it hold for them, going groping into the grounds of this house on this day, and afterward what glorious silver portent? They heard the pure voice of a Mexican singing somewhere on a balcony, as if rejoicing that the world had relinquished its shadow and the moon was with them again. And after the eclipse, standing on the roof balcony, the sense of space and light, of being almost up in the sky. Long vines were waving and making shadows on sun blinds. Stars were winking like jewels out of white fleecy clouds, silver clouds; and the wide *near* sapphire-and-white sky, a white ocean of fleece, and the brilliant full moon sliding down the sapphire sky.

VI

*E*nchiladas with mole sauce
. . . *Fama est enceladi seminstum fulmine corpus, Urgeri
mole hac, ingentemque insuper aetnam . . . Enchiladas
—Enceladus, identified with Typhon, or Typhoes, who was
imprisoned under Mount Aetna, remember* The Valley—
*and the thousand heads and voices. Peach, ho! The moon
sleeps with Endymion. . . . Like angry golfers the Cyclops
hurled their clubs into the sea. . . . Thus, whilst Endymion is given an opportunity of rising out of his own fatal
self-absorption to help another, the fate of Glaucus throws
additional light upon the problem, which is before Keats's
mind all through the poem, the relation of love in its different forms to higher ambitions of the soul. . . . La Luna
ilumina la noche. Enfolded by her light he slid swiftly with
her once more into total eclipse. Then the horrible shadow
of the earth fell over her.*

Gradually things moved into a sort of place, as they do to a
seaman, after having drunkenly joined a strange vessel the night
before. Sigbjørn lay there with the moonlight of a month later
streaming in upon him. Gradually he became aware that he was
half dreaming, and at the same time that he actually was
in Cuernavaca itself. Quauhnahuac! And not in Cuernavaca

113

merely, but in—was he?—was he?—he tried to lift himself on
his elbow but found he could not move—in Laruelle's tower, in
Jacques' madhouse, in the tower of Chapter VII. Where the
devil was he really? A blaring light came through the window
and he shut his eyes. A blinding light from where? He was asleep
in the morning? What kind of blinding light? He was ill; he was
drunk. He was drunk; that is, he had been drunk. "And I took
this stekel, stekel means stick, and hit this man, and that's the
time I sent my overcoat to Berlin." Who had said that. Why, he,
Sigbjørn Wilderness and no one else had said, or written it, in
some story. Still, well, it wasn't that kind of stekel. What it was,
he had been *reading*, Stekel, the writer, just before he went to
sleep, if indeed that could be called sleep. Sleep means reexperiencing one's past, forgetting one's present (which he certainly
had done), and prefeeling one's future, he had read, was that
true? He could not say exactly that he had been asleep, probably
it was the effect also of Hippolyte's phenobarbital that he
had taken. But so far as reexperiencing the past was concerned,
it was valid enough. It had all happened—Suddenly he opened
his eyes, that light must be the full moon, he remembered, he
shut his eyes again, extremely loath to be fully conscious. On the
other hand, he was wide awake. Music started outside; it was
that posada, it had been going on when he went to bed. There
were dogs barking too, other noises too, God what noises; even
with the earplugs in his ears that he used while swimming in
Eridanus he could hear them. Cuernavaca was an infernally
noisy rowdy place at night. The dream, if it was a dream then,
but it was not a dream, he had been awake, was all true, absolutely true in every detail.

The full moon—they had first come to the house at the full
moon, so that was a month ago—was that light. And it was the
light or the noise that had wakened him. It seemed to him his
life was beginning to have more and more the character of a
dream. He reflected a little on this too. On the whole, it was too
damned obvious. Perhaps life indeed was to most a condition of
sleep, and while it was not true, thank God, that for that reason
the majority of what men call dreams were, so to speak, valid
functions—His mind came to a full stop. The trouble was, he

had a little more time than most people to reflect up
really extraordinary character of human destiny and it w
like fate to play a trick like this on a man without any philo-
sophical gifts, a man, in short, who was so stupid that fate felt
fairly safe from his ever revealing the truth. It was too bad: per-
haps the sensation of writing that he had had in connection with
the letter was related to a half memory that seemed now to come
to the surface, as if he had been writing it all down, as if indeed
he were writing this down or as though somebody else were writ-
ing it down, or writing through him.

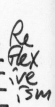

Re
flex
ive
ism

It was a hideous thought, and without waiting to speculate upon how far he might have been prefeeling—horrible word—the future, he made an enormous effort to wake up, though still without opening his eyes, for he could feel the wild light of the moon almost boring at his eyelids. Well, perhaps Jupiter had bestowed upon him, like Endymion, the gift of perpetual sleep, as well as that of perpetual youth. In fact, at times, Sigbjørn did feel rather like Endymion. Middle age, at all events, was a thing impossible for him to contemplate so that, middle-aged, he did not contemplate it. Certainly nothing in his experience had been so dramatic as that eclipse of the moon, on the very day they had first come to the Quinta Dolores. It was a moment of pure ecstasy, and Sigbjørn held it in his mind now, reliving it. He lay perfectly still, and then, since his ears were paining him, he removed the plugs from them, very gingerly, so as not to wake Primrose, and being careful not to open his eyes.

Christ. Great God, what a tumult! It was as if he had, by removing his earplugs, opened the door of an engine room and all of a sudden the full dumbfounding clamor of the machinery had burst upon him. Or it was as if he had been lying semiconscious in some sealed cabin on a ship during a hurricane and someone had opened a porthole through which suddenly he heard the full roar of the sea, mingled with thunder, the splintering of gear, shouts and cries for help. Sigbjørn lay in a sort of stupor. The noises diminished a little. And because of the character of the steep walled old town of Cuernavaca, the sound poured over him in great echoing waves while at the same time they were diminishing with a whine. It was the same every night. The whickering of sleepless vultures seeking warmth on the roofs and of those smaller birds, even worse, apparently practicing to be vultures, and of which that bird he had seen the first day was the forerunner that each evening, through the same celestial purple passage of sunset, the same bleeding bloody-minded sunset against which the gold cathedral, or gold-cupolaed cathedral was silhouetted—each night the cathedral tower was seen against pure pale turquoise, and gold stars, and the light fading from the volcanoes as the light came on in the watchtower of the prison, and the shabby simple arcades of Cortez Palace and the great gray stone golem they were sculpturing beside it—flew home, accompanied by those tiny, jumping, lyrical birds, to roost in the square: what a spectacle, Sigbjørn thought, sunk in bed as if it were a shellhole, of those horrible abominable long-tailed sooty birds, so ugly in flight, wobbling like badly ridden bicycles, a cross between a starling and some sort of loathsome insect. Yes, and it was especially horrifying when the sun was going down in a blaze with cyclones of dust sweeping up the street and the rainbow in a deep blue sky overhead—can it be that I affect the elements since they hadn't had such tempestuous, if occasional, breaks in the weather of mid-January here within living memory?—and masses of wild wind-swept cloud and these bloody birds dropping out of the sky, scattering, and the wind, wind, wind! Down the street the people turned up their collars, struggling, and a brief hard pattering shower, the little rain, or lluvia, came before the sunset itself, when these birds multitudinously settled in the trees in the square to gibber and quack with a mechanical unbelievable screeching like myriad insane crickets, against the loudspeakers, and the loudspeakers themselves—it was they that were in his ears still—Jesus, the jukeboxes and radios turned on full blast, a maddening aeolian horror that would almost have kept even his poor Consul out of a cantina, however much he needed a drink: all these noises that had not ceased, or even if they had ceased, were still echoing in his brain, and in the ancient delirious town: yes, he seemed to hear them all at once, all the noises of the blaring darkness of all the chilly nights: and now, here they went, the turkeys, that seemed to tear through the very fabric of your sanity, just as they tore through the blue fabric of each afternoon —hubblebubblepoppergetsthebottle!—great God, what a bird, part vulture, peacock, and the rest baboon, and seemed, moreover, sometimes almost to bark; and the yowling, the howling, the meowing even of certain kinds of dogs, the explosions of rockets, all this together with the pandemonium of hurdy-gurdies, motor horns, cutouts, and that blasting again of apparently five million loudspeakers turned on full blast, together with the searching moan of the eternal train in the valley that had apparently been equipped with the siren of the *Lusitania,* and the cocks that began to crow, and for all he knew the hens too, at 8 P.M. (or 8:20, if it was the train) and went on till dawn, (it was still early yet, he thought) and the interminable ticking of termites in the roof above, in the stringers, under the fire-proof plaster, and this was one good thing about this place, it wouldn't burn down even if you set fire to it. But he mustn't forget the termites, neither in themselves, nor to mention them to Señora Trigo, or rather, since he was becoming increasingly afraid to mention anything, get Primrose to mention them.

In bed Sigbjørn tried to move, to stretch out toward his wife lying beside him, but he could not: he could not even move a little finger. Though bits of the ceiling crumbled, sifted down ceaselessly on his face, still he did not, or could not move.

The city is of night, but not of sleep. Occasionally he rose, that is to say, he thought, a moment after that he had risen on his elbow to say something like "Christ help!" quite loud, or "It wasn't as if—" or "The thing," or "The bubble," or "Seize the theme, Emily"; his hangover had caught up with him in the middle of the night. But now he thought he remembered again. It was not the middle of the night. It was still quite early, early enough, he thought, waking slightly more, for the sounds of the party, the posada, still to be going on next door, or over the barranca, wherever it was: the clarinet soared. "Smoke gets in your eyes." (I'll say it does.) The clarinetist had made quite a good break; it was a significant tune, had, indeed, been Ruth's favorite tune, he said aloud; then, hoping that Primrose hadn't heard, suddenly came still more to his senses and stretched out his hand really for her, to touch her. But she was not near enough to touch, it was a wide bed, and he did not feel capable of moving over. Ah, my sweetheart and my love, are you why, whom?

That was what had been written on the wall in the sad Borda Gardens where he and Primrose had wandered the next Sunday, the Sunday after the eclipse, because it was only open on Sundays, and as he subsided half into sleep again, the blackened dead branches and empty dead fountains of the gardens where the doomed Maximilian and Carlotta, pale royal ghosts of the Consul and Yvonne, had wandered, began to weave a pattern of mournful music through his consciousness: all the more mournful since, during a hangover this was the memory of a hangover, for he had, indeed they had, much increased their drinking since moving into the tower, even if half against their will. Indeed the Borda Gardens appeared to him much as the House of Usher had appeared to Poe: gloomy, no flowers, grassless, even the trees were dark, the flowers died in the very bud here, even the geraniums in the pots wouldn't bloom, the pillars supported nothing, and the roots of the old trees pushed up the pavement in broken waves; a few ducks swam in the shallow long pool, a few lonely old women sat here and there, some American tourists tittered and talked loudly and stupidly, an artist showed horrible bright prints, and Primrose and he wandered past the dry fountains, reading on the low leprous walls: *3/24/16 Recuerdo Julián Medina, el amor es la excelsa sonrisa del espiritu, miradme compasivos ojos claros que por el vasto mar del amor mio de mis deseos al gentilnavio providente quiais como dos faros.*

But what had he been trying to avoid, to prevent her seeing, what drew him to these walls and yet made him afraid of them, was it not that he was afraid of seeing carved there—or afraid that she would see—at the end, by the arbor, on the tree, the nine-year-old words that would, after all, have *grown: Recuerdo Ruth and Sigbjørn, November, 1936.*

Remember me.

That afternoon, on the day they had gone to the Borda Gardens, as if to complement the later experience, Sigbjørn had taken her to Maximilian's Palace, past the Consul's house; the old continuation of the Calle Humboldt had been discontinued, the road proceeded straight ahead into new vistas with new planted trees, a bus even ran down it, the old continuation over the bridge on which Hugh had jumped and from which Yvonne had seen the horses was now simply a path, through the drop, now more like a crevasse, was still terrifying; outside Maximilian's Palace a notice:

> *Quinta de Maximiliano*
> *Vivero de la*
> *Comisión Nacional de Monumentos Históricos.*

The stove and the roof gone, the walls with grass and vines growing along the tops, small trees growing up through the rooms, the bougainvillea, pink bricks, more names and arrow-pierced hearts on the walls, washing hung out to dry in one room, shock of corn in another . . . Sigbjørn thought of Carlotta and the Pope and her definition of hell.

Sigbjørn Wilderness was quite awake now. Why was his wife not there? Because she was in the next room but one. And why was she in the next room but one? Oh oh, oh ho, rosebuds sing so loudly.

Then he remembered everything. Or nearly everything. The weakness and the unreality are the worst; shame came upon him in great crowded chill waves. How could he have sunk like this, have become his own "character," nay, far worse. A sense of grief and shame so agonizing it was as if his whole soul was being stretched on a rack . . . But who was that *other* Wilderness! A sense of fear of him, utterly ruthless was this Wilderness. . . . It was this Wilderness, not him, who—for what?—wanted the tower. A sense of waste, too: as if his life too were being consumed by flames; like the man at the fair in Guadalupe whose body was being gnawed by rats. The guilt over telling lies, for he did tell lies, almost every time he opened his mouth. And the guilt also in this other sinister form; this feeling he is being watched. . . . Trying to pray, the heart beating so wildly: what if it stopped? had already stopped? The sense of pathos was almost obscene. He tried to pray but could utter only obscenities. How can you struggle with death, when surely death itself is in

"character" en sensa doble

the weakness and cowardice that has you in its grip? And the
sense of involving Primrose in it. Oh Jesus, why had he ever
come back to Mexico? Why have I come back again, he cried
soundlessly to the ceaseless termites, and the specters already beginning, it seemed, to stand round the room. My sweetheart and
my love, are you why, whom? Sigbjørn realized that he was having a unique experience—he was actually too frightened to go
and get a drink. And perhaps this sense of absolute panic was the
worst.

Sigbjørn Wilderness, somehow or other, was out of bed, wide-
eyed, looking back out of the window into the street, down the
Calle Frey de las Casas, down the Calle Humboldt. The street of
The Valley of the Shadow of Death! His street! Street of the
Land of Fire!

So he was living in the tower, of course. M. Laruelle's tower.
The famous Calle Nicaragua and the Calle Tierra del Fuego.
For a moment it was as if he were the Consul himself and the
next thing Dr. Vigil would be on the phone, asking him to go
to Guanajuato. A desire to drink endlessly, to talk endlessly,
to someone, anyone, overwhelmed him. Dr. Vigil! Fernando!
He would see Fernando soon. For the first time he noticed that
as if by magic there stood a drink by the side of the bed: he
tasted it. Odd—how had that come about. He remembered
anyhow: it was not a drink strictly speaking, but an infusion
of boiled orange leaves, prescribed by Dr. Hippolyte, in case
he became sleepless, and administered by the nurse. The nurse!
No, that was a long time ago; how long? It was Primrose who
now administered the ochas, for that was what it was, ochas of
Oaxaqueñan-Farolitan memory, but without the raw alcohol.
There was a blank however in his more immediate memory;
that was bad; there used not to be such. He felt the ochas lulling
him a little, steeping the pain away. It was not, however, dawn,
he saw—some kind of moonlight simply. Well, he had known
that before, perhaps only a few minutes ago, since when there
seemed to have been another syncope, blank. It was, in fact,
bright hellish moonlight—the bilingual moonlight, that spoke
at once the language of love and madness!—in which, outside
the panadería, the shop where they bought their morning rolls,

among the crucificial shadows of telegraph poles, the same three
dogs, two male and one female, were still furiously copulating
that had been doing so when he went to bed: it had been going
on, just like the posada, before he turned in, and must have
been going on ever since, only now, in addition to this infernal
din, were added the frightful howls and yelps of yet another dog,
who must have scented the concourse from a distance: renewed
shouts, laughter, dancing, stamping—the Raspa, they were playing now, and how well that rasping name suited Mexico—came
from the posada itself too, from the court behind the tintorería.
What the hell were they doing, and why couldn't they sleep?
But why, for that matter, couldn't he? It didn't help, if indeed
he knew, and if indeed, after the ochas, he wanted to go to sleep.
De *boom!* De *boom!* de boomditty boomde *boom!* Te *boom!* Te
boom! Te boomtitty boom te *boom!* The Raspa, the Mexican
Sir Roger de Coverley—one note had been altered from what
used to be the Mexican "For he's a jolly good fellow" and they
had made a rag out of it. On debombditty boomditty boomditty
boomditty, boomditty boomditty boomditty *bomb!* That was
the middle, people were stamping and shouting, and how the
dreadful repetitious thing began booming out again!

> *The bomb!*
> *The bomb!*
> *The bombditty bomb de bomb!*
> *The bomb!*
> *The bomb!*
> *The bombditty bomb de bomb!*

Sigbjørn, under the impression that he had lit a cigarette, immediately upon rising, now began to hunt all round the room
for it. Humanity today was like that, he reflected, like a man
who suddenly remembers that he had left a cigarette burning
and cannot remember where. Who had said, Life is like anything, if you look at it like that? Copperfield. Christ, was it not
enough to have lost the house and his book, but above all their
house, their dear little house, by fire, without on top of it to
have this dreadful fear of fire—and Christ, how fire seemed to
follow him around.

Was it not enough to have conquered that—not to say, after having formally conjured it—to have had the courage to go back and rebuild, with their own hands, their house—and here was the thing, the thought again, not so much a thought by this time, but like truncated exposition itself in this novel the daemon was writing—though someone had already agonizingly built on part of their burned site, to have rebuilt it in six months with their own hands and the fishermen's aid, and then perhaps to have the whole thing taken away from them, the forest they had saved to be broken up into auto camps of the better class, to be turned out as undesirable squatters: no wonder the poor house left there unfinished beckoned to him with its memory of another house, and with its hint of the last house of all, the grave.

Yes, was it not enough to have endured all this without having to expose himself to further—*supernatural* was the only word—torment. Supernatural. Christ. Sigbjørn, having failed to find the cigarette, sat down on the bed, groaning aloud, and wished the house would burn down with him inside it, only this was one house that wouldn't burn. A cold tickling horror leaped in the bed and he hugged it to him. Ah, to be tied—often this was wished, like by Stendhal and later Gide—to be tied to the bed, to be chained to it not because he wished to be confined to bed, but so that the chains, the ropes, would crush out the anguish of his thoughts. *A little jitter bounced and yapped. About the room. And Carthage slept. And all the rigadoons were still. And God was playing on the harp. And in the fishbowl sank the carp. And rose again to sink no more. Immortal on the bestial floor.* Nonsense like this: unbelievable in an educated man, he thought. There was the tequila bottle in the kitchen—why not? He had no intention of stopping drinking. It was the only comfort he had. Everything he had written about drinking was hypocritical. But this time, yes, it was too far.

But that his torment was supernatural, or at least inhuman in some sense, there seemed no doubt in his mind. It wasn't good art but it was the truth. Anybody more bloody well damned than himself, he considered, it would be next to impossible to find on this planet. What had God been up to in creating such a man and what was his purpose in keeping him alive, if alive he could be said to be? Was He so kindly that He would do it for his wife? Yet what strange power was it in him, strange, and it could not but be evil—Yet, was he not good, were they not good, had they not sacrificed their own house, their work, to the forest, for others' good—he had forgotten this, this was something else again—was this a power that was wasted on writing and that God had determined must in some sense serve chaos.

Sigbjørn got up, moved to the window overlooking the garden. The mailbox was the most brilliant thing in the garden, more brilliant than all the flowers, like, by day, a tiny orange birdhouse, by night all you could see was one rectangle of the peaked roof, still brilliantly orange under the light. . . . Underneath it at night broad leaves, of cannas: over it a jacaranda tree that disappeared into the night sky, over the top of that, a star—no, it was the light in the prison watchtower. "I do not want to remember."

But in the prison in Oaxaca there had been no watchtower. No one could escape from there. Or could they? He thought of the time the police arrested him in the Covadonga, not for being drunk, but for an expression of genuine political opinion in what was a pro-Franco joint. He did not have his papers, and they were within their legal rights in imprisoning him.

But the prison in Oaxaca, the "worst" prison: the murderer, covered with blood, thrown in the jug, getting mescal from the guard, wiping the bottle politely, but there was blood on the bottle—there was blood, not on his lips but on his arm where he had wiped the bottle, to be courteous. . . . Sigbjørn Wilderness tasted this blood.

"Sí, hombre."

"Sí, hombre."

"Noche bueno."

"Merry Christmas."

"Feliz Navidad."

"Es sangre."

"Es verdad."

Then the alcoholic child, not more than six or seven at most that had been thrown in, and the murderer had comforted him all night as the shadow of the mescal-producing angelic policeman swung against the wall as he made his ceaseless rounds on Christmas morning and then the blue blue sky and the beautiful country air coming into this pigpen of the prison, with outside the fountain blowing, and a butterfly hovering there in the air alive with Christmas bells, black velvet with sapphire-studded wings. Then, the door opened for all but him, and instead of Christmas bells wildly hot music coming from the prison radio.

Then when he was let out to the excusado, the stool pigeon. The place swarming with these spies in dark glasses he had seen outside the Hotel La Luna where he was staying with Hölscher. They would get their orders then dodge off again and mingle with the hot shuffling blanketed crowds and sunlight. Then trying to take a walk. A single step seemed to take him about a minute.

Then the Captain of Police had hauled him out of jail and given him a drink at the cantina opposite. "We have founded out, that you are a criminal and escape through seven states. . . . You say you are—ah, a wrider. We-ah read-ah your wridings and they don't make sense." Yes, brothers under the skin were his publishers and the Oaxaqueñan military police. "You no-ah de wrider you are de espider and we shoot-ah de espiders in Mexico. . . . Where are your friend?"

No reply.

"Where is he for?"

Silence. The silence of Sidney Carton—Sigbjørn Wilderness.

Earlier Sigbjørn had renounced all knowledge of Hölscher; he judged the situation a truly dangerous one, the more so because the Communist was using his passport.

"You want-ah to escape. Escape! Escape now!"

Fortunately—or unfortunately—Sigbjørn hadn't or by the law of ley fuga, which the Captain was itching to invoke, he would not be here now.

Of all this, Sigbjørn had not written, but were he to try to do so, a word would have been as difficult as each step to the excusado. What liars writers are sometimes, and what feeble accounts they give of their despairs. His agonies must be far from unique yet it seemed to him that if but one person had survived such a thing to breathe purer air and love the light that there was hope for the human race. For one man's agony belongs to all men and to God.

Sigbjørn became aware of a slight throbbing pain in his left wrist and also, for the first time, that it was covered with plaster. He drank a little more ochas, then turned on the light. He turned it off again. Well, I do not want to remember. The light flickered off, then, as usual, came on twice before dying. Though he scarcely needed it, he looked at himself in the flawed mirror: something horrible looked back at him. *Little ham who made thee, dost thou know who made thee?* He would not remember.

He sprang, dashed, not wanting to wake Primrose, on tiptoe, through the living room. The door of Primrose's room on his left was half open—held by some gadget of string—moonlight flooded through the window and he could hear her even breathing. In the kitchen, in the gloaming, gleamed the tequila bottle, and Sigbjørn stood motionless beside it scarcely daring to breathe himself. She would have got used to the Raspa, the dogs, all the explosions, the jukeboxes, the gallinaceous cacophony, claver, of nocturnal Cuernavaca by now, it would be part of whatever sleep she was having, yet the slightest noise within the house might disturb her. What if she should wake and catch him drinking tequila? But the tequila had water in it, and if he drank, he would certainly choke, and in that case Primrose would certainly wake up. Just as that afternoon he had stood, while Primrose was away at the market, trying not to drink it, so he stood now, and there was something unspeakably dreadful about this simply standing by the bottle, gaining a kind of dismal comfort from its proximity, almost too weak to make supercession to weakness, which would have at least comprised some action. Now, as then, while there seemed a hush, again as between armies in the night, in the mortal (and puerile) conflict within him, he stood like a ghost beside the half-empty bottle. From the next room he still heard Primrose softly breathing. "Write and tell me if you have not killèd yourself with drinking." He had repeated Fernando's words aloud before he could help himself, and he listened again, taking a soft step nearer the bottle, so that he could touch it, and if he had waked her, perhaps snatch a quick drink without her knowledge under cover of the noise she would make turning over or getting up. But her even breathing continued and Sigbjørn still stood, frozen, with his hand on the bottle. Eight years ago in his Fernando-Oaxaca days, he would have drunk unthinkingly; three, four years ago, in Eridanus, had he felt as vile as this, it would not even have occurred to him, he would have had a swim, and for a moment he thought of this, the run out to the end of the pier at Eridanus, the dive into the green cold delicious salving element, and the climb back up the ladder; the dripping swift return into the warmth of the house—the invariable remark, "God, how marvelous, that knocks the nonsense out of you"—for they had built their pier to come right out of the front door, whatever morose problems had precipitated him into the inlet now at the bottom of it, or, perhaps, on the way to being solved.

But what had gone wrong? For a moment it struck him as loathsome and unfair, that such a thing could possibly happen, that such a thing could ever become a problem. For it worked both ways. A good and merry and constructive and admirable friend, it was not to him that it was a bad, so much, as an unworthy enemy. Yet since he had accepted, at least in part—his thought weakened slightly—its challenge, its contemptible challenge, he couldn't appease it, without some oblique moral treachery—nor can you, Geoffrey Firmin. In short, he couldn't take a drink when he most needed it, and when indeed it would, such as now, do him the most "good." (Whatever was meant by good.)

> *The bomb!*
> *The bomb!*
> *The bombtittybombtittybomb!*
> *The bomb!*
> *The bomb!*
> *The bombtittybombtittybomb!*

Nonetheless that the tequila had water in it at all was not, from one point of view, a good sign: this was the case because yesterday, alone in the house all afternoon, he had not indeed left the house for several days, he had finally succumbed and taken several drinks and had filled the bottle to its previous level because he had not wanted Primrose to know that he had had those drinks before they started on their regular—where was it, by the way?—habanero (but not tequila, and certainly not mescal, he would not think of that, he took a half step nearer the bottle even put one hand on it) drinking at six o'clock in the evening. On the other hand, it *was* a good sign, That there was not more water in this tequila was a good sign. And that in spite of the water there was any tequila there at all was a better sign still, was it not?

"Sickness is not only in body, but in that part used to be call: soul," he murmured, involuntarily again, and this time took yet another step nearer and grasped the tequila bottle more firmly; yes, indeed, Fernando had been right. That was precisely what it was, though what a complicated sickness he, Sigbjørn Wilderness, was suffering from, even Fernando, Dr. Vigil, even Hippolyte himself would have been at a loss to specify. (Ah, to be on some old freighter, rolling through the cerulean sea to Pijijiacic, with a cargo of cherries-in-brine, old marble, and wine.) Ah, old maker of tragedies, are you making more tragedies? That evening he and Primrose had drunk a good deal of habanero. They drank officially while she prepared dinner, as indeed she prepared everything, but the catch was, with this way of drinking that with each succeeding day the hours that stretched out before six o'clock became longer and longer and more intolerable, so that laterally he had even taken to setting his watch ahead, with the further result that it was rather like being on the plane again, it was four o'clock, the next moment five, it was five, but hey presto—how swiftly time passes in Mexico—thank God, it was six. "Last night I got such terrible drunkness I shall need three full days of sleeping to recover myself." No, it was not so; he did not have to think this. For at that moment he had caught sight of the tequila bottle on the sink and saw that it was still half full. Strange though, how he kept remembering Fernando's words all these years, and would have remembered them, doubtless, even had he not made him a character: but stranger still was it to think he might actually be meeting Fernando himself in person in a few days—for had he not proposed at dinner that they set out in the morning, by bus, for Oaxaca?

"Primrose, I've been thinking," he'd said suddenly, at dinner, "I'm bloody well not going to spoil your holiday for you any more by this kind of thing. I've been reading in the folder, this *Guía de Turistas*, and I've got a real trip for you up my sleeve."

"Oh, have you darling?"

And Sigbjørn had outlined, from the folder, how it now seemed possible to him to get from Cuernavaca to Oaxaca by road, a road that had not been there before, and had taken as long to build as his book had to write, a point that perhaps has some bearing on human effort. They would go, at all events, through Yautepec, of happy and complicated memory, to Cuautla, and thence to Matamoros, so far only by terrible unpaved roads and second-class bus, but at Matamoros, he had calculated, if they were lucky, they could connect with a first-class bus from Puebla and Mexico City and proceed on to Oaxaca, a distance that upon the map at least, looked negligible.

Primrose had been excited and so had he, when he had turned in early, too drunk to sleep with Primrose, who was however quite drunk herself, in this other bedroom, with its spotted mirror in which everything appeared broken and not quite right, amid the serapes and perfume bottles and chinches and termite sawdust that rained down all night in an unceasing shower; it had seemed a good, even a glowing, even a warming idea, but suddenly, now, he was seized with horror at the notion of sitting, bouncing and jouncing, in that dreadful second-class bus; but above all it was the thought of the initiative to be exerted that was intolerable to him, the courtesy, the por favors, the perdone mes, the dónde está el salón or los camiónes para Zuxtepecs, the adiós, the necessity for avoiding all the time being cheated at every turn—what about that fat man at the deserted Cerveza Barril telling him that beer was only sixty cents a tarot but on the plea of no change only giving him three pesos change for his ten for his beer, then filling up his tankard before he had proper time to drain it, pretending he was going to treat him, pouring cognac for himself, and Sigbjørn only just succeeded hypocritically from cognac being poured into his beer, that for once he did not want, and still no change, and then when he made to go, charging him fifteen pesos, and then when he demurred, nineteen, then throwing his three pesos to a waitress and, saying twenty-five pesos, he was threatening to call the police, was indeed ringing them up—Sigbjørn had run away. Or robbed! Yes indeed—the necessity of having to face and come to grips with the extraordinary mélange of chivalry, hatred, fear, grace, admiration, chicanery, obsequious pimpery and boundless contempt that is manifested in the Mexican's attitude toward the gringo and that was so often if not largely—he had shouted "—the fault of you bloody Americans who try to impose your beastly mythless loveless sanitary way of life and cheap tawdry expensive goods"—Primrose was at the door and he shook his fist at her—"and Coca-Cola bien fria that's always warm and mass produced noisy horrors and shallow selfish philosophy and moronic movies and execrable manners on a world that would explode in your face before accepting it!"

"——"

"It's all your fault, the fault of you bloody Americans who for some reason think you're great! You keep trying to impose your bloody little way of life on everybody—"

"Nosotros no somos americanos ricos," Primrose said.

"Oh Jesus, let's get out of this. It's killing me. It's killing us both. For Christ said, oh Jesus, it's awful. Let's go home. Let's get away from this. . . . Why did we ever come to this God-awful country?"

"But you've got to write your new book. You've got to, Sigbjørn, you've got to! And I thought you wanted to see Juan Fernando Martinez."

"——"

"And we've probably got no home anyhow, anyway."

"Why do you *say* that?"

"But, Sigbjørn—"

"It was your fault. You should have done what I told you," he shouted.

"You know you burned the house down yourself."

But this was getting beyond a joke. He would not remember.

Ping! Bing! Puzzle! banglejangle jingle started from the cathedral.

"God help me," Sigbjørn said now. "God help me. I don't

want your help, I only want a drink. But help me just the
same."

Primrose bent over him, she kissed him as silently, as softly as
if a bird had closed its eyelid against his cheek.

"There is no mail," he said, reaching up for her. "There is no
sail—"

Pingle-bangle-jingle-jangle-puzzle-bangle-jingle.

"She is the Virgin for those who have nobody with."

"—for those who have nobody them with—"

"—for those who have nobody with—'

"—for those who have nobody them with—"

"I like to work them with."

"Then pray to her."

"But I am not a Catholic, I am a heretic, a Communist, a
conservative, an Englishman, a draft dodger, a stealer of dog's
dinners, Christ knows what I am."

"Then pray to her."

Sein oder nicht sein, das ist die Frage. That was not the question now, however it might have been before, it was irrelevant.
His getting up, as it were, symbolized the struggle between life
and death. Now he remembered it all; five days ago tonight, he
had made a very nearly successful attempt at suicide, in fact two
attempts, one to hang himself with a dressing gown cord, the
other to slash his wrists; the second had followed in fact his failure at the first due to an unconsciously (deliberate perhaps) ill-
tied knot.

At the same time his eye lit on his bathing trunks, which were
dry, he hadn't been in since the tenth, it was now the fifteenth; a
bright idea struck him, perhaps he could have his cake and eat
it, he could swim and take a drink, or rather vice versa, he would
need a drink in order to be able to take a swim. And, damn it, he
had at last waked Primrose: Sigbjørn, his sounds covered up by
her stirring, as quick as a grebe diving, snatched the bottle, swal-
lowed a horrible-wonderful mouthful of tequila and replaced
the bottle without a sound on the sink, and controlling his nau-
sea, turned on the light as a covering alibi, should the telltale
gurgle have been detected.

"What is it, darling?" he heard her say.

"Nothing. I was just fooling around. I can't sleep." Sigbjørn opened the door and looked in. Primrose, moonlit, had risen on her elbow.

"Are you all right, darling?"

"Yes—are you?"

Primrose fell back on the pillow. "I'm just so frightfully exhausted, that's all. God, this awful noise."

"How beautiful you are."

"Am I?"

"Don't forget we're going to Oaxaca tomorrow."

"Oaxaca." Primrose had seemed about to say something but had fallen straight asleep again without turning on the light.

Sigbjørn hesitated on the threshold. Here bright hellish moonlight scarcely described it. This room, the one of the degenerate machicolations, of what incredible extraordinary significance in his book, had been equipped with panes of stained glass, set in machicolations, the chevron-shaped windows of his Chapter VII, or what was left of them, now seen from the inside with the moonlight pouring through a filter of blue, yellow, and red: through the red it was as if for a moment one saw the street down below with its copulating dogs less through a film than through one of those veils, flashing with hellish fire, black as soot, and livid as a corpse, through which those in the Swedenborgian spiritual world, who had acquired a rooted belief in nature alone, looked downward from "heaven"—their understanding being closed above to spiritual light—to the earth (though it was dark nonetheless and infernal); it was not real, no, surely Sigbjørn could not be in *this* room.

At this moment he saw on the Feliz Año Nuevo calendar, ironically from the liquor store, the Casa de la Vega, the only calendar that had been sent them, with its picture of Pátzcuaro upon it. Did undertakers and executioners send out New Year's greetings?

VII

SUDDENLY THE FRONT DOOR
rattled softly and terrors knocked in Sigbjørn's brain. He tiptoed
into the alcove of the dining room, froze another moment in
terror near the tequila bottle, then peered from the window in
the recess (the house seemed fuller of such little recesses today
than usual): it was Eddie—Eduardo Kent—and he opened the
door softly, putting a finger to his lips; Eddie was evidently
quite plastered, perfectamente borracho.

"I saw a light so I thought you both might be up. I know you
sometimes both read in there late and you asked me to drop
in."

"Primrose is asleep in there."

"Well, come down and have a drink. . . ."

Sigbjørn held his breath a moment. If only she would be sensible and treat his drinking as Dostoevski's second wife did his
gambling. After all he stood (a giant perhaps) to gain by it
someday. Greatest strength equals greatest weakness. Or, he reflected, realizing that he had just been on the point of asking the
question now answered triumphantly in the affirmative by
Eddie for him "Is it anything important?", he might ask her,
"Do you mind?" and she might reply, "No, darling—of course
not—run along and have a good time." Might, but then that
would wake her.

Sigbjørn grabbed his topcoat of Irish tweed, Man of Aran—
none but he knew what had been concealed in those capacious
pockets—this coat rescued from the fire while *In Ballast* hadn't
been—swiftly from behind the door and put it over his pajamas,
and leaving the door half open so as not to be heard returning,
and without giving more than a passing thought to the possibil-
ity of thieves, they descended the winding red-clay steps of the
tower apartment, M. Laruelle's tower: Sigbjørn felt a pang as
they passed the earthenware pot of boiled water on the parapet
that Primrose put out each night to cool and pushed through
the gate that banged all night, a relic of the last tenant before
Eddie: perhaps in the belief that it might prove useful to him
one of these days Sigbjørn had never removed it, availed himself
of Señora Trigo's permission to remove it: at the bottom of the
steps they had to jump over a puddle made by the overflow from
the cylindrical water tank on the flat roof, usually there was a
waterfall too, but tonight it had stopped.

"What time is it?" Sigbjørn, who had forgotten his wristwatch, asked, turning around and gazing through the open gates
of the Quinta Dolores down the Street of the Land of Fire, quite
deserted, in spite of the noise from the posada, and the amorous
hubbub of the dogs, and one lone, bewildered, melancholy looking and terrifying old woman standing at the corner of the Calle
Nicaragua—really the Calle Humboldt—under a sole dim street
lamp. Cross Road Puzzel.

"Nearly eleven. . . . There's such a hell of a noise. . . . I
don't see how anyone can sleep."

"Is that all it is?" Sogbjørn said, thinking oddly then it must
be about time for the train to go. "Surely you can't have closed
up for the night so early."

"Now I've got help, I'm keeping open *all* night. I thought I
told you. How are you, by the way, I heard you weren't too
well."

"I've been a bit under the weather."

"Not the old trouble, I hope."

"Old trouble? What—no. Not that old trouble, thank God.
Incidentally, it was clever of you to see the light in the tower."

"Why?"

"There wasn't one."

"It must be the moonlight. If you look now, it looks as though there was a light."

They walked down the drive, through the ghostly garden, past the gnomed ghostly fountain, there was a dim light only in the room of poor Dr. Parragas, who never had any patients, and the ghostly car of Dr. Hippolyte, who had too many, including, recently, Sigbjørn himself (according to Hippolyte, Sigbjørn had never had any disease more serious than varicose veins, which he had sclerosed again, with good effect, so that Sigbjørn could now walk without difficulty), past the ghostly letter box with its tragic ghostly light, where despair alone arrived, while Sigbjørn, taking in the silhouettes of the angels on Señora Trigo's house that complemented those that had been removed from their tower, wondered if those latter had their existence now alone in his work, or had they been transferred; they stepped off the rugged parapet down onto the dark little wet lawn and the garden of Eddie's bungalow, fringed by the poinsettias, with the leaf-laden pool beyond, in which the moon was swimming under water; they went into the bungalow and Eddie turned on the light.

"It's too big for me now."

"I noticed they've taken your ladder away," Sigbjørn said. "But perhaps you don't go up much on the roof."

"In God's name, why should I?" Sigbjørn could feel Eddie's brown eyes staring. Then he laughed. "Oh, I see what you mean. No, I can't take too much sun. . . . In fact, if I sat out in the sun all day like you do I'd be dead in a week."

"'Nor I," Sigbjørn said absently, considering, not unpleased, the whimsy of this, under the circumstances, the impression he made of being someone who healthily sat out in the sun all day, when if truth were known, only five days ago he had attempted to kill himself. As Eddie went out onto the porch again and into the kitchen, which was at the end of the porch nearer the tower to get glasses, Sigbjørn studied the bottle of Four Roses whiskey on the table.

Suddenly there was a calamitous noise of hooting and wailing from the valley. It was the important little train—Sigbjørn felt a stab of love because it was beloved of Primrose—that with a clapping and a puffing that seemed to carry all the way to Popocatepetl and return redoubled in volume came in to Cuernavaca station at exactly twenty past eight every night, doubtless he had heard it earlier in his wild dreams, and went out at eleven: four hours it took to get to Mexico City—it was in part the meandering selfish little railroad of his novel—this was the train Hugh was supposed to have taken to Vera Cruz. And there it went— chug! chug! chug! chug! The moonlit train on the moonlit track through the moonlit cactus under the moonlit maniacal mountains. Well, at all events, when Primrose and he returned, they would not go by train, they would take the plane again, if they could afford it. Dostoevski (and he could have comforted himself by remembering what he had not till this moment, that he too had once planned a book on drinking, to be called *The Tipplers,* the book that had turned into *Crime and Punishment,* so that the hero was not Marmeladov, but Raskolnikov—the son of Pulquería), Dostoevski had termed his years of travel "worse than deportation to Siberia." And indeed for him, what could have been better than Siberia? Sigbjørn thought. Damn it, he could almost work up a sort of vicarious nostalgia for Siberia himself: the genteel Siberia. No responsibilities, and why fear about being "watched," cantering about the steppes with the attorney-general, falling in love with the wife of Captain Issayev, swimming in the high-banked river Irtich with that same attorney-general, the angelic Baron Vrangel, or watering the flower beds in his cotton shirt, and then going back to his little windowless room blackened with smoke to write his infernal bathroom scene in *The House of the Dead,* with the poor Jews and Poles howling and spewing and clanking their chains as they climbed ever higher and higher out of the mephitic steam, then shoveling snow and playing snowballs—at a pinch you could even throw a snowball at a policeman—or working in alabaster: it was the ideal life, especially for a writer, all the more so since, not being allowed to publish a word, you were spared the continual anguish of rejection. Sigbjørn's eyes again sought the phantom orange postbox and he found he had indeed taken a step toward the Four Roses when Eddie returned.

"Chin-chin."

"Lhiat myr hoillin!"

"What does that mean?"

"Success as thou deservest. . . . How's business?" Sigbjørn asked, chuckling inwardly at Eddie's polite look as he spoke the Gaelic.

"It's falling off. . . . It's because of the milk. I can't get fresh milk from the dairy any longer."

"Primrose will be sorry to hear that. . . . But I wasn't aware you relied on milk for your profits."

"And I can't make my girls stay with me."

"Who can? Tut, tut, who can. Well . . . After all . . . That's not quite a new story. Why don't you buy a pulquería and put a sign outside, English spoken," he suggested. Sigbjørn was thinking of Dostoevski again.

"A pulquería! Jesus, Mary, and Joseph!"

"I'm serious. All the pulquerías here are full from morning to night, they're gay, at least, guitars twanging all the time, and cheap—you'd be turning Americans away by the thousand. And you won't have to bother about milk for your profits."

"The police wouldn't allow it—"

"But aren't *you* the police?"

"I have permission for twenty slot machines. . . . And I'm putting in a jukebox," Eddie said gravely, and Sigbjørn thought he sounded rather hurt. Eduardo Kent, reputed to be a murderer, five times married, and a crook ("If there's one thing I hate, it's a crook," he liked to say), was also, if he could be believed, a policeman ("I use this restaurant simply as a cover-up for—well, not exactly a cover-up—that sounds a bit phony, doesn't it?"), the Chief, in fact, of Judicial Police in Cuernavaca, with a job that consisted partly in bailing American tourists out of jail and partly in tracing murderers, and a cultivator of prize carnations, a sideline whose incongruity was only not complete etymologically since, unlikely though it may sound, the word derives from carne, while on the side too he kept the noisy, uncomfortable pavement cage in the square called La Universal, mostly patronized by Americans, to whom he served expensive hamburgers cooked by himself with a trembling hand. Both Primrose and Sigbjørn, who bought their agua selice there and milk, though not their drinks, for it was too expensive, liked him immensely and it was in fact due to him that they had come to the Quinta Dolores in the first place.

Sigbjørn had heard a story about Eddie. Once, when he was nineteen, in Puebla, he had seen a woman run over by a streetcar. Both legs of the woman had been amputated. Everyone hesitated to do anything because of the law and, indeed, since Sigbjørn himself had dramatized a similar scene it was this legal question that had given rise to the story. Eddie had dashed into a neighboring tiendita, bought a ball of twine, and placed tourniquets upon the poor woman's stumps. He did not escape the law, even for this, albeit the judge had commended him for his humanity. Actually what both Sigbjørn and Eddie had in common was the fictitiousness of their lives: yet strangely, this story, Sigbjørn was convinced, was true—if for no better reason than that he had not yet heard it from Eddie.

"Have you recovered from Taxco yet?" Eddie said after a while, smiling, as they settled down with the Four Roses.

"It depends what you mean by recovered."

"Helen and Guido couldn't get over you two. They said you were simply the happiest couple they'd ever met in their lives."

Sigbjørn took a long drink. "That's something one always likes to hear."

"I've been married five times. . . . I've got a boy of twenty, and I was first married at twenty, so that makes me—forty, doesn't it?"

"Not necessarily. Still, I'll take your word for it."

"Yet I can't say I've ever been so very happy, what with one thing and another—you know," Eddie went on musingly. "But it gives me real pleasure to be with you people. Yes, that's what I like—to see people *happy!*"

Sigbjørn was thinking how little happy poor Primrose had actually been on that particular trip to Taxco with Eddie. "I don't know if you quite realize what you got us into when you found Primrose this place for us," he said.

"Your wife said she'd like to take an apartment here in Cuernavaca. I like to live here, I speak English, so I walked her down here that day and she said, 'I can't believe my eyes. . . .' "

"She didn't tell you *why*."

"I never have quite got the story. Were you here before? Or was it something to do with the book you were writing?"

"Both, in a way. I told you I was here ten years ago. That is, not precisely. . . . Let me see, it's now January, 1946. I was here from September, 1936, to the end of July, 1938."

"But not staying at this house?"

"No, I meant I was here in Mexico," Sigbjørn replied, "although I was in Cuernavaca part of the time. In fact, most of the time. I lived farther down the Calle Humboldt. I don't know if you'd know the house—anyway they've changed the number." Sigbjørn was silent for a while, remembering the recent occasion he'd taken Primrose down there to see the Consul's house, number 65, now 55, 52 in his book, the gate had been mended, the bougainvillea still there, the gardener had been working on the drive, and he had been surprised when they had suddenly thought better of it, turned round and gone out again without once looking back, although they'd had another furtive glance at it from the other side of the barranca. The house seemed unchanged, save that another small wing had been added. "I'd never set foot inside the Quinta Dolores until Primrose brought me here a month ago," he went on, "and said, 'Well, here's a surprise for you!' On the other hand having lived in the street and written about it I was as familiar with it as if it had been my own house. Of course it was not called the Quinta Dolores then."

"I'm not sure I follow you," Eddie was saying.

"Yes, when I said 'house' I meant the tower," Sigbjørn said, "the apartment where Primrose and I are living now. The tower was there all right in the old days, in fact it was about all you could see from the street. But so far as I know there were no rooms for rent in it then. It belonged to an artist and I supposed the bottom part to be a studio since it was glassed in."

"That would be Señora Trigo's brother, but he's dead."

"Years ago," Sigbjørn said, accepting a Bohemios, and half to himself, and walking about restlessly now, "there were two towers with a sort of catwalk between, joining them on the roof, and on the one that seemed to be used as a mirador, there were all kinds of angels, and other round objects, carved out of red sandstone. The funny chevron-shaped windows are still there, but there used to be some writing in gold leaf below them that you read from the road. And they seem to have knocked down one of the towers, though I notice some of the angels have reappeared on Señora Trigo's house."

"And so the tower gave you an inspiration?" Eddie said. "It fired your imagination, isn't that the phrase?"

"Or my imagination fired the tower. . . . But unfortunately it hit our house in Canada: however that is another story. . . . What I wanted to say, Eddie, was this. For some reason I made a rather important character of mine live in that blasted tower over there. And also one of the most important scenes in the book takes place in it," Sigbjørn said, "a scene where my hero has to choose, to put it rather stupidly, between life and death. . . . And now I'm living in the thing myself."

Eddie's croupier's eyes narrowed with interest, though whether with interest precisely at what Sigbjørn had said, even though he had repeated him, saying, "And now you're living in the God-damned thing yourself, eh?" or at some train of thought of his own that his words had set in motion, "That's what you would call a coincidence, isn't it?" he added sagely.

"Or something worse."

"What is the book—is it a sort of detective story?" Eddie was asking.

"I'll lend it you. . . . I've got a copy of the manuscript but I lent it to Hippolyte. But there's a question I want to ask you. In fact I've got it here, what am I thinking of?" Sigbjørn pulled a crumpled piece of paper out of his pocket.

Eddie importantly put on his glasses, and read, " '¿Le gusta este jardín? ¿Que es suyo? ¡Evite que sus hijos lo destruyan!' No, that's wrong."

"But I copied it down. Incidentally, how would you translate it?"

"Do you like this garden which is yours? See to it that it is thus: that your children don't destroy it."

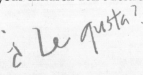

Sigbjørn looked over Eddie's shoulder. "But I copied it down straight from the notice in Oaxaca."

"Well, that explains it. . . . You have to get it right."

"It alters everything—I can see now that it's an absurd mistake, but for at least eight years it's never occurred to me that it could mean anything else but 'Do you like this garden? Why is it yours? We evict those who destroy!'"

(handwritten in margin: Not evict!)

"It doesn't have anything to do with evict."

"Still, that gives me an idea. . . . I'll have to alter it of course. But I could have my Consul *think* that's what it means at first. Yes, I can see that that would be better still."

"You've got to get it right. It's no use unless it's right."

"And then somebody else can make the real translation. It's going to be a hell of a nuisance but I can see the real translation's even worse."

"I thought you said it was better."

"I mean more relevant and terrifying," Sigbjørn said as he folded the paper. "Thank you, Eddie, can I help myself to a drink?"

"That's what the bottle's for," Eddie said, taking off his glasses. "Smoke Gets in Your Eyes" suddenly burst out again from the neighboring posada. "But I'm interested to know. And now tell me what the book is about," Eddie said, replenishing his own glass.

"Drink, mostly," answered Sigbjørn Wilderness.

"Of course, I wouldn't know anything about that. It's a terrible thing to say, but I drink a bottle, yes, a bottle of Berreteaga a day. Never get drunk. Never have a hangover," Eddie said.

"Primrose and I only drink a liter of bulk brandy," Sigbjørn said, sitting on the parapet with his hands clasped across his knees, and gazing up at the moonlit tower, "and have hangovers."

Yet Sigbjørn's mood of depression had now left him, and he felt almost a mood of ecstasy stealing over him, together with a sort of morbid pride, looking up at the ghostly garden, the maniacal dark tower in the moonlight. "*And* get drunk," he added. It was as if indeed he were moving in the midst of his own creation, and even if that creation were a failure, the sensation was almost Godlike. For did not, conceivably, God himself move within His own creation in just such a ghostly fashion, and how should we see Him, when we dimly sense that He has the power at any moment to cut us out altogether from His strange dark manuscript?

"When is it going to be published?"

Sigbjørn shook his head. "Probably never," and Sigbjørn knew what was coming now too.

"I shall expect a signed copy. . . ."

How often Primrose and he had sat here waiting for the postman, who happened, incidentally to be his own little postman of Chapter VI and looking no whit the older for the years that had passed, the same charging stride, the same goatee beard, and with the same air of always being the bearer of tremendous news. And the news from England, the rejection, had come on New Year's Eve, they'd found it in the box when they came back from Yautepec. "And Mr. Wilderness, while imitating the tricks of Joyce, Sterne, the surrealists, the thought-streamers, gives us the mind and heart of Sir Philip Gibbs. On top of that it inevitably calls to mind the recent successful novel and film, *Drunkard's Rigadoon*." But up to then, up to that moment, what a lovely last day of the old year they had had! Rousing himself in the morning with a tremendous effort—as he meant to tomorrow for Primrose's sake—to make her a present of a glorious event, seeing, from the bus the golden corn spread out in the yards, Popo and Ixta appearing and disappearing, and then Yautepec itself, the little town, undiscovered by tourists, the huge drifting white butterflies like flowers of the wind. And then the glimpses into the patio of the church, cool, shaded, the walk along the little river. They had returned so happy, in the crowded bus, and there was his book rejected, and worse, the gratuitous insult and promise only of the continuation of the tension. For the news from England had not been quite final. "But in spite of this, it seems to me that the book has a certain quality," the reader concluded, "the chief trouble seems to be that at least two thirds of the book is irrelevant to the main issue. The author has overreached himself. Though the author may gibe at this, my suggestion is that he rewrite it, even at the risk of its becoming even more like *Drunkard's Rigadoon,* by which it is obviously influenced, and that until we receive his reply we hold the manuscript."

Sigbjørn had written back at length, anatomizing the book chapter by chapter, and making it clear that since it had been rewritten ten times already, it must stand or fall as it was. And oh God, that New Year's Eve, then the rockets, the noise, the terrible train whistles blasting, the drunken horror, and yet, after all, final love! And the even worse horror of New Year's Day. But why should anyone *want* to sober up in Mexico. If you were not drunk on tequila or mescal you would be on sun or the cobalt sky or moonlight or volcanoes unless you wanted to sleep all the time! Or go mad . . . And then, right on top of the other, had come the usual bad news from America, this time something new in the language of rejection. The American editor, or reader, even pretended to have read it twice (which he might well have done without knowing it, Sigbjørn had said, since the same firm had rejected it before in a previous version as far back as 1940). "I do not give this opinion merely because I think it wouldn't sell. . . . My sense of its second-handedness deepened on rereading. . . ." Second-handedness! Jesus, Sigbjørn thought again in anguish. But no, by second-handedness he meant something else. "Judging by our files, it seems, after the publication of *Drunkard's Rigadoon,* every young writer who ever had a hangover seems to think that an account of a drink is the short road to success." Sigbjørn could only send a mute appeal to Jason Wilkes himself: "Was that what you call a short road?" And on the other hand, he might have asked, what was there so good about Sigbjørn's bloody book in that case that the editor had to read it twice? A sense of poignance, of loss, of absolute failure now came over Sigbjørn again. He began to feel maudlin. And how disappointed Primrose had been, how brave, and selfless. Eddie was now moving about in the kitchen.

"A signed copy"—Eddie was saying in a loud tone from the kitchen, "of the first edition."

"There isn't going to be any edition at all, I shouldn't think, unless of an anthology entitled *King Alcohol,* to be composed entirely of novels published in the last two days," Sigbjørn called back. All he needed now was Eddie to ask him, and sure enough, Eddie was asking him the question:

"It's a bit on the style of this, what do you call it, *Drunkard's Rigadoon?*"

"Et tu Brute. . . . Don't tell me you've heard of that this far south."

"Sort of, what do you call it, a plagiarism." Eddie was persistent as a hornet.

"Ha ha . . . No, again, ha ha, just another, what you would call a coincidence."

"Eh."

"Nothing."

"Drink," Eddie now said, emerging from the kitchen. Being a restaurateur Eddie was very neat, and seemed to have been washing up. "Well, what about it?" Eddie sat down.

"Nothing. Everything that's been said about it's all wrong. Including any conclusions I may have once come to. If I were to write my book again, I'd argue that in the main it's a constructive thing. I never can trust teetotalers. And people who can't drink usually make a tyranny of something else, make people who can, unhappy at all events. Though I must say I'm having a bit of a struggle myself. Or like to pretend that I am."

By the way," said Eddie, "I have a new Janey." And, producing it from his holster, he laid a new shining pistol on the parapet. "I can introduce you to a man . . . I could tell you a story —Say! I could write a book. I'll tell you now. He shot twenty books—twenty men in as many seconds, bang! bang! bang! like that. Chief of Police of Yautepec"—and had Sigbjørn been talking about Yautepec too, when he thought he'd been merely thinking—". . . And, do you know what? A perfect gentleman . . . Once I shot fifty men—and if ever Uncle Sam wants me again . . . Still, that's another story. You know, Sigbjørn, if I can call you Sigbjørn. Can I call you Sigbjørn?"

"Go right ahead."

"I hate a crook."

"So do I. But why don't you put that thing away. Now, what I was going to say was—"

"Say!" Eddie said (and at this moment he sounded precisely

like Stanford, was becoming more and more Stanford, was, indeed Stanford). "Say . . . That's what I want to speak to you about, in fact that's what I wanted to speak to you about when I took the liberty—no, no, it was liberty, to knock on your door, Sigbjørn. May I call you Sigbjørn?"

"My name is Thorbeard," Sigbjørn said in a deep voice.

"Say!" interrupted Eddie. "I'm going to Acapulco tomorrow. Why don't you two come to Acapulco with me and forget all about it."

"Wonderful idea," Sigbjørn said hesitantly, and as it were against his better judgment, came to his senses for a moment. "Wonderful—but—" He thought of Acapulco, the last time he'd been there—Stanford, of course, had been there; 1938 Stanford—when he was still wearing the white suit—what was it made of, not seersucker—that Fernando had sold him for five pesos in Cuicitlán ("My poor horse, she is biting, biting all the time"): Acapulco was his first port of entry (like Yvonne's) in 1936: it was, indeed, in Acapulco that he'd had his first mescal: he thought of mescal: then he thought of Taxco. If he went to Acapulco with Eddie, as they had gone to Taxco—and they would go through Taxco again willy-nilly; perhaps they could even redeem Taxco—there would doubtless be plenty of drinks in the morning, just the kind of drinks and the number he would want tomorrow but about which Primrose was going to be tough: on the other hand, no, he couldn't do it. He would, would he not, for was he not going to take Primrose to Oaxaca. Oaxaca! For what would Primrose remember of Taxco—in spite of being a member of the happiest couple Helen and Guido had ever seen—actually, of that time with Eddie, save how imperially drunk he, Sigbjørn, became: perhaps the two towers of the cathedral, first the sunset light on them, on the domes (watching from the delirium tremens café), the cobalt sky, the light fading, the stars!—Mars and Saturn between the towers, and perhaps Sirius and Canopus beyond—yes, and even though he had not seen them, perhaps the stars through the palm leaves, and the light of the city below from the terrace of the Victoria, but shown her by Eddie, not by him. Dancing the Raspa. "The happiest couple I've ever known," Guido had said. Yet Primrose had been—in a sense of course, always in a sense, brokenhearted. Sigbjørn thought of the clipper folder, with the photograph of the young man taking the photograph. This certainly had not been that kind of ideal Taxco. No, no, no, he wasn't going to disappoint her like that again. Besides, trips that they hadn't planned themselves rarely "worked out." They were happier alone.

"No, I'm afraid not, Eddie. You see, I'm thinking of taking Primrose to Oaxaca tomorrow," he said.

"Can't you go to Oaxaca another time? . . . I've got the car, you know. How are you thinking of going to Oaxaca?"

"By bus from here in Cuernavaca."

"You can't do it, you've got to go to Mexico City," said Eddie, "and either take the train or the bus from there. The train takes you all night—though I've never been to Oaxaca myself—but in either case you have to go through Puebla."

"I know all that." Sigbjørn smiled, reflecting that he had perhaps already seen a good deal more of Mexico than Eddie, himself a Mexican, who had not even bothered to go to Oaxaca while, born in Puebla, relatively nearby. "I've been by train before from Mexico City. But last night I was looking at a map and I figured you could go from here to Matamoros by second-class bus and connect there with the bus coming from Puebla."

"It's a dreadful road from here to Cuautla. And from Cuautla to Matamoros I don't think there's a road at all, to speak of. You'd be half dead anyhow by the time you got there in one of those overcrowded buses. No Mexican would think of doing it."

"Apparently they do or the buses wouldn't be overcrowded. Mexicans do or they wouldn't be sitting even on the roofs of the buses I see going to Matamoros," Sigbjørn said, "and anyhow it will be an adventure."

"Not for me!"

Sigbjørn now felt reasonably sober, and glad that he had not weakened about Oaxaca. "But I've got another reason for particularly wanting to go to Oaxaca. There's a character in my book I call Doctor Vigil—he is a real person, a very dear friend of mine I knew when I lived here in Mexico before, that is when I was in Oaxaca, for he's a Oaxaqueñan. While I was writing the book in Canada I wrote him several times but got no reply for some reason—his letters were always sent back."

"See who's here."

The white figure was that of Dr. Hippolyte himself, although he was not standing close by, but approaching over Eddie's lawn, a package under his arm, and as he approached Sigbjørn seemed to hear the sound of drums—indeed he did, though these were not voodoo ones. Dr. Hippolyte was a Haitian, had been the Haitian chargé d'affaires in Mexico at one time, but for some reason had not returned and still lived in Cuernavaca, a gigantic Negro, clad all in classical white, and with a black tie; an essence came with him, as it were, a murmur of trumpet trees and a vision of a tiny Negro up one saying five cents please, tin-roofed houses made out of lace among flamboyant trees, the five funerals going into the burning white cemetery, and the susurrant hush of white-clad women like gulls ceasingly climbing up to and coming down from Kensikoff: Sigbjørn had visited the country—he had half meant to take Primrose too—years before as a sailor: the tambours did not cease.

"Hullo . . . Hullo . . . " said the man who only five days before had saved Sigbjørn's life. "I brought your manuscript. . . . I'm sorry, I spilt a little tequila on it."

"Something like the person who returned *Ulysses* the day after it was lent him and remarked, 'Very good.' "

"I haven't volunteered an opinion yet. . . . Perhaps"—Dr. Hippolyte smiled—"I am not worthy. I too am an exile. I thought I hated the white man because he is the conqueror of the world and because he produces both superiority and inferiority complexes in the Negro. . . ." Dr. Hippolyte was tasting his rum with a professional air. "I thought I was a Negro. But now I discover they think I am a white man and it is a tragedy for me. You see, I also have tragedies, though I do my best not to make them. Perhaps that is because I haven't got the talent. . . . We have a revolution now, at this moment. A bloodless one. We shivaree the President from his white mausoleum simply by marching the school children round and round the square banging drums and giving him a sense of shame. Hence my demijohn."

"Was Vigil a real doctor?" asked Eddie.

"No, he wasn't. He often had to act as one."

"I too, of course," said Dr. Hippolyte. "I don't think I'd like to be your Doctor Vigil."

"I was going to say that you would have thought they would have forwarded your letters to his new address if he was known in Oaxaca," Eddie said.

"No, that's the reason I didn't worry. In real life, although he was trained as a chemist, he worked for the Banco Ejidal, and they send their men all over the state hundreds of miles away where there is no post office at all to deliver the money for the collective farms—which was his job, I once rode with him myself up into the hills—actually in fact he was two characters though I don't see that that can be of much interest to you. . . . He also acted in Eisenstein's *Thunder Over Mexico*."

"I borrowed a smoking from Eisenstein," said Hippolyte.

"Still, you would have thought the bank would have kept in touch with him."

"He was always on the point of resigning his job and I came to the conclusion he must have done just that. But I felt I'd have a good chance of tracing him if I went to Oaxaca again myself. And if we don't find him in Oaxaca, I know some friends of his up in the hills there who might have some idea where he is."

"It's asking for trouble—I won't use the word gringo—to go up into some of those places, especially with a woman."

"No Mexican would do it."

"Negroes do it. In fact there are many Negroes living in Oaxaca. Once I thought I was a Negro—"

"No." Eddie laughed. "No Mexican would do it. . . . But when Americans come here they seem to lose their heads anyway. I have to bail an American out of jail on an average of twice a week. For instance there was a young American fellow in the Universal Bar the other night and some farmer was borracho and got him into a trial of strength. One of these little policemen here arrested him for fighting and disturbing the peace. He wasn't fighting or disturbing the peace any more than I am. It was simply a put-up job to get some dollars out of him. There's no mystery about that part of my job—it comes straight from the Governor. They want the tourist trade and they don't want Americans to get into trouble. If it comes to that it's all a matter of dollars. Afterward this American offered me five hundred dollars. Yes, five hundred dollars not pesos. Of course I didn't take it."

"Well I'm not the sort of person that gets into trouble, at least not on account of drinking. The only trouble I ever got into in Mexico was for not having my papers with me. That was in Oaxaca but that was a very long time ago and I hope they've forgotten it. Anyhow everything was all right when my papers finally arrived from Mexico City." Sigbjørn realized that he really must be pretty tight if he was talking as lightly as this, could dismiss that dreadful incident as lightly as that. "Still I made my Consul get into enough trouble here for ten."

"Your Consul? What did you do to him?"

"My Consul in the book."

"What happened to him?"

"Someone shot him and then they threw him down a ravine."

"Bad luck always waits you in the barranca," Eddie said grimly. "How did he come to get in that spot?"

"He drank. Well, Hippolyte knows all about the Consul by now."

"Yes. I liked him very much. I was sorry to see him go. In fact it was my opinion that your character Yvonne should have gone over the ravine and the Consul and his half-brother lived happily ever afterward, the house and the mescal and everything to make them happy."

"He got into trouble. Mescal was his nemesis. . . . And he had the misfortune of course not to have you to help him." Sigbjørn laughed, taking a sip of his drink. "Of course, strictly speaking he was no longer a Consul. If it comes to that he was, almost, no longer a man. He had lost his wife: she divorced him, but on the day the story really opens, she had come back to him. His friends, Monsieur Laurelle up in that tower over there, and his half-brother—that is to say me, I might say the same of all the other characters too, in a sense—who happens to be staying with him, and of course Doctor Vigil—whose real real name, did I say, is Juan Fernando Martinez; he had an Indian name for me, by the way, being a Zapotecan, because I was a writer, the 'maker of tragedies,' he would always say—'Hullo, are you making more tragedies today?' was the way he liked to greet me, usually in a bar—all these people, including the Consul's wife, try to help him, in various ways, to stop drinking, to go away, to Canada, to cultivate new interests, to drink something else, to go, so to speak, to Acapulco. For instance, Doctor Vigil invites him to go to Guanajuato with him, by car, just as you've invited me to go to Acapulco, and so on."

"I think I am going to write a book," Eddie was saying.

"I wouldn't, if it does to you what it seems to do to our friend here," said Dr. Hippolyte.

"I wouldn't, if I were you." Sigbjørn slid the package back along the parapet.

"How did you come to write it in the first place?"asked Dr. Hippolyte.

"One day about nine years ago, it was the end of 1936, when I was staying at number fifty-five down there"—he nodded towards the Calle Humboldt—"I took a bus to go to Chapultepec. Not the big Chapultepec, the little one near here. There used to be a waterfall and so on, but it's gone. There were several people with me, a person extremely dear to me, whom we will call X, Señora X my first wife, I wasn't really married to her, but still that's another story, and two Americans, one of whom was dressed up in cowboy costume—which was the costume also of a character I had named Hugh: he'd come down here in a cattle truck on a bet from Texas, and they'd impounded his clothes at the border. We were going to a bullthrowing, this side of Chapultepec. The arena's still there, because I saw it on New Year's Eve when we were going to Yautepec. About halfway there we stopped beside an Indian who seemed to be dying by the roadside. We all wanted to help but were prevented from doing so, to cut a long story short"—Dr. Hippolyte laughed at this point—"because we were told it was against the law. All that happened was that in the end we left him where he was, and, meanwhile, a drunk on the bus had stolen his money out of his hat, which was lying beside him, on the road. He paid his fare with it, the stolen money, and we went on to the bullthrowing."

"Go on."

"That's all. The whole story grew out of that incident. I began it as a short story. It then occurred to me"—Sigbjørn laughed, though without a great deal of humor in his voice— "that nobody had written an adequate book upon drinking, upon which I was now, to say the least, a considerable authority, and so while the first short version of the book was getting turned down by publisher after publisher, I began to elaborate upon that theme of drunkenness, both in my life, and in the book too, if you understand me. There's far more to it of course than that, but out of this kind of thing came the character of the Consul, to forestall you, Hippolyte, you might say that I invested my vices in a figure of authority so as not to feel too bad about them myself."

Eddie yawned but more perhaps at the story, Sigbjørn felt, than because he wanted to go to bed, for he poured himself a large slug of Four Roses. On the other hand since it seemed Sigbjørn's destiny to cast his work before people who had not at bottom the slightest interest in it, he pursued doggedly.

"After having written the story about the Indian by the side of the road, and first got the inspiration to make the whole thing a larger novel, I wrote the end of this book"—he indicated the manuscript that was lying on the parapet—"first. I had him, the Consul, shot by a bunch of policemen in a pub. I placed this cantina above the barranca, and in a place that was something like Chapultepec—the one near here, not the place of the battle, that is. Later, after having gone to Oaxaca, for the last time, I changed the nature of the cantina all around again and made it like one in Oaxaca itself called the Farolito, and which used to open at four in the morning. I had been myself up to the Universal and fallen in conversation with a bunch of complete borrachos, who far from being annoyed that I copied down every word they said in a notebook seemed flattered by this. They were attempting to talk English. I myself, Spanish: and the resultant confusion was precisely what I wanted. It must be admitted that I was perfectamente borracho myself."

"But remember what I told you, Sigbjørn. In Voodoo, there is a great lesson. There is discipline. The dancers do not leave the blazing circle. If you like to call it neuroses that they get rid of then that is what they do. And even if the priest becomes possessed, the ceremony goes on. A bell is rung when it has reached a certain point beyond which it might become dangerous. You have to be your own priest and ring your own bell. Yes, I will tell you. You are possessed too. You are possessed by Sigbjørn Wilderness. But not by Baron Samedi nor yet by Papa Legba, the Minister of the Interior of Death. You are possessed, by Sigbjørn Wilderness. That is to say, Sigbjørn is possessed by Wilderness. That's all right too, though you have to make up your mind whom you prefer."

Though Sigbjørn felt that in this enchanting fellow he had made a friend for life, he nonetheless felt rather irritated by him, perhaps because he had made that possible.

"I had to protect you from yourself. A little matter of suicide is nothing in Haiti. My own brother shot himself right through the heart when he thought he had caught a disease. But he is quite all right now. And in fact he had no disease. Just like you."

"How do you mean, just like you?"

"Don't you remember, that's what you told me. You told me you went out and got it deliberately." Eddie went inside and could be heard moving about in the kitchen.

"Oh my Christ, did I say that?"

"It's true, of course, love can go no further," said Hippolyte.

Sigbjørn, as a writer, tried to describe Eddie. Starting with the head—well, he had a head-shaped head upon which he had scattered rather more than the normal amount of oil. He had a body-shaped body, of medium height, but since he never exposed even the smallest part of it to the sun—perhaps significant in itself—you could not tell precisely what kind of body. One suspected it, however contrary to what might have been expected, to be innocent of bullet wounds. Feet-shaped feet, enclothed in huaraches completed the picture, but if he ever wanted to write about him he would have to ask Primrose what he looked like. It betrayed a lack of normal curiosity. Yes, curiosity to Sigbjørn (—despite his inordinate vanity) was a form of sin. It was much the same, though, on a different scale, with the Quinta Dolores itself. He could say, "to the left was so and so" or "to the right." Or "toward the southwest," But such devices, when Sigbjørn encountered them in any of the few books he had read right through, only resulted in his turning the book upside down, in becoming confused. Anyhow, it would not be your north-northwest, not your east by east—why try? Primrose would know anyway, and again, if necessary, he would ask her.

"I notice a peculiar thing in you, Doctor, a Haitian, that you are not superstitious. With me you have to deal with someone at least ten times as superstitious as anyone you have ever met, even in Haiti."

"Oh, I have my little possessions. . . ." Dr. Hippolyte chuckled. "Once, in Port-au-Prince, I saw a headless woman dancing outside the Hotel Olaffson."

Sigbjørn thought that there was perhaps something in all this weirdly reminiscent of the scene between them and in his book between the Consul and Dr. Vigil.

"Perhaps you will go into the business of the supernatural a bit further."

"Ah, supernatural," said Hippolyte. "Unfortunately, while the frontiers of science are always pushing forward, are governed at a given time, science can only help the person whose experience is beyond it, by advising him to comfort himself with a lie, temporary and useful, that is a rationalization, until it has caught up."

"Of course, writing a book about it, I daresay, constitutes a very good attempt at a cure."

"But even the supernatural is governed by the rational, according to its dictates. For example, in conversation with you, I see you are haunted by coincidences, numbers, etcetera."

"Yes, even this is an eerie coincidence."

"How so?"

"I wrote a book about running into the past."

"Of course, as an intelligent man, you would agree all this number business is absurd. Actually one of the best cures is sympathy and what is known as a good example, such as the value on the part of someone who knows what it is to suffer. Hence those anonymous clubs and so forth. However, since most authors are constitutionally opposed to anonymity, they would seem to have a difficult problem. Though I venture to say that had you yourself been less constitutionally opposed to it, you would not suffer so much from *Drunkard's Rigadoon.* . . . I am interested in the part where your doctor says, 'More alcohol is perhaps best.' Did you know that was true?"

"I'll say I did."

"Intravenously speaking"—Hippolyte chuckled—"that is. They use it with rather a lot of success, it is called ethyltherapy, if I translate correctly. It is like equalizing the liquid contents of two vessels. . . . But what are you doing now? How do you go about writing such a book?"

"Part of the artist's despair," Sigbjørn said, half to himself, and walking restlessly now, "in the face of his material is perhaps occasioned by the patent fact that the universe itself—as the Rosicrucians also held—is in the process of creation. An organic work of art, having been conceived, must grow in the creator's mind, or proceed to perish. It was all I could do to finish *The Valley of the Shadow of Death.* . . . Thank you for refraining from saying, 'Me too.' In fact, of course, it is always doing both so that the author, while working, is like a man continually pushing his way through blinding smoke in an effort to rescue some precious objects from a burning building. How hopeless, how inexplicable the effort! For is not the building the work of art in question, long since perfect in the mind, and only rendered a vehicle of destruction by the effort to realize it, to transmute it upon paper?"

"Drink," Eddie said, again emerging from the kitchen.

But overwhelmed by the desire to talk, Sigbjørn shook his head.

"It would seem this building is a peculiar one, not susceptible to mundane laws, and bearing indeed in one respect some relation to the creature of Dante's *Inferno,* for while it continues to go on burning, as if in an external hellfire, so long as the author continues to exert his efforts, it continues just as fast as the walls are falling down, to be pushed up by him, as it were with one hand, while with the other he is trying to catch the treasures that are being disgorged by it upon his head. It is true too that the

fire as metaphor

artist must sleep, which is perhaps the main difference between him and God. Drinking, as Waldo Frank has pointed out, represents one of his futile efforts to bridge this gap."

"Did you ever try writing that as a story," interrupted Eddie. "Of course, I'm not an expert."

"No, I didn't. For the simple reason it wouldn't make a good story. . . . But to render this image even more ridiculous—for by now it has become ridiculous in the same way that anything set down on paper ceases from that moment progressively to be true—we must consider what happens each morning when the artist is confronted with his work again. Has it not changed in his absence? Of course it has. Even on paper something has happened to it. . . . Even if he were to throw out by now absolutely incomprehensible stuff about the burning building and look upon his work simply as an effort of a carpenter to realize a blueprint in his mind, every morning he wakes up and goes to look at his house, it is as if during the night invisible workmen had been monkeying with it, a stringer has been made away with in the night and mysteriously replaced by one of inferior quality, while the floor, so meticulously set by a spirit level the night before, now looks as if it had not even been adjudged by setting a dish of water on it, and cants like the deck of a steamer in a gale. It is for reasons analogous to this perhaps that short poems were invented, like perfectly measured frames thrown up in an instant of inspiration and, left to suggest the rest, in part manage to outwit the process."

"You don't mean to say you didn't know this?" said Dr. Hippolyte. Eddie was silent, the silence eloquent even though he was not listening; it was a silence that could be felt; Sigbjørn walked restlessly.

"There was sound pragmatic truth in the statement that poetry is the highest form of literature, and to a lesser degree, in Poe's dictum that a poem should be short. If God lends less material from the source of all creativity to the poet who writes a sonnet, say, of genius, there is also a minimum to be destroyed in its creation, and what truth it suggests is as indestructible as the chrysalis, or the salamander, while between the two-by-four's of the lines the necessary fire blows harmlessly. . . . I don't know what a two-by-four is. And hence the cunning within, the even greater cunning—dear to the true poet—of writing plays which, so long as they are being played are never quite the same from night to night, neither in themselves, nor in the transformations lent the characters by the actors. Of course, what I am saying is absolute nonsense. For that matter a reader is likewise an actor. . . . You see, everything I said has fallen down already. It seems to be my curse."

"Perhaps you try to get too much in," Hippolyte said. "That at least was my first impression of your book. That's what I feel about some of our Haitian painting too. A little more selectivity might be in order."

"Selectivity!" Sigbjørn burst out. "But my God, suppose that you were in my position, haunted at every moment that a fire or some other disaster would step in and destroy what you have already so laboriously created before you have the chance to get it into some reasonably permanent form—which is the case with my house too, though I'm not going into the matter of the house at the moment," he added, wandering around. "Jesus, where am I? But to continue the analogy, of the house, also just for the moment: would you not tend also to 'get too much in'—for one thing the house is too small as yet to contain what was saved from the other, little though that was—on the basis that it's better to get too much in than to get too little out, the more especially if, so to speak, just as I was living in the house that I was rebuilding before I'd finished it, you are at the same time *living* the book you are writing, or supposed to be writing"—Eddie was snoring—"and that's the whole point, I suppose, that I am living what I should be writing. Even now in this conversation. But how can I do both at once?" He paused and added humbly, "Would you mind telling me exactly what I'm driving at?"

"Driving yourself mad at the moment," Hippolyte said, "and me too. For example, you were not, I take it, haunted at every moment, as you say, while you were writing the book I've just read, at least when you were making the final draft, for the other day you spoke to me of the sense of security you had when you were writing it, and which was destroyed by the fire. Still it can only have been a relative sense of security at that particular time. However you make me want to read it again."

"I wouldn't if I were you. That's what one publisher did and he didn't like it any better. . . . He said his sense of its second-handedness deepened. Anyhow," he added, "you're not going to, not just now at any rate. I've a few additions I want to make."

"Don't tell me you don't remember what happened the last time you took a book out of the publisher's hands to rework it. Wouldn't it be a good idea to leave it alone now you've finished it? At least you don't have to bother about its getting lost if you've got copies both in America and England and one here."

"No, these are not important additions. . . . Just one or two things that occurred to me just now. . . . That sign, for instance, and something else. . . . Besides, I'm going to Oaxaca tomorrow, and I may be able to verify the words on the sign, if it's still there."

"And by the way, to answer your former question about doing both things at once," Dr. Hippolyte was saying, "Is that such a unique position? Aren't we all more or less in the same position, haunted at every moment, in one way or another, that a fire will step in and destroy what we have so laboriously created? But continuing, with faith, to go on building just the same."

"No, it isn't. It's too obvious," Sigbjørn said. "It isn't what I said, either."

"Even so. What about the new work?" Dr. Hippolyte went on, counting on his brown fingers. "It seems to me you have to take things, one, two, three, four. In order. Are you going to do some more work?"

"I don't suppose so. Because this would seem to be it."

"What would you call it?"

"*Dark As the Grave Wherein My Friend Is Laid.*"

"Again you are being greedy. Why not just *My Friend Is Laid.*"?

They laughed and Dr. Hippolyte indicated the demijohn, but Sigbjørn shook his head: a dirty story came into his mind but he refrained from telling it—that too would lead to another ¹
Eddie woke up and offered him some Four Roses,

refused this too, all these, the temptation perhaps seeming easier
to resist for his having previously resisted the temptation to say
Yes to the invitation to come to Acapulco.

Sigbjørn made his way back through the garden to the tower,
groped his way up the red clay steps being careful of the gate,
and somehow through Primrose's room without waking her, to
the room with the chevron-shaped windows, somehow up the
ladder to the roof, once the mirador of his book, and here in the
moonlight he looked out over Cuernavaca. He had a bottle up
here, but he didn't drink from it; he felt just pleasantly tight,
conscious of a great sense of relief in having got all this off his
chest, thinking upon the exposition and the significance of the
tower from which he could still dimly see the form of Hippolyte
talking to Eddie. Were they talking about him? He couldn't hear
because of the noise from the posada. He looked north, south,
east, west, even to the pyramid Teopanzolco. He thought of
Christmas, New Year's Eve again, and what had been the New
Year—the rockets bursting in the sky while he had quoted Bergson—and even of the Easter they had planned to spend here, all
the festivals of hope. Then his fear, his sense of persecution suddenly came back in full force, and as if in response to this he
found that he was looking straight toward the light on the skele-
tonic prison watchtower, but this prison was an enlightened one,
Pedro, while the prison in Oaxaca, and that Christmas morning—Perhaps soon he would see Fernando again, but this
thought made him thirsty and he wanted to drink Fernando's
health. He allowed himself one small drink and then felt no fear
—for when I am weak then am I strong, at least I am not hiding
up here, am I, God, you can see me up here? Ah, if only he could
believe in his work—north, south, east, and west, he looked back
over the rolling barren hills and tragic clefts, and broken roads,
and cactus plains, and false volcanoes of his own life, and saw
little light—since the moon was shining—save that afforded by
madness: yet this was a fertile valley. Was he really looking over
toward Oaxaca, were those dark plains Oaxaca?—Oaxaca, where
was really Parián—and terror struck him again—his image for
death, though in his book, seen from the tower (and he had
never had the feeling so strongly that he was standing *within* his

book) in daytime it had appeared quite near to Hugh, through his binoculars. The jingle-jangle-pingle-pangle-bangle of the bells for matins came furiously from the cathedral—it was the madrugada, the hour before the dawn, the last hours of the condemned. How many now were waiting for death?

VIII

SIGBJØRN STOOD BY
Primrose as she slept. How beautiful she was, and peaceful, as if
wrapped in a dream of wild flowers in spring. The moon looked
in on her. She had wide, frank, long-lashed eyes that changed
color, like a tiger cub's; she was a vivid and exciting person. A
girl like a flame. Despair had at one time carved care on her face,
but during the last years the signs had almost vanished. Sigbjørn
had perhaps done her some good. Sometimes he thought she
could make these signs come or go, at will. They were never
there when she was "alive," and Primrose was uniquely
"alive." She had the wonder of a young girl—her face could
be chaotic with frowns.

He smiled as he recalled Primrose's Christmas Eve: there had
been Primrose's heroic struggle to get the charcoal stove to
work, fanning it, now the lights had gone out: fuse: and after
she returned—for Sigbjørn would not go with her for the fuse;
his eyes seemed fixed on that letter box—Sigbjørn following her
in his mind as she described it, walking up through the extraordinary sunset to get the fuse: pan, tortillas, and wishing everyone, how beautifully like her, Feliz Navidad—such a sense of
excitement, love and joy, people carrying firecrackers, throngs in
the zócalo, the volcanoes superb, the people in the panadería
pan dulce, and the tacos woman outside El Vacilon, the pulquería

161

where the guitars were going like mad, all so happy, it seemed to her, it would seem to her, of course. And after dinner the fireworks going off all over town like the Fourth of July and the church bells, ringing, clanging, clapping, booming. Sigbjørn had no reply yet from Bartleby, Dismas and Bull, and they watched the letter box, agonizing for him. They ate, as they had done their first night at El Petate, chorizos and frijoles, very good: and the noises all night, the explosions, music from dozens of loudspeakers, laughter, shouts, noises getting worse.

Even now she was trying to make the tower a *home;* always the difficulties with the charcoal stove, the kitchen drain overflowed, there was the difficulty of obtaining carbon, and then the greater difficulty of obtaining D.D.T., or whatever it was, and it was she, Sigbjørn thought, she the stranger, who gladly or nobly or both attended to all these things. Perhaps there were many husbands who could attend to a charcoal stove, as she said, and it was true that helping successfully with a charcoal stove did not necessarily compensate for a larger spiritual neglect. Nor was Sigbjørn slow to admit his failings, but his admission of them, it seemed too often, was a form of technique too, as if, since he never improved, his admission—this frank bringing of his failings clearly into the open—of these failings actually was an equivalent of the help itself: and the admission once made, one needed to do nothing further about the matter. And these things began to add up. It was far more moment to him, for instance, than the D.D.T. or the carbon, that he had discovered that it was possible to buy bulk habanero for one sixty a liter actually in the market, whereas it was one seventy-five at the liquor store, the Casa de la Vega. And in spite of this, it was she who even got the liquor, just as she had done in Canada.

Sigbjørn had found it more and more difficult to move at all. He did not want to; in fact he never did unless he could not help it. On the other hand, he never quite gave up. But things began to edge into a form of order. They managed to budget at about fifteen pesos a day, and this included someone who did the washing, one Concepción, which, now he thought about it, was a bit too much like Concepta, the Consul's servant, to make one altogether easy in one's mind.

Of the weird way they cut meat in the market, of how hard it was to get milk, even finally with the assistance of Eddie Kent, of the very existence now of the flowers in the garden, the tulipan hedge that screened Eddie's lawn from the swimming pool, for instance, the zapotes like chocolate jello but tasting of delicate flavors (so she said), of all these things, he would have known nothing, had she not told him.

It was true too that while Primrose did most of the work she delighted in it and also in her conversations with Señora Trigo, which she would report to Sigbjørn:

"The charcoal men do not come with the carbon on their mulas since they are not going to the hills now it is the Noche Buena. They are walking, walking all the time to church. But they have promised after the Año Nuevo they will come here with the carbon."

"But what shall we do in the meantime?"

"¿Quién sabe? You can buy dos kilos down the street. You take your bollito and are going, but is more expensive."

"The two little girls who stole our bag and basket and threw them down the barranca—por que?"

"They are full of devils, those girls, because they live all the time with servants and no one cares. Their papa, he is very rico, dos millónes, he gets for a factory where they are making the chewer—you know—the chewer?—and when he comes here he stays at the Bella Vista and the mother she goes there to sleep with him."

Primrose asked where she was the rest of the time.

"¿Quién sabe? But she is not here, and these girls, they are full of devils."

The woman who once had had the tower house had a boy of twelve and an infant one year—such a beautiful strong boy!— "otherwise he is dying, for he is sitting in the ice water, you know, all one morning and crying." Señora Trigo had gone to find out if the child was all right while the mother was in Mexico City, and the servant was getting breakfast while the baby was on the floor and icebox has overflowed. "Why is he here?" "He sleeps here, Señora. On the floor—the Señora does not want him in her room" (something like Sigbjørn, one might point out).

"When the Señora have come I think she is such a nice lady-woman because she is so pretty and young and talking so nice and these two beautiful boys. But then Mexican men are coming —ah, very handsome! But not, you understand, of good family. They are policemen and taxi drivers! Who knows what they will do? And in the night they are drinking and fighting and I think someone will be murdered. So now she goes with her friend-boy to Mexico City and I am glad and I say do not come back!"

And even when she told him these things, his interest was a mere pretense, and he would find his eyes on the mailbox—still no mail: why? he would say. And had the remarkable child gardener remarkable eyes? Was he really remarkable? Did he sweep the jacaranda blossoms from the pool every morning? Had the drain, right now, at this moment overflowed again before his eyes. He supposed so, since she said so. Otherwise he would scarcely have known. And anyhow, it was not he who would do anything about it.

Did Primrose, on the way to market, go up the steps of the new terrace outside Cortez Palace for the view of Popo and Ixta, and find them always there, always different? He was glad she did, but to him they were what they were, just volcanoes, dead and extinct. Luxury, a kerosene stove, the kindly loan from Señora Trigo! Disaster, but we can't buy any kerosene! It was all the same to him. With dull eyes he watched the cats, dogs, turkeys wandering around the garden without molesting each other. Well, so they didn't molest each other. Anyhow they'd mostly wind up in the barranca in the end. Everything went into the barranca. Two garbage trucks, one called Cruel es mi Destino, and the other Mi Amigo, called for the garbage from time to time, but only to throw that garbage down that same barranca and since they could do that themselves more easily, why bother with the garbage truck?

Even as the garbage would, Sigbjørn found himself sinking more and more into fear, into a barranca, his own, a barranca of fear of he knew not what! Ah, the strangeness of Mexico, and this fear that possesses one like a paralysis—who spoke of the neuroses of travelers, how seasoned travelers hated traveling, their only unity of place in perpetual escape. . . . The blaring darkness of the chilly nights . . .

The jukeboxes—he could hear them now—the terrible terrible noise of jukeboxes and radios turned on full blast, a maddening murmuring horror, only the pulquerías with their guitar music have truly Mexican flavor, but no es elegante, definitely, for foreigners.

With a certain kind of acceptance of his damnation, and yet an absolute determination not to let Primrose know he accepted anything of the sort, when he did make the agonizing effort, walking agonizingly also on his feet, and even the greater effort of humbly accepting that relatively speaking it was not worthy of the shame of effort at all, when he did go with her to the market, how delighted it made her! To see, through a gap in the walls of a steep cobbled street, a little adobe house, below street level, a cat in the window, a chicken pecking in the yard, the washing strung out to dry across a neighboring roof, and above and beyond, Popo and Ixta; how delighted it made her feel, at least, that she was sharing these simple things with him, that he was participating. How she delighted in the old women, or two old men reading letters with such an agonized expression, the baskets of sweetmeats, arranged on bright papers and then on green leaves, carried on the heads of two laughing young men running down the steep hill, or she would pause for minutes at a time before some vinelike small flame trumpets; how, unselfish as she was, she delighted in treading these walks Sigbjørn had brought alive for her or that she herself had made alive: all these things made her heart dance, to sing, as she put it, like the calandria, if that brilliant yellow-and-black bird was a calandria, in the tulipan. This was her life. This was her rebirth, her becoming the phoenix. And yet, while Primrose was being renewed again, Sigbjørn seemed to see nothing, to love nothing, to sway away from her into some anguish of the past, into some agony of self, chained by fear, wrapped in the tentacles of the past, like some gloomy Laocoön. . . .

The lone trips at twilight too, how Primrose loved them, the trips at twilight down the steep hill for charcoal, even standing in line for their three kilos, in that infernal scene in the dusk at the edge of the barranca, to be doled out a shopping bag full of charcoal dust by a man black as a coal trimmer: all this was life and adventure for her, and fresh, and what did this mean on the spiritual plane? And how much life and adventure, for him, therefore, was not he, Sigbjørn, missing? For more and more those little experiences that were the stuff of memory were being stored up by Primrose alone, so that when she looked back upon all this, it would be, sadly to say, "The times I used to go down to get the charcoal," or this, or that, not "The times that *we* went."

Every night, after he had his third habanero or so, Sigbjørn fully intended to take arms against this state of affairs with everything in his being: every morning he was further from doing it than ever, so that it had become, almost, that he was literally afraid to go out: he had even given up little but significant things that related him to marriage and holiday, getting the fresh rolls in the morning from the panadería, unable to create, even to dress, to buy anything for himself, afraid even to buy a bus ticket: his life was becoming nothing. A piece of sodden driftwood washed up on the beach had more life than he; for even the horrors that fastened upon him seemed inert, ghosts of old horrors. And why, why, why, he asked himself.

The night before the day—last day of the old year dawned of the fateful year of 1945—that would be New Year's Eve, he tried hard to stand right outside himself, outside themselves, to see the situation as objectively as if he were watching a film with themselves as the actors. Since nothing is sadder somehow than the spectacle of a long-awaited and well-deserved holiday that is being wantonly spoiled, the effect was poignant in the extreme: so great was one's sympathy for Primrose, and one's exasperation with Sigbjørn it was enough to make one groan aloud: for God's sake do something to make the poor girl happy, take her on a longer trip, take her home, do the washing, stop drinking, buy her a present, start working again, say even one kind word, stop thinking of yourself, but for God's sake do something truly unselfish for her. And so Sigbjørn determined in the way of good resolutions, but this time once and for all, to roll all his waverings, all his past, into a congeries, and jettison it then and there —much as he made the resolution tonight to take her to Oaxaca tomorrow—and so he would start off clean, even in anticipation of the New Year, by taking her to Yautepec on New Year's Eve.

Yautepec was a pretty little town to their south, half way between Cuernavaca and Cuautla. Sigbjørn's former memories of it were all horrible, of missed appointments, a beastly interminable fiesta, of an outrageous quarrel, of sleeping on the cold stone of an immense high room floor, of trying unsuccessfully to buy drinks with an obsidian ring of Ruth's that had later been stolen, of sitting up half the night with a borrowed copy of *The Golden Ass,* never to be returned, imagining he was reading it, but it was not necessarily disqualified on that account. In fact had it been, he would have had to disqualify half of Mexico of which he had any conscious knowledge. But he would, he thought, exorcise even these recollections. Partly he had already done this by using bits of them in a constructive manner, a road here, a cantina there, a building there, in *The Valley*—how he had made them sing!

What excitement in the bus at Cuernavaca before it started, the people with baskets, the babies, the bundles, even a cake of ice bound optimistically for Cuautla, that melted steadily, solemnly on the floor beside them, as they sat at the back and from whose steady deliquescence they had, from time to time, to withdraw their feet. Many women and children got in and settled, about six of them, with much shuffling and conversation, then suddenly all got up and got out again; vendors sold ice-cream sticks and sweet oranges; a basket of cakes, with butter and bread, was thrust through the window; everything seemed utterly arbitrary, but, as was the way nowadays with Mexican buses, they left promptly at eleven.

The bus, the Flecha, whose number was seven, Sigbjørn saw ("Come seven come eleven," he cried gaily), was ancient, or rather being no more than a mass of old scrap iron thrown together and placed on a powerful chassis, it was difficult to determine its age, the roof, so low their heads continually bumped against it, was actually falling in, pieces of the bus flew out after them, through the narrow streets, barely missing other trucks, actually scraping one. But all was well, Sigbjørn pointed out, next to the sign *No Destraija el Chófer.* They forged, jumped, out into the open country. Goats, pigs, cows, a little donkey, untethered, were standing alone by the road. Sigbjørn, his usual hangover still at bay with two surreptitious habaneros under his belt, happily knew that Primrose was thrilled and taking it all in, and even began to observe a few things himself, as it were with her, but on his own account. Not very interesting, or surprising to him, since he'd written about it all, but still, he had been seeing them, Sigbjørn thought, not just remembering them, which was something, and with fresh eyes. The trees thick with white flowers like morning glories, only lovelier, the cobalt convolvulus, yellow and orange flowers, the country was now hot-looking and covered with dust, white with dust, the thatched huts like the South Seas, low stone fences, golden corn spread out in a yard. Popo and Ixta appeared and disappeared— they were coming closer.

Sigbjørn glanced automatically from side to side. Perhaps, because this was in a sense "the road to Tomalín"—ah yes, for now there was where it went on, to Chapultepec, and there, on the right, was his arena, still there, after all these years, and it looked much as if preparations for a bullthrowing were going on too, perhaps on the morrow—he looked from side to side, as if half expecting to see an Indian lying beside it, with his horse near, on which would also be the number seven. But the ditches on either side were being excavated for a drain. Progress would not afford room for even an Indian to sleep. Morelos was keeping up with the times. But apart from this, it all was much the same as before.

They rounded the corner, away from Chapultepec, toward Yautepec. It was at this point, now or later, on the hill, that he had the brilliant idea for the first time (which he meant still, and, still now, at the moment, after the tequila and the Four Roses, more vigorously than ever, to put into execution tomorrow) of going all the way to Oaxaca by bus. This bus said *Matamoros* on its forehead, though doubtless it did not go farther than Cuautla, and they would have to change, and he would have to look at a map, just as he had done last night for the road to Yautepec. It should be possible. But meantime let this be, as it were, a little dress rehearsal of the larger trip. This, all over again, was the beginning of a new life, and so far everything

boded well. To a casual observer, these little trips on the side,
visits, these little excursions, were simply trips, visits, excursions.
But that morning, on this last day of the old year that had given
birth to a new age, they had not appeared to him in this light.
They were indeed like attempts, not only on their own part but
on the part of their marriage, if such a union could be thought
of as a sensate entity, since the catastrophe of the fire, to arise, to
be reborn. Going to Niagara had been like that. And returning
from Niagara to rebuild their house had been like that. Or it
was like the tide at Eridanus. The farther it came in, the farther
it went out. Each time was like a rebuilding, each time had a
fire. Nor was this symbolism, if one could call it such, confined
to trips or excursions. The act of finishing *The Valley of the
Shadow of Death,* after the fire, had been like that. And then
again, after Primrose's accident, of going on building their
house. And once more, after his illness, of coming to Mexico.
And then of coming to Cuernavaca, and so forth. All these little
flights had something in common: and their rhythm had been
something like this: starting with disaster, reaction, determination to transcend disaster, success, failure; it had become effort,
apparent success, something happens, failure. Every time, just as
with a person grappling with a vice, say, drinking (though drinking could not be called a vice, or could it? of course) the effort
became greater, and the subsequent failure worse. And each time
the effort became greater so was the temptation. It was like the
action of a pendulum, for each time the pendulum swung more
violently on the one side or the other. Just so—as between the
pit and the pendulum. It was not exact of course. All the more
reason then why he was determined to break this pattern, if
one could compare it to a pattern, to put them on an upward
spiral, if one could compare this to a spiral, flight spiral, pendulum pattern, it was no use Sigbjørn bothering to reflect upon
how muddled his thought was. The thing was to do it, to bring
it off.

He remembered how they came to the final gradient as they
left the valley and began to cut through the pass up, then down
into Yautepec. There had been another thing about that day
also that had occurred to Sigbjørn, which made it memorable. It

was a little anniversary of its own. One year ago, he had, in Niagara-on-the-Lake, in the Riverside Inn, Mr. Sherlock, proprietor, made his last correction upon Primrose's typescript of *The Valley of the Shadow of Death,* and sent it off to the publishers. It was true that the year before that, and the year before that, and the one before that, and so on as far back as 1936, and each time with the feeling, how many more years will I be doing this? he had been doing much the same. But this year there had been this difference. It had been sent off and it had not come back again.

Yautepec had come in sight, and with it the feeling, for it was quite necessary that some excuse be made for a drink and that soon, for the sake of the trip itself, that this anniversary might prove useful in a certain respect. He put away the thought on one side and it jumped back through the opposite window. He discarded it again, as it were to the left, but like a cigarette thrown to windward it came back almost in his face. He sought a way to lose it on the right, and a cantina looming up on his right that he thought he knew, and from behind whose bar a yellow bottle winked at him, confirmed only the more strongly that it was so.

They came to the square. The little town appeared undiscovered by tourists. There was a lovely bandstand with fountains underneath in the little zócalo bordered like Cuernavaca's with huge fresno trees. Only a loud jukebox proclaiming to the emptiness, and the omnipresent signs for *Bebe Coca-Cola, Bien Frio,* as if it were a town that had been evacuated by victorious armies, proclaimed that it had once been invaded. They climbed out of the bus and then, precisely, there was nowhere to go, unless of course it was that little cantina over there. However, he piloted Primrose loyally twice round the square. Squaring the circle, or was it circling the square?

"This is the square," he had said rather obviously, and "I see the old bandstand's still there—I remember—" But since he didn't like to remember he added, after a while: "There's a nice little cantina down there. . . . It's possible the proprietor's still there. . . . I thought perhaps, I know it's morning. But I thought we might break a rule today. For do you know what, it's the anniversary of the day I sent off *The Valley.*"

"I know that too, Sigbjørn. I was saving it as a surprise to remember. I was just about to suggest that we have a drink myself."

"Well, it wasn't an alcoholic drink I had in mind, Primrose," Sigbjørn went on feverishly, "at least, not exactly. It's a kind of concoction like Advocaat they have here, something very special." They had now reached the cantina and went inside. "You see, in that yellow bottle. It's called rumpope."

"Come off it, Sigbjørn. I know rumpope's an alcoholic drink."

"How do you know?"

"Don't you remember your own book?"

They only had one drink, however, or at most two or three—Sigbjørn had really forgotten but he had been honestly restraining himself. Besides, if not nonalcoholic, it was at least a digestif, so even if they hadn't had a meal yet, as on that particular morning he hadn't, one could feel it was just as if one had, which meant therefore (he forgot for a moment the other drinks) that it was not like drinking before breakfast.

To the side of Yautepec nearer the volcanoes, there was a large rocky hill covered by brush, and leading to this hill, Sigbjørn remembered, was a street, very steep and sunny and lined by adobe and thatched huts, and composed of enormous volcanic boulders. It was a cruel-looking hill and had once moved Sigbjørn to write, transposing it to the Calle Humboldt, which he had visualized the Consul at that moment climbing, and then falling down: "His life stretched before him like a hill of tossing stone that went on forever like a life of agony"—something of that nature, at all events the word agony was in it.

In spite of the agony, it was to this hill, without the rumpope he couldn't have done it of course, but it was to this curious hill he had trudged for their morning's fun. It was to this hill he had piloted Primrose, and this hill he proposed they should climb, right to the very top and in the heat of noonday, where they could see a cross, and from which there was doubtless an excellent view. It proved to be called the Calle De Mirador, and Sigbjørn was right. It was certainly not a street, no vehicle could possibly climb it, huge boulders, very steep and sunny, adobe thatched huts, cats, dogs, chickens, lizards, children. Mexico was a sestina of these words, if it came to that, just as Sigbjørn was becoming one of horror, drink. Then these fell away and there was a path mounting through steep rocks that were piping hot. It was absolutely deserted. Wary of snakes they climbed up, and in fact both they and the sun reached their meridian at the same time. You might have thought that their tempers would have been in the same position, having ascended this Pisgah; on the contrary, they had felt happy. The walk had done them good. And they had a sense of accomplishment. Here was the cross, dedicated to a general who had once captured the hill, but it seemed like a token of their new life, or as though they had captured the hill themselves; it seemed no one had been there since the cross was erected. Behind them, and far below, was the empty town; to the left the rocky treeless mountains, immediately in front the flat green fields and trees, a river, and the road winding away, and ahead Popocatepetl and Ixtaccihuatl, rising straight from the floor of the valley.

There was not a sound in the theater of the noonday, the stillness was absolute, the solitude complete, only up here, even up here, on top of the hill, penetrated the sound of the jukeboxes, indeed sounding loud, it was a harsh and ugly challenge to this solitude, and coming from the emptiness, almost ludicrous, and so loud, as they listened, it seemed to have kept the birds awake in the fresnos of the zócalo, from where their voices, borne on a sudden cat's-paw, sounded like doors swinging on rusty hinges. They laughed and then stopped. For beyond the volcanoes far, far beyond the horizon, impossibly far away, almost like the White Sea and Arabia, almost like a dream, beyond the farthest mountains, as might have appeared the Promised Land to the Children of Israel, or Ceylon at three bells to the seaman chipping rust, it had seemed to Sigbjørn, pointing, that there, dimly and for the first time, was a shadowy hint of Oaxaca.

They had come down to lunch in a little nameless restaurant in the shade of the square where they had a slight quarrel. Sigbjørn was thirsty after their climb and wanted a beer and thought it reasonable Primrose should want one too.

"You have one if you want one. I'll cheer."

"But won't you have one? Just now you were saying how hot and thirsty you were."

"Well, I'm not now. I'm cold. Anyhow, it's too much trouble: they have to send out for it."

But for some reason Sigbjørn took an antagonistic air. "Well, damn it, it's only a beer. You speak as though I were having a tequila or something." Moreover he did not want to drink alone, perhaps because he wanted two beers, not one: or even three.

"It doesn't matter what you have, drinking in the morning, it only leads to the same shambles in the end."

"Oh, you're off on that track now. But this isn't drinking in the morning. If you'd said that before when we had the rumpope I could have understood."

"Well, you had your rumpope and now you want to get tight before lunch."

"I didn't say anything about getting tight."

Lunch, which consisted of soup and huevos rancheros and was good, though beerless, went off mostly in silence, though Sigbjørn, who had been inwardly furious, and as though he'd been rehearsing this all the time, once burst out savagely with: "You only have to think how much more dreary and gruesome Jack Charleson's weekend on the farm in *Drunkard's Rigadoon* would have been to realize the wisdom of his choice." ~Chas Jackson~

"Oh Sigbjørn, must you? On New Year's Eve?"

"And on the anniversary of the day I finished I don't even know or care what the name of the bloody book is any longer."

This made them laugh and they made up and went out. But it was true, part of their trouble did lie in Sigbjørn's drinking in the morning. But what was wrong with that? Where would she have been now if he had not had a few drinks before breakfast today? It was a subtle pleasure—who knew better than he? Drinking before breakfast could be compared sometimes only to swimming before breakfast. And this had not even been that, but only in the morning, when thirsty, before lunch, as an appetizer. Drinking before breakfast indeed— A loathing of all people who did not drink before breakfast or in the morning came over him so strongly he stopped dead in the street when Primrose spoke.

"I don't want to be a bitch. And now I *am* thirsty. Let's go into your little cantina and have a beer."

"My contrary darling. But don't do it for my sake."

"No, you do it for mine."

"But I don't do it because I'm thirsty."

"Who's contrary now?"

When they could have had the other, comfortably, without any fuss and been wandering around that much sooner!

They came out into a mass of huge drifting white butterflies floating past over the bridge, like flowers of the wind, across a sparkling little stream. Good heavens, good heavens, how lovely! And in the face of such loveliness he asked himself, everywhere to be found in the world, and himself free to find it for them, and with Primrose, and having Primrose, why any need to drink? Having had his beer, or rather his habanero, because taking advantage of Primrose, at the last moment he changed his order, at the same time seeming to be absorbed in deep conversation with the barman, so that she could raise no objection publicly, and thank God it hadn't come to that yet! (while in fact the only word he understood of the barman's was the word, the rather singular word, "resulta") after this, were the butterflies any more lovely? Or seem so? Yes, they did. Indeed, they did. Without the magic habanero, he told himself as he walked, the progression would have sounded to a spiritual and omniscient listener somewhat as follows: butterflies fire: butterflies fear: butterflies liar: butterflies Primrose: butterflies ruined holiday: butterflies guilt: butterflies Erikson: butterflies Eridanus: butterflies auto camps of the better class: butterflies failure: butterflies anguish: butterflies no one will ever buy *The Valley of the Shadow of Death:* butterflies Erikson: butterflies Fernando: butterflies I am failing Primrose: butterflies plagiarism: butterflies will they find out?: butterflies after all: butterflies middle age: butterflies feet: butterflies where is that resolution I made last night: butterflies still kept, or is it: butterflies nonsense: butterflies middle age: butterflies disgrace: butterflies death: butterflies Erikson: to which might be added butterflies Communism: butterflies am I: butterflies people being tortured in China: butterflies atom bomb: and so on, round and round, even though he was walking in a straight line, just like poor old Samson grunting round the wheel in the Saint-Saëns opera. But as it was, hey presto, there were only butterflies. Or were there? For it was true that he was even now thinking like this, and had had the habanero, but now these thoughts seemed like thoughts of someone else, some gruesome mutterer who went by on the opposite side of the street, wagging his head into the shade. These thoughts then were so carried away, but others came in their stead. Still now at least he could consider them clearly, relatively without pain. Since the fire, often the world, as nature had appeared to Blake, had seemed to him curiously dead. It seemed the end; nothing whatsoever would lift his spirits. And Primrose had been in the same boat. She, however, did have the compensation of travel—of achieving a life's ambition, or what she thought was a life's ambition. And be Mexico never so dreary and dull, and Sigbjørn likewise, this thought of Mexico's foreignness would come to her rescue. It was like when he'd first been to sea, when he'd first seen Sokotra, after knowing nothing else but the desiccated miseries of an English public school, and lately the even worse ones, if possible, of a fo'c'sle: "It is worth it!" And so, he felt, Primrose could say come what may, It is worth it.

Now, watching her sleep, he reflected that she might have been driven too hard too and she no longer could say within herself, It is worth it. Actually it was the first time in their lives, during these last weeks, that alcohol had become a problem between them. During the greater part of their half decade together he hadn't drunk at all. Now suddenly he wondered if she had been afraid on her own account. She must have had a bit of a hangover, a quite large one in fact, but yet had been trying on her own hook—after the resolutions of that night—to do something about it. And he had not helped her. And it was this that had caused their nearly sordid little quarrel. It seemed inconceivable to him that they could have such quarrels. Yes, looked at objectively, clearly, how bloody sordid! Why make such a fuss about it, about a bottle of beer, which if truth be told he hadn't really wanted? It was not worth spoiling lunch about. Far less their day, how much less their lives. Now it seemed to him it wasn't even a worthy theme for a book. Well, it wasn't. As a social problem he cared less than a tinker's damn in hell for it. It killed more people than tuberculosis? Good, so many the less people! Employers lost more man hours through it than through industrial accidents and venereal disease. Splendid! Bugger their self-important selfish souls. And all the more leisure for their employees—and hard drinking to them! And what cock, the idea that only people who in the obvious sense couldn't handle their liquor were the problem drinkers. Problem arseholes. It had been a challenge to him, because it seemed something that had never been done before. *Drunkard's Rigadoon* had killed it; he would never have written it if he had believed anyone capable of doing the same thing, whatever he'd said at lunch. Even now, had it been only about drink, had not drink meant something else, been related to something valuable, knowing about *Drunkard's Rigadoon,* he would never have sent it off, he would have had the courage to admit failure. Now, the ground broken, there was going to be a lot of other books on the same dismal subject that was no less dismal for being symptomatic of the times. It was true that to him, without Eridanus, and without the sea, and without work, the world had become again nearly unbearable; but if it meant a choice between accepting the world being unbearable and Primrose, he would give it up. Cut it right out. He was convinced that this would do no good—it hadn't stopped the fire, had it?—but he was prepared to make the sacrifice, if he could be sure it was a sacrifice. It was a sacrifice. With the beer, he thought now, or rather the habanero, the butterflies had become more than butterflies, the stream more than a stream, just as with the rumpope, the hill had become more than a hill, and earlier thanks to his matutinal inspirational habanero, the bus drive more than a bus drive. And for that matter, of course, Sigbjørn more than Sigbjørn, and Primrose more than Primrose.

But "shambles" no. God knows he didn't want any "shambles," as Primrose called them. To tell the truth, he loathed getting drunk. And there were those "blanks." They were bad. So that after all, when they had walked over the bridge, hand in hand and happy again and began to follow the river, for the first time in his life Sigbjørn would have really been convinced that he'd missed anything in Mexico because he drank too much in those days. In the first place, he'd never known that this part of Yautepec even existed.

First there had been the glimpse into the patio, cool, shaded. The little river, narrow, deep, went on winding between stiff thick overhanging trees, making pools of shade like on the Cam, and they tramped along the bank. Ah, would they ever forget this walk along the little river? For a moment, if you don't look too closely, Primrose said, Mexico might be Michigan, where she had been born. Did not this beautifully hint that in spite of him Primrose was "getting something out of her trip," was, in a fashion, perhaps, this time, being reborn herself? It made his effort all the more worthwhile. Yes, she was thinking, Mexico might be Michigan, the green trees bending over the sparkling stream, the grass, the ducks, the sense of peace and sweetness—then you turn and there are the jagged precipitous hills, treeless and blasted, ahead, the little burro, gray with a white belly and little black hooves, walking demurely down the street: a dog chases it, and, unafraid, it turns aside and lopes off like an antelope. But ah, the river, free, sweet, never-to-be-forgotten little river!

It was late afternoon when they returned, walked through the hot dust, so hot it burned the feet through leather shoes, had tired out his feet, but he wore a smile, and was determined not to spoil anything by complaining, or even risking it again by suggesting they have a drink, though the heat and glare of the sun on the white walls was now more intolerably hot than noon. And in fact, seeing how happy Primrose was, he had begun to enjoy it all over again. Though the sleepy town was trying to wake up: the pigs and sows trotting down the street, the man carrying a bunch of tuberoses, children smoking marihuana in a doorway, the hideous blind beggar woman in the doorway of the restaurant, her filthy rags and bare swollen feet, the girl who gave her a roll, these men in their light clothes—often very clean—and white sombreros who sit all day in the square. Ah, if they could go on walking forever like this through the sunlight. Then El Cielo—a pulquería, orange walls, in the blazing sun, dark green trees against the cobalt sky, and a glimpse of dark forms drinking from pottery jugs and a garden beyond, the paper fringes overhead, the music—it was one of those pulquerías too, rare and delicious to Sigbjørn, as a rare stamp, that sold likewise tequila and mescal, just like the Farolito in this regard, and there was a glimpse, through the open door beyond, as in "The Last Supper," of the sky: ah, how he had wanted to join them, to drink their dreams with them, to understand, to plunge himself into this cool oblivious world. Who else but a Mexican would have thought of calling a tavern the Sky?

He had been paying the penalty too for the drinks he had before: he felt twice as hot, twice as weary, and twice as thirsty. But anyhow it was against the law for women to enter that particular pulquería. Knowing Primrose's passion for cool Mexican soft drinks, before they should have any altercation about the cantina in the door of which stood the proprietor, bowing to him, he procured—and be this remembered for him on the Judgment Day!—two fruit concoctions, refrescos, while they were waiting in the bus, that were served from a great glass jarros from which a girl was continually having to pick flies. . . . It choked him, but he gulped it down.

At sunset, tired, they had returned, so happy (these were Primrose's very words), in the bus more crowded than the other. The roof of this bus was even lower, and at the back there were no seats, simply a long bench. In order to give Primrose more room, Sigbjørn attempted to sit on the floor, but since as was the case with the other bus, the chassis and the body seemed to obey different laws of motion, they soon found themselves sitting on top of each other, Primrose somehow on Sigbjørn's lap, utterly unable to move, save at the sickening behest of the two battling, swaying, jellylike gymnastic personalities of the camión. In spite of this within the racket they managed to hold hands. The gradient down to Yautepec that morning had been very steep; climbing it in reverse direction, and with a much increased load, was full of difficulties. Every time they changed gears the bus stopped, tottered, seemed almost about to slip back, recovered itself, the powerful American engine taking hold, and then began to inch forward and upward, almost as slowly as a woman crawling, through the churchyard to make her prayer to the cross. (How a Soviet writer, a decade or so ago, when such things were more fashionable, would have delighted in this symbolism: the broken ramshackle bus, by which everyone was tortured, borne by the inflexible powerful American engine.) This thought made him attempt to raise himself and see if this bus also kept faith to the Saint of Dangerous and Desperate Causes: there he was—he sent a prayer to him for them both—next to a sign, surmounted by a pretty girl showing her knees, saying in this case, *Distraija el chófer!* Sigbjørn laughed loudly and gaily as a Mexican at this, but there was such a pandemonium he wasn't able to point it out to Primose, who for her part was taking it all as a great adventure.

Finally they had reached Cuernavaca and the Quinta Dolores and this time the little gnomed postbox contained a letter, a letter postmarked London, and because it had not been sent airmail, the kindly face of King George VI eyed him birdlike from a blue two-pence-halfpenny stamp. The letter had been forwarded from Eridanus, and could only be from— Unable to open it, he took it into the bathroom to regard it alone. What an end to the day if this were indeed a letter of acceptance. And there was, in fact, no accompanying manuscript. A good sign. Then he came back to the kitchen, poured himself a glass of habanero, and took it to the bathroom again: he drank half the habanero, returned to the kitchen, replenished it, finished the glass at a gulp, and opened the envelope. "Your book is regarded here as having potential importance and integrity." His heart leaped, he almost shouted out loud to Primose, who was as excited as he and waiting for the verdict in the bedroom, but—at this point, yet another letter fell out. It was the reader's report, and he seized upon it. "The author has overreached himself. This book will naturally call in mind the recently successful novel and film *Drunkard's Rigadoon. . . .*"

It was not an outright rejection, but it was in a sense worse. The book had possibilities, and although they would not give an outright no to it, on the other hand he was being invited to rewrite it. What! To rewrite it again? His mind traveled right back nine solid years of continual failure from New Year's Eve, 1945, to New Year's Eve, 1936, when he was here also, in Cuernavaca. Nine years, time to grow up, time to die, time to fight three world wars in, time for a child to have grown up and become a drunkard. And I wonder how many more New Year's Eves I'll be wrestling with this damn thing, he had observed

prophetically to a friend. But then it had been in a state, or
nearly a state—yes, he could see by the letter—in a state they
would have accepted it outright. For what they wanted to do, in
effect, was for him to undo all the work he had done since then
upon it, and put it back into its simplest, or at any rate its first
form. But, he thought, here was temptation indeed, to give in.

What was of far more importance than the acceptance or non-
acceptance of the book at this particular point, he was able to
think, thanks to the habanero as he took the letter to show Primrose, though it was pretty hard to see the truth of this on New
Year's Eve, especially when a triumph, and the day after all *had*
been a triumph, at this junction would have fitted in so beautifully with his line of thought and his "resolutions," was how he
took it; it was easy to see, if he was noble enough about it, how
an outright success just at this particular moment would have
been as dangerous as an outright failure. And here this was neither one thing or the other. What made it worse, and yet, yes,
better, at the same time, as he had pointed out to Primrose, was
that of course there was some truth in what the reader had said.
It was all something like this case of the Italian composer, Pietro
Rinaudi, as wonderfully described by the English writer Cecil
Grey in the book *Contingencies,* who, like the white termite ant
that when its habitation is disturbed builds a fantastic kind of
tower—(and here, so to speak, was the tower)—had taken to
building a fantastic tower of music; three oratorios, on the first
day one being performed, on the second the second, and on the
third the third, and on the fourth evening, all three being performed at once with different conductors, under the direction of
yet another conductor, the composer himself. Or the two operas,
an opera buffo and opera seria, to be performed at once. In this
case of course it was failure and nothing else that had made his
book more and more complicated and added all the different
levels of meaning: and all the "reader"—that is the publisher's
reader, he couldn't speak of any others as yet—the reader, because it went without saying that neither Bartleby nor Dismas
nor Bull had ever read a book right through—was quite properly asking for was that he should write the single, first oratorio,
his Potiphar so to speak: to cut down his score by three feet or
so, the original one being according to Grey, some five feet five.

"But you're not going to write it again?" Primrose had said.

"Why not, I'm not doing any other work. It'll give me something to do," he had said bravely, only he knew how.

"Over my dead body."

"Well, perhaps you're right. Just the same—"

"They're just plain fools. Oh, I could kill that reader for hurting you, Sigbjørn. . . . You said yourself that English talent has all run to literary criticism. And that they're jealous of anything really good that comes out. And you said something about the national ethos just at present, that while it's always deploring the fact that your national literature has become so feeble when anything threatens that seems to be just the answer to their prayers, they'll do their damndest to kill it."

"Did I? Well, perhaps I was right. Unless of course it happens to be American. . . . And then only if they felt that they have discovered it themselves. But—"

"And what about America? Are you going to rewrite it for America too?"

"If they want it that way—of course I'd forgotten—"

"Well, the Americans are more generous."

"You didn't say that when we got Mcguire's letter."

"I didn't get Mcguire's letter. Don't you remember you opened it and wouldn't let me read it for months," she said, "and besides 'Nosotros no somos americanos ricos,'" they said together, laughing. "'Nosotros somos canadianos *pobres.*'"

But it did no good. Cheer themselves up as they might there didn't seem much hope, only continuation of the tension. Their gloom and tension but part of the great gloom and tension, as if waiting for some disease to incubate. He had forgotten this too. And it was impossible to sleep, for the rockets and the noise, no, they couldn't get rid of the year 1945 rudely enough, they were blasting away an old age and letting in a worse one. And there was no one to talk to, nothing to do at night, unless it was to drink or sleep. No darkness has the same quality of hopelessness as the darkness in Mexico.

"Well, anyhow, all right, I'll write and tell them I won't change it. I'll explain what each chapter's about, since they don't seem to know."

"And I'll help."

to Cape

And so they got paper and pencil and tried to work out what was to be said. But how hopeless and dreary it seemed—all these explanations. And he sighed in despair. And Primrose, who really on the whole appeared to be taking it worse than he, said: "Come on now, Sigbjørn, do be sensible. Let's look at it as a *test*."

"Well, my Jesus, am I not looking at it as a test. I've had nine years of it—in fact nine years and two months. I'd forgotten the two months. But even two months can be a hell of a long time."

"Just think how free we are, we're the freest people on God's earth, and if we keep on squawking about each little thing that happens, a brick will really fall on our head and give us something to worry about. It's just like before the fire."

"What's like just before the fire?"

"I said then if we kept complaining we'd really get something to worry about."

"I dare say you're right, Primrose, but who was squawking, as you put it—not I."

"Well, let's have another snort and get on with the letter."

And then the train whistle started blasting away like the *Lusitania,* and it was "Happy New Year," instead of "Happy Anniversary." They embraced each other in the kitchen, but immediately afterward they were quarreling: seeing the rockets Sigbjørn tried to put a stop to their quarrel by quoting Bergson, but this only made matters worse.

Then came the worse horror of New Year's Day. For as if he had imposed on her that unconscious longing, outside El Cielo the day before, to enter into that world where no women could enter, he had persuaded her now to drink in the morning. And they had actually hidden, yes, hidden, drinking all morning in this house, Laruelle's tower, and then he had gone to the Casa de la Vega, the liquor store, and got two more bottles, and this time his hand was trembling violently even as he accepted his obsequio; it was beginning to get a bit serious: he didn't only feel that people were watching him, but as in the case of the Consul, that people were. Only now, when he had the responsibility and Primrose was even getting mild illusions (an imaginary baby turkey) was he able, by virtue of sobering themselves, to sober himself up; but as if anybody should want to be sobered up in Mexico again, and if he sobered up that would not prevent him from seeing double.

Sigbjørn sometimes felt that he drank much as a Russian peasant used to beat his wife. And Primrose—but he thought it tactful to change the subject at that point. Still after New Year's Day they drank a little less. For one thing what these two good people, artists themselves, lacked, Sigbjørn had advanced the argument one day, was precisely the solace of art.

It took them four days to straggle out of the New Year's bog. Meantime Sigbjørn went on trying to explain to his "English publishers" why they should not have been bored with his novel and why he did not propose to alter it and why it must stand or fall precisely as it was. He made an exhaustive analysis of each chapter. The waste of time often seemed to him appalling— looking now at the very desk where he had sat down day after day made him feel almost physically sick—he could have written the first draft of another short novel in the time it was taking him, and only the illusion that it gave him that he was beginning to write again *creatively*, that and the fact that it pleased Primrose, had kept him at it, if only for the practice, though what he imagined he was practicing was another matter. Poverty of the creative faculty—or was it inversion of the sensibility—could go no further. On the other hand he persuaded himself that upon the impact of this letter might depend the acceptance of his book in England. What made it worse, and wasted even more time, was that during each evening, during their drinking period, he would invariably forget what was supposed to be the purpose of the letter, and find himself engaged in tearing his book to pieces and even thoroughly agreeing with the reader. Imbecile! Confronted with this dichotomy the next morning, he would discover that a third of the previous day's work was wasted and have to do it again. Moreover the book, upon which he had once based so many hopes, began to appear in the light of an enemy and he even found himself wishing it had been burned together with *In Ballast to the White Sea*. In so far as he felt bound exclusively to concentrate on the letter, to that extent, it was depriving him of the far more important business of "concentrating" upon Primrose's and their holiday. Yet, since time was of the essence (he saw nothing ironical about this) he felt it unwise, perhaps a fatal mistake, to leave it unfinished, for instance, and go to Oaxaca. And anyway Primrose, for his sake, would not have gone. Yes, the book was spoiling that too.

One evening they stood high on the tower and watched the sunset. Swiftly the color and light was changing on Ixtaccihuatl and Popocatepetl: white to gold to rose, with shadows deepening from blue to violet. The cathedral tower was outlined against pure pale turquoise and gold clouds. Now the light was fading from the volcanoes, and like a huge star, the light came on in the prison watchtower. Long pearl-colored clouds streamed across Popo. The little black cat on the roof below awoke, stretched her front, then her hind paws, strutted off for her night's work. Mauve appeared in the east, blue, delicate rose, gray, pearl in the west, vermilion, and the sky still flaming: God how she loved it, all these colors that he scarcely saw and she recited one by one, as if she had never seen a sunset before. The street below was already dusky. A man with a white shirt on a burro went down the Calle Humboldt, the Calle Nicaragua. And then two children carrying a bucket of carbon. A drunk staggered out of El Vacilon. And now a woman came walking heavily, tiredly, leading a tiny girl by the hand, down the Street of the Land of Fire. Calle Frey de las Casas. Which was real? And now the wind was ruffling the trees and the serape on the balustrade; Popo and Ixta were fading, fading. Even Cortez Palace, where a few late stragglers were looking at the murals, took on a somber dignity lacking in daylight. A woman, far below, was walking across the roof of the tintorería across the street to take in the washing. A truck lurched down the hill: Canada Dry, and then another one: Cruel es mi destino. The last light from a now colorless sky picked out the eternal puddles in the street and now the first bats were flittering across it, over the low brick chimneys and corrugated water tanks on every roof. A two-tone motor horn tooted, brayed. A bell clanged deeply twice for vespers, when the priest should be hiding for his life. The man who sold Primrose frijoles and rice now stood, as was his custom, halfway up the Street of the Land of Fire, while behind him an orange light fell across the steps and caught the skirt of a woman leaving his little store. And so the sun went down. But Sigbjørn, he had come up, hadn't he? Wasn't it like a promotion to be here, standing on this tower, living in this tower? Was it not like an ascension of the soul, after the ordeal of fire, to a realization of its true purpose? But who was this other Wilderness standing beside them? A sense of fear of him, utterly ruthless was this Wilderness. It was this Wilderness that had wanted the tower, not he. And what for? And for what purpose? Who knew? But anyhow, since it seemed that there was some purpose. And anyhow, it was an occasion for celebration.

So the sun went down: and the horrors of the night came closer. And while Primrose wrestled with the difficulties of the charcoal stove he went on with his analysis in the tower of what Chapter VII meant, concerning the tower, the tower built against the coming of the second flood, knowing perfectly well it would have to be rewritten the next morning, and that what it meant was all but incommunicable, for what it meant was *this*. Talk about the projection of the unconscious upon reality! And to his great detriment he did talk about it, and to the London publisher, thus wasting even more time. But he went on working and drinking. Even after Primrose went to bed he was still working. And at three o'clock in the morning he was still drinking.

Yet he didn't give up. On the next day, Eddie had invited them both to drive in the afternoon to Taxco by car with him, staying overnight and returning the next day, and this not proving a success at least from Primrose's standpoint, last Thursday, which would be the tenth, he had taken her to Zampoala, just as he thought he would that first time they had passed Tres Cumbres in the bus. Actually this was the first trip they had made north, back in the direction of Mexico City, by extension, of Canada. All their other trips were still south, still *toward* their destination, whether Oaxaca or Acapulco. And taking her had been almost in line with a half decision on his part to give up, actually to return to Canada very soon and it was curious how this little trip had seemed to illustrate how dangerous or even impossible this turning back was, until at least whatever strange discords had been set playing by the original error, inherent in his return to Mexico at all, had been somehow resolved. Or possibly it was just too late. Had they turned right round at Mexico City and gone home by the next plane perhaps no serious error would have been committed and it would have been different. But come what might there was no return yet, and this is what this little day seemed to have to tell them. The day had indeed started off dreadfully, everything had gone wrong, while they had remained geographically in this line of return, of going back; he had hopelessly misjudged the distance to Zampoala to which it turned out there was no bus from Tres Cumbres, and in fact they never even saw the lake, let alone reached it; they had run into a high wind, almost a blizzard, glass had cut their feet, they had both lost their tempers: but when they actually began to find their way southward again, walking by an old disused Aztec road, and miraculously this dispelled one's yesterdays, home-ward—for this was now homeward—to Cuernavaca, everything had gone into reverse, had seemed to go right, and had come right. It had been one of the happiest times they had had·in their lives, something to look back on with joy forever, and he was going to need the memory of it tomorrow morning if he began to waver about Oaxaca.

Sigbjørn looked over toward the postbox again. Of course, the old pattern had finally repeated itself once more: of course, it would, it had to, since it had not been broken. This time there had been bad news from America. Only with this difference: this time he was on his guard; he had almost been prepared for it. And he was not going to let it spoil that day. So he had not said a word to Primrose about it, even forced himself, so he thought, to forget it.

It was unfortunate, though, that Sigbjørn had gone out and bought another bottle, stopping at the Cerveza Barril for a beer, and then, coming home, there was the terrible hysterical scene with Primrose over the incident, and that night, he remem-bered, he had become inordinately drunk, drunk in a way that he hated, and which used to be extremely rare with him, so that there were blanks in his memory, and there were blanks still. All he remembered was waking on the floor, with an empty bottle of mescal in his hand. Primrose was asleep in the room she was sleeping in now and it had immediately occurred to Sigbjørn though he had been drunk he had not, for him, drunk very much, that his drunkenness must have been occasioned by fatigue. At all events had he been drunk, or even half drunk, on waking he would have had a large snort and gone to bed. Remorse, at least for the time, would have been subsumed and postponed. And then playing his guitar—all out of tune—the sum of all guilts he had ever experienced. Trying to pray, the heart beating so wildly—what if it stopped?—had already stopped? The sense of pathos was almost obscene. He tried to pray but could only utter obscenities. "Well, who can help?" "God will help you if you ask him." "But that's what I mean," Sigbjørn said, tears running down his cheeks. "You didn't say that. Fernando Martinez did." "I have my tragedies too." "Well, we all do." How can you struggle with death, he asked himself, when surely death itself is a weakness and cowardice that has you in its grip? And the horrible sense of involving Primrose in this. And the sense of being, yes, even now, watched. But the weakness and unreality were the worst. And then the coincidences began to weigh upon him again, the fatal declension of work. The money too, that was being willfully cast down the drain, it was as if he were gulping his whole life down. The fiasco of Taxco, and now to have spoiled this day. Well, at which rate it was better to spoil eternity. So that instead of taking a drink he had taken a razor blade and savagely cut a vein in his wrist. In doing this, however, he knocked over his guitar and woke up Primrose who came running and bound up the wound and rushed out to get a doctor, but fortunately met Hippolyte, coming back from the Red Cross Ball, who while he didn't live there, parked his car outside. Primrose thought it was an accident and afterward Sigbjørn thought that he had not been wholly serious in what he did. He had, and he hadn't. At first accidentally—he was using the razor blade to cut one of the strings of his guitar—almost experimentally, as it were, he had cut his wrist and watched it with some fascination, not very deep, and he had probably no intention of going farther—yet how could one be sure? For one thing, at that very final moment when he had thought: "What did you think then?" "This is where I come to an end, this is the point of the whole thing," he had had two simultaneous thoughts: one of Primrose, "This is a cowardly wrong," the other that, if it came off, even his death would be, as it were, derivative. While he had not seen the film of *Drunkard's Rigadoon,* he had read that there too, the protagonist had been on the point of suicide. Hippolyte had given him phenobarbital ("So stop going on about *Drunkard's Rigadoon,* my dear fellow. It's written and I don't see how you can very well unwrite it, even with the aid of—") and the next morning, ochas. And all Friday he had stayed in bed. In fact, Hippolyte had sent a nurse to sit up with him. During the weekend somehow he had gone on with the letter; today it was finished, and now it was off. The letter was finished and he was going to Oaxaca tomorrow.

He sat beside Primrose, watching her beauty and trying not to wake her, but he did, and it was as if she was guarding him, for "Where's Sigbjørn?" were her first words.

"Here. Quite safe, sweetheart."

"Is the little boat all right?"

"We're in Cuernavaca, darling, not in Eridanus."

"Did you really say we were going to Oaxaca tomorrow?" she murmured sleepily. "To find Fernando. . . . But do you know," she was still speaking with her eyes shut, as if in a trance, "I dreamt you said, 'Never mind, darling, if this trip doesn't work out, I'll take you all over Sweden flying on the back of a goose.'"

"Oh, I will, I will, but it will work out, you'll see."

"Sigbjørn?"

"Yes?"

"Tell me the story of the shearwater."

"The one they took to Rome and that found its way home by itself from Rome to Denmark."

"But oh, let me get some rest. I'm so tired."

"I can't very well do both."

"It's all right, I just wanted to think about it, that's all."

"You haven't had enough sleep," Sigbjørn said softly. "I'm so sorry I woke you."

"It makes no never mind." She smiled tenderly and sweetly. And she was asleep. No bird so wild but has its quiet nest.

My God, he didn't deserve her. Sigbjørn sat there in dead silence a little while, holding her hand, scarcely daring to breathe. He would sit a little longer to make sure she was asleep, then go. It must have been the way she spoke, he thought, that brought that time, when everyone had thought she was dying in the Vancouver hospital, when he'd been summoned that night, and now he watched over her, in this room with the strange stained glass windows, remembering that time when he kept his vigil, on that very first day when she had run the nail through her foot when they had started to get lumber from the old mill for the new house. How thankful he was to have her, that they had each other still! But then he had sat, half dead with anxiety, but also with remorse: he had not been able to get a doctor, or had not got one soon enough, and if she died, his last memory would be of a quarrel. The feeling of this other time was so vivid that it was again as if death were in the room.

Death with its delirium, its madness, its apparent finality: yet how idiotic to be afraid of it, to suppose that it ended there, to suppose that it was even death. What was meant by death? Quite dispassionately he wondered, sitting there, if he had not died, died in fact, some time ago , he couldn't exactly say when, and that this was it. It seemed even reasonable to him: here he stood, in the tower of his own creation, surrounded by these ghosts of the past, of his life—it was a dream—and about to set off to meet one of his characters. Surely this was more what was meant by death. Death in life, for you could be dead, and yet have existence on earth too, at least according to Dante. Such was death, such was life, he thought, sitting quite still by the bed. But Primrose, that was another matter! She was not dead; she had been spared, and he had been allowed to know the joy of her being spared.

Suddenly, it occurred to him that he could have the best of both worlds at once—Primrose was alive, and he would be her guardian angel. As for his thoughts at the moment he would put them off on the Consul; he must strive to give a center to their lives, realizing the impossibility of amending his life by himself.

The posada was still going on; the moon still shining; it seemed nearer, though this was absurd. He remembered—*The flickering candle flames!*—in the little church opposite the Cinema Morelos, next to the Borda Gardens. They had stopped there, that afternoon on the day they had gone to the Borda Gardens. This church was exceptionally tawdry and compared ill with the other churches in which clean starched lace-edged altar cloths and vases of paper flowers were somehow sincere—and if you liked—pathetic, certainly moving; but this whole church was tawdry, with odd murals painted above the usual altars along the sidewalls. One showed at bottom the round world with Mexico in the foreground and above an enormous heart with open wound and wreath of thorns showering down a rain of blood onto the world. The top of the heart was like an open jarro out of which flames were spouting. The whole was surrounded by bodiless angels. On the opposite wall was another heart of equal size; rays of yellow light, pointed and rigid like lances shot out all round it; it was pierced by a sword, encircled by a wreath of gardenias, and round the top was a garland of pink-and-blue forget-me-nots. A third mural showed at the top a lamb, lying peacefully and demurely in an open blue box. From its side, however, from a great gash, came a surge of blood, flowing through a kind of xylophone into an enormous chalice, which overflowed on the scene below, which presumably was hell, for there were flames, but solid, like twisted maguey, through which unhappy people peered out. From beneath the chalice, angels were trying to pull up one of these unfortunates.

There were the usual saints in glass-enclosed niches; one who looked like Hamlet, dressed in a bejeweled gold-studded Roman toga complete with laced sandals coming right up his legs, seemed to be—in fact was—stabbing himself in the stomach with a pen. Undoubtedly, Sigbjørn had said, another writer.

A man and a woman, with his handkerchief over her head, stood reverently regarding these things, with three Indian women—two sharing a rebozo over their heads. There were also two young boys who knelt, crossed themselves, and went right out again. Leaving the church, Sigbjørn and Primrose encountered a very, very large pig in the doorway, which Primrose was afraid of and sidled past gingerly, whereupon the pig trotted amiably enough into the church through the open door.

Then the tortured and anguished face of the dark Christ in the glass case at the door looked at him.

IX

AS SOON AS SIGBJØRN
awoke, he decided to get up and wash, and, after drinking his
tea, to think matters over, taking various things into considera-
tion . . . altogether, to go thoroughly into the subject. He lay
for half an hour tormented by his decision.

"She is the virgin for those who have nobody them with."

"—for those who have nobody them with—"

"—for those who have nobody them with—"

"Then get up."

Sein oder nicht sein, das ist die Frage. That was not the question now, however it might have been before, it was irrelevant.
His getting up, as it were, symbolized the struggle between life
and death to him. He finally did get up with a tremendous effort and sat on the edge of the bed, too exhausted to move,
shaking like a factory. "But what to do now? I have forgotten
what to do, what one does, when one gets up."

"Throw away your mind," Fernando seemed to be saying,
"my maker of tragedies. Do you want to make more tragedies?
Have a shower, no, better have a swim. Then the necessary
drink. . . . Sí, hombre, you have overlooked that you are a creature of luck!"

Certainly, Sigbjørn thought, I have overlooked this, that
every time I have tried to pull myself together, and have—but

191

wasn't I thinking about the last night, or an hour ago?—and have set out with Primrose somewhere, then it is as if God himself were trying to help us.

Every rising in the morning is thus like a new birth. Freud. Sleep is a sinking into one's self. Hebbel. Sleep means reexperiencing one's past, forgetting one's present, and prefeeling one's future. Stekel.

He lay down in bed again. "Last night I got such terrible drunkness I will need three full days of sleeping to recover myself." Strange, how he kept remembering Fernando's words, how he had remembered them all these years—years of work, years of high hope, years of courage and pride and disaster.

"Then get up."

"I shall arise now and put on my rejection slips, my erection slips," he said aloud. Sigbjørn found his swimming trunks; he had a towering hangover, but then he had had worse hangovers in his life, ten years ago, for instance, not to say a fortnight ago. He had difficulty with his swimming trunks, with his rejection slips, his erection slips, but the thought of meeting Fernando again warmed him, the lifeward, whatever it was, principle reasserted itself.

Primrose was in her room with the door shut. He went down through the patio haunted by his characters, and on the way down, staggering, he said absurd things aloud, like, "Totter totter totter." "See what Sigbjørn is doing." And once, aloud, "Walking stalking death." And he had—it was a tremendous effort of will—a swim. He was a good swimmer. "Have I done nothing good?" he thought, toweling himself. "I rescued three men from drowning anyway." (The funny part of this admission was that it was untrue.)

Sigbørn was having trouble with his shoes, which had become unlaced. "Shall I do my exercises?" No. He was embarrassed. People might be watching him. The proximity of Señora Trigo's house worried him, and Eddie's bungalow again down there, the bottle of Four Roses still on the parapet.

Señora Trigo appeared and began a fatuous conversation. "You are so strong!"

"It is a wonderful tonic," he said, toweling himself. Sigbjørn's super-modesty was torturing him: and Señora Trigo, widowed, seemed to be studying him.

"You look so wonderfully well."

He felt glorious for the moment—about five seconds—and with real Paracelsian heroism he even tried to exercise now that Señora Trigo had gone. He half bent to the ground once, slipped in the water that had overflowed the pool. "I have done my exercises, I have one good bicep"; and returned to the tower, past the gnomed fountain, feeling self-conscious about his cord shoes flapping—was his tool hanging out?—and unable to resist looking at the postbox once more, no mail, and trying to avoid the eye of Dr. Hippolyte, already going to his car on the other side of the patio.

As he opened the door, the thought of Primrose's holiday being spoilt after all she'd been through together with him, the fire, and the water, the firewater, the aguardiente, was unbearable and heartbreaking, but now the thought that she was going to have her holiday after all and he would give her a good trip was glorious.

Her door was still shut. The tequila bottle, why not? He picked it up. Take the necessary drink. He put the bottle down.

He had a shower, dressed, and went in to Primrose. She was flattened against the window. Down below, where the dogs had been copulating all night, outside the tintorería, seen through the chevron-shaped windows, half rose-colored, he had described, there seemed a lot of excitement. He had forgotten in his ecstasy what had been going on outside. He approached her, placed a hand on her shoulder.

"See, it's a wedding," she said, obscurely, not to him.

So that was what had been going on all night. "So I see," he said. "Well, darling, don't be so mournful."

Was she thinking of their own wedding in an apartment house, with a Unitarian minister, now defunct, who after the ceremony had offered them a glass of carrot juice?

And it was indeed a wedding. What was more to the point it was a wedding in the very place where, in *The Valley of the Shadow of Death,* he had put a funeral. . . . Near the abarrotes too, with the scene, *you are a man who like moch wine!* But what indeed was everyone waiting for? The car, done up like an Easter basket, the men dashing to and from the Mínima, phoning possibly to the bridegroom—yes, it must be the bride's house—the men in the tuxedoes at this hour (just like the Consul) and glistening black hair, the man coming down the street in a pseudo tuxedo, who, important, suddenly spat. A flower girl, a mere infant, shyly peeping out of the doorway.

There were several fine shiny cars clogging the street, one of them bound round with white paper ribbon and decorated with wreaths and flowers of white paper. There was a fluster in the whole street with people, mostly women and children, standing and peering out of doorways and balconies. Such a clashing and glittering of black and white elegance. Shoes like mirrors, black trousers, knife-pleated, black hair oiled and shining, and white shirts sparkling.

They stood by the tower window, watching: the splendid young man had on his tuxedo coat and was sprinting up the street every few minutes to phone; a friend in a tuxedo with a white tie and bright brown shoes, and two older men in business suits arrived; a larger crowd gathered and the tension grew— were they waiting for the bride? the bridegroom? the priest? Yes, the bride in a long full white dress and yards and yards of veilling ran out of the door and into the car; someone was arranging her veil. The little flower girl—a tot of about three or four— dressed in imitation of the bride was bundled into the car. As the bridal car pulled away out of the door came four bridesmaids looking very fine and important in long shell-pink taffeta dresses garlanded with deeper apricot roses and each complete with small pink veil and flowers in their black hair and carrying bouquets; with much giggling and solemn excitement they fluttered about, swirling their skirts while the crowd of women and children watched and commented delightedly. Then they got into another car, other people emerged from the house and got into cars, and off the whole procession of shining cars went bumping and trailing up the street.

"I put the coffee on," Sigbjørn said. "I'll just dodge out to the Miramar and get two pan dulce and one blanco while you fix the turkey eggs. I've got it all set. We're going to Oaxaca."

"Oh, *are* we?" Primrose was joyous again.

When Sigbjørn returned, the eggs were sizzling. Should he take another drink? No, to escape the temptation he climbed once more up to the roof and looked over the city. How different he felt from last night; in spite of the hangover remaining, he felt joyous. Here he was, enclosed in his own book. In one sense it gave him a feeling of power, and in another he felt like a puppet. Or would God close the book upon him, as if he were an insect? It was a glorious day, scudding clouds, blue sky, Cortez Palace, and the good birds of morning. He drew deep breaths and vowed again that Primrose should have a good trip.

It was not until they were actually sitting in the sweat-smelling rolling bus with its pictures of the Virgin of Guadalupe and the Saint of Desperate and Dangerous Causes that he remembered again that in his book too Oaxaca was supposed to represent, in so far as it was supposed to represent anything, death—*The Valley of the Shadow of Death!* And the number of the bus was seven.

The Flecha Roja bus writhed and shook and jerked down the precipitous hill alongside Cortez Palace, the street "desperate as a winze," Street of Dangerous and Desperate Causes! The bride's car passed, then the bride's mother crying happily within it, and everyone looking pleased and triumphant. The wedding was now completed and Primrose and Sigbjørn smiled at each other. The iron, malleable, the feeling that the bus was alive, slippery, but a jellyfish or sea dragon, a harshly voluptuous motion. Sigbjørn with a tremendous effort had brought Primrose ice cream and they sat hunched up at the back eating it. After a while Sigbjørn's hope seemed to wear off slightly. It was replaced by a feeling as though God were tired of one, like a magistrate, Sigbjørn thought, who says to the husband, returned, found guilty of assault for the fifth time, and put on bond of five hundred dollars to keep the peace: "I hope I never see you again. I've seen all I want to see of you and your friends. I've had all I want of you."

But after a while as they rattled with uneasy purpose through the bypaths of Sigbjørn's eighth chapter, the hope returned, or a sense of it, not great, rather poignant. They did not take the way in his book past the market; the Avenida Guerrero, blocked by awnings, an overflow of the market, was closed to traffic. But they were heading for the same road that would take them to Chapultepec, which had been in his book, Tomalín, and which was also the road to Parián that had been death. There were of course actual towns called Tomalín or at least Tomallin, also Parián, the last place where he had seen Fernando, waving to him on the station platform with a bottle of mescal after their wild adventure in Nochitlán, but those were in Oaxaca, whereas in the book they had been in a mythical state called Parián—as it were the state itself—which was Morelos, and more particularly Morelos and Oaxaca: and they were going by a route that had not formerly been possible, to the city of Oaxaca itself. The point that each of these places had long occupied in his mind as a symbol of some chamber or niche of the human spirit was doubtless, to most people, even to Primrose, incommunicable: such thoughts being akin perhaps to those that trouble the dead rather than the living.

On the hill they were climbing now there did not seem room for two buses to pass abreast, but with a wriggle and a swerve this was achieved continually: it seemed like luck, it was as if the patient iron simply bent out of the way on both sides: but these Mexican drivers were portentously good.

The good feeling that they were off, not so uncomfortable as one might have expected, their bag on the rack above them, the window open. They went at first toward Chapultepec. Toward Yautepec. Popo and Ixta appeared and disappeared growing closer. The final gradient as they left the valley and cut through the pass up, then down into Yautepec. Sigbjørn thought of that day on New Year's Eve. The little town undiscovered by tourists. The lovely bandstand with the fountain underneath in the little square, the fresnos, the huge white butterflies drifting like flowers of the wind, the sparkling little stream, and the view of Popo like a dream. Ah, Yautepec was where they could live and love in forever, so happy in one another!

The bus was now plowing through the dust of boring hot country crossed and recrossed by a stupid railway line that sometimes, however, gave them the names of the towns: Oacalco,

Tenango, Calderon, Cuatlixo, Isabel Jauregui: but the names were the only beautiful things for the towns were all the same, the country was flat and dusty, and he squeezed his wife's hand. Isn't this good? Aren't we having a happy time?

They arrived at the flat dead heat of Cuautla. In the arid park, there was a man playing with a child on the grass, and a woman wearing a Stetson hat carrying a glass of lemon ice cream. Where were the buses to Oaxaca? There was no way to tell which way they were going. They ate, drank beer, and anxious to be on time, they got on the wrong bus and were nearly taken to Mexico City—finally, in spite of the chaos, they set out for Matamoros. It was getting on toward evening, as they plunged over the roads into the wilds of Mexico; Sigbjørn dreaded it all, hated it all with one part of his mind, but with another part he was having a good time. There were, of course, people in the bus, but he did not notice them: they sat there like blocks of inchoate, illegible notes. Phrases and paragraphs bumped by: and the unwritten octet of the bright dark blue sky.

[margin annotation: writing as metaphor]

Fernando was perhaps the last friend he had alive or alive somewhere on these cactus plains, these hills, in this hell or heaven, he who had called him "the maker of tragedies." "Are you making more tragedies? Sickness is not only in the body." Perhaps Fernando was the only person who could help him. Sigbjørn remembered the projected trip to Tehuantepec: "When you have founded the right girl, comprende? If you have not killed yourself with drinking, I will resigned my job." Terrible memories: his first poem here: *the tick of real death not the tick of time* on the piece of notepaper, the frightful horrors, the insects like flying machines, the lidless eye of God, falling down the hole in the road and being rescued by the Indian—the rain, rain, rain and the thunder crashing in the Gothic mountains, but that trancelike sense of consciousness, of ecstacy, and the moon, a prophecy of Canada after the Stanford experience, *risen to bring us madness none too soon,* the film directors and the drunks he had been with in the sulphur baths, playing the piano, Willard Robinson's "Jubilee," in the thunderstorm.

At Yesera, crossing a barranca, with cattle on the bridge, with this cheery crowd in the bus, somebody was hauling something up—a bull had gone over the bridge; then Axochiapan and El Muerto, the dead, and terrific organ cactus at suitably named Organo, then beyond all this wild dead desiccated country, with the sun going down over it, to see ahead country where it was *green,* with water. This was Lagunillas; they took a long turn to the left and proceeded along a fertile valley, Popo was near and vast to their left, but sloping from them; the workers were coming back, their hats over their eyes to shield them against the sun, riding two up, on mules, along the railroad track, mules loaded with sugar cane, as they approached Ahuehuetzingo— and ah, the beauty of these Ahuehuete trees, the *green.*

Sigbjørn watched the lost prose sliding past the window; worse even than the sorrow that quite goes by is the beauty the poet no longer wishes to express. Sigbjørn tried to have the air of intensely searching for something, an air of concentration. Actually he "saw" little, or nothing, observed but little, or superficially, or nothing, and was searching for nothing at all, unless it was, out of somewhere, anywhere, an excuse to drink himself to death: or was it for that consciousness that had been released at the Farolito? Had he not been a writer, or had not accepted the lie or the illusion so long that he had come to believe in it, he would have observed more. But since he still thought of himself as such, "to observe" came into the category of work and the emotions that hovered around that prospect were themselves too loathsome for words. It was something like the obverse of it he thought, perhaps the error was to think of it as prose, not as poetry, that had ruined his friendships. He had no sooner made an interesting friend than he began to think of that person as a character. But Sigbjørn had been brought up as, so to speak, perhaps even in a sense was, an English gentleman. Perhaps it went against some inherent sporting instinct in him to use that friend for his own purpose, to write down his foibles, to annotate (even mentally) his bad taste, to learn enough about his work to identify himself with him.

Consequently, since he was reluctant finally to find out anything at all about that friend, he never got to know him, he faded into an abstraction, and he lost him. But perhaps it would be more true to say that the moment that the observation of the friend became work—and this was true even before his fire—he lost interest in him: to make the effort for friendship alone was beyond him (though perhaps because of this subconscious feeling that he would be anyway *essentially* a writer), and in this sense too Sigbjørn Wilderness, who often thought of himself as less a man than some species of daemon, was almost inhuman. But if inhuman, how be good, how be witty, how, even adventurous? It was for reasons something like this too that Sigbjørn would probably have been at a loss to describe Juan Fernando Martinez adequately.

The sun was setting and there was the unearthly beauty of feathery sugarcane tall against the green evening. They sank below it themselves, the whole evening brimmed with wavering sugarcane, as they turned off the paved road into dust and darkness and obscurity. The road led to a little town called Chietla, with a beflowered square at dusk, which Primrose loved, but Sigbjørn feared the bus's stopping because that involved responsibility, and he had a quarter of an hour's paralyzed panic in which he could not even buy Primrose a torta, in which he feared they were going to be left there the night. Then: "bangbang" on the iron bus's back by the conductor, "Vámanos," and they retraced their path down the dusty bumpy road, out of the beautiful town of Chietla—lost, they will never return!—past the feathery sugarcane once more; but now it was quite dark and then they were back off their detour, on the paved road—it must be, but no, it cannot be that they are going to turn back to Atencingo. Is the same thing going to happen as at Cuautla, should they have got off at Chietla? Sigbjørn was in a momentary panic but saw, by a flash of headlight for the first time, the sign, not *A Matamoros*, but *A Oaxaca*—and what a strange moment that was. But obviously it meant Matamoros too.

A bumping began again, as when a plane is landing, old walls rose up on the left side, endless high walls, the road became absolutely incredibly bumpy, as if they were driving over a volcano. Sigbjørn turned his eyes away from certain possible hotels before they reached the square simply because responsibility was after all postponed until they stopped, and though he dreaded that, still more he dreaded having to act on some decision made now of what might prove the right thing to do then, for "then" he could not accept: after all there might not be a then—the bus, happy thought, might never stop. The bus herded indignant but unbudging women down the narrow ancient streets and finally they reached a dark square round which they seemed to drive several times before they finally got out, stiff, tired, but "happy."

Sigbjørn, though, was nervous, so much so that much as he longed to he couldn't even propose a drink. It was a dark town indeed, the darkest he had ever seen, no street lights at all, and only flares in the square, and an occasional gloomy light from a cantina. They began to look for the Hotel Iturbide, which Sigbjørn had at least had the foresight to remark had been recommended in a folder.

"How clever you are."

"So clever I don't even know what state we're in."

"What state did it say on the folder?"

"Wait a moment. We can't be in Morelos still—I'm sure we're not in Oaxaca—is there a state of Tampico?"

"I don't know. Why?"

"It said, *Matamoros, Tamps.* on the folder. I should know, but I don't, what is meant by Tamps."

"Well, surely, Tampico."

"Of course it might mean Tamaulipas. In which case we're several thousand miles out."

"Of course, the Tamaulipas warbler."

The Hotel Iturbide was indeed in Matamoros, Tamaulipas, and this fact somehow demonstrated how lost, in one sense, they were.

"I'm a bit sad we may never go to Tamaulipas though," Primrose said.

Hotel Reforma, the only hotel in town, was a long sky-blue building with a long, wide stone corridor between the rooms opening to the sky, and down this corridor a runnel, at one end the excusado, with latticed doors, so that everyone could see you in there, had no lock; obviously the place had been once, like the ex-convent of Santa Monica in Puebla, a brothel. At least the tradition still, happily, persisted, three pesos and no questions asked. Having procured a key and paid the three pesos, they went out into Matamoros. They walked several times round the dark square in a daze. Now Sigbjørn was afraid even of entering a cantina, so dark was it, and Primrose herself was thirsty and wanted a drink.

"Do you mean that you are actually more afraid of going in and asking if I can come in and sit with you than you want a drink?"

"Yes."

First they sat in the square and unhappily drank two warm limonadas. But finally Sigbjørn plucked up courage and went into the cantina opposite.

The night, a quiet night, the quiet dark-walled hush of Matamoros. Every now and then Sigbjørn awoke, thinking of the delirium of Cuernavaca nights, but there was no sound, only the delicious hush of the ancient walled town until when, in the early morning the cock crowed, and when it crowed, crowed thrice.

Matamoros, and the dark, and Sigbjørn thought once more of Juan Fernando. Occasionally in the States or Canada, you see such a person driving fast, usually in a rather dark and lustrous car, a person with unusually dark and lustrous hair, and as often as not accompanied by two beautiful women; there is something in the ease with which the car is driven, the abandonment and gaiety between the three as the car disappears around a corner forevermore, the flying laughter that hints of the romance they will find in things familiar and second-rate to you, this, and something in the extra skill with which the car is driven, tells you that above the number plate is the word *Mexico*—Fernando had come into Sigbjørn's life as swiftly as that car, and almost as swiftly departed, but he had never forgotten him.

Sigbjørn's hangover for tonight had not yet caught up with him; he was still slightly tight, but sleepless. Nonetheless he felt a certain sense of peace. He thought of hangovers. Some hangovers are cold, as if the soul had descended into the Mayan hell, there to contemplate its loss, its lies, its sins, the waste, the secession from love, from its salvation, and its final derision of life.

Cold like a hermit who sits in an icy cave hung with stalactites of remorse, terrified that anyone may enter—ah wish the poor devil a little whiskey, for that is his only warmth. It is cold in a way that the drug fiend knows coldness: sad as Poe's vision of the House of Usher. Roderick Usher rose at six, and found his house in a hell of a fix. Nay what was the House of Usher but a hangover. Poe did not mean that the scene, his feeling, was like the hideous dropping of the veil after a prolonged bout. No, the House of Usher was the state of his soul in such a hangover, the tarns and the mists were his hideous thoughts, and its fall was his soul's fall. While Roderick Usher was of course none other than Poe himself. Poe too must have known this hideous superposition of reality. What else could he mean by Roderick Usher's pictures, which became more and more lifelike?

Here, in this bed, he felt none of the strangeness of Mexico, the fear that passes all understanding, the fear that possesses one like a paralysis. It was silent and in this silence he felt safe. It was a silence like the silence of the dark grave itself. He thought of his wife sleeping so silently beside him and threw an affectionate arm around her. How happy they had been! How happy they could still be. My sweetheart and my love, are you why, whom? . . . How beautiful and generous she was in her responses to life. Ah, the times they had had before the fire. The quarrels after, when he was going to pieces, and he had come near, perhaps, to driving her actually insane. "Why don't you leave the man?" "Because I love him." It was, because of the fire, too late to have children, but that was of small matter: if anybody in the world represented that abstraction "life," it was Primrose Wilderness. She was for him the spiritual life principle, still allied to the earth, once one of the elements too. And again she was, as it were, herself a perceptiveness of life, this perceptiveness of what life remained to him. She was a person whose creative perception was simply that of creative life and living, not a writer, but a person who loves life, who expresses her creative life in the *living* of life. That was the contrast—how much better she observed it. "Life" is thus attracted to the person who can take her formless vast creative principle and give it a form and a mold. How she responded when he was happy! How she *lived* poetry.

How had she ever put up with his dreadful glooms, his pro-tracted supercession from every kind of order or organization that can bring joy into married life or even into life itself? Why was he not a more tolerable fellow?

They set off the next afternoon at three thirty finally with a tremendous sense of adventure, sitting in the back seat, as usual, some kind of lawyer on the right with briefcase, the priest and possibly his brother in front. They recrossed the river, saw the old walls, endured the terrible bumpiness, which they retraced till again they saw the sign *A Oaxaca* with all the horror and excitement as if one should see *To Death—To Die*—then into gear, a paved road, and uphill, up, up, through cruel cactus country; at one moment when they were very high apparently everyone in the bus saw something horrible, or frightening; they all rushed to one side of the bus pointing, panting with excite-ment; the priest (in mufti) with his dirty black coat woke and crossed himself, but Sigbjørn did not know what it was, and Primrose couldn't see, and that innate delicacy that had once inhered in him as an artist now forbade him to ask.

What had appeared to be a small route on the map was enor-mous distance to be traversed in reality. Was not this too sym-bolical—how simple our journey seemed and yet how long, how dangerous it was—or would it be better to say, in our blindness, our dumb unawakened lives, how mean our journey seemed, how great in reality? And fast, sure, powerful, they were going. Getting up into the high country. Corn was stacked in organ cactus as big as a house. There was now no mistake about it, they were going to Oaxaca. Cactus, cactus, cactus. Nothing is more dead than a dead organ cactus. Country turned to red soil—colorado. Primrose said: "Look how the soil ranges in color from faded brick-red to pure vermilion. It's all that lovely color I've only seen in old bricks, and now we've lost the art of making them." In this country of tierra colorada, because the houses and even churches are made of the soil itself, they partake of its color, so that every dusty poor village glowed like the dawn and the very adobe had this same ruddy warm color, and the color of dawn, if you like of hope itself.

In spite of the hope however, twilight was coming on.

Gliding downhill at at least seventy and taking a detour into some town gleaming below, its churches below the first stars, suddenly they blew a tire.

They bumped on, however, into a kind of marketplace, into a town strange as any beheld by the grim Doughty in his travels through Arabia Deserta. Cold stars, white and blue churches like a child's thought of Turkey, like Poland: Chagall and marzipan. Cold blue chimes and a wind blowing in the mountains and blowing dust through the windy blue mountain town. A man peed behind the bus with graceful gesture but Sigbjørn could not follow suit. Out of this anxiety sprang another one: what if this were actually Huehuepan de León? Fearing it might be the terminal, Sigbjørn said to the priest:

"Por favor, señor, es esta puebla Huehuepan?"

"Sí, es Huehuepan."

"Es Huehuepan? Dónde, por favor, está un hotel?"

"Hotel. No hotel aquí."

"Pero nuestro terminal is Huehuepan y es necesario para mi esposa y yo encontrar un hotel."

"Huehuepan, sí."

"Pero, usted ha dicho que aquí es Huehuepan."

"Oh no, no es Huehuepan, aquí, es Acatlán."

It was Petlalcingo. Una hora a Huehuepan and they set off once more.

Darkness, and strange lights were moving in the hills; lights were flashing in the fields beneath the bus. Wandering lights, like lighthouses, caused by light behind latticed windows. Sometimes these lights seemed to be signaling as to a plane. It was caused by the motion of the bus, but strange illusions were bred in the cactus plain seen from the dark, swiftly moving, powerful bus with its well-behaved passengers. A thatched hut seemed at one moment to tired eyes to be a house at home. Rows of white stones set at corners fled from some vision of returning to some place once called home so slowly that the illusion seemed to overtake it and become reality. It seemed to Sigbjørn that the cactus had dropped away and been replaced by trees like small palms. But now it was night. Men laughing with wild unfinished sombreros, like green crowns of thorns on their heads, visible only by its light, stopped the bus. The conductor was nervous, saying "Vámanos! Vámanos!" but the driver stopped and they got on just the same, laughing, all of them a little high. Sigbjørn wondered if they had actually crossed into Oaxaca. Somehow he had that feeling, that subtle sense of change, almost imperceptible, as perhaps when you die you don't know you're dying, it's the same kind of darkness, and you don't know you're crossing.

Then Huehuepan. And yes, he saw it was Huehuepan, Oaxaca. The darkest city Sigbjørn had ever seen: darker than Matamoros. Strangely the bus drove right up to an hotel called El Jardín, where over the door there was just enough light cast by the bus for him to see the word Parián, for the first time again—and what a strange feeling this gave him—on a notice:

> *Camiónes a Parián, Nochitlán.*
> *Matamoros, Oaxaca, y Anexas.*

So dark this Mixtec city, absolutely and so utterly dark and sinister it was almost beyond belief. At night, at ten, as in the Middle Ages, the great doors of the Hotel El Jardín were shut, and double-bolted, and a great haft of wood propped against the giant door. But no matter how great the hafts of wood they would not shut out the past. . . .

X

THEY LEFT FOR OAXACA THE next morning at eleven thirty. At first it was all desert, too high even for trees, just a few scrub oaks and cactus and mesquite and sage. They had seats in the back, as usual, this time in a first-class bus, which was still climbing, going up and up and up and round and round and round; beyond Huehuepan the driver, tired—he had driven from Puebla that morning—Godlike, took his hand off the wheel altogether and the bus conductor just steered from the right: Sigbjørn had the feeling the bus was steering itself: up, up, up, into the cruel strength of the country, but suddenly they saw a green valley, a sparkling river and then a waterfall. Afterward the country seemed still crueler; it was as if the bus were driving into a gigantic slab of stale cake, or a country the color of a rusty gasworks, cliffs, parched earth, sheer hillsides of rock, and dead trees; the bus always in second or first gear, very very slowly, winding, purring, then down and on, on, on, and up. This is the Tierra Colorada.

Nonetheless, it was Oaxaca, and Oaxaca, he kept saying over and over to himself. Oaxaca! Grand canyons opened off to the right, where vast cataclysms had cracked the earth. A cool breeze blew in through the window. They passed small villages of adobe, with tiled roofs and neat farms, and the cattle seemed well fed. True he had not been this way before but it seemed to him there was a vast improvement in the human lot, and all this he put down to Ejidal. Fernando had his hand in this, he thought; everywhere he seemed to read the work of his friend. What a contrast too from the terrible railroad journey through Puebla he had taken with Hölscher, the eternal fields of cactus, the fetid, slow, crowded train stopping at every desolate boiling station, the delirium, rubbing the baby with tequila, the heat, and the misery. It seemed to him that there was a lesson in this, that he had won through to this, he was taking the same journey, and yet by a more elevated route, it was almost as though he were flying. It was much, indeed, the same feeling that he had had on arriving in Mexico.

This feeling became more intense as they began slightly to descend again, with the tremendous sense of space, and range after jagged blue range for hundreds of miles in every direction. Nowhere in the world, not even on the sea or on the prairie, was such a sense of boundless immeasurable heavenly space as this, and his very soul seemed free as a bird within him, and it was Fernando he was inwardly thanking for all these marvels, it was as if Fernando knew they were coming and had sent something of himself to meet them to guide them.

Then Nochitlán (which Fernando used to pronounce Anochitlán), and the memories of having ridden there on the last trip for the Ejidal came flooding in, the room in Nochitlán, the ride to Andoa and Chindoa (no one would believe these things, that they had any organic truth, so why write about them; nobody would believe about Cuicitlán or the fellows who sat up in the church tower at Andoa and Chindoa and shot at them, because they feared an invasion of buccaneers; no one would believe that they made peace between those two warlike towns, and even Elizabethan politeness). "The poor pig, poor my friend"; and seated in the theater, "Are you making more tragedies?" Sleeping in the graveyard in Andoa, the purple sorrowful hills of death and his lost life. But, "we will go riding up there."

Fernando. Only twenty-four when he knew him (Sigbjørn recalled with a shock), Fernando stood six foot three—thus contradicting ethnology, for the Zapotecans are supposed to be short, shorter than the Mixtecans—and in features he rather resembled an Italian. He thought of himself as Zapotecan, but he owned Spanish and English blood as well. He had been well educated, but for sleeping under the stars and eating tortillas and beans he had a literal preference. The job to which Fernando was frankly dedicated provided a strange link with the past. This was with the Banco Ejidal, whose historical function was based on an old Aztec system, a bank that differed from another bank in that instead of your going to it, it went to you—if you were a remote Oaxaqueñan village—largely on horseback in those days, and across widely dangerous mountain terrain. Fernando had a genius for languages, and he needed it, for his part was that of the horseman, often combined with that of a doctor, and there are fourteen different languages in Oaxaca; he spoke them all, including Chinanteco, Popaloco, and Zoque, and the mournfully majestic old Spanish of the conquistadors. In addition he spoke Italian and French fluently, and had mastered English, though in speech he had that haunting habit of putting prepositions ("I like to work them with") at the end of a phrase.

Sigbjørn had once gone with Fernando on one of his more hazardous journeys. On the way they had run short of a horse, and rather than wait longer for another, Fernando had insisted that Sigbjørn use his, while Fernando ran. A mere matter of twenty miles, mostly uphill. Moreover every time Sigbjørn prepared to dismount, Fernando would urge his horse, who was enjoying the whole thing after a rest, to a canter once more; and when Sigbjørn would inquire if he were not getting tired, Fernando would laugh, and had the breath to do so uproariously. He liked, he said, to run his horse with. . . .

From Nochitlán, though it was in the foothills above the valley of Etla, it was still necessary to climb once more, with Parián somewhere away to the right, *A Parián* a sign said in a melancholy fashion, and here climbing, the view back the way they had come passed all belief: it was boundlessness beyond boundlessness, mountain beyond mountain beyond mountain, they could see so far that even Popocatepetl, or what looked like it, was perhaps visible hundreds of hundreds of miles behind this childhood dream of heaven, and rolling valleys, the dream of the

sailor sleeping on the poop in the vast violet of the Indian
Ocean as it deepens at noon . . . (or like the temptation that
the devil showed to our Lord). The sight afflicted Sigbjørn with
a terrible thirst for the first time in hours: he wanted to gulp it
all down, to drink these mountains and meadows. . . .

Down, down, down, they were winding down toward Oaxaca.
Dark faces paused on shovels and looked at them. A car nearly
hit them coming round a crag. And again, the mountains! the
mountains! It was like seeing beyond the farthermost abysses of
sense, a tremendous rolling green dumbfounding crescendo of
all the vast seas and meadows of the mind, inexhaustible, mea-
sureless as the human soul, yet seeming to stretch beyond its ut-
most limits. Down, down, and with sunset came the valley of
Etla and the memories of scratching the ground. "This is the
hour I love when all the men begin to sing and all the dogs to
shark." Etla and the memory of the fossilized head—again what
a symbol of the past was this head!—being carried through the
sunset that Sunday evening when they had fenced at the Banco
Ejidal in the morning and drunk in the Farolito all afternoon.

And now in the late afternoon they were going down along
the valley itself, down, down, gently down, on the last lap to
Oaxaca.

They were traveling at sunset along the valley of Etla with the
mountains on either side, though flatter immediately to the
right, the mountains with their great indentations shadowed
like enormous gods with their hands on their knees.

At the very far end of this lush green evening land there was
the merest hint of Oaxaca, as if it were the celestial city in an
illustration in a child's *Pilgrim's Progress*.

Why should he be drawn to it so? Apart from Fernando, why?
It was not the happy memories of Oaxaca that he had had with
his first wife—first wife, that was wrong too, according to Swe-
denborg at least he had not properly been married—that he
wished to revive; it was the misery of remorse, it was the memory of that old consciousness of fatality that he wished to revive,
the stimulus of the old wine of complete despair whose cold in-
ternal glow he sought, and the memories of the Farolito.

Was it that he wanted to return there, as if to gloat over the conquest of these things, as he might have looked down from the mountains upon the valley, upon the narrow-gauge railway line—that now, as if the past had joined him, ran parallel with the road here to Oaxaca itself—that had carried him on his first, his second, his third, last, and disastrous trip to Oaxaca, with a feeling of pride, thinking that all this had been transcended? How much better I am now! No—for surely if this were so, he would never have run his head like this into the noose of temptation again. Had he really transcended it? Was he coming here with a pride of accomplishment with Primrose, and a gesture of defiance, to fling his gage in the face of fate and say (and say moreover in clichés), Look, I have succeeded, I have transformed, single-handed, my life-in-death into life, nay what is more I am going to make that life-in-death pay for the future, in hard cash, I have come back to show you that not an hour, not a moment of my drunkenness, my continual death, was not worth it: there is no dross of even the worst of those hours, not a drop of mescal that I have not turned into pure gold, not a drink I have not made sing.

Would that he were saying that! But he could pray only that he might be really good and bring himself to say it, for Primrose's sake.

Even here at this very point, where his memories were as nostalgic as those of a lover, those memories were all of disaster. With what absolute despair, after the devil dancers at Etla (the daemons dancing in the mud at Etla, the mountains, Coco's "Don't be careful!"), he had seen those mountains turn, even as they turned now, to purple, a despair so great that he would need another language to describe it, the despair that his life was finally gone, his life ruined, his love lost, his work hopeless, and that he was looking upon such beauty for the last time, a despair and sense of ruination that was insanely heightened by the knowledge and remorse of how much that beauty might have meant had it only been shared with the one he loved but whom he had willfully, that day at the Hotel Cornada, sent away.

He now remembered a peculiar thing: the huaraches, bought in Canada, that had come wrapped in an Oaxaca newspaper gave him the very information he wanted for *The Valley of the*

Shadow as if Oaxaca itself had sent it to him, wrapping the precious pious symbol of the sandal indeed in the very words that Sigbjørn required. Sigbjørn had not traversed these mountains before, he had scarcely seen the beauty of Oaxaca: now this beautiful trip was going into the immediate past; if only, starting now, he could build a life of such splendid memories for Primrose and himself; but now they were in the valley, and the past, symbolized by the mean little railroad that crossed so slowly and agonizingly the terrible cactus plain with its memories of heat and anguish and drunkenness, was running parallel, so that he was flooded with these memories of the past, the past was keeping pace with him, he could not for a moment outdistance it, it would follow him indeed all the way into the city of Oaxaca itself. . . . *Is that Oaxaca in the distance?*

There was the statue of Benito Juárez with the lamp and the outstretched hand in the distance, far far away on an eminence on the left: Sigbjørn pointed it out. They were excited, it was after all, an adventure!

On the right they passed a kind of aqueduct leading to a little town half hidden by poplars or willows, with its church hiding there as if it were Tewkesbury. And over there, once, one afternoon, among these poplars, in the grasses, he had taken the big omnibus edition of Keats and Shelley and, immersed in the fury of the sounds of the words that he had half pretended to be reading, as if, with the bottle of mescal beside him, he were even making the pretense of starting a new life—God what irony— that very day, that afternoon so to say; while the unspeakable melancholy of the trees and clouds and grasses tossed about him, a melancholy ten times greater because here in this outlandish spot of dead civilizations to which he bore not the faintest relation but which, nonetheless, so dispossessed was he, had the power to bring the deep meadows of kingcups and buttercups and willow trees of Cambridge heavily about him, he was half unconsciously obeying a boyhood habit, an old lost call of his adolescence, to go out in the country, and read. And there were other reasons too, for being attracted to Shelley.

It was this same undergraduate instinct that had bade him that Sunday morning (Lawrence himself who sought his contemptible oranges—oranges!—had not been free from it, and who was contemptuous) to the bank to find Fernando that Sunday when they had "scratched the land" in Etla and found the petrified head after drinking at the Farolito; and then to take a spin in a two-seater, which was precisely what they'd done. How extraordinary: they had taken a spin, and precisely in a two-seater. With what contempt Fernando's friends had dropped him off at the Farolito again on the way home—unless this was in his imagination—unkindly, it seemed to him, they had tried even to run over him. . . . There was little generosity 'in so many Mexicans: even though they were clap-stricken drunkards themselves, their innate angry sense of inferiority made them contemptuous of any gringo who was likewise: was this too, intrinsically, because they coveted our beastly little civilization, because we were their superego, and they were consequently distressed to see it misbehave?

> *At dawn the east wind rises with the sun*
> *Blowing blue smoke downstream*
> *Sinks with the turning of the tide at noon*
> *Into our dream. . . .*

And along here, somewhere, too, would be the barbershop where so often he had been shaved, and where his shavings had so often deteriorated into aguardiente drinking both in the barbershop and at the pub opposite. Un hombre noble, they had called him—what lies he had told. A hero of the Spanish War. God knows what he had said. Was it those lies he was now expiating! And the police always after him. And the little barber had made him exchange his good leather belt for his own inferior one. . . .

This then was his past, to some it must seem as sad and hopeless as a poor ravaged city, but to him a matter of evil excitement.

But Sigbjørn, peering eagerly this way and that, as though this had been the scene of some passionate triumphant love affair, or of some great transaction that had changed his life once and for all into successful courses, could not now find the little barbershop.

Oaxaca indeed—even though he had approached it before by that old parallel road (though they had now lost it); perhaps at this point the two had merged once more, so that now past and present and future were one—seemed very different as they were now approaching it: the dumb blank red walls built against cataclysm, the station on the right with the cantina opposite—and the mysterious strange depths of these Oaxaqueñan cantinas—where he had bought, for five pesos, the wonderful machete, where he had drunk, that day he came back from Parián and his clothes had been stolen, wearing Fernando Martinez's clothes, afraid to go back to La Luna (suddenly Sigbjørn remembered he had a blind man of his own, the man with dark glasses outside the Hotel La Luna who would keep pace with him every morning but on the other side of the street; there seemed no movement outside the hotel until he came out, then everything would start up in motion, people following him on either side of the street as if his morning exit in the sun were awaited by an invisible orchestra leader somewhere who then set the hosts in motion). Ah yes, yes, yes—these red walls, the impassive façades of these houses—the one where Fernando and his sweetheart had left notes to each other, "My sweetheart and my love"—with their iron grillwork, but the complex, deep and beautiful beyond, and this was true even of some of the meanest pulquerías.

Bouncing, bouncing at dusk down the interminable streets—how long they were only he knew: the squares were different, there seemed more of them, and there was the curious sense of it being no longer Oaxaca. Now Sigbjørn had his usual anxiety about hotels. *Hotel Monte Albán, donde el turista vive en un ambiente legendario*—memories of having picked up the American there who had taken them to Etla—but it was too expensive, but now, my God, what were they doing?

They were stopping at the Hotel La Luna itself. Yes, there was no doubt of it, the third-rate Hotel La Luna—where once Lawrence had written his famous letter to Middleton Murry, and Sigbjørn himself had died, and literally perhaps, were not these sensations a foretaste of what the dead may feel?—was now the terminal. They pulled right up at the door and got out. The bus ticket office was now in the lobby where the old man used to sleep at night and Sigbjørn used to walk over him on his way to the Farolito. But they were actually met by the old man himself, with his bare feet, and Sigbjørn hoped he was not recognized. As if by force majeure they were going in.

"Nosotros no somos americanos ricos. . . ."

Antonio Cerillo seemed no longer there: the rather effeminate-looking manager, if he was the manager, wanted to charge them twenty pesos, which seemed far too much to them.

"I am a friend of Antonio Cerillo."

"He sold the place five years ago."

"And his nephew?"

"Oh—he is still here in town."

Sigbjørn was still carrying the actual bag he'd bought off Cerillo—or his sister—for five pesos, on the day of his departure back to the Hotel Cornada.

"We have a room but it is very bad. Ordinarily we don't show this to tourists."

I'll say it's very bad, thought Sigbjørn.

But they were shown upstairs, and Sigbjørn knew what was coming. They were shown into his old room. It was number 40. Where was Mr. Waterhouse, the silver miner, who had typed his life away in the next room? It had not changed save that the window was broken: there seemed no privacy there at all. The barefooted man now arrived with the bags. He said:

"It is better on the roof. There you can see Monte Albán. There is a papagayo on the ladder."

The parrot was on the same ladder that always led down to the kitchen from which the sounds of slaughtering came.

"Y posiblemente un xopilote después!" said Sigbjørn, remembering the vulture in his washbasin, and the old man laughed.

"Music," said the old man, inclining his head and hearing some music.

It was here too that Juan Fernando and he had drunk so often —as they had drunk early the day he saved Hölscher's life—and he had other memories: how he had dressed him that day before the posada. . . . "I get so horrible drunkness the next morning I fall off my horse."

It was decided to change the room for a better one—if someone evacuated one—but Primrose wanted hot water immediately, and got it, and washed herself in Sigbjørn's old room: was there any meaning in this cleansing process?

Later they went up on the roof with the old man and looked up into the mysterious purple mountains, where Fernando rode. Darkness was drawing in swiftly over Monte Albán, the seat of the Zapotecan kings.

After having changed to a better room, Sigbjørn and Primrose walked around the town before dinner, which went on until nine. How strange was this walking into the past . . . how different the town was from what it had seemed in his delirium. He avoided the Covadonga where he had met Juan Fernando and had been, all those years ago, arrested. Primrose wanted a drink, Sigbjørn was afraid of finding a cantina, though he too wanted one. No, the town was not so fearful nor so beautiful as he had wanted to present it: it was a fake: death was a fake too, that was why he always had to wear a mask, the image of man's fear; did he, Wilderness, make that up, had he read it somewhere, or Primrose said it? They went to the Salón Modelo: Sigbjørn was half dead with fear; he went into the bar to find the barman, walleyed and charming, and they drank habanero.

Sigbjørn now wanted to find Independencia 25, the Banco Ejidal. But there seemed for one thing more squares. And those squares were astonishingly ugly: the garish electric lights, the white lime on the trees. It was only when you left the squares for the back streets that climbed the hill that the old sinister quality reasserted itself.

"We must have overshot Independencia then."

"I haven't seen the name."

"I thought it was farther but then I suppose it took me longer to walk in those days."

Avenida Matamoros, Avenida Morelos . . . but no Independencia. And no Cervantes's place. Though drawn as by a remorseless purpose to find it they could not in the dark.

> *La persona que destruya*
> *Este jardin sera*

consignada a la
autoridad. . . .

Le gusta este jardín
Que es suyo? Evite que
Sus hijos lo destruyan!

Sigbjørn was staggered. It was an understatement to say that they were wrestling with an invisible enemy. He felt more as if, like Hudson's fabled fox in *The Purple Land,* biting the air, struggling, yet becoming more and more exhausted, he were being, by some strange magnetism, sucked from a distance into the maw of a lampalagua, that serpent which in fact resembled the Mexican Immigration that while extremely sluggish in its motions, it yet captures its victims by following them into their burrows.

Yes, he had come back a great deal farther than the Consul to verify the sign . . .

They returned to La Luna unconsciously by a back street that Sigbjørn used to take for fear of being recognized, and in La Luna dinner already had begun. How often had he walked through this dining room with his shoulders thrown back pretending not to be dying and up to the "very bad" room to have another few mescals before dinner?

But this time they walked in quickly without going upstairs, and took their places while the barefooted old man, now dressed as a waiter, flashed them a smile.

The La Luna was an hotel like a railway station: glassed-in patio; at night the snores, the murmurs rose, and were echoed each by the station dome. At this point, though, it was more the thoughts and memories that seemed to rise and echo from this dining room to the roof and make a muttering, dismal, yet furious echo there; for this phenomenal dining room, so full of loathsome memories, had not changed in any major respect, even down to the tiny bar at the foot of the stairs where the pale slattern woman made such a fuss about serving him tequila before breakfast, and would keep him waiting for a quarter of an hour at a time: it was a bad place to drink, in full view of the dining room, most of whose denizens eyed you with contempt.

In the dining room sat John Stanford.

Sigbjørn had not been more astonished when once, at sea, in the middle of the Pacific, he had stepped out on deck into a hurricane of young owls being blown into the rigging.

John Stanford, his face half turned away from the Wildernesses, sat with three women at the next table but one, at the larger table by the wall upon which was a huge, obsolete map of Mexico. Stanford had, however, not yet recognized Sigbjørn, and Sigbjørn was relieved to see that Stanford's party was well through dinner, was indeed now waiting for the dessert.

He seemed to have changed little: he was a little more beefy perhaps, a little balder, though his hair had always been slightly receding: but he looked ruddy, sunburned, even quite fit, although he was the type of man who was quite capable of practicing the most continued dissipations and these of highly esoteric and taxing nature, without in the least showing it: how horrible a man was Stanford! A drunkard who never had the shakes, a debauchee who was never called upon to pay the piper because —who knows?—he was the piper himself.

How horrible to see him here—and yet—Sigbjørn knew only too well what he was suggesting to himself, the illimitable tequilas, the mescals, the glorious debauch that would be the result of meeting him, and which would make this yet another Taxco for Primrose.

Suddenly Stanford rose, had seen him: there was a moment of tension so unbearable between the two men that it was almost beautiful, beautiful because it became immediately obvious to Sigbjørn that either Stanford felt exactly as he, i.e., that he had made up his mind not to recognize him, though his sense of guilt must have stemmed from very different sources, or that actually the man had not recognized him. But the thought of the special guilt that Stanford must be suffering, was another thing: and Sigbjørn, turning to his soup that was growing cold, with a hand not shaking for the usual reason but with pure anger, felt also a sort of terrified amusement.

"Do you know who is sitting over there, Primrose?" he asked finally, admonishing her to silence.

"No, who is he? Someone you know?"

"Yes."

"Then why don't you speak to him?"

"Ssssh."

"Who is he?"

Well, after all, when it came down to it, how could he explain? Who *was* Stanford? Stanford was hangovers; Stanford was lies; Stanford was the prescience of disaster and its coefficient. Stanford was everything that had occurred since he had left La Luna before and gone to Acapulco, after saving Hölscher from the police. In fact, Stanford was an accomplice. Stanford was the past and the difficulty of transcending it: and here he sat—the sorrow of his life, together with all its evil, everything that before the fire at least he thought so miraculously transcended. In fact Stanford went further back than that, because he was even a blood relative of a terrible sort. It was as though the lowest ebb of his life had returned to reveal, in the mud, precisely the same horror that time had not had power to disintegrate and disperse, and more frightening even than the impossibility of the whole thing was this urge to greet it cheerfully, tactfully, above all to celebrate with it. The temptation was indeed colossal but Sigbjørn resisted it: he wondered if however they had any of the old vino de la casa at the hotel, or that wine whose identity as nonsinful fare was sanctioned by the monks on the label; and then it occurred to him that he did not want Stanford to see him drink either—while noting that Stanford was not drinking at the table—he wondered with a gnawing curiosity even unbearable, whether Stanford was "drinking."

All this time Stanford, who had risen and was looking at the map, seemed to be standing there longer than was necessary: yes, he was fatter, more "meaty" was the word—but doubtless still attractive to women—at all events he had three with him: but now it was apparent that the big man had recognized him. Well, let him stew in his own guilt. (Another odd point was that Sigbjørn was actually wearing one of Stanford's shirts.) Hereafter Sigbjørn subtly avoided his eye.

And now Stanford, having left the map, was sitting down again and calculating the bill: totting it up over and over, with a

professional, and yet too meditative, worried, air: that was what
he loved, at least to do, to give this impression that he was a
"business" man, and Sigbjørn remembered the scene in the
Tarleton—"I didn't come down here for this"—an exhibition
of hysterical rage on the part of an American in Mexico.

The Wildernesses went on with their dinner: now Stanford—
bloody coward—was walking over to the desk: but there was
certainly no mistaking Stanford, not with that walk, for that
rolling sailorlike gait had been copied from Sigbjørn himself
eight years ago in Acapulco and undoubtedly never abandoned.
Should he, Sigbjørn, go over to him—but he remembered: *La
persona que destruya este jardin sera consignada a la autoridad.
. . . Le gusta este jardin?*

He had saved Sigbjørn at least from losing *In Ballast,* about
Erikson, Erikson who had died, his mind went round in a circle;
moreover Stanford himself had only just escaped being a character in *The Valley;* it was impossible to escape the conviction
that there was tremendous meaning in all this, on the other
hand it dimly ocurred to him that if he really understood what
Stanford meant, he would go mad on the spot. *Naturam expellas
furca, tamen usque recurret*—Horace had said (translated by
Arnold Toynbee—*You may throw nature out with a pitchfork
but she will keep coming back*). Very true, worse than that, on
another plane, it seemed that the past was liable to come back,
armed with a pitchfork itself, in the guise of the devil. Moreover
the past grows too, and confronts you in all kinds of strange
forms, at the times you least expect it, when you thought at last
you were rid of it, like the child who only yesterday, it seems,
was a little boy afraid of the dark, but who today looms up behind you, gigantic, accompanied by a whore, in the liquor store
where you least by the way want to be seen yourself. "Don't you
remember me? I was about so high." To which you reply, "Yes
. . . no . . . well, you certainly have changed"—not remembering until afterward that yourself on the contrary are dressed
in the same shabby old tweed jacket you were wearing on the
last occasion you saw him, the coincidence of nondevelopment
by which he alone perhaps has recognized you, as it were *caught
up* with you.

Sigbjørn lay in the dark, deeply in bed, with Primrose beside him, in the Hotel La Luna. Carefully avoiding Stanford, they had gone to bed immediately after dinner, Primrose being tired. What did Oaxaca really mean to him? All the agonies and anguishes associated with it, being chased by pseudo Franco spies —the blind man—but also the profound death wish, the sense of grief after being left alone at the Hotel Cornada, that had made him accompany Hölscher to Oaxaca in the first place, and the almost unbearable associations of the place, originally almost happy. Sigbjørn went down through layer after layer of his mind. He had been wearing the suit Fernando had sold him for five pesos when he first met Stanford, the sight of whom made all these thoughts even more agonizing; indeed there was no end to those thoughts, they seemed to go on forever like the Sierra Madre. The prison experience, which had been the end of his little pilgrimage to free humanity: *"You are a man who like moch wine!"*—the horror of the people fighting locked together in El Bosque—the terrible scene with the murderer in prison— the Virgin for those who have nobody them with—La Luna and the Farolito, and that latter the symbol of death, although because of the fact Primrose was so determined he should turn death into life she had said almost gaily: "How I long to go to the Farolito!"

One source of Sigbjørn's guilt he thought was that he had a disordered imagination and lived a phantasy of a life: a liar is the better word, as the judge said. He thought of La Vida Impersonal and then he wondered: What dreadful force moves me? He decided he was the evilest and the saddest man in God's creation, remembered Stanford again, and suddenly thought, "God, were I to meet Fernando, would it not only prove the same thing!" Fernando was one of the greatest men he had ever met in his life: a man of wild courage, humility, and greatness of soul. But Fernando was merely the bright side of the same medal: and that medal had equally been forged in hell: the two men were linked together with invisible bonds, save that one was good, the other evil, and suddenly he thought, Wouldn't it be running my head into the noose of temptation again? And on the decision that he perhaps ought not to find

Fernando either he sat up and said aloud with a cry, waking Primrose:

"Christ, I can't go on. This Stanford business is the end."

"Oh, why is there always something, always something?" murmured Primrose.

"But why does it have to happen to me? . . . We're going back tomorrow. And then we've got to go back home."

"Home, without seeing Fernando!"

"Even if we did see Fernando, it would mean only another bender. And if I spoke to Stanford that too would mean another bender. There is no nucleus of peace in my whole life but those years and the house and then that had to burn down. I am damned. And when I say that I am damned I mean that I am still burning. My soul is not a soul, it is a conflagration."

"Oh, pile on the faggots, Jeeves," Primrose said disgustedly, wrapping herself up in the blanket on the far side of the bed, while Sigbjørn wondered what Henry James would have done with such a conversation.

"Perhaps I have not got a soul." Sigbjørn was struck with another idea.

"But you can't go without *trying* to find Fernando. You know, that's why we came."

"No—no—let's go—let's go at least back to Cuernavaca!"

"I won't let you. You've *got* to *try* and find him." . . . And so Primrose went on.

"Oh Jesus, oh Holy Mother. Go to sleep then," Sigbjørn said finally.

Primrose went back to sleep but Sigbjørn had to go on torturing himself. He thought of his habits regarding drinks when he was not drinking. Why was it he loved to talk of drinks and deliriums? He thought of his burned book: the god in the mescal was a jealous god who disdained that Sigbjørn should make use of him while remaining sober. He thought of the reasons for his earlier anguish before, left alone here in Mexico. It could be described as the solitary anguish of first love, delayed in Sigbjørn's case, false, unreal, but in terms of suffering, an almost Promethean agony, or his inability to cope with the country coupled with his feeling for his friends, dying in Spain. He thought of how he had sent his wife away and tried to join a ship, accompanied Hölscher to Oaxaca, his delusions, his sober terrible perceptions, his imprisonment, "Mescal possible, mescal impossible." *"You are a man who like moch wine!"*

It occurred to Sigbjørn that perhaps not three days had passed since they had been married without his having mentioned Fernando with friendship and love, then a terrifying thought followed it—was this but another manifestation of his secret desire for death? *El Alcoholismo es el enemigo no. 1 del proletario*—the poster in the seguridad—and his being thrown into jail on Christmas Eve, his bemused self-sacrifice, his disdaining to be bailed out—ley fuga—"You are no de wrider"—the Captain actually took him out of the prison for a drink—contestar el telegrama—and finally his poem, the alcoholic child and the murderer. What had he done with that? And yet these terrible things were not so terrible in memory. So unimaginably frightful and intense had been his suffering that he looked back upon those days almost as he looked back upon the beauty and health of their Canadian life. They were days as beautiful as vultures circling in high sunlight, as beautiful as death that flies just for the love of flying. And of all these things Fernando was in some way the symbol. No one could be more alive or life-giving in spite of all than he was. Which made it all the more puzzling that what all these things were that he loved so much should also so obviously be death. . . . They had met in the square at the pub called La Covadonga. . . .

"No, hombre," Martinez had said, having given him back his change. "I looked at you—perdone me—and I think, if you don't mind, throw away your mind."

"Who are you?" Sigbjørn said then, a little later, "What are you? Do you work for the Government?"

"No, not for. With the Government."

Fernando then said something so beautifully in such mournful accents and with such a dying melancholy fall, with all the music that there is in the word Oaxaqueñan or desconsolado, pronounced, or sung, as only the Oaxaqueñan can, that to this day Sigbjørn could not be persuaded—there were perhaps other reasons for thinking so—that his friend had not said something profound and great: "I am a drunk."

Sigbjørn Wilderness's loyalty was, he told himself, terrific.

The few friends he had made he cherished and would have died for at the drop of a hat. But he had few friends left. Two in Canada, one an American now in England, and his own brothers, and two or three more in England, who never wrote and were dead, and his mother and his wife. He was careful of making any friends, people liked him, often loved him. But he did not like to think of what it was in him they loved for the saying had got around that even to meet him was disaster. Erikson! It was all too true, it happened with material events too. Not Faust was a man more accursed than he: but was he not blessed also, perhaps he was an experiment of God's and it was not beyond paranoia to imagine that God must often have wondered about him, that perhaps not since the infant Horus had he had such a thorn in his side. The things he had survived would have smitten most men dead with fear: even to contemplate. But on the surface he was merely a drunk and an unsuccessful writer.

The light grew greater: pale and nasty. In the morning the hotel awakes early, and the flushing and belching from the Caballeros y Damas started, with such a noise of knocking on the doors: Señor! A las cinco y media—a las seis—a las seis y media —and hoiking and trumpeting and banging and no water running in the shower or toilet and freezing cold and bells clanging.

"This is a good address," he remembered Lawrence having written (before the climate got him) who lived here and here wrote his famous letter to Middleton Murry.

Perhaps Lawrence would help him.

"God will help you if you ask him," he remembered Martinez saying. Suddenly he found himself quoting Lawrence: *And I say to you it is not easy, it is not so easy.*

And I say to you too it is not easy. . . .

He had a half-waking vision of the daemons dancing in the mud at Etla, and among them, one, the Devil of Devils, whose shuffling footsteps did not conceal his slightly nautical swagger.

Making an effort analogous to his first effort when he decided to take Primrose to Oaxaca, he got up, had a slippery, rather awful shower (in the Damas) but afterwards felt much better.

Keeping a wary eye out for Stanford, they went down into the dining room and breakfasted on ham and eggs. This was different to his old entrances to breakfast which were made, after solid five-hour bouts at the Farolito, and generally a tepache or two with a beggar on the way home, from the street. During breakfast, which they were having early, Stanford and his party did not make their appearance: but once he saw him emerging from a room—a better one than theirs on the balcony—apparently catch sight of him a moment, and bolt back in again, as if he did not want to be seen; and this reversal of the persecution motive, when he thought of his old life, was a source of considerable satisfaction to Sigbjørn.

After breakfast, after more efforts, and more indecisions, they set out, avoiding Stanford everywhere, to find the Banco Ejidal.

They found Independencia and also Cervantes' old joint, The Salón Ofélia, turned into a drugstore called the Farmacia de la Soledad.

They were told that the new Banco Ejidal was in the Avenida Juárez. They were tired and could not, finally, find it; the address they had been given, number 25, was a closed green horrible obtuse building. Sigbjørn thought of Fernando standing outside it with his sword unsheathed toward the sun, standing there for a moment, but the sword always went back into the sheath: "I like to work them with. . . ." It was terribly hot. Sigbjørn—remembering Fernando's twenty miles' run—was turned toward life: he would not let the day be ruined and asserted he would take Primrose to Monte Albán.

At lunch Stanford was hiding himself behind his paper, the Mexico Herald—had he been out at all?—probably not, he had been staying in his room all day, as at the Tarleton. Was he drinking? Sigbjørn could not be sure, though certainly his friends seemed to be.

After lunch, and various directions from the old barefoot man they set off walking to Monte Albán. This was not a very sensible thing to do: Sigbjørn thought he remembered how, the first time he had been there with Juan Fernando, his foot had pained him and the Rimbaud suspicions he had had. Now the injections for varicose veins seemed to have worked well, and he was setting out walking again; the ecstasy of this, the feeling of setting out, in the heat, and the man in the bus station who said, "Es imposible—para usted, posible; pero para mi, no!"

So off they went happily into the heat and the sun and

Sigbjørn found the path. They wouldn't go by taxi because it cost 20 pesos. They crossed the hot railway line and a cinder heap, and obliquely a field with a cart track across it, where an Indian was burning sugarcane in the sun. Ah, those disc-wheeled bullock carts that stood outside the Farolito! They forded a dry stream, and then came to a sort of lane where they got stones in their shoes. They inquired of two Indians if they could get up and down by sundown, who said no, mucho tiempo, but they walked on, past a school and a queer little square and a blue church—and up, up, a hot road cut into the side of a great hill. Primrose rolled Sigbjørn's trousers up and they went on and on endlessly around and around; then thank God they were picked up by taxi with some tourists. Buen amigos! They stopped at the thousand foot summit and walked up to the top of the ruin, vista encantadora! The valley spread out all around them with a river and villages and the far blue mountains.

To Sigbjørn the fact that Monte Albán was Zapotecan, the great seat of the Zapotecan kings, was more important than its size or antiquity; it was of Fernando, of him alone, that he thought in the presence of all this majesty.

And it was of Fernando that he thought too gazing at the view far, far down below in the valley and on every side, the sweet green fields, the sparkling river, the villages deep in trees with a church spire to show one where the village is: it was Fernando he saw in all this peace, this fulfillment over the whole great hundreds of miles of valley one saw from the top of Monte Albán.

Fernando had helped to make this life fruitful and good as men should have had it in the Garden of Eden: this was progress as God wanted it on the first day when he saw that the world was good. It was the Garden of Eden. *Le gusta este jardín que es suyo?*

And it was of Fernando too that he thought as following the guide, he descended into the dark tomb number seven, where gleamed the guide's one candle.

The guide explained the mysteries of Monte Albán . . . "One of the strangest finds at Monte Albán was relief sculptures of human beings, all of whom have some bodily deformity.

Some show the heads too flat, while others show them extraordinarily elongated. In some the extremities, usually the feet, are twisted, others were bent, and so forth."

These sculptured stones, utilized in the north platform merely as construction material, were evidently torn from some yet older edifice. Nor could their hieroglyphics be deciphered by any of the keys to the writings so far known in Mexico or Central America. Who were the authors of these writings, and why did they prefer to show cripples in their sculptured stones? Was it their intent to ridicule certain enemies? Or should we see in these sculptures a representation of the sick who came to a temple in which there was a god who performed miraculous cures? Could Monte Albán be a kind of Lourdes? Was there not some identity with modern art—yes, and modern writing—in this? Was art at bottom a form of propitiation?—God, what depths beyond depths of meaning there was in all these things.

But the guide was saying that frequently in the tombs of the Oaxaqueñan region there are found the bones of a man or a dog, together with several other articles near the principal grave. The Mexicans believed that in the journey taken by the spirit in the realm of the dead there came a time when a wide river, difficult to cross, was reached. For this reason they killed a dog to accompany his master on the last journey. The spirit of the dog was supposed to reach the far side of the river in advance of the man, and upon seeing his master would jump into the water and help him across. This startled Sigbjørn, for it tallied so closely with *The Valley*. Something to think of at night.

Back in Oaxaca, and with various directions from the old barefooted man, they set off walking about three P.M. to the museum to look for the petrified head.

On the bottom floor the glass cases seemed full of cabezas petrificadas—heads from Parián, Etla, Cuicitlán, Nochitlán. They searched frantically for the fossilized head Sigbjørn and Fernando had found, but couldn't identify it—perhaps it was this one, no, this one. The arch from Etla was surely the one they had found, however.

They were taken in tow by the curator who told them about las joyas from tumba number seven—how modern they are—

and Primrose, in spite of all, was delighted; they were mounted as if in a Fifth Avenue shop. However, still there was no trace of their petrified head.

"And let me tell you this . . . they are pheasants. And there eagles. . . . And look at here—the birr. The birr take the babe . . . Do you understand me?"

But all the while, Sigbjørn was thinking of that scene at sunset, the natives carrying the petrified head through the purple still evening.

"And now, I am going to show you this-a . . ."

Suddenly, Sigbjørn thought if thousands of years hence some descendant of Fernando should be prowling around Cambridge, what significance would he attach to the gold-and-silver rowing challenge cups that had survived: would he deduce from surviving pictures that the dons had been high priests, that the oars were used for flailing slaves, that the coxswain of the eight at the head of the river was sacrificed to propitiate the Cam, and that one and all had worshipped Gog and Magog? It was not an original thought: Sigbjørn felt he had probably once read something of the sort in the *New Statesman* or the *New Republic*.

"And now I am going to show you . . ."

They went to an upper floor and found themselves looking at the beautiful black pottery from Ocotlán. The next moment, however, Sigbjørn found himself staring at a gigantic golden object, a sort of breastpiece: it seemed to represent a human head wearing a jaguar's-head helmet with imitation feathers of golden thread.

And all the while, the refrain from the curator: tumba, tumba, tumba.

A skull, bored by syphilis germs, had survived: the oddity and the meaninglessness of it.

Tumba, tumba, tumba.

How different was the city of Oaxaca itself, Oaxaca of the Farolito. Where would Fernando be now? At evening the purple mountains seemed again as they had on that first day at evening from the bus, like great gods with their hands on their knees: yet this had once been for Sigbjørn the Valley of the Shadow of Death.

XI

STANFORD'S LIGHT HAD been on in his room even during the day: as the Wildernesses returned from the museum down to 20 de Noviembre to the Hotel La Luna, his light was still on. Was the man then going mad, staying in his room like that? He had French doors giving on a balcony, and Sigbjørn heard his deep silly tittering voice, and heard the clink of bottles: he was absurdly pleased by this but exhausted by his trip had a sudden access of fright at entering La Luna; he was afraid of drinking, afraid of what might come, afraid of Oaxaca, afraid of the Covadonga, afraid even of getting a drink at the Modelo.

The fright, as if it stemmed from the tombs of Monte Albán, had taken the form again of a mysterious fear of trying to find Fernando. He had not yet even taken the most sensible means that it might be thought should be taken to find him: this was accounted for by his fear of his former awful life at La Luna; but Primrose, knowing how much at bottom he wanted to, of course, encouraged him.

"And we can't go without your taking me to the Farolito."

Habanero and a terrible night, in spite of no hangover; Sigbjørn said again in the middle of the night, waking Primrose, that he wouldn't look for his friend: he was afraid, and it was Stanford who, on top of everything else, made him afraid of his past.

God, what if he should become like his Consul and be buried
with a dog at his feet too, only first having been thrown down a
ravine? Was he afraid of Fernando because he too was his "character"—even if an innocently good one, the doctor—but had
not Fernando called him "the maker of tragedies"? This time in
the hours before the dawn, la madrugada, he gave way to his fear
and did not get up but let Primrose do so first.

While she was in the shower and Sigbjørn was lying in bed
listening to the usual sounds echoing to the glass roof, someone
knocked on the door.

Full of his usual terrors Sigbjørn got up, tried to jump into
his trousers with the usual complication between himself and his
clothes.

"Excuse me, does Mister Sigbjørn Wilderness live here?"

Sgbjørn put his head out of the door. It was Stanford.

"Are you Sigbjørn Wilderness?"

"Why, yes," Sigbjørn said, falsely vacant, and trying to throw
a look of surprise and half-baffled recognition into his face.

"I'm John Stanford. Don't you remember me?"

"Why, good God, John—" Then he was seized for a moment
with embarrassment that Primrose might come back half
dressed; moreover he didn't want to be seen talking to Stanford
at all, or rather he didn't want to introduce Primrose to him.
"Just wait a minute."

"I live just down the corridor," Stanford said from outside
where, however, he was obviously waiting.

The door had been half open during this period: now
Sigbjørn stepped back into his room, he had one shoe on, he had
a moment of indecision, of shakes, grabbed at his other shoe, and
went out on the balcony. John was standing a little farther down
it, the glass roof did not seem so far over his head, but Sigbjørn
gently maneuvered him round the corner to the head of the
stairs where Primrose could not be seen by him should she return, embarrassed, from the bathroom. John was already chuckling hoarsely and bowing in a manner once already borrowed
from Sigbjørn—who was a young fellow at his best, or drunk,
with rather German manners—though with one shoe on, it was
indeed rather difficult to click one's heels together.

"Well, well, well, well."

"Why, well, good God, John, I half thought it might be," Sigbjørn began to lie, though he was enjoying himself enormously; the obscene old boor had evidently been having an uncomfortable time of it the last few days, in fact must have begun to doubt his own sanity slightly; it was difficult to tell if he had been drinking or not though, for he looked remarkably well, as if staying in his room with the light on had deeply bronzed him.

"Well I saw you but I couldn't believe my eyes." Stanford said, "But I went and asked the manager. Is there anybody called Sigbjørn Wilderness here? . . . Well, well. You certainly look a hundred percent better than when I saw you last."

Sigbjørn, who in spite of his relative abstinence had the shakes slightly, started. "Thank you. Thank you very much, John."

"I suppose you never take a drink. I can't afford to take a drink anymore. That was my wife and her mother-in-law. I work. I don't have to work, but I'm making a lot of money. . . . I have a mine now. . . ."

"For God's sake, what kind of a mine?"

"A silver mine, and—"

"Good going."

"People say bad things because I wasn't in the war and I show them these two hands." He giggled deeply, bowing, and rubbing his hands, which he showed to Sigbjørn; they were large and beefy, kept in good trim doubtless by smacking female bottoms and stroking female thighs, but they did not look as though they had done much work apart from that: even Sigbjørn's right hand had a callus on the second finger. Sigbjørn also had calluses on his knuckles and often wondered if they were caused, like Milton's, by gout.

"Quite so," Sigbjørn said appreciatively. "Well, it's damn good to see you looking so well too."

"Were you in any of the services yourself?" Stanford was asking.

"No."

"What did you do?"

"Bugger all."

"And your books?"

"Books? Ah—that one, *In Ballast,* the one you sent off to the agent—that one was burned."

"Burned."

"Yes, it burned up on invasion day—no connection—with our house. We built the house again, with these two hands as the saying is, but the book was a dead loss."

"Oh, that's too bad," Stanford said sympathetically. "Then where are you living now? And who's 'we'? I thought you were divorced."

"In Canada, with Primrose, my wife. I went to Canada about a year after leaving here—after a period in the States. We hadn't much money, so we bought a little cabin, the one that burned, and we've lived there ever since, that is to say."

"What about the other book you were writing that what's his name saved from the Consul's house in Acapulco?"

"I finished it a year ago and so far it's been rejected in both England and America. Though that is tentative so far as England is concerned. They will accept it perhaps if I rewrite it."

"I read that *Drunkard's Rigadoon* and thought of you, ha ha."

"Thank you," Sigbjørn said, though he was reflecting that this was a purely gratuitous remark, that actually Stanford had never read through a single book in his life.

"By the way, they've pulled down the old Münchener Kindl, you know."

"You mean the place where I left your hat as security." Sigbjørn said, thinking at the same time how poorly it spoke for his memories, how poverty-stricken they must indeed be, if he could look back upon a place with such nostalgia for no better reason than that once, having been both drunk and broke, he had left someone's hat as security, and at that the hat of an enemy: "Yes, I know. I went to see what had happened to it immediately we arrived. It hasn't been pulled down, it's just another sort of cantina, that's all. But it isn't the same any longer. I went along to the Petate too, where you were good enough to save a few poems for me. The ones I wrote on the menu."

Stanford chuckled with delighted reminiscence, although the

Petate had been simply the loneliest of homes for both their tragedies where they had swilled all night when they were staying at the Tarleton. "Yes, the Petate, my God, the Petate."

"And by the way, in case you wondered about the bill at the Tarleton, I paid it in full before I left Mexico," Sigbjørn said. "I mean in 1938. I paid your bill too. The manager gave me some of your shirts, white ones, like Arrow shirts."

"What!" Stanford said, and flushing. "But that's funny, I paid it too, for God's sake."

"Good," Sigbjørn said. "Well, that's what it's like in Mexico."

"He's dead now."

There was a silence: then—

"Well, by God, it's good to see you anyway. . . ." Stanford began again heartily. "And what about all those poems you were writing?"

"I lost a lot of them in Mexico before I met you, if that makes any sense. . . . But I hope at least that some of them may be coming out."

"Well, we're staying at the Gillow in Mexico City. We must meet and have a few tequilas for old time's sake at some of the old haunts."

"Yes, indeed. If there's any left." Sigbjørn now got out of telling Stanford his own address in Cuernavaca but mentioned Eddie Kent as a way of contacting them.

"By the way"—Stanford began laughing, again, bowing and rubbing his hands—"we're still *characters* in Acapulco."

Sigbjørn was silent, for this was a dramatic moment. "They still remember us there, do they?" he said finally, scarcely daring to ask where in Acapulco and inwardly wincing at the word "characters." Why did he have to say "characters"? It was here in Oaxaca that the German had said, "But now you are becoming like one of your own characters."

Wishing Stanford good luck Sigbjørn parted from him hurriedly, wanting to get back to Primrose. He had saved Sigbjørn at least from losing *In Ballast,* even if he had only saved it for a worse fate in Canada, *In Ballast,* written about Erikson, Erikson, who had died, December 7: his mind went round in a great whirlpool as though there were killer whales beating and leaping in it; moreover, Stanford himself (Stanford-Hugh) had only barely escaped becoming a character in *The Valley* himself. It was impossible to escape the conviction that there was tremendous meaning in all this, indeed meaning in all our lives: for one thing what ghastly and barren, destructive and even suicidal memories can be made to shine simply because they were shared. Still, it was not without a certain feeling of, so to speak, belief in humanity that he returned to their room: after all, in a sense Stanford had done the noble thing. He knew that he had cheated yet that had not prevented his finally knocking on his door in the end—if only to satisfy his curiosity, that was still something.

But the main strange point about all this was that it had reconciled Sigbjørn to going to seek Fernando and he was in a happy mood again. After breakfast, again on ham and eggs, Primrose asked the rather effeminate manager (most of the Oaxaqueñans seemed slightly effeminate, or to have become such, it was not unfrequently that one saw them in the barbershops openly having their hair waved while not a few of them— Sigbjørn remembered Coco—carried hand mirrors; Juan Fernando had certainly been an exception, an exception even as a Zapotecan) to find out precisely where the new Banco Ejidal was; he phoned, was informed, and said: "Juárez y Calle Humboldt."

"y—" Sigbjørn asked, staggered for a moment.

"Calle Humboldt."

Sigbjørn and Primrose looked at each other: it was not only that they lived in the Calle Humboldt in Cuernavaca, where their tower was, and that Sigbjørn had lived in the Calle Humboldt eight years before when living in Cuernavaca, but that the Calle Humboldt *was* the Calle Nicaragua of his book: consequently it was a name he'd dwelt much with for the last years in his mind; Juárez was of small significance by itself, but Juárez y Calle Humboldt, as one should say Sixth and Main, meaning in this case the place where Avenida Juárez was crossed by the Calle Humboldt, seemed to portend something strange to him: moreover though Sigbjørn's novel concerned almost equally Oaxaca and Cuernavaca, he had only known there was a Calle

Humboldt in existence in the latter city. "But señor, we live in the Calle Humboldt, in Cuernavaca," Primrose said.

"Then that is good luck," said the manager.

Sigbjørn felt that it probably was good luck. After the interview with Stanford a tremendous sense of well-being was released within him. He realized the sentimentality of his feeling that it was a renewed belief in humanity—though there was this too, Sigbjørn was still slightly resentful that Fernando hadn't written, generous view though he had immediately taken of the whole thing—that prompted this happiness. But he did have a certain sense of having come to terms with his past: both, if Stanford were to be believed, had paid the same bill and paid it to someone moreover who was now dead: the past was now dead too, he could tell himself, or if not that he had at least, as it were, met it face to face, and in one of its worst aspects and even found it not too bad.

And so they set out, feeling happy and hopeful, to find Fernando, and Humboldt and Juárez. Sigbjørn realized again how afraid he had been to look for him after the first covert glance at the shut bank. They went down, after getting their bearings by the cathedral, past the old El Bosque, now turned, to all appearances, into an innocent lonchería of some kind. God, if they had only known, those passersby! El Bosque—many a happy hour had he spent in there with Fernando, this indeed was the original of the Farolito in another sense, but he'd never had such an affection for it, since he'd quarreled with the proprietor, whereas in the Farolito, hellhole though it was, he had never received, thanks to Fernando, an unkind word. When he got too drunk, they simply put him to bed in one of the beds off the patio and charged him fifty cents for it. El Bosque was another hellhole: it was where, that night—"Remember," Juan Fernando said, "you are among friends"— there had been that indescribable scene of terror with ten mescal-drunk people locked together in bloody fight. Mucho escandalo, as Coco had said, sighing and looking in his hand mirror. The next morning, at El Bosque, Fernando had been in love with Coco's sister and had been mostly afraid of Coco's knife in his throat. Sigbjørn smiled, he almost purred indeed at the memory. He even composed a bit of a poem, or rather the end of it, in its honor—*is shut and with it how much of remorse that now no more shall wander from its source.* They passed an office of the Compañía de Aviación, another little garden with *Le gusta este jardín* on it, and a big brown lace-looped, curtained, closed bus going to the Isthmus, to Tehuantepec, and this now recalled Fernando's "We will go riding down to Tehuantepec," and the plan, that had been half formulated between Primrose and Sigbjørn that if they found him in the city of Oaxaca, they would propose that they all ride down together.

All this time the two friends and lovers, the husband and wife, Sigbjørn and Primrose Wilderness, had been walking merrily along a main street that Sigbjørn thought was either the Avenida Hidalgo or Matamoros. At last they came to the Avenida Juárez, and they turned up it. It was one of Oaxaca's broken and hot streets and it went on interminably without meeting the Calle Humboldt. At the corner store Sigbjørn went in and bought cigarettes: "¿Qué marque?" "Alas," he replied, almost automatically, in his voice out of the past—for it was his and the Consul's brand of cigarettes; the Wildernesses usually smoked Bohemios—asked the way to the Calle Humboldt, was told it was straight ahead, and found that at this point Juárez crossed a street called Calle de los Muertos.

A little farther on through the sunlight past this Street of the Dead, which was in fact a rather pretty, merry little street, they came to a beautiful square planted with great trees that Sigbjørn faintly recognized, or rather the Avenida Juárez at this point became indeed a great avenue of trees that ran down the left side of this shady square with a bandstand under the trees to the right and to the center a kind of cage with bears, a sort of zoo. Then a little farther on they saw a sign in blue, *Calle de Humboldt,* and immediately beyond, the Banco Ejidal.

It was certainly in a much better site. Overhung with trees, there was a Victorian look to the place. Or rather, in a sense, American. It was like an old brownstone house set down upon the shady edges of Parker's place in Cambridge and though it was not covered with ivy that was how it always seemed to him in memory. Stone steps ran up to the entrance from the street, as if it were a quiet "unlicensed" hotel, and a peon sat waiting outside on the parapet. They went up the steps, past this peon, into the dark cool interior and addressed themselves to a man, sitting at a desk on their right.

This man, who had been writing, stood up courteously, listened to Sigbjørn's labored query as to whether a certain Juan Fernando Martinez still worked for them, explained that he had only been with the bank a year, and saying, laughing: "No sé. Posiblemente la señorita—" motioned them toward a pretty dark-haired girl typing at a small desk against the wall on the hither side of the big desk, presumably the manager's, set against the large windows that looked down the way the Wildernesses had come.

Sigbjørn was not sure whether he recognized this girl, but evidently unable to make her understand Fernando's name with his own pronunciation, taking a seat opposite her, he wrote down in pencil on a sheet of yellow paper the girl placed before him:

Juan Fernando Martinez

At this the girl's eyes became bright. "Ah, Juan Fernando Martinez!" she said. "El Zapotecano. . . . Ah, mucho tiempo."

"Sí," Sigbjørn said excitedly, "El Zapotecano."

"Sí, le conocí bien." Of course she knew him. She knew him well.

"He is well and still working for you?" Sigbjørn and Primrose almost clutched each other with delight.

"En Villahermosa," the girl answered.

Sigbjørn and Primrose exchanged looks. "Dónde está Villahermosa?" Sigbjørn said.

"En Tabasco."

"Then we will go to Villahermosa." "How do you get to Villahermosa?" Sigbjørn and Primrose said eagerly and almost simultaneously, meantime the disappointment that he was not in Oaxaca city itself was drowned triumphantly in the dawning of the knowledge that there Fernando was, after all, in Villahermosa, and Villahermosa could at all events not seem so far away from Oaxaca as Cuicitlán had once seemed from Canada.

"So he is still working for your bank, but in Tabasco, is that it?" Sigbjørn persisted.

The girl shook her head. "No, Don Fernando has—how you say—murió."

"Sí. Comprendo. He has moved. We understand. But will you please write the address, por favor," Sigbjørn said, and she took the paper from Sigbjørn and began to write under where he had written *Juan Fernando Martinez.*

"You knew his parents?" the girl asked suddenly, looking up.

"I? No, they lived in, I think, Sonora," Sigbjørn answered.

Just as Sigbjørn had received back the paper from the girl and was saying, "So he moved to Villahermosa in 1939. But I wrote him to Independencia twenty-five when your bank was still there and still they do not forward my letters. How is that? They sent them back with a—with—with a hand on them—" the manager of the bank came in, came in with a flood of memories of those Sunday mornings too, for he was the whiskerando; Sigbjørn had immediately recognized him, but was too engrossed in reading again what the girl had written in slanting difficult handwriting on the yellow paper either to continue what he was saying or to greet him.

Juan Fernando Martinez—murió en 1939 en Villahermosa, Tabasco.

"No, what? You mean it is not in Tabasco?" Primrose said, reading over his shoulder.

"He has moved, but when?"

"1939," Primrose said.

The girl shook her head. Her eyes filled with tears.

"Murió. Muerte!" suddenly almost shouted Sigbjørn. "You mean he is dead!"

"He died."

"You mean Fernando is *dead!*" cried Sigbjørn, "Ah, my God, no!"

"_____"

"What happened?" Sigbjørn heard himself asking finally.

"Ah, he was enfermo," said the girl, crying. "And—"

Tears sprang to Sigbjørn's eyes and after another silence filled as if with clashing sabers, Sigbjørn broke out: "When? Why? What month?" He added, "How did it happen?"

"What month was it?" the girl turned to the manager.

The manager was not sitting at his desk. He did not seem to have aged since the old days of the saber lessons. He was a stalwart, handsome man of about fifty, with brown skin, gray hair, and waxed gray handlebar moustaches. His eyes were full of sorrow also as he looked at Sigbjørn and then, after hesitating, answered the girl:

"Diciembre."

"Sí, señor. Diciembre."

Primrose gripped Sigbjørn's hand: December was also the month in which they had been married. It was the month, for that matter, in which he'd first met Fernando, in 1937, and the month when Erikson had died. And what could have been more desolate than the manager's hesitation? For here was Fernando to their own minds and hearts still so very much alive, yet to someone who had known him better than Sigbjørn, he had been so long dead he couldn't even remember when he had died. Fernando had been dead for six years, had been dead indeed when Sigbjørn wrote him his first letter. Moreover, during these years since he had died, Fernando had grown, mysteriously, and Sigbjørn had got to know him better.

"And he was working for your bank then in Villahermosa," Sigbjørn said.

The manager nodded, stroking his gray moustache: "I remember you well. Un buen amigo. You were a good friend to Fernando."

Sigbjørn too remembered him well, the Sunday fencing, that day they had found the fossilized head at Etla, and Fernando revered him: "I have resignèd my job to my boss, but he will not accept it." It was he, too, who had introduced Fernando to the philosophy of La Vida Impersonal, that of the "throwing away of the mind," where every man was his own Garden of Eden. Personal responsibility is complete, though the life is all interior.

"I didn't know him very long. But I've always looked on him as my best friend. My wife—this is my wife—and I—we both live in Canada—came here to Oaxaca on purpose to visit him. But—but I can't believe it. Was it paludismo?" And Sigbjørn remembered Cuicitlán, which had been lousy not merely with malaria but tuberculosis and even cholera: Fernando had to build him a bed in the bank.

"No . . . no paludismo." And the manager made a gesture precisely similar to one Sigbjørn had made Dr. Vigil use, his right forefinger and thumb making a sort of cup, while he flicked his wrist over several times rapidly with this cup near his mouth, as if suggesting the act of quick or continuous drinking. "Mescal," he said, "Muchas copas—he go loco. Mescal y mescal and so—"

"But—mescal couldn't kill Don Fernando," Sigbjørn said. "I ought to know!"

"Loco. Crazy. He was drinking much mescal. . . ." The manager tapped his temple. "Muchas copas . . . y . . ." The manager suddenly shut his right eye, simultaneously raising his right elbow, almost imperceptibly at the same time his curled right forefinger, his thumb curling to meet it, went through the motions of shooting downward through the sight of the aperture with his left finger and thumb of a trigger, being pulled twice, though the motion took less than half a second. "Un hombre le mató."

"Christ almighty!" Sigbjørn started to his feet. "A man—do you mean Fernando was murdered?" he said.

"A man killèd him."

It was the killèd that did it, Fernando's own accent, which was peculiar to some Oaxaqueñans. It was as if Sigbjørn had been walking in a trance with his mouth open for the last few minutes to verify something in the distance that his eyes could not believe, something unimaginable, like that Calgary farmer who had crept up on his own brother, struck by a bolt of lightning while controlling the harrow's four horses from behind, his brother dead in the saddle, the horses lying in pairs to left and right where the lightning had cut a swath, his clothes spread over the summer prairie, his cap cut in two, as though by a pair of scissors. At the same time Sigbjørn seemed to hear Fernando's own soft, mournful, amused voice saying: "Throw away your mind, old maker of tragedies. Are you making more tragedies? . . . Write and tell me if you have not killèd yourself with drinking."

"He was un hombre noble," Sigbjørn said finally.

"Sí. Fue un buen muchacho."

"Sí, un hombre muy noble y mas que simplemente simpatico y esta es una calidad la mas major." Sigbjørn didn't know what he was saying.

"He was a son to me, a brave boy." The manager put his head down and waved his hands in a gesture of finality and grief.

Everyone was crying in the bank.

"Muchas gracias."

"Buen muchas gracias."

"Muchas gracias."

"Adiós."

"He gave me his horse and ran himself," muttered Sigbjørn. "He sold me his best clothes for nothing. He gave me his friendship and advice I will use for the rest of my life. And he is dead like that."

Outside in the square Sigbjørn and Primrose looked blindly at the two bears chasing each other round their cage: they were without interest, the bears, without merit altogether. They stopped and had a brandy at the corner shop, then went on down the Calle de los Muertos. They walked on through the hot blue Oaxaqueñan midday. Sigbjørn felt he evinced such absolutely heartbroken misery that a passing priest in black mufti, whose hand had just been kissed by a desperado with one arm in a black windbreaker and high leather small boots, crossed himself, but did not fail to say either, as they met him and passed: "Adiós."

Though it was blazing noon and hot as flaming hell outside, in the little dirt-floored church it was cool and dark. They knelt down and prayed; it gave Sigbjørn cramps in his thighs but he prayed on. He prayed that the Virgin Mary might hear this humble prayer and that in some obscure way it might benefit Fernando in whatever niche of the next world he was. Tears ran down his cheeks. Then, while Primrose still prayed, he looked up, and around the somber obscure church. There had always been something between Fernando and him to which Sigbjørn could give no name. Now it occurred to him that it might have been the shadowy presence of precisely this—but with what joy he would have greeted him!

In the front of the church, before a tilted dark bleeding

Christ, a man knelt with his arms raised high, like an abandoned plow, in endless supplication. Before an altar on the right, a woman knelt on the stone floor with her hands outstretched. She had a little child with her and on the floor too was an habanero bottle. In the pew in front of him, he saw as they stood up, a drunk was huddled asleep, and yes, on his face too was an expression of infinite pity and peace. His sombrero had fallen to the floor so Sigbjørn picked it up for him. How many times and in the same way had not Sigbjørn himself in this terrible city taken sanctuary! At the door in the gloom they paused once more before the Saint of Desperate and Dangerous Causes. For only more dangerous and desperate than the most dangerous and desperate of this world might be those of the next.

But this time in his prayer, childlike, Sigbjørn included not only Fernando, himself, and Primrose, but the man in supplication whose hands were still held high, the woman with the child and the bottle of habanero, and the drunk, but the manager of the bank and even the world. Then almost as an afterthought, he included John Stanford.

XII

MURIÓ IN VILLAHERMOSA.
The beautiful city . . .
Where had Fernando been buried? A longing to see his grave,
to say a prayer there, overcame Sigbjørn. One day on the way
back from a waterfall in Cuernavaca, they had decided to go to a
cemetery. One part was very garish and full of blue and other
colored monuments and great trees and flowers, next to it a pitiful one, hot and dusty with only poor wooden crosses. . . . In
the fine cemetery Primrose was fascinated by a sort of shining
crypt made of blue and white bathroom tiles, large as a room,
with open walls, ceiling tiled, and at the back a sort of cache,
glass-fronted and padlocked with a large photograph of a man.
Below was a notice: Recuerdo a mi Querido, and the usual vase
of flowers.

But Sigbjørn found the prize: a building as large as a small
house but open at the sides, a glass roof like a greenhouse covered with flaking green paint. But the structure itself was made
of millions of tiny mirrors cut in every geometrical shape and
fitted together in intricate mosaic patterns, balustrade, pillars,
down sides like a green temple, even a huge jardiniere containing flowering plants, and in the center of the building a crypt,
also covered with mirrors. The whole great thing glittered and
flashed in the sun and looked like some M.G.M. set for the Zieg-

feld Follies. It was meticulously cared for: someone had even
been watering the garden set inside the back of the place, but on
one side were an empty tequila bottle, old rags, tin cans, even a
broken basket—Sigbjørn remembered that it was waving a tequila bottle from a station platform in Parián that he had last
seen Fernando. Ah, poor humanity. The blue painted stucco
monuments—the man asleep by a grave—the old building like
a grandstand in the cemetery, the sign outside—"It is forbidden
to ride bicycles in the cemetery." Was Fernando buried in a
place like this?

The gigantic tragedy of life goes too fast for those who must
merely sit down on some tomb and between scenes try and interpret it, especially when they themselves are actors: Villahermosa! Sigbjørn thought of the loneliness of that death. Un hombre le mató. Perhaps a cold wind blew in Villahermosa as Fernando walked with his high long swift unsteady step, his western
tasseled jacket open with the tassels blowing, on his way to that
last final cantina, through the high dark night wind—passing
through the squares perhaps at night with their uncertain wavering lights, and the wind-blown raucous music from the loudspeakers, the queerly named popcorn wagons, and the merry-go-
rounds empty, perhaps newly painted that morning, under the
dark waving trees, the lights were going out one by one, and
then one red light glowing by some new road, and beyond the
brilliant light of that last fatal cantina, past which two men were
urging forward their mules with milk cans, and Fernando moving in step to this sad music through this darkness made for
drunkards. . . .

Before dinner, tired as they were, they set out for the San-
tuaria de la Soledad. They passed the closed and dark green
Ejidal. They passed Cervantes' Farmacia de la Soledad. They
entered the church of the Soledad. A service was going on. The
priest was intoning: everyone was saying: "Santa Maria, madre
de Dios, ruega por nosotros pecadores, ahora y en la hora de
nuestra muerte, amen. Santa Maria, madre de Dios, ruega
por . . ." Pray for us sinners now and at the hour of our death.
Pray for us sinners now and at the hour of our death. The candles were being lit, one from another, some candles were even

thrown away: nothing seemed sadder than one of these cast-off candles, and Sigbjørn was glad that they had bought a generous one for Fernando; they lit a great candle and prayed for him. "A candle is a statement of faith," Primrose said softly, "a way of saying: 'my dear one, I have not forgotten.' And like the cross, it is a symbol of acceptance of suffering, but it's also of resurrection. . . ."

Primrose and Sigbjørn walked slowly out of the Soledad, leaving the candle burning behind them, down the steps, into Independencia, past the Farmacia de la Soledad, toward the old Ejidal: though the one was shut and the other turned from a cantina into a drugstore, Sigbjørn was struck by the fact that the relative distance between them was not changed.

But the old Banco Ejidal at number 25 was not shut. The great green doors stood open, they had been thrown wide. The Banco Ejidal was no longer a bank—but it was no longer a house either. No one apparently lived in what had been the old bank itself for here the windows were boarded up. But one glance told Sigbjørn that the high rooms beyond where Fernando had lived and where they had fenced and the shack opposite in the courtyard where the Indians who served Fernando his plate of beans they were always cooking, and of whom he said, "I like to work them with," had been pulled down. The whole place was in glorious bloom, packed along its entire length and breadth with blossoms and riots of roses. Independencia number 25 had become a garden. "Remember Parsifal," Sigbjørn told himself.

It was the next morning. A wild cold wind blew the dust of the ruined city of Mitla into their faces. They halted for a moment, turning their backs to it, and to the broken whistling road, walled with organ cactus, by which they had come. The man who had followed, then preceded them toward the ruins, repeated, "Then let's go, meestair." Zapotecan women approached to sell leaden-colored whistles, fake idols, junk embroidery. But Mitla itself was a sensational ruin, testifying to the Zapotecans' extraordinary intelligence and culture and to the rapacity of the Spaniards.

Ruined city or no, it was difficult to understand why anyone would have built a city here for any purpose whatsoever unless it were for that, perhaps, of mourning. And mourning, precisely, was what it had been built for. In the Aztec tongue, the guide was saying Mitla means sad place, lugubrious landscape, or inferno. No bird had ever been heard to sing there and the atmosphere, save for this steady chilling, shrilling, dusty wind, was one of sadness and quiet. The Zapotecans called it *lyoba* or tomb, *lyovaana* or place of rest. It was not used as a temple. It had been built as a sumptuous dwelling for the most important personage in the Zapotecan kingdom, the high priest. It had been erected over the graves of the Zapotecan kings, but had continued to be used as an elaborate burial ground for the rulers and great nobles. When some important person had lost a member of his family, or some dear friend, he would come to this splendid palace of Mitla to grieve and meditate.

The inconceivable yet magnificent desolation of the whole place, an image, indeed, of death, reminded Sigbjørn for the first time, perhaps, since their fire, of the even greater magnificence of being alive.

The sun shone brilliantly, and the wind seemingly was drawing lugubrious tones out of the organ cactus. There was a feeling of something Renaissance and yet Teutonic in the atmosphere —heroic, the sense of the heroic.

As they moved among the ruins and mosaics that Aldous Huxley imagined had influenced the patterns of tweed, and to which the Wildernesses bore about as much relation as a couple of Hottentots on Salisbury Plain "doing" Stonehenge, Sigbjørn felt himself as if questioning Fernando's spirit, as well as sorrowing for him, questioning some essence of him, drifting with them here, mournful himself, yet responding with gladness to the fact they were here.

Mitla was a place where one could imagine the dead stagnating in its dismal barren Usherlike quality, with the cold wintry little church, also built on ruins: and yet there was a romantic element to it, a Keatsian "La Belle Dame Sans Merci" quality to it too.

They wandered around in the blazing sun and howling wind, in the birdless dusty blue, gazed at conical hills, truncated stone pyramids, like archetypal golf tees, gigantic broken columns, like huge chicken croquettes in stone, walls with always the same design, walls made out of pieces of stone cut and fitted without any binding material whatsoever, remains of painted walls, delicate works of filigree without explanation, as if they were the work of some master novelist laboring in conjunction with a sculptor, the whole thing as inexplicable, as mysterious as God himself.

"The library" with pictures—could it have been a library?—in red and white brick; the priest with the head of an animal and hand with ruffled cuff—with Anubis-looking hieroglyph—the realm of the dead: Sigbjørn reflected what a truly dreadful place this would be to have a hangover in, and this made him want a drink: he would like to drink Fernando's health in mescal.

They walked among pillars whose significance had been long forgotten, columns out of place, with round tops, which could have supported no roof, scattered round the ruins, of unbearable evocation for our time, in this ghostly strident place.

Roaming round the ruined walls, they picked up their Zapotecan guide again, who was charming, with gestures like a dancer. He took them out of the sun into the dark cruciform tombs oriented north, south, east, west, his refrain through the whole being, "The Spaniards destroyed!"

But if these ruins of a great city, in fact prehistoric, for nobody knows for certain by whom it was built, or for certain to what use the enormous buildings were dedicated, no legend even existing relating to the builders, though the designs seemed more Grecian than anything else, if they stimulated the imagination, scarcely did they do it in any normal sense.

They came to a subterranean passage, leading to another cruciform tomb. In the center of the junction of the arms of the cross, a great column called The Column of Death was erected, about eight feet high. The guide pointed out that there was a tradition that if one embraced The Column of Death, the number of fingers that could be placed in the space between the hands denoted the number of years the person embracing the stone would live. He wanted them to try, Primrose wanted to try too, but Sigbjørn would have none of it. He was too superstitious; but also believed that it might superimpose something suggestive on the will that might beget one's death at the time indicated. "I am not superstitious,"Sigbjørn said.

Even though they had not done it, the column was still there; and had they done it, a number of fingers could still have been placed in the space between—potentially the guide's fingers had been placed there—so did it really make any difference? Was the oracle only valid when consulted?

Suddenly it struck Sigbjørn that perhaps they were not there for no reason at all, that this was a landscape, so to say, to which they did bear only too pointed a relation: but if this gave one cause for despair, what conceit was it drove man to such extremes as postulating the end of our civilization as almost the end of the world, or even the "end of the world" as the "end of life"?

It was absurd to think of all this, as one did, as the "beginning," because it was prehistoric, even though the walls seemed woven in a pattern formed by the continuous repetition of a simple unit of design—a diaper pattern: Sigbjørn was trying to work out something about the "infancy of the race."

Cruciform tombs. Cruciform tombs—Christ—what was this strange persistence of this symbol? What was the real significance of the cross? Sigbjørn realized he wasn't seeing anything at all, or listening to anything at all. He was going into the Shaftsbury Avenue Pavilion in Charing Cross to see *The Fall of the House of Usher.*

Then he realized he was not only walking in this unreal landscape, withdrawn into a daydream, but that this daydream was framed as it were in yet another withdrawal, by the cinema, in which again he was watching a shadow show on a screen, not even then an original story, but as the director had it, a transcript of themes from Edgar Allan Poe. No matter how despairing Poe's story, the genius of the director had managed, and with triumphant aesthetic success, to impose—as no Mexican director would have ever done—a happy, or a hopeful ending upon it. Sigbjørn had been so absorbed in his daydream that his awakening from it amounted to an awakening from an illumination, as if he had a message, given him in these grotesque terms because they were terms that he could best understand. What was the theme of *The House of Usher?* It was, or so it seemed to him at the moment, of the degradation of the idea of resurrection. But in the film, when the entombed was Usher's wife and not his sister, she came back in time, as it were with the doctor's help, to save him: they went out into the thunderstorm, but into new life.

Were we not empowered as the director of that film at least to turn the apparent disaster of our lives into triumph? Suddenly it occurred to him that this was what he was doing in Mexico: was it not for him too a sort of withdrawal into the tomb? Was he the director of this film of his life? Was God? Was the devil? He was an actor in it, but if God were the director that was no reason why he should not constantly appeal to Him to change the ending. Perhaps only if he lived up to his higher self constantly, that was at all times, the best kind of actor that he could possibly be—given his limitations—perhaps only then would God think him worthy to listen to, worthy of being saved, whatever he meant by saved, and of saving Primrose.

free will

This strange and confused rumination had not solved any of the questions he had put about the cross: the multiambiguous cross: but his thoughts now passed tenderly to Primrose, so disappointed because she had not yet seen the Southern Cross.

Yet they had seen Eridanus, all down the horizon: river of life: river of youth: river of death: how strange Eridanus would seem over Mitla. Then he thought of the cruel criticism: Sigbjørn Wilderness, while imitating the tricks of Joyce, Sterne, the surrealists, the thought-streamers, gives us the mind and heart of Sir Philip Gibbs. Well so be it. Perhaps Sir Philip Gibbs, in spite of any belief in spirits, had not seen *The House of Usher,* certainly would not have thought a day's hunting worth giving up to go into the Shaftsbury Avenue Pavilion to see it.

They came now to the cold dreary windy gusty white church, the Catholic church, and the Wildernesses entered to pray to the Saint of Desperate and Dangerous Causes. The church had been built upon a foundation of one of the great buildings of Mitla. The guide told them there was a legend regarding one of these rooms of this building, set aside as that in which the bodies of the defunct kings were deposited. When a king died, his body was borne to his tomb with much ceremony, placed on a funeral pyre, and the ashes placed in the tomb. In another room there was a door to a dark enclosure, closed with a large stone that was opened only when the bodies of heroes killed in battle were conveyed there to be deposited in the murky cavity below. It was said this cavity extended indefinitely under the ground, and it also was said that some were thrown into the tunnel alive, of their own free will, sacrificing themselves to the gods, in the hope of resurrection, rebirth.

Perhaps—in fact, undoubtedly, it was the case—Fernando's ancestors had been buried there.

Suddenly Sigbjørn found that they were all looking at the candles in the church. What was the meaning of the candle, the light burned to the dead? Was it the symbol of the mediation for life? Perhaps man was not so irrevocably alone, he thought, even men poured their hearts out and threw their pistols on the floor in the Temple of the Virgin for those who have nobody them with. For between man and man, and woman and woman was the mediating influence of the dead. And between the gulf that separated each of the dead from each other was the mediating influence of the living. And between the gulf that separated the dead and the living from the unknown and from the ineffable was the mediating spirit of what was known as the Holy Virgin, mother of us all.

Outside, they wandered round alone and on one stone found signs of recent worship—a wreath of flowers of the kind known as zempoaxcochital, which still are used by the Indians in their burial ceremonies, and the remains of a wax candle that some pious soul had lighted to appeal to the gods of Mictlan, for the eternal rest of his relatives.

In the Hotel La Luna Sigbjørn waked with a start, as if automatically, as if obeying some habit, some impulse out of the past. Everything in his being told him why he was getting out of bed, what time it was, and what, as if he were sleepwalking, he was going to do. And also out of this same habit he walked to the washstand and carefully, silently, so as not to wake Primrose sleeping, poured himself, as once before he had poured tequila, a tumbler full of wine. Everything was still, but he knew instinctively what time it was. It was about four in the morning—his old time for going to the Farolito and he had waked out of habit. The desire for a drink was unassailable. Sigbjørn drank down the wine which warmed him right through immediately.

He dressed, drank another half tumbler of wine and went out on to the gallery, shutting the door carefully. What was to prevent him going, just to have a look at least, to the Farolito by himself, or just have one drink there, and return, just as last night he could have returned from the bar of the morning slattern without Primrose being any the wiser, as if in short nothing had happened. Or he could go at least "to see if it were still there so as to prevent Primrose making any useless journey."

As he went down the stairs—he found he was taking the stairs heading down from the "very bad" room—he reflected upon the miracle of this: how could he be going down these stairs, alive, a relatively hopeful happy man, that he had once descended dead. How had such dreadful nights and mornings as he had endured been survived at all. And the memories of the dining room too came back to him, the nephew asleep on the couch waiting for the morning train and himself drinking out of somebody else's bottle . . . and he remembered the clock ticking. Only in those days he would not have had to dress: he always slept fully clothed in the "very bad" room, and when he went out to the Farolito, it was with a blanket over his head, like an Indian.

Out on the sweet-smelling street in the early dawn Sigbjørn had turned the corner to the left on his way to the Farolito before he knew what he was doing. Why did such a grim inexplicable ecstacy attach his mind to these early morning debauches of his, he wondered. Was it because it was partly associated in his mind, not with evil but with consciousness? It was consciousness born of and intensified by sorrow and despair but it was still consciousness. Though he had lost most of his work done in this kind of manner, it was doubtless worthless anyway, perhaps he had not entirely wasted his time at the Farolito. Perhaps he had grown in some inexplicable manner there. Or perhaps what he had experienced was tantamount to some kind of illumination, perhaps it was some sort of mystical experience that suffering had caused him to undergo. Another thought now struck him, as unerringly, having reached this point where the open sewers stopped, he crossed the street. Why had he said to himself just now that he was a relatively "hopeful and happy man." He had not been saying that to himself lately, in fact, had not said since the fire, or at least the very latest since they had begun again to rebuild the house. Had something changed in him, been purged away from him—or was it just the wine? No. The Farolito was somehow associated with freedom.

Sigbjørn walked on. It was very cold and clear and there were piled clouds between walls. He had wasted some time in getting up or over his wine, or it had been a little later than he had thought, for a few women were already sweeping in the streets and there were the oxen already, with heavy yokes and mild sweet eyes. And there—he had almost run as he rounded the corner—was the Farolito. The outside of the cantina was the same, with the blue strips across its façade, and the two low entrances, only the entrances were boarded up. The name El Farolito had been however almost painted out, or had all been peeled off: and on the wall was the legend, scrawled cursively in paint: movio a Calle Humboldt, numero 7. On one side the long cold streets led to the country and the fields, and on the other up to the hills and there too was the big wall beyond which was the potter's factory where so often he had gone with the potters after drinking. Could that have been called happiness? If not, why did he look back upon it with such an inexplicable yearning? For here Fernando was not the only or even the strongest tie to the Farolito. It was himself, his lonely dying youth.

Calle Humboldt! This was strange too: once more the Calle Humboldt had come upon the scene, as if the street possessed some queer magical reference of its own that he could not fathom but of which it alone was aware: or as if it had been a password among his own guardians or daemons that they caused him to be aware of when they wished him to know they were watching; or it was as if it were something that some force within him or them, or without, brought to their notice to ring its own changes of memory, or as a warning.

Sigbjørn took to the streets leading uphill toward the Oaxaqueñan Calle Humboldt. He had not remembered how near the Church of the Soledad was to the Farolito but he could see the steps leading up to it even from here. Ah, these walled closed streets of Oaxaca that did not give out their life at all, these blank thick-walled cantinas behind which lurked such deepness, such complexity, such beauty of patios and sawdust rooms when you entered them, depth beyond depth, those barred prison windows, and huge worn wooden doors through which how occasionally you would see some enchanting vista of stone courtyards, arches, and gardens—what was all this an image of? It was not enough to ask. Did not men too have such walled closed streets, such hidden gallantries, such concealed gardens and cloisters and misericordes, and rooms wherein took place such invisible debauches? What soul, moreover, did not have its invisible Farolito, where it drank itself to awareness in the dead watches of the night? And here was the Church of the Soledad, of the Virgin for those who have nobody them with. And yet man was alone—how could he be so? Perhaps what was meant was that he was alone so far as the living were concerned. Or perhaps there was something wrong about the meaning of the word alone.

Feeling that the Calle Humboldt number 7 might be too far —for he was already tired; or with a feeling even stronger than his desire to discover the new site of the Farolito—he went up the steps to the church itself, toward which a woman already was advancing slowly, millimeter by millimeter on hands and knees toward the portal, past the little stall that sold medals and candles, scarcely giving a glance down Independencia toward the Banco Ejidal, or at the Farmacia de la Soledad, up past the barracks, which was now a convent again—the prison or barracks turned into a convent; a man had been in there for twenty years, in the "worst" prison. With a good feeling that their great candle would still be burning for Fernando, he went into the little church where he had once taken sanctuary when he was being pursued.

When he returned to La Luna, Primrose was asleep and it was about six thirty. He woke her up, and they took the same walk he had made himself as far as the old Farolito with "moved to the Calle Humboldt" upon it. They returned to the La Luna, ate an enormous breakfast, and after saying farewell to the barefooted old man, who said, "que lástima" that they were going, and that it was a fine fresh day—fresco—they paid their bill— "Nosotros no somos americanos ricos"—which was larger than they had thought: they were charged extra for the ham and bacon, and for their second cups of coffee, and Primrose had cracked a mirror unfortunately, the day's only flaw. "Then that is—ah—seven years bad luck" said the effeminate manager, handing their papers to them. But Sigbjørn was not even put out by that. . . .

Once more the Wildernesses were off, this time going back the way they came so that once more they saw the sign *Le gusta este jardin* and *La persona que destruya este jardin sera consignada a la autoridad.* They had front seats, a fresh wind was blowing through the window, and something seemed to have changed in Sigbjørn, he felt glad to be alive, he was enjoying the trip, though it was shot through with sadness.

Etla again and the mountains, mountains, mountains of mysterious Oaxaca. Sigbjørn remembered eight years before the dreadful poverty of the villages, the pitiful few fields of corn and the sense of so much of the land that could be used to bring fruitfulness to the people lying idle simply for want of a little help. This time he was conscious of a great change, directly the result of the work of the Bank. Everywhere one saw rich green fields, felt a sense of fruitfulness, and of the soil responding and of men living as they ought to live, in the wind and sun and close to the soil and loving the soil. Those farms were lovingly tended too and cared for, showing exquisite care and instinctive knowledge in the way the fields were terraced and contoured, the earth displaying the feeling and genius of the people for their land—but they never could have done it without the Banco's help, and not merely the kind of help one gets from mortgaging one's house in order to spread out a little bit, because then there's always the terror and pressure and fear of losing it through the very force of the earth itself in powers one can't control, drought or storms: the earth, subject to cataclysms, is a cruel master. But here the farms were real, the houses, instead of being thatched, corn-shocked shacks, as in Morelos or Puebla, were nearly all adobe and many of them, most of them indeed, had tiled roofs; and were beautiful, growing out of the very soil, for adobe was the earth itself.

"Look, Sigbjørn, see where they're making adobe. Molding it and drying it in the sun."

It was all so different from eight years ago, and also the look of the animals, which were not shabby or starved looking but had strong well-fed looks and shining coats that came from proper feeding and care, and the fields themselves were rich. Oaxaca had become the granary of nearly all of Mexico and the Valley of Etla had become the granary of Oaxaca.

"That's all the Ejidal!"

And then a field of young, new wheat—pale green in contrast to the dark green of alfalfa—and then a field of ripening wheat dimming to gold, then quince and peach orchards, young trees, obviously planted within the last ten years and blossoming. . . . The Banco Ejidal had become a garden.

Then they were leaving the state of Oaxaca behind them, and behind them too, in the dark church of the Virgin for those who have nobody them with, one candle burning. . . .

ABOUT THE AUTHOR

Malcolm Lowry was born in England in 1909 and
attended public school in that country.
At eighteen, before going to Cambridge, Lowry
went to sea. That voyage of a year, on a freighter to the
Orient and back through the Indian Ocean and
the Suez Canal, was used as background material for his
first novel, *Ultramarine,* which was written while
he was at Cambridge and published in England in 1933.

During the nineteen-thirties, Lowry came to the
United States, living in New York and Hollywood.
In 1938, he went to Mexico and wrote the
first draft of *Under the Volcano.* In 1940, Lowry
married Margerie Bonner (also a novelist) and
they lived much of their life together in British
Columbia, Canada. At Dollarton, near Vancouver,
Lowry rewrote *Under the Volcano,* which was
published in 1947. *Hear Us O Lord from Heaven
Thy Dwelling Place* was written for the most part in
British Columbia, between 1950 and 1954.
Dark As the Grave Wherein My Friend Is Laid
reflects a catastrophic trip the Lowrys made
to Mexico in the winter of 1945–46.

Malcolm Lowry died suddenly in England in 1957.